PENGUIN CRIME FICTION

THE BABY IN THE ICEBOX AND OTHER SHORT FICTION

James M. Cain was born in Annapolis, Maryland, in 1892. After graduating from Washington College in 1910, he taught journalism at St. John's College and later wrote political commentaries for the *New York World*. His novels are often characterized by the violent interplay of his middle-class characters' enclosed lives and the crimes they commit out of desperation or passion. Among his most acclaimed works are *The Postman Always Rings Twice* (1934), *Double Indemnity* (1936), *Mildred Pierce* (1941), *The Magician's Wife* (1966), and *Rainbow's End* (1974). James M. Cain died in 1977.

Roy Hoopes is an accomplished journalist and editor who has published hundreds of articles and half a dozen books, including *Americans Remember the Home Front*, a civilian documentary of World War II. He came to know James M. Cain during the last years of the writer's life, and he is the author of Mr. Cain's first full biography, *Cain* (1982).

THE BABY IN THE ICEBOX

AND OTHER SHORT FICTION

BY

JAMES M. CAIN

EDITED BY ROY HOOPES

PENGUIN BOOKS

Penguin Books Ltd, Harmondsworth, Middlesex, England
Penguin Books, 40 West 23rd Street,
New York, New York 10010, U.S.A.
Penguin Books Australia Ltd, Ringwood, Victoria, Australia
Penguin Books Canada Limited, 2801 John Street,
Markham, Ontario, Canada L3R 1B4
Penguin Books (N.Z.) Ltd, 182–190 Wairau Road, Auckland 10, New Zealand

First published in the United States of America by
Holt, Rinehart and Winston 1981
First published in Canada by
Holt, Rinehart and Winston of Canada, Limited, 1981
Published in Penguin Books by arrangement with
Holt, Rinehart and Winston 1984

Copyright © Alice M. Piper, 1981
Introduction and Prefaces copyright © Roy Hoopes, 1981
All rights reserved

LIBRARY OF CONGRESS CATALOGING IN PUBLICATION DATA
Cain, James M. (James Mallahan), 1892–1977.
The baby in the icebox and other short fiction.
I Hoopes, Roy, 1922– II. Title.
[PS3505.A3113B3 1984] 813'.52 83-25662
ISBN 0 14 00.7055 9

Printed in the United States of America by
George Banta Co., Inc., Harrisonburg, Virginia
Set in Caledonia

"The Robbery," "Vanishing Act," "Dreamland," "Joy Ride," "Queen of Love and Beauty," "Santa Claus, M.D.," "Gold Letters Hand Painted," and "It Breathed" copyright 1928, 1929, 1930, 1931 by Press Pub. Co. "The Hero" copyright 1925 by The American Mercury, Inc.; copyright renewed 1953 by The American Mercury, Inc. "Theological Interlude" copyright 1928 by The American Mercury, Inc. "Pastorale" copyright 1928 by The American Mercury, Inc.; copyright renewed 1955 by James M Cain. "The Taking of Montfaucon" copyright 1929 by The American Mercury, Inc. "The Baby in the Icebox" copyright 1932 by The American Mercury, Inc.; copyright © renewed James M. Cain, 1959. "Dead Man" copyright 1936 by James M. Cain; copyright © renewed James M. Cain, 1963. "Brush Fire" copyright 1936 by Macfadden Publications, Inc.; copyright © renewed James M. Cain, 1963. "The Birthday Party" copyright 1936 by The Curtis Publishing Company; copyright © renewed James M. Cain, 1963. "Coal Black" copyright 1937 by Macfadden Publications, Inc.; copyright © renewed James M. Cain, 1964. "The Girl in the Storm" copyright 1939 by James M. Cain. "Money and the Woman (The Embezzler)" copyright 1940 by James M. Cain; copyright © renewed James M. Cain, 1968. "Joy Ride to Glory" copyright © Alice M. Piper, 1981.

Except in the United States of America, this book is sold subject to the condition that it shall not, by way of trade or otherwise, be lent, re-sold, hired out, or otherwise circulated without the publisher's prior consent in any form of binding or cover other than that in which it is published and without a similar condition including this condition being imposed on the subsequent purchaser

CONTENTS

Introduction   1

Sketches and Dialogues

    The Robbery   24

    Vanishing Act   28

    Dreamland   32

    Joy Ride   36

    Queen of Love and Beauty   40

    Santa Claus, M.D.   44

    Gold Letters Hand Painted   48

    It Breathed   51

    The Hero   55

    Theological Interlude   68

Short Stories

Pastorale	94
The Taking of Montfaucon	104
The Baby in the Icebox	120
The Birthday Party	139
Dead Man	153
Brush Fire	167
Coal Black	177
The Girl in the Storm	188
Joy Ride to Glory	201

Serial

Money and the Woman (The Embezzler)	221

THE BABY
IN THE ICEBOX

INTRODUCTION

James M. Cain, conceded by many writers and critics to be one of the most influential of America's popular authors, is remembered primarily for his four controversial novels of the 1930s and '40s—*The Postman Always Rings Twice, Double Indemnity, Serenade,* and *Mildred Pierce.* However, Cain was essentially a writer of short fiction. This is confirmed when we recall that two of the above stories—*Postman* and *Double Indemnity,* which Ross Macdonald described as "a pair of American masterpieces"—are really novellas, barely qualifying as full-length works of fiction. In fact, when Cain sent the manuscript of the story later published as *The Postman Always Rings Twice* to Alfred A. Knopf, the publisher maintained that at 35,000 words it was too short to qualify as a novel and refused, at first, to pay Cain the $500 advance called for under an option clause in an earlier contract. *Double Indemnity,* which has only 29,000 words, was first published as an eight-part serial in *Liberty* magazine, and *Serenade* has only 44,000 words. Even Cain's two biggest hardcover sellers—*Past All Dishonor* and *The Butterfly*—are slim little books, more accurately described as novellas. (*The Butterfly* hardly looks like a conventional novel, even with the twelve-page "preface" Cain added, in part, to give it additional heft in the bookstores.) His longest novel, *The Moth*, published in 1948, never achieved the impact or the sales of his earlier shorter books, and in a letter to a friend Cain offered one explanation for the book's limited success: "If you ask me, a simple tale, told briefly, is what most people really like."

In addition to writing eighteen novels (six of which were originally written as magazine serials), Cain was a prolific producer of sketches and dialogues, as well as dozens of conventional short stories, seventeen of which were published. The short-story form appealed to Cain and, as he wrote in the introduction to *For Men Only*, an anthology of stories he edited in 1944, "In one respect . . . it is greatly superior to the novel, or at any rate, the American novel. It is one kind of fiction that need not, to please the American taste, deal with heroes. Our national curse, if so perfect a land can have such a thing, is the 'sympathetic' character. . . . I take exception to this idealism, as the Duke of Wellington is said to have taken exception to a lady's idealism when he told her: 'Madam, the Battle of Waterloo was won by the worst set of blackguards ever assembled in one spot on this earth.' The world's greatest literature is peopled by thorough-going heels"—as are many of Cain's stories.

Cain was born in Annapolis, Maryland, in 1892. When he was eleven, his family moved across the Chesapeake Bay to Chestertown, where his father became president of Washington College. Cain graduated from the college at the age of seventeen, after four miserable years in which he said he felt like a "midget among giants." Then, at an age when most intellectual kids still are in college, Cain spent four years in Maryland and Washington, D.C., drifting from one job to another before finally deciding what he wanted to do with his life. That decision came one day in 1914, when he was sitting on a bench in Lafayette Park, across Pennsylvania Avenue from the White House. He had abandoned his ambition to become an opera singer and had just quit a job selling records at Kann's department store, when suddenly, from nowhere, he heard his own voice say: "You're going to be a writer."

It came to him, "just like that, out of the blue," he later said. "I've thought about it a thousand times, trying to figure out why that voice said what it did—without success. There must have been something that had been gnawing at me from inside. But if there was, I have no recollection of it, nor did I have any realization that the decision I'd made wasn't mine to make. . . . [It] would not be settled by me, but by God."

Having decided to become a writer, Cain was faced with the problems of what to write and how to support himself until he became an established author. He went back to Chestertown, where his family welcomed his decision. His father found him a job teaching English and grammar at the college, after which Jamie, as his family and everyone around the little college town called him, settled down to try his hand at his new trade. "In the afternoons," he said, "I played the typewriter, on which I was becoming a virtuoso, writing short stories in secret, sending them off to magazines, and getting all of them back. In a year or more of trying, I didn't make one sale, until the thing became ridiculous and I was horribly self-conscious about it, to the point where self respect, if nothing else, demanded that I quit."

So Cain abandoned the typewriter, temporarily discouraged and wondering whether he had the talent for fiction. But those early, drifting months had not been completely wasted. While teaching at the college, he became a walking encyclopedia of grammar and punctuation, which he always maintained was at the root of good writing. There are no copies of his early stories in existence, but we can assume he had taken the first step in developing the famous James M. Cain style. And the four years he had spent drifting around the Eastern Shore in a variety of jobs, even an aborted singing career, provided abundant material for his later stories.

What to do next? He decided that a newspaper career might be a good way for an aspiring writer to make a living, so in 1918 he went to work as a cub reporter for the *Baltimore American*, then later, the *Sun*. But his newspaper career ended even quicker than his fiction-writing career when America entered World War I and Cain soon found himself in France with the American Expeditionary Force. After seeing action in the Meuse-Argonne offensive, he built something of a reputation as an editor of the 79th Division newspaper, the *Lorraine Cross*.

Returning to the States, Cain spent three postwar years as a reporter for the *Baltimore Sun*, and soon he felt ready to resume his efforts to write fiction. He was sent down to West Virginia in 1922 to cover the treason trial of William Blizzard, a young man who had led an armed insurrection against the coal mine operators, and after the trial, encouraged by H. L. Mencken, who was also on the *Sun*, Cain took a three-month leave to go back to West Virginia and try to write a novel about life in the coal mining communities. He wrote three drafts, but threw them all in the wastebasket. "The last one," he said, "I wouldn't have written at all if I hadn't squirmed at the idea of facing my friends with the news that my great American novel was a pipe dream."

There are no copies of these early Cain efforts so we cannot assess Cain's first attempt at a novel, but Cain did say later that part of the problem was his journalistic approach: "I was so preoccupied with background, authenticity and verisimilitude, that I had time for little else." There were also questions of style and structure. "I didn't seem to have the slightest idea where I was going with it," he said, "or even which paragraph should follow which." His people "faltered and stumbled." They were homely characters, who spoke a "gnarled and grotesque jargon that didn't seem quite adopted to long fiction; it seemed to me that after fifty pages of ain'ts, brungs, and fittens, the reader would want to throw the book at me."

So once again, James M. Cain had failed to write successful fiction. However, his reporting of the treason trial for the *Sun* and articles he subsequently wrote about the coal mines for the *Atlantic Monthly* and the *Nation* attracted considerable attention in the literary community. H. L. Mencken was especially impressed, and the two men became good friends. Later, after Cain quit the *Sun* and joined the faculty of St. John's College in Annapolis, as a professor of English and journalism, he began writing for Mencken's new magazine, the *American Mercury*.

Cain's first contribution to the *Mercury* was a series of iconoclastic articles attacking some of Mencken's favorite targets—labor leaders, academicians, editorial writers, do-gooders, and politicians, especially female politicians. Then, in 1925, Cain turned his typewriter loose on county and town commissioners—with a significant change of approach. Instead of ridiculing his subjects in a conventional essay, he satirized them in fictional dialogues, which were, in effect, one-act plays. Many of them have been performed over the years by theater groups.

By 1925 Cain had resigned from St. John's, spent a summer in a tuberculosis sanitarium, and, at his doctor's urging, gone to New York in search of a job that would be less strenuous than newspaper reporting. Through an introduction from Mencken, Cain met and impressed Walter Lippmann, then the editorial-page editor for the *New York World*. Cain spent six years, from late 1924 until early 1931, writing editorials for Lippmann, and in 1928, in an effort to earn more money to help pay for a divorce from his first wife, Mary Clough, Cain started writing a column for the "Metropolitan" section of the

Sunday *World*. Most of his columns consisted of sketches about New Yorkers and, eventually, people on the Eastern Shore—the same kinds of down-home country rubes he ridiculed in his *Mercury* dialogues.

During this period, Cain also wrote his first two conventional short stories for *American Mercury* ("Pastorale" and "The Taking of Montfaucon") as well as articles for the *Bookman* and the *Saturday Evening Post*, all of which contributed to his growing reputation as a biting social satirist and master of dialogue. His *Mercury* pieces were especially popular, and Cain told Mencken that he hoped to write enough of them to eventually make up a collection. When Mencken mentioned this to his friend Alfred A. Knopf, also an early Cain admirer, Knopf urged Cain to contact him first whenever he was ready to do such a book. Cain eventually did write enough sketches, and the result was *Our Government*, published in 1930, which consisted of most of his *Mercury* dialogues, the short story "The Taking of Montfaucon," and four additional dialogues done especially for the book.

Not only did the publication of *Our Government* further enhance Cain's reputation, it also helped bring his name to the attention of Hollywood producers. His New York agent, James Geller, obtained offers from a few studios, and soon Geller started pressing Cain to take a job in California. Cain was not interested at first, but then, in 1931, after the *World* folded and Cain spent nine months at *The New Yorker* learning, among other things, that he could not get along with Harold Ross, he decided to take his agent's advice. He went to Hollywood, where Geller found him a $400-a-week job at Paramount Pictures—twice what he was getting at *The New Yorker*.

Cain's first assignment at Paramount was to work on a new script for *The Ten Commandments*. The project ended in failure, and within six months of his arrival in Hollywood, Cain was out of a job in the middle of the Depression, forty years old, and supporting a second wife (a Finn named Elina Tyszecka) and her two young children (Leo and Henrietta). Although broke and discouraged, Cain was sickened by the thought of returning to New York, and going back to a Baltimore paper appealed to him even less. As he wrote Mencken: "I have always disliked Baltimore with a venomous unreasoning dislike that goes beyond anything that can really be said against it. So here I stay for a while." In Hollywood ("as good a place to find out where I am at as any") at least the living was cheap.

The Cains moved from their two apartments in Hollywood's Montecito Hotel to a little house in Burbank, and Cain settled down to try to make a living as a free-lance writer. But whenever he began to think about articles, he became depressed at being in the West, three thousand miles from his usual coordinates, ideas, and sources of information. Then he began to think: "Unconsciously," he wrote later, "I assumed that the East was the only good seat for the show that started in 1642, and the white man began his reduction of the continent. But actually, if the Atlantic was the starting line of the great trek, the Pacific was the goal, and just as valid a place to study it from as the other side of the country."

Cain began to study the West, especially California, and decided he had been making false assumptions. "I had supposed the West to be a bit naïve, a bit recent, a bit wild, wooly and absurd. When I examined these facts, however, I found them rather different. Actually the country is the heir to a prodigious, rich, colorful civilization that sprang into being with the first gold strike on the American River in 1848 and, indeed, back years before that, for the life that was led by the Spanish ranchers, to say nothing of the contribution of the Russians, was wholly charming."

Gradually, as Cain continued his research, he gained more and more respect for the West, an appreciation which would soon work its way into his magazine articles. But first, he wanted to try fiction again, having been encouraged by favorable responses to the two short stories he had written for the *Mercury*.

Even as early as 1932, one of the principal forms of recreation in California was driving around in an automobile—through the canyons, out into the valleys, or down to the beaches. Cain loved to drive, and he took hundreds of such trips, alone, with Elina and the kids, or with friends. As he drove around in his 1932 Ford roadster, he began to feel more and more that California and its people provided a natural milieu for his writing. And there was one gas station, where he regularly stopped, that provided a spark that would eventually ignite Cain's phenomenal career as a writer of controversial best-sellers. "Always this bosomy-looking thing comes out—commonplace, but sexy, the kind you have ideas about," he later told an interviewer. "We always talked while she filled up my tank. One day I read in the paper where a woman who runs a filling station knocked off her husband. Can it be this bosomy thing? I go by and sure enough the place is closed. I inquire. Yes, she's the one—this appetizing but utterly commonplace woman."

He began to think: What about a novel in which a woman and a typical California automobile tramp kill the woman's husband to get his gas station and car? Cain and Elina discussed the idea for months, but he was still not ready for a long story. At the same time, he only felt comfortable in his writing when he pretended to be someone else, telling his story in the first person, in the manner of Ring Lardner. He preferred to write about Eastern Shore rubes who spoke the dialect of the common man, and was most comfortable when he could pretend to be one of them.

Although critics later would say that James M. Cain was a disciple of the "Hemingway school," the two men who had the greatest impact on the development of his literary style were Ike Newton and Ring Lardner. Newton was a bricklayer who had put a walk on the campus of Washington College while twelve-year-old Jamie Cain sat fascinated for hours, listening to Newton talk. "Later," Cain wrote, "my dialogue would be praised off and on by critics, and I would save myself argument by acknowledging debts to various experts on the 'vulgate,' as H. L. Mencken called it. But actually, if a writer owes a debt to what his ears pick up, mine would be to Ike."

Cain had become a fan of Ring Lardner just before World War I, when Lardner's stories about a fictional baseball player named Jack Keefe were appearing in the *Saturday Evening Post*. In France, Cain wrote letters to his brother, Boydie, a young Marine pilot destined to die in a tragic accident after the Armistice. In these letters, Cain imitated Lardner's style, and he later said it was the "only time I consciously imitated anybody." Lardner obviously had an impact on his early dialogues and short stories written for the *World* and *Mercury*, but as Cain found out when he tried to write his novel in 1922, the colloquial dialect invariably became tedious in a long story.

So Cain put his idea for a novel in the back of his mind and decided to try another short story. The result was "The Baby in the Icebox," and, like "Pastorale" and "Montfaucon," it was written in the first person, Ring Lardner style. But unlike his earlier stories, "The Baby in the Icebox" was set in the West and had characters who were western in origin. Suddenly Cain found something happening in his fiction. When he wrote about the western roughneck—"the boy who is just as elemental inside as his eastern colleague, but who has been to high school, completes his sentences and uses reasonably good grammar"—the first-person technique did not begin to grate after fifty pages and he did not have to drive the reader crazy with all the "ain'ts," "brungs," and "fittens." Maybe now he was ready for long fiction—at least longer than he had been writing, if not a full-length novel. In fact, James M. Cain did not really need to write a full-length novel; he had developed a style which enabled him to tell a story in about half the space required by the average novelist.

Cain sent "The Baby in the Icebox" to Mencken, who liked it and wrote back that it was "one of the best things you have ever done." The story attracted considerable attention when it was published in the *Mercury* in 1933, and Cain's agent immediately sold it to Paramount for $1,000. The studio gave it to screenwriters Casey Robinson and Frank Adams, who turned it into Cain's first movie—*She Made Her Bed*, starring Richard Arlen, Sally Eilers, and Robert Armstrong. Paramount had wanted to cast Baby Le Roy as the baby who ends up in the icebox, but he had outgrown the part, so they gave it to Richard Arlen, Jr., instead.

The success of "The Baby in the Icebox" convinced Cain that he was now ready for his novel about the California drifter who conspires with the wife of a gas station owner to murder her husband. In endless discussions with his friend, screenwriter Vincent Lawrence, Cain hit on an approach to the story. Lawrence had mentioned a curious fact about the famous Snyder-Gray murder case (which had dominated the newspapers in 1927): When Ruth Snyder had sent Judd Gray, her lover, off to Syracuse the night she murdered her husband, she had given Gray a bottle of wine—and later, when the police lab analyzed it, they discovered enough arsenic there to kill a regiment. When Lawrence told him this, Cain said: "Well, that jells this idea I've had for such a story; a couple of jerks who discover that a murder, though dreadful enough morally, can be a love story too, but then wake up to discover that once they've pulled the thing off, no two people can share this terrible secret and live on the same earth. They turn against each other, as Judd and Ruth did."

So Cain started his novel with an opening sentence that would eventually be quoted over and over again in college writing courses: "They threw me off the hay truck about noon." The novel, of course, was *The Postman Always Rings*

Twice, and the young man thrown off the truck was Frank Chambers (played by John Garfield in the 1946 MGM production of *Postman* and by Jack Nicholson in the more recent Lorimar version). And when the little 188-page book came out in 1934, it created a sensation that is difficult to comprehend today, when almost every other big novel seems to make news, with a six- or seven-figure sale to paperbacks and a rich contract for TV or movie rights. In 1934 that kind of success for a book was scarcely known. In fact, *Postman* was probably the first of the big fiction successes in American publishing, the first novel to hit for "the grand slam," meaning a hardcover best-seller, paperback best-seller, syndication, play, and movie. It scored more than once in all media, and still it goes on and on, selling today both in a Knopf hardcover edition called *Cain X 3* and in a Vintage paperback.

If there was one single review that started *Postman* on the way to its dizzying success, it was Franklin P. Adams's in the *New York Herald Tribune*. Adams was positively ecstatic in his praise, calling it the "most engrossing, unlaydownable book that I have any memory of." And that was just a starter. Whereas the *New York Times* review (as did many to follow) quoted the now-famous first sentence of *Postman*, Adams said: "I once thought the first chapter of Hardy's *The Mayor of Casterbridge* was the greatest first chapter in English fiction." But now he thought *Postman*'s first chapter might be literature's greatest, and to back up his case, he *reprinted* the entire chapter in his review.

Other critics were equally enthusiastic. Gertrude Atherton, a popular novelist, was shocked at the story but recognized the book's power nevertheless. "There are several disgusting themes and the characters are scum," she wrote, "but that book is a work of art. So beautifully is it built, so superb is its economy of word and incident, so authentic its characters and so exquisite the irony of its finish, it is a joy to any writer who respects his art."

Postman started slow in this country and then "took a

standing broad jump," as Cain put it, onto the best-seller lists, and it stayed there for weeks. MGM, carried away by all the excitement over the novel, bought it for $25,000, knowing full well it would be difficult to produce a script the Hays Office would approve and, in fact, it was twelve years before the studio finally filmed *Postman*.

With *Postman*, Cain had produced that rarest of literary achievements—a best-seller widely acclaimed by the critics. As a result, he was immediately in demand everywhere: Knopf wanted him to write another novel; MGM hired him to work on a film to star Clark Gable and Jeanette MacDonald (which was never completed); a Broadway producer wanted him to do a play based on *Postman*; and magazine editors were clamoring for Cain short stories and, especially, serials, having noted that *Postman*'s compactness and periodic plot twists made it ideal for six- or eight-part installment stories, a genre very popular in the 1930s.

So began one of the most unusual literary-cum-Hollywood careers in the country's history. From 1933 to 1948, when he left Hollywood, James M. Cain wrote more than two dozen short stories (not all of which were published), six magazine serials, seven novels (most of which were best-sellers), and two plays (one of which, *Postman*, was produced on Broadway, while the other, *7-11*, was staged in a summer production in Cohasset, but never reached New York City). At the same time, thirteen movies were made from his stories, including the classic *Double Indemnity*, starring Barbara Stanwyck, Fred MacMurray, and Edward G. Robinson; *Mildred Pierce*, which won an Academy Award for Joan Crawford in 1945; and the first version of *Postman*. All of these movies were scripted by other writers while Cain was going from one studio job to another, working his way up from $400 a week to $2,500. From Hollywood alone, he made an estimated $388,000 in those years, approximately one-third of it from the sale of his stories to the studios and two-thirds from salaries earned while working in the studios. Yet in all that studio work, he achieved only three shared credits—for *Stand Up and Fight* (starring Wallace Beery and Robert Taylor), *Gypsy Wildcat* (Maria Montez), and *Algiers* (Hedy Lamarr and Charles Boyer). Cain's studio career, by his own estimate, was a total failure. "I wanted the picture money," he said, trying to explain his Hollywood experience, "and I worked like a dog to get it. I parked my pride, my esthetic convictions, my mind outside on the street, and did everything to be a success in this highly paid trade . . . [but] even working in a whorehouse, the girl has to like the work a little bit, and I could not like pictures."

While he was living and working at such a pace, Cain's personal life, not surprisingly, also turned chaotic. In 1942 he divorced Elina, and then after three years of excessive eating and drinking, he married the silent-movie star Aileen Pringle. He separated from Aileen a year later, then married a former opera star, Florence Macbeth, who had been one of the idols of his youth, after meeting her quite by chance at a Hollywood cocktail party.

He and Florence were ecstatically happy together, and in his newfound tranquillity Cain made one of the most critical decisions of his life. One day in 1947, he said to Florence: "Either I'm going to wind up as a picture writer or I'm going back to novels and amount to something." Florence, who did not like Hollywood, voted for a return to the novels, and so, after he had completed *The Moth*, the Cains left Hollywood and headed East in 1948. They went to Hyattsville, Maryland, because Cain wanted to be near the Library of Congress, where he planned to research a Civil War trilogy. This project, however, proved the most exasperating, difficult task Cain ever undertook, and it was fifteen years before *Mignon*, the resulting novel, was eventually published—and then it was condemned by the critics and never became a best-seller.

By the early 1950s it had become painfully obvious that

Cain was not going to be able to support himself while trying to "amount to something as a writer." From time to time he wrote to H. N. Swanson, his new Hollywood agent, asking him to watch out for something in the studios, but nothing turned up. Finally, one day, he mentioned that it might be time to return to Hollywood, and Florence said: "It's not there . . . the Hollywood we knew does not exist any more."

Cain agreed and they decided to stay in Hyattsville, a decision he regretted for the rest of his life. "California is a neck of the woods everyone is fascinated with," he said. "It was El Dorado. You can put it in your book, 'It was nothing but a wayside filling station—like millions of others in California,' and that's O.K. Any piece of California, no matter how drab, prosaic or dull, is California just the same, the land of Golden Promise. I don't know anyone who is holding his breath over Prince Georges County, Maryland."

Cain was right: Maryland was not his milieu. From 1953 until 1977, when he died at the age of eighty-five, Cain wrote nine novels set in Maryland, only three of which were published—*Galatea*, *The Magician's Wife*, and *The Institute*. He also wrote *Mignon*, which was set in Louisiana, and *Rainbow's End*, set in the mountains of eastern Ohio. And none of them achieved the impact or the sales of his California stories. But he kept writing to the end, never wavering from the decision he made "out of the blue," while sitting on a bench in Lafayette Park in 1914. Late in his life he wrote an unpublished novel called *The Cocktail Waitress* and occasional nonfiction pieces for the *Washington Post*, and he was working on his memoirs when he died. To the end he retained his zest for writing: "It excites me and possesses me. I have no sense of it possessing me any less today than it did fifty years ago."

Cain also felt that those who can write must write, and for him the most important thing in writing was the story. "[Stories] ought to be about personal relations rather than broad issues," he said. He had a horror of becoming a writer

Introduction

with a message; and oddly enough, considering his reputation as an author who dealt with murder, adultery, homosexuality, prostitution, and incest, he maintained that his storytelling model was always *Alice in Wonderland*, a favorite which he professed to have read once a year throughout his life. "I . . . remind myself, it is about a girl who followed a white rabbit down his hole—about as unpretentious an idea as could be imagined. It is, so far as I see now, devoid of any significance and lesson to be imparted, or wisdom—those pitfalls for every writer. Whenever I feel an impulse to be important, I remind myself of Alice."

—ROY HOOPES

SKETCHES AND DIALOGUES

I N 1924 CAIN BEGAN writing for H. L. Mencken's *American Mercury*. His first contributions were typical magazine essays, but right from the beginning he showed an unusual talent for capturing the speech and dialects of the average man. For example: In his first piece—"The Labor Leader," which appeared in the February 1924 *Mercury*—Cain compared the labor leader with the businessman and said that just as the businessman had come to the point where everything was "a proposition," the labor leader had reached the point where everything was "a matter."

> This Matter you speak of, now, I don't want to be quoted in it, see? but if there's anything going in I want it to go in like it is, the truth about it, I mean, and not no pack of damn lies like the papers generally prints. What I say, now, don't put it in like it come from me, because I don't know nothing about it, ex-

cept what I read in the papers, not being notified in no official way, see? Besides, it's a matter which you might say is going to have a question of jurisdiction to it, and I don't want to have nobody make no charges against me for interference in no matter which it ain't strickly a point where I got authority. But, I can give you a idea about it and you can fix it up so them that reads the paper can figger out their own conclusion on how we stand in the matter.

With his talent for dialogue, Cain eventually suggested to Mencken that he be allowed to do his iconoclastic, satiric pieces entirely in dialogue, and the *Mercury* editor agreed. The result was a series beginning in the April 1925 *Mercury* lampooning various aspects of town and local government. The pieces were essentially little one-act plays and attracted considerable attention in the literary world, establishing Cain as a humorist and master of American dialect, both rural and urban. He continued to write these dialogues until he had amassed enough for a book, *Our Government*, published in 1930. Two of them, "The Hero" and "Theological Interlude," are included here. The first was included in *Our Government* under the title "Town Government: The Commissioners"; the second, he intended to include because he felt the book needed some sort of offbeat piece "to wash it up," but then decided that religion has very little to do with American government and dropped it. Another, "The Governor," was included in Katharine and E. B. White's *Subtreasury of American Humor*, which pleased Cain immensely. "The piece," he wrote Katharine White, "is one of the few things I have ever written that I have real affection for."

The dialogues also impressed Phil Goodman, a friend of Mencken's who produced Broadway plays. Mencken introduced the two men, and Goodman encouraged Cain to write a full play. It was about a modern-day Messiah who comes to the coal mines of West Virginia to save the miners and their families. He called it *Crashing the Gates*, and it was produced in 1926, a year before Sinclair Lewis's indictment of the clergy in *Elmer Gantry*. Clearly, the country was not ready for it. It shocked theatergoers in Stamford and Worcester, many of whom hissed, booed, stomped their feet, and then walked out. *Crashing the Gates* closed before it reached Broadway, but Cain never lost his urge to write a successful play. It was a dream he never realized.

Cain was also developing as a writer of short fiction in another outlet—the *New York World*. In 1928, partly to help meet his alimony payments, Cain started writing a regular column for the Sunday section. It consisted almost entirely of short sketches, as he called them, similar to the longer dialogues he was writing for the *Mercury*. They were, however, rather tepid versions of his *Mercury* pieces, given the restrictions of a family newspaper. For his *World* sketches he could not write about "niggers," murderers, and burning "stiffs" in a county poorhouse as he did for Mencken; he had to be more conventional. In the first year, his column was devoted entirely to a neighborhood centering around a fictional Bender Street in a city which was obviously New York. The recurring characters included: Mr. Schwartz, proprietor of the Bender Pharmacy; Mr. Fletcher, the popular bootlegger, his wife, and son, Herbert; Mr. Kallen, Grand Exalted Scribe of the Bender Lodge, The Loyal and Royal Order of Bruins; Hans Krumwielde, the director of the lodge's band, the Bender Red Pants; Police Sergeant Joyce, his daughter, Rose, and son, Benny; Mr. Albright, Bender School history teacher; Winny the Ninny, a friend of Rose's; and Dolly Dimple, an advice-to-the-lovelorn newspaper columnist who advises Rose on her many problems, most of which are told to "Dear Diary."

The dialogues centered around such issues as Rose Joyce trying to fatten herself, at Dolly Dimple's suggestion, with milk shakes, or the problem in the Bender Red Pants caused by the first trombonist not being able to play because he was being fitted for new false teeth. Reading them today, it is hard to imagine that these sketches were written by the author of *The Postman Always Rings Twice*. Yet the voices are authentic, the dialogue excellent, and each little sketch holds your interest once you get into it.

After a year, Cain, or perhaps someone higher on the *World* staff, tired of the Bender Street gang. So Cain shifted to other characters and locales, and from 1929 to early 1931, when the *World* folded, the subjects of his sketches fell into three categories, examples of which are included here: New York and New Yorkers ("The Robbery," "Vanishing Act," and "Dreamland"); Eastern Shore rubes and roughnecks, most of which begin "Down in the country . . ." ("Joy Ride," "Queen of Love and Beauty," and "Santa Claus, M.D."); and fictionalized accounts of personal experiences ("Gold Letters Hand Painted" and "It Breathed").

These sketches were extremely important to Cain's development. In the first place, he discovered that he was at his best as a writer when pretending to be someone else, and the person he felt most comfortable imitating was some Eastern Shore rube or mountain roughneck who spoke like one of Ring Lardner's characters. A perfect example is the sketch "It Breathed," about something that happened to Cain while he was in France in 1918. Instead of writing it in perfect diction, using the kind of grammar and phrasing that had so impressed Walter Lippmann, Cain pretended the incident had happened to some yokel and wrote the story in the first person in an Eastern Shore dialect.

Cain's *World* sketches were widely read around New York and are still being read in writing classes, where teachers use them to illustrate how a story can be told through dialogue alone (see "The Robbery"). The sketches also helped draw attention to Cain when he was still a relatively unknown writer. One day Claude Bowers, a *World* writer and historian, brought an eminent editor named Robert Linscott, from

Houghton Mifflin, to see Cain. Linscott had read Cain's sketches and wanted him to try a novel. Cain told Linscott of his earlier unsuccessful attempts at longer fiction and said he was not capable of it, but Linscott disagreed and predicted that someday Cain would write a novel—and he expressed the hope that Houghton Mifflin would be its publisher.

However, by 1931, when Cain left New York for Hollywood, he still felt his colloquial first-person approach to storytelling would not stand up in longer fiction. He was also convinced that New York was not his milieu, and that of all the sketches he wrote for the *World*, the ones about New York and New Yorkers were the least successful. "I'd been gradually coming to the conclusion," he later said, "that if I was to write anything of the kind I'd been dreaming about for so long, it could not be based in New York. . . . Those killingly funny drivers of New York cabs, the secretaries, bellhops, and clerks behind counters, were completely sterile soil. I drew nothing from them." On the other hand, he took pride in the country sketches, especially the dialogues he had done for the *Mercury*. They were, he said, in the "down-home idiom of Anywhere USA—anywhere but New York." Writing had to have roots—"it can't wriggle down from the sky, as Alice did, in Wonderland." And he felt that, just maybe, he would find his roots in the West.

Moving to California in 1931 proved to be the wisest decision James M. Cain ever made. Once in the West, he was ready for more conventional short stories, but he also discovered something that surprised him. The dialogue for which James M. Cain had become famous was essentially written for the printed page. It would not play to the ear, as Billy Wilder and Raymond Chandler found out when they were scripting *Double Indemnity*. This curious fact was perhaps at the root of Cain's frustrating inability to achieve success as a scriptwriter or playwright.

R.H.

The Robbery

"Good evening."

"Good evening."

"I guess we've seen each other a couple of times before haven't we? Me and my wife, we live downstairs."

"Yeah, I know who you are. What do you want?"

"Just want to talk to you about something."

"Well—come in."

"No. Just close that door behind you and we'll sit on the steps."

"All right. That suits me. Now what's the big idea?"

"Today we was robbed. Somebody come in the apartment, turned the whole place inside out, and got away with some money, and my wife's jewelry. Three rings and a couple of wrist watches. It's got her broke up pretty bad. I got her in bed now, but she's crying and carrying on all the time. I feel right down sorry for her."

"Well, that's tough. But what you coming to me about it for?"

"Nothing special. But of course I'm trying to find out who done it, so I thought I would come around and see you. Just to see if you got any idea about it."

"Yeah?"

"That's it."

"Well, I haven't got no idea."

"You haven't? That's funny."

"What's funny about it?"

"Seems like most everybody on the block has an idea about it. I ain't got in the house yet before about seven people stopped me and told me about it, and all of them had an idea about who done it. Of course, some of them ideas wasn't much good, but still they was ideas. So you haven't got no idea?"

"No. I haven't got no idea. And what's more, you're too late."

"How you mean, too late?"

"I mean them detectives has been up here already. I mean that fine wife of yours sent them up here, and what I had to say about this I told them, and I ain't got time to say it over again for you. And let me tell you something: You tell any more detectives I was the one robbed your place, and that's right where the trouble starts. They got laws in this country. They got laws against people that goes around telling lies about their neighbors, and don't you think for a minute you're going to get by with that stuff no more. You get me?"

"I'll be doggone. Them cops been up here already? Them boys sure do work fast, don't they?"

"Yeah, they work fast when some fool woman that has lost a couple of rings calls up the station house and fills them full of lies. They work fast, but they don't always work so good. They ain't got nothing on me at all, see? So you're wasting your time, just like they did!"

"What did you tell them, if you don't mind my asking?"

"I told them just what I'm telling you: that I don't know a thing about you or your wife, or your flat, or who robbed you, or what goes on down there, 'cepting I wish to hell you would turn off that radio at night onct, so I can get some sleep. That's what I told them, and if you don't like it you know what you can do."

"Well, now, old man, I tell you. Fact of the matter, my wife didn't send them cops up here at all. When she come home, and found out we was robbed, why it got her all excited. So she rung up the station house, and told the cops what she found, and then she went to bed. And that's where she's at now. She ain't seen no detectives. She's to see them tomorrow. So it looks like them detectives thought up that little visit all by theirself, don't it?"

"What do you mean?"

"I mean maybe even them detectives could figure out that this here job was done by somebody that knowed all about me and my wife, when we was home, when we was out, and all like of that. And 'specially, that it was done by somebody that knowed we had the money in the house to pay the last installment on the furniture."

"How would I know that?"

"Well, you might know by remembering what time the man came around to get the money last month and figuring he would come around the same day this month, and that we would have the money here waiting for him. That would be one way, wouldn't it?"

"Let me tell you something, fellow: I don't know a thing about this, or your furniture, or the collector, or nothing. And there ain't nothing to show what I know. So you ain't got nothing on me, see? So shag on. Go on down where you come from. So shut up. So that's all. So good-bye."

"Now, not so fast."

"What now? I ain't going to stay out here all night."

"I'm just thinking about something. First off, we ain't got nothing on you. That sure is a fact. We ain't got nothing on you at all. Next off, them detectives ain't got nothing on you. They called me up a little while ago and told me so. Said they couldn't prove nothing."

"It's about time you was getting wise to yourself."

"Just the same, you are the one that done it."

"Huh?"

"I say you are the one that done it."

"All right. All right. I'm the one that done it. Now go ahead and prove it."

"Ain't going to try to prove it. That's a funny thing, ain't it? Them detectives, when they start out on a thing like this, they always got to prove something, haven't they? But me, I don't have to prove nothing."

"Come on. What you getting at?"

"Just this: Come on with that money, and come on with them jewels, or I sock you. And make it quick."

"Now wait a minute. . . . Wait a minute."

"Sure. I ain't in no hurry."

"Maybe if I was to go in and look around. . . . Maybe some of my kids done that, just for a joke—"

"Just what I told my wife, old man, now you mention it. I says to her, I says, 'Them detectives is all wrong on that idea. Them kids upstairs done it,' I says, 'just for a joke.'"

"I'll go in and take a look—"

"No. You and me, we set out here till I get them things in my hand. You just holler inside and tell the kids to bring them."

"I'll ring the bell and get one of them to the door—"

"That sure is nice of you, old man. I bet there's a whole slew of them robberies done by kids just for a joke, don't you? I always did think so."

Vanishing Act

"THIS HERE," said Mr. Kemper, after contemplating for a time the rear elevation of the Public Library, "is a bum park. You can twist your neck around till you got a crick in it and still you can't tell what time it is. Let's go down to City Hall. It's plenty clocks down there."

Mr. Needles said nothing.

"What the hell you doing with that paper anyhow?" continued Mr. Kemper fretfully. "You been gawping at it for a hour, and in the same place. If you can't read it, then say so, but don't keep looking at it that way. That there annoys me."

"This here," said Mr. Needles, "is a terrible thing."

"What is it?" said Mr. Kemper.

"A guy what's getting littler all the time," said Mr. Needles. "Look at him. 'Living at Soldiers' Home in Sawtelle, Cal., he was five feet seven inches tall in 1914; now he is four feet ten inches. The case is of rare type.'"

"Rare and then some," said Mr. Kemper. "More like raw."

"How you mean?" said Mr. Needles.

"I mean it's so rare it ain't so," said Mr. Kemper. "That there is just one more of them lies what the guys would get tired of that devilment after a while."

"That there is so," said Mr. Needles.

"H'm," said Mr. Kemper.

"Because look at them pants," said Mr. Needles.

"Well," said Mr. Kemper, "them pants is for a bigger guy than he is, that's a fact. H'm. And that coat don't fit so good, neither."

"That there is true," said Mr. Needles. "I know it's true. I feel it in my bones."

"Well, then," said Mr. Kemper, "what of it? Maybe that guy is better off little than he was big. He don't eat so much, and that makes it easier. Or would, anyway, if he had to panhandle his grub off these eggs around here, 'stead of getting it free in a old soldiers' home. Bryant Park. Was this here William Jennings Bryant a Scotchman, do you suppose?"

"I ain't thinking about him," said Mr. Needles. "I'm thinking about myself."

"What you got to do with it?" said Mr. Kemper.

"Plenty," said Mr. Needles, and lapsed into a gloomy silence. Then, after a long time: "I been worried about myself a long time. I ain't as big as I was. Not nowhere near as big. And suppose I got this here disease too? 'The case is of rare type,' but if they got one, why can't they have two?"

"No reason at all," said Mr. Kemper. " 'Cepting what ails you is you don't get enough to eat. If you would get offen that bench more and work up and down Forty-second Street, panhandling enough nickels and dimes to get some grub what would stick to your ribs, why, then, you wouldn't have that there disease. Nobody can't stay the same size on coffee only."

"He's getting littler all the time," said Mr. Needles. "Maybe I am too. And that there is a terrible thing."

"What's so terrible about it?" said Mr. Kemper. "I already told you maybe he was better off. And maybe so are you."

"But suppose he would shrivel clean up like a balloon what has a leak and the wind all goes out?" said Mr. Needles. "Or maybe go away altogether, like a . . . like a . . . well, what the hell is that there like anyway?"

"Like a hole what somebody et the doughnut," said Mr. Kemper.

"Yeah," said Mr. Needles.

"Well, then," said Mr. Kemper, "suppose he would? The next war what he fights in, nobody couldn't shoot him. Looks like to me he would be still better off."

"But how about his soul?" said Mr. Needles.

"That guy," said Mr. Kemper, "he don't look to me like he even got a soul."

"But I got a soul," said Mr. Needles.

"How you know?" said Mr. Kemper.

"Never mind how I know," said Mr. Needles. "I know, and that's enough."

"Well, then, if you know, that's enough and you ain't got nothing to worry about. You never hear tell of no soul going out like a hole what somebody et the doughnut, did you? A soul, why that there is something what's built to last."

"I know," said Mr. Needles, "but if I all shrivel up and go away like that, am I dead yet or not?"

"Well, now," said Mr. Kemper, "that there is a question. It sure is. Of course, if you ain't there no more, I guess you're dead legal, all like of that. But are you really dead, let's see now. I got to think about that."

"I ain't even sure I'm dead legal," said Mr. Needles. "If it ain't no dead body, how can a guy be dead legal? No coroner wouldn't give no verdict without no remains."

"That's right," said Mr. Kemper. "It's funny I didn't think of that myself. Must of been because I was figuring on this other side of it."

Vanishing Act 31

"What's that?" said Mr. Needles.

"Suppose after you shrivel up and go out like that," said Mr. Kemper, "suppose, then, you would start growing again. How about that?"

"What was that again?" said Mr. Needles.

"Suppose," said Mr. Kemper, talking very slowly and distinctly, "after you went away and you wasn't there no more, why maybe you got cured of this here disease and begun growing again. How about that? Would you be the same guy or would you be another guy? Or like the fellow says, a couple of other fellows?"

"Holy smoke," said Mr. Needles. "Holy smoke, I never thought of that."

"This here," said Mr. Kemper, "is a very rare case. This here interests me a whole lot."

"Let's talk about something else," said Mr. Needles. "I . . . I . . . I don't like this here. It's got me worried."

"Then let's go down to City Hall, like I said," said Mr. Kemper, "so we can see what time it is."

OCTOBER 20, 1929

Dreamland

VINNY FELT HIS MOUTH GO NUMB as he entered the apartment and saw what was on the table. He stood for a moment moistening his lips as he stared at it.

"Piece of mail for you," he heard his sister-in-law call. "Looks like a phonograph record."

"Sure," he replied, and was surprised at how casual he sounded. "I been expecting it. How's everything?"

"O.K. Dinner'll be ready in a few minutes."

He picked up the record, went to his room, and sat down on the bed. He had been expecting it all right. Or hoping for it anyhow. Ever since that day in the store.

He hadn't covered himself with glory that day, that was a cinch. He just hadn't had the nerve to make the grade.

He had gone in to make one of those personal phonograph records, a record to send his brother Ike, who had moved to Cleveland. But he had had to wait.

Then the girl arrived. She was a pretty girl, and she sat

down so close to Vinny that he could smell the fur of her little summer neckpiece. He wanted to speak to her, to start a little conversation that would lead to his asking her if she didn't want to go with him and have an ice-cream soda. He opened his mouth to say it was hot, wasn't it. Nothing came out of it. He tried to catch her eye, so he could shake his head and fan himself a couple of times with his hat. Then he would probably have the nerve to say it was hot. But she didn't look at him.

Pretty soon the radio announcer came out, with his accompanist and the lady in charge. The girl stood up.

"But I think this gentleman was ahead of you," said the lady in charge.

" 'S all right," said Vinny. "I'll wait."

When she came out she would probably stop to thank him or something for letting her go first. Then he could say it was hot, wasn't it, a pretty good day for an ice-cream soda.

She came out with her record under her arm, stopped, started to speak, and fled without saying a word.

"It's your turn now," said the lady in charge.

He sat down in front of the microphone and took out of his pocket what he was going to say to Ike. He had it all written out, so he wouldn't get rattled and forget it in front of the machine.

"When the red light goes on," said the lady in charge, "it's time for you to begin. I'll turn it off ten seconds before the record is used up, so you'll have time to finish."

"All right."

The red light.

"Hello, Ike! you old son of a gun; how are you and what do you think of this for pulling a fast one on you? It's cheaper than calling up on the long-distance telephone, hey, Ike, you old son of a gun?"

It had seemed pretty funny when he wrote it out, but it sounded stale and flat now.

The red light out.

"Well, so long, Ike, this is all they allow me this time and don't take any rubber nickels."

"That'll be seventy-five cents unless you want a package of needles, and that'll make a dollar."

"All right. Put the needles in."

"A dollar, thank you. And now, if you don't mind writing your name and address here in this book . . ."

"Aw, never mind about that . . ."

"Well, we usually ask for the name and address—"

"I know, so you can send me a lot of that advertising junk and—"

He stopped. Looking up at him from the book in a threadlike, feminine hand, were a name and address:

Miss Amy Clarke
130 East 35th Street.

"All right," he said, and photographed this signature in his mind's eye as he wrote his own beneath it. A fat chance he would forget it.

"Say," he said innocently, "I believe I'll make another record. Just remembered somebody else I want to send one to."

"Why, surely."

This time he sat down at the piano. He could play a little, well enough for this job anyhow.

The red light.

He started up "You're the Cream in My Coffee." It sounded lousy, but it would give her the idea. Then he stopped singing and turned to the mike. "I'm the guy," he said with a guarded look at the lady in charge, "that wanted to speak to you today and didn't. And that you wanted to speak to and didn't. Believe me, I want to speak to you and if you feel the same way about it, you meet me at the Dreamland

Dreamland

dance hall, up on a Hundred and Twenty-fifth Street, on Saturday night, at . . ."

He mailed it, then spent three days of agony. Most of the time he felt like a sap, but sometimes he would play with the idea that the girl would go back to the store after she received the record, find the name and address after her own, and mail him a postcard saying "I'll be there" or something like that.

Now, here it was Saturday night and instead of a postcard there was a phonograph record, addressed in the same threadlike hand.

Trembling he cranked up his phonograph and clipped a needle.

A few bars of piano music. An old tune. Where had he heard it?

A thin, pretty, trembly voice:

> *Meet me tonight in Dreamland*
> *Under the silvery moon!*

"Dinner's ready," called his sister-in-law.
"I don't want any dinner!"
"But it's ready!"
"Sorry. Can't wait!"
Vinny was gone.

SEPTEMBER 15, 1929

Joy Ride

Down in the country when they built the state road it was a couple guys worked on it name of Luke and Herb Moore. And they was brothers, but their old man was stingy and wouldn't never give them nothing for their work. Because they didn't hire out to the contractor direct, but drove teams for their old man and the contractor paid him and he paid them. And he got thirty-five cents a hour apiece for both them double teams, and paid them $12.50 a month for driving them.

So all them other guys that worked on the road was all the time giving them the razz, and letting on their old man must be pretty rich by now, account he's got a big farm but don't never spend nothing, and goes to church every Sunday but don't never put nothing on the plate, and all like of that; until Luke and Herb got so they hated to see the old man show up on Saturday afternoon to sign the payroll. So along about the first of October they begun mumbling to each other in the lunch hour, and then they give it out they was going to

Joy Ride

do something that would make them other guys on the road look pretty sick. And what they was going to do was go on a bender. They had just got their month's wages, and that was $25, and they was going to swipe one of the old man's horses, after he had went in the house that night, and drive down to the railroad station what was about six mile away, and hop the 6:46 in to Washington, and then come back on the owl what got in at 12:22, and then drive on back and put the horse in the stable without the old man knowing nothing about it. Because they figured that $25 would pay for a pretty classy drunk, and then they would have a comeback if they heard any more of this tightwad stuff.

So they done it. They et some supper in a hurry, and then they sneaked out and geared the old man's best horse to his new buggy, and then they walked the horse on the grass so the old man couldn't hear them going by the house, and then they hit for the station. And on the way down they passed Will Howe and Heinie Williams, what was rolling the road in the nighttime on account it was getting late in the year and the contract had to be finished before frost, and Will and Heinie blowed the roller whistles for them and it looked like their trick was going to work. Them razzes would be changed to cheers. And they caught the 6:46, and down in Washington they must of put on a swell drunk act, because some people heard them arguing in the Union Station just before the owl pulled out, and Herb was for staying and spending the rest of their money, but Luke says no he wouldn't give the old man the satisfaction of knowing they stole the horse.

So they come back. And they was all set to get away with it, until they drove up to the piece of road they had built that day, where Will and Heinie had been rolling up to twelve o'clock. But then they seen something they had forgot about. Them two rollers was parked across the road with red lights hung on their water boxes to keep people from driving over the new piece of road that had just been rolled down. And it was a detour they could take, but Luke wouldn't hear of no detour.

"What?" he says. "Us turn back and drive a half mile further just for a pair of measly steam rollers? Nothing doing."

So he jumps out, grabs off the red lanterns, and commences waving them around.

"Engineer," he hollers, "do your stuff, I'm too drunk. 'Stead of us getting out of the way of these here rollers, we'll make them get out of our way."

So Herb, he climbs up on the little Buffalo roller what was on the left, and he can't see so good, and he's pretty drunk too, but he's seen Will and Heinie do it, and he grabs a couple of bars, and pulls them, and sure enough the little Buffalo roller begins to move and slides right back in the ditch.

"Whoa!" says Luke, waving his lights out there in the middle of the road. "Engineer, you done great. Casey Jones couldn't of done it no better. Now get on that other one."

So Herb climbs up on the big five-ton Acme what was on the right-hand side of the road.

Now a Acme, it don't work just the same as a Buffalo. The throttle and reverse bar is placed a little different, so when Herb grabbed aholt of them and pulled, he didn't have no such good luck as he had the first time. 'Stead of going backward, that big five-tonner went frontward. It give a jump and run across the road and whanged right up alongside that other one. And Herb, he got throwed plumb out of the cab on the road. And it wasn't nothing but steam coming out of both them rollers on account the bump had strained the boilers and they begun to leak. And it was dark all of a sudden. And Herb, soon as he remembered where he was at couldn't see nothing of Luke. Because that roller, when it jumped frontward, had knocked Luke down and put out his red lights. And it had rolled him flatter than a German pancake.

So the horse give a jump when them two rollers come together, and helloed past them up the road, and turned in at the home gate. So the old man got up and went out, and then he begun ringing all the rings on the party line telephone, and it wasn't long before him and a bunch found the rollers, and Herb, and what was left of Luke. And then he begun to rave.

"Oh, God," he says, right out in front of where Herb was crying on the side of the road, "what have I done that you do this to me? Ain't I always done right? Why did you send me a pair of worthless rascals like this when I asked you for sons?"

So Will Howe, he stood it as long as he could, and then he says: "Well, if God made you, it ain't much else that I would put past him."

"Come on, kid," he says to Herb; "you better stay with me tonight."

So Herb, he stayed with Will; and the coroner held him, but the state's attorney turned him loose. And after that, he done some work on the road, but he didn't never get no razz.

Queen of Love and Beauty

Down in the country they used to have every summer what they called a tournament, and it wasn't much to it, only a bunch of farmers calling theirself knights, and riding work plugs down a course and spearing iron rings off hooks with a pole they said was a lance. But they generally always had a pretty good time, because the knight that spread the most rings could crown the Queen of Love and Beauty at the dance they had in the Grand Opera House that night, and them that speared next to the most rings could crown the maids of her court, so it was a little excitement anyway, and what with plenty of fried chicken and deviled eggs at the supper they had in between, everybody made out pretty good.

So sure enough, right after wheat-thrashing time one July, they put it in the county paper the tournament would be held the next Saturday, at a farm name of Three Hills what was owned by Mr. Glynn, and when Saturday come it was a big crowd out to Three Hills, and all the women giggling about who was going to get crowned Queen of Love and Beauty.

But what shows up on top of a runty-looking horse with a pole in his hand but a guy name of Bert Lucas. And the committee didn't hardly know what to do. Because Bert, he wasn't really no guy to be riding in a tournament. When he was young, he had been kind of wild, and one night he swiped a car and went on a joy ride, and then didn't have no more sense than to wreck it. So the Grand Jury indicted him and he done the only thing he could do, and that was to skip. And when he come back about five years later to work the little farm what his old man had, nobody didn't have much to do with him. The indictment, nobody done nothing about it, because his old man had scraped together enough money to pay for the car before he died, so they just kind of let it drop. But there it was just the same, and a guy under indictment don't hardly look like no knight.

Still, here he come cantering in, and the committee was all crossed up and couldn't think of nothing to say, so it wasn't nothing to do but let him ride. He said he was the Knight of Hawthorne Bay and they passed him in.

Well, the first tilt wasn't hardly over before the whole place knowed that was a big mistake. Because where Bert had went when he skipped was out West and if it was anything he couldn't do in a saddle that runty-looking horse could pretty near do it for him, because it wasn't nothing more or less than a cow pony, what he had rode all the way back East from Texas. He could spear them rings so easy he made all them other guys look ridiculous, and he wouldn't come loafing up on a slow singlefoot either, but on a dead run. And he would kind of holler when he got in front of the people, like them circus cowboys does, and that was kind of a new one in that neck of the woods, and nobody knowed what to make of it.

They couldn't get away from his score, though, so when the judges read out that he was the winner, they tried to give him a little bit of a hand. So that went to Bert's head just like it was liquor. I guess it had been pretty lonely out there on the farm without nobody to come and see him, and when Mr. and Mrs. Glynn set the supper out under the trees, he was laughing and cutting up like he was drunk. So all hands thought they might as well kid him along, and pretty soon somebody asks him who is he going to crown Queen of Love and Beauty.

"I ain't made up my mind yet. I don't know which one I'm going to pick. It's so many good-looking women here I'm afraid I'm going to have to shake up all the names in a hat and pull one out."

So with that, Mr. Glynn went behind the house and got a bunch around him.

"Listen, men," he says. "Do you know what? That simple-looking nut thinks that winning the tournament gives him the right to pick any woman here and name her Queen."

"What!" says two or three.

"He certainly does," says Mr. Glynn. "And I don't know what to do. Suppose he picks my wife? I can't have her leading the grand march with that jailbird."

"Say," they says. "We got to think about that."

So Mr. Glynn was grand marshal of the tournament, and of course he had to make the speech handing the crown over to Bert after they had all drove in to the Grand Opera House for the dance. And so he made the speech. And he made it long and flowery, because he was pretty good on that stuff on account he liked to make Fourth of July speeches. And Bert, he just ate it up. Because it look like to him that everything had been forgot and nobody didn't hardly remember if it was him that was indicted or maybe somebody else. So he kept his eyes glued to Mr. Glynn and kept smiling to hisself. And while Mr. Glynn was talking, Mrs. Glynn and a couple other women kind of tiptoed through the little door that led back of the stage. And two or three more followed them, and then some more, and in a minute they was all slipping through the door like ghosts.

And when Bert took the wreath of flowers from Mr. Glynn, and turned around to pick out some woman to give it to, it wasn't a single woman in the hall.

So Bert looked around, and his face got red, and a kind of a silly-looking grin stayed on it. And then he swallowed a couple of times, and dropped the wreath down on the floor. And then he walked straight out of the hall. And then he went to the hitching rack, and got on his horse, and rode out into the night. And nobody down there ain't seen him from that day to this.

Santa Claus, M.D.

Down in the country one time they got a new principal to the high school, name of Hartman. And he was a kind of funny-looking guy, and he taught science. So pretty soon he began to teach them pupils in the higher grades all about how the animals has little ones, and he was wasting his breath if you ask me, because if it was anything them tough mugs didn't know about the animals and all the rest of it, why it wasn't much. But along about Thanksgiving it begun to be some talking around. A whole lot of people, they let on they didn't think much of it, teaching boys and girls stuff like that. And pretty soon, the board of trustees, they held a couple meetings.

So just about that time Hartman, he stood up in the assembly hall in front of the whole school, little children and all, and give them a little talk on Christmas. And he says the best thing is to know the truth about Christmas, and the truth is that it ain't no Santa Claus, but only your father dressed up,

Santa Claus, M.D.

and the real way to celebrate Christmas was to quit thinking so much about presents and to go to church and give thanks that Jesus Christ was born that day.

Well, did you ever cuff a hornet's nest with the butt end of a fishing pole while you was trying to jerk a big one up on the bank? That's what it was like when Hartman made that little talk. Them little children went home bellering to their father and mother, and a couple dozen big Ikes showed up at the school and wanted to fight, and things got hot. So the trustees, they made up their mind what they was going to do pretty quick. They fired Hartman, and took the key to the school away from him, and put one of them woman teachers in charge till they could get somebody else.

So that kind of eased things off, but Hartman ain't left town. He hung around and he would come over to one of the stores from the little house where he lived at on the edge of town, and buy some stuff, and then duck away without speaking to nobody. So the day before Christmas some of the boys fixed it up that they would kind of give him the idea that he better beat it. And what they was going to do was go around that night and take him out, and maybe fan him a few times with a strap, and then make him kneel down in front of Doc Merritt, who would have on the Santa Claus suit that he used to wear up to the festival at the Methodist church, and then let him take his pick would he leave town hisself or get rode out on a rail.

So they done it. The Doc put on his suit, and him and about a dozen others sneaked over there. And when they beat on the door, they could hear some running around upstairs, but not nobody come to the door.

"Come on out, Hartman!" they hollers. "We brung Santa Claus with us and we want you to look at him."

But still nobody come to the door, and they was getting

ready to break it down. But all of a sudden a light showed, and through the glass in the door they seen Hartman running down the steps, fast as he could come. And he opened the door and come running out without no hat.

"Grab him!" one of them hollers, and a couple of them made a pass at him.

But he throwed them off like they was puppy dogs or something, and went running up the street fast as he could go. And they was so surprised all they done was stand there and look at him.

So it seemed like it was something funny about it and they opened the door and peeped in. And right away they could hear something upstairs. It sound like a woman crying.

"Hell," says one of them. "Let's beat it."

"Wait a minute," says Doc Merritt. "Shut up, you guys." And he listened, and then he tiptoed upstairs.

"What's the matter?" they says when he come back.

"Boys," he says, "this party is off. It's his wife. She's having a baby."

So he sent a couple of them over to his office, and give them the key, and told them to bring him his kit, and went back upstairs. And the rest of them, they felt kind of ashamed of theirself, and they beat it.

So Hartman, where he was heading for was Doc Merritt. And he run over to his office, and didn't find him there, and then he helloed over to the boardinghouse where the Doc lived at, and didn't find him there. And then he got kind of wild, and went running all over town, in stores and everywhere, trying to find the Doc. And not nobody could tell him where the Doc was, on account this fanning bee had been kept pretty dark, and everybody was wondering what was up.

So in about a hour, here he come running back, and he didn't have no Doc and he didn't have nothing. And when he went upstairs he almost fainted. And then he begun blubbering and crying and carrying on like he was crazy, and the more the Doc tried to calm him down the worse he went on. Because it was all over, and what he seen was the Doc, wrapping up the new baby boy in a little piece of woolen cloth. But what the Doc had forgot was, on account he had been working so hard, that he still had on the Santa Claus suit, with the whiskers still sticking to his chin, and for all Hartman could see it was Santa Claus hisself that had brung him his child and made everything all right.

"It is a Santa Claus," he kept saying over and over, even when he got it straight what happened. "Oh, God, after the way I ran and prayed, and then come back and find—" And then he would just cry.

So them eggs that was going to fan him, they was trying to tell theirself it was all a joke by that time, and they showed up with a lot of Christmas stuff, and a drum for the kid. And it was all over town in an hour about how Hartman has changed his mind about Santa Claus, and maybe ain't so sure how little ones gets in the world no more, so Christmas Day the trustees held a special meeting and took him back. So after that he done fine. So it looks like to me Santa Claus pulled a fast one on him.

DECEMBER 22, 1929

Gold Letters Hand Painted

WHEN I WAS ABOUT FIFTEEN YEARS OLD, I and all the other young men about town used to resort to various schemes to give the impression that we had reached man's estate. Some of us acquired girls, some took jobs, some played poker, and some just talked. But Bob Plummer, son of one of the Metho-preachers in town, made the mistake of hatching a scheme so grand that it challenged the gods; and that, as we all know, is merely storing up dynamite against the lightning bolt. Bob's scheme was an individual shaving mug, no less. He went away to Wilmington, Delaware, with his father one spring, to attend the annual conference, and when he came back he had it in his suitcase. He didn't show it around, of course, and boast about it. That would have been a gross strategic blunder. He merely strolled around to Johnny Vandergrift's barber shop in the most casual manner, left it there, and told Johnny that from now on he would come on Saturday nights to be shaved.

Well, that, as you may understand, was a bombshell; it made girls, jobs, poker games, white pants, and all such things seem childish nonsense by comparison. By twos and threes that afternoon we all had a look at it, coming to jeer, remaining to be struck dumb with awe. There it stood in plain view, among the hundreds of cups belonging to Johnny's regular customers, and on its pearly face, in beautiful gold letters, was his own individual name, thus:

ROB'T P. PLUMMER, JR.

And for a whole week we were so groggy that our faculties were practically paralyzed. But then duty called: we had to organize some sort of counteroffensive. And presently we had one that we thought very neat. It was called the Foggy Club, and it was formed for the sole purpose of affording the members an opportunity to foregather occasionally for the sociable smoking of cigarettes. And the beauty of it was that Bob, since his father was a minister, could not very well join.

The next thing, of course, was to select a propitious moment for inviting him to join, and we decided that none could be better than when he was reclining in Johnny Vandergrift's best chair, having himself shaved out of his precious blue mug. The next Saturday night accordingly, having made sure that the operation had actually started, we all trooped into the shop.

Red Lucas led off. He yawned awhile, and then put down his magazine and looked over at Johnny.

"Who's that you got in the chair?" he asked, in a puzzled sort of way.

For answer, Johnny held up the mug.

"Oh," said Red. "Bob Plummer. Damn, I didn't know that was Bob Plummer. Hello, Bob. How you was?"

"Hello," said Bob. "I'm all right."

"Say, that reminds me," Red went on. "We haven't got your ante yet for the Foggy Club. You'll let me have it in the next couple of days, won't you?"

"Yeah, I heard about the Foggy Club," said Bob. "If you don't mind though, I think I won't join."

"What, not join?" said Red. "Why, we were counting on you."

"No, thanks, I'd rather not."

"Well, gee, I sure am sorry. Old man won't let you smoke, hey?"

"No, that's not it. He says I can smoke, if I want to. But you know how it is. He's a minister, and it would make trouble, so I just don't do it. Not regular, anyway."

Well, there we were, licked before we started. Somebody said something about Mamma's boy, but just then Johnny dipped a brushful of lather out of the mug, and it wilted away to a few weak snickers. The game was over and we hadn't scored a point.

"No," said Bob, after he had got up out of the chair, and carefully inspected his face, "it's not so easy, being a minister's son. There's a lot of things you can't do."

He leaned close for a look at his chin. We had an uneasy feeling that more was coming, and that we wouldn't enjoy it a bit. And in a moment, we saw what it was. He had given Johnny a quarter, had received fifteen cents, and was fingering his change. He was going to tip Johnny Vandergrift!

The room reeled around us. Johnny Vandergrift, who had brought the first automobile to town! Johnny Vandergrift, who had once seen an airplane! Johnny Vandergrift, who wore a brown derby hat on Sunday! . . .

"Here you are, John," said Bob. "That'll pay for the wear on the razor."

"Keep it," said Johnny. "There's no wear on the razor, because I've shaved you three times now and haven't clinked a whisker yet."

There was more, but on the whole I prefer to draw the veil at this point.

MARCH 2, 1930

It Breathed

IN THE WAR I put in some time on observation post, and it was in top of the tallest tree in France, and you climbed up by a ladder, and they had a little iron box up there what look like a coffin, and you could go in there when the shells was falling, and they generally was. And how we done was to have two hours in that box and six hours off. Only a guy name of Foley got sick, and that give us two hours on and four off, on account we only had three men instead of four. And that there wasn't so good, because even doing two and six we didn't never get no good sleep, and doing two and four we didn't hardly get no sleep at all.

So it went on like that for two days. And then Katz, he called up headquarters on the telephone again to ask them to come get Foley, and they put up a argument or something, and he kind of got a little wild.

"So you ain't got no car you can spare, hey?" he hollers. "Well, you better get one, and get it quick. Because this guy is sick. He's got the flu or something and if you think three men can run this post and take care of him too you made a mistake and you can tell the Captain I said so."

So Foley, he was laying right there in the bunk in the little shack we had under the tree, and of course, he heared everything that Katz was saying. So after he hung up, Katz begun to blubber, on account he didn't want Foley to think we minded bringing him water, and bathing his head, and all like of that, and he asked Foley not to pay no attention to what he said. So Foley, he wasn't paying no attention to nothing, and all he done was nod his head a little bit and wave his hand like he didn't want nobody to bother him.

So then me and Katz went over to draw the rations, and where we drawed them was from a infantry field kitchen, and it was in a trench about a half mile from where the tree was at. So we ain't hardly started before he begun some more of his wild talk.

"Damn this thing!" he says. "Damn all of it! How did it ever get started anyway?"

"It won't be so bad," I says, "after they send for Foley and give us another man so we can get some sleep."

"Sleep!" he says. "Ha, ha, ha!"

"Well," I says, "what else seems to be bothering you?"

"Plenty," he says. "Them shells, for one thing. Always going off. I got so I jump every time a twig falls off one of them trees on the ground. And another thing: That would be fine, wouldn't it, to get knocked off right at the end?

"Two weeks!" he keeps on. "After a while only one week. After a while only one day. Then pft! Just like that. Knocked off. And then this."

"This what?" I says.

"All of it." And he waves his hand over the whole front, where it was kind of stretched out in front of us. "Yeah, that's the worst. The rest, that ain't nothing alongside of that.'"

I didn't have no idea what he meant, but I give a kind of a look around and says: "Oh, I don't know. It wouldn't be no bad-looking country if they would fill up them shell holes and leave the grass grow a little."

"Not by daylight," he says. "But at night, ha, ha, ha! Listen." And he stopped still and looked at me with a kind of a crazy look in his eye.

"Listen," he says. "You know this whole thing is alive? You know it's alive and it breathes?"

"Well," I says, "I never noticed it."

"That's because you ain't got that two o'clock watch," he says. "Oh, my God, when that fog comes down and you can't hear a thing, and all of a sudden it turns over and breathes! And me up there all alone in that tree—"

"Katz," I says, "it ain't a thing the matter with you except you're blotto from not having no sleep, so—"

"Blotto!" he says. "Yeah, I'm blotto, plenty blotto. But that ain't all. I've been feeling like this a long time, and—"

"And," I keeps on, "you can damn well snap out of it. Hell," I says, "you think you're the only one that's got it tough?"

And I spoke pretty short, because I was good and tired of listening to him bellyache. So we fixed it up that we would switch that two o'clock watch and I would take it 'stead of him. And at first he didn't want to, but I made him do it because if it would make him shut up, the two o'clock watch was same to me as any other watch.

And that night when two o'clock come I went up and started the watch. And I wasn't hardly up there than I seen what he meant, all right. A whole lot of people, they got the idea that on a battle front it's a hell of a lot of noise going on all the time. And most of the time it is, like shelling in the afternoon when the balloons is up, and machine guns at night when they're sending up flares to spot raids, and all like of that. But from two o'clock in the morning on to dawn it ain't nothing so still as a battle front.

Still, I made out all right, because it didn't mean nothing

to me. But then all of a sudden I felt my lips go numb and my heart begun pounding like it would jump out of my throat. I was just looking at my watch, and it was 3:28 and I was getting ready to make my 3:30 entry in the book, when I heared it, just like he said. Maybe you think I'm lying, but I tell you it give kind of a sigh and then went right quiet again. And I was still pretty shaky when he come up to relieve me at four.

"Well," he says, "you was right." And he wasn't wild no more, but stood there looking out at it.

"How you mean?" I says.

"Plenty of them got it tougher than I got it. Foley, for instance."

"Did they send for him?" I says.

"No," he says. "He just went."

He went in the box and lit a cigarette. "You better enter it in the book," he says. "I took note of the time. It was three twenty-eight."

NOVEMBER 17, 1929

The Hero

The office of the town commissioners, second floor, Water Witch Fire Engine House. It is an afternoon in May. The members of the board, who are Mr. Hinsch, chairman, and Messrs. Matchett and Oyster, have just returned from lunch after a public hearing which lasted all morning, and are now about to go into executive session, from which, of course, the public is excluded.

Mr. Hinsch: Well, gentlemen, the way I get it, we got to act on this matter of a pension for Scotty Akers, what I mean for his family. And I say let's not have no more bum argument like we had this morning. It's too damn hot.

Mr. Matchett: I never seen the beat of them people, a whooping and a-hollering, and a-carrying on, the way they done.

Mr. Oyster: And it don't make no difference which way we settle it, we got one side or the other sore as hell at us.

Mr. Hinsch: That's right. It don't make no difference what we do, we got ourself in Dutch.

Mr. Matchett: And us only trying to do the right thing.

Mr. Hinsch: It's this here goddam fight that makes all the trouble.

Mr. Oyster: This here fight makes it bad. Wonder why the hell Scotty couldn't of been squirting water in the fire when that string-piece beaned him, 'stead of on them Water Witches.

Mr. Matchett: Scotty sure was a caution, thataway.

Mr. Hinsch: How come that fight to get started? I ain't never got that straight in my head yet.

Mr. Oyster: Scotty started it.

Mr. Matchett: Yep, Scotty started it, just like he always done.

Mr. Oyster: You see, when them Semper Fidelises drives up in their truck, they finds them Water Witches already at the fire. Well, Scotty, he was driving the Semper Fidelises' truck. And soon as he seen them Water Witches, he hollers out: "Hell, ain't you got the fire out yet? Get out of the way and let some firemen get to it."

Mr. Matchett: That's what Scotty said. I was there and I heard him.

Mr. Hinsch: It's a wonder Scotty couldn't of shut up once in a while. I always did say Scotty could of shut his trap and improved hisself.

Mr. Oyster: And with that, them Water Witches turns the hose on the Semper Fidelises. And they had a fight. And right in the middle of it the roof of the house that was on fire falls and a string-piece beans Scotty on the head. And when they pick him up, he's dead.

Mr. Matchett: And the house burns down.

Mr. Oyster: That's the hell of it, the house burns down.

Mr. Hinsch: What I say, if them two companies got to have a fight every time they go to a fire, why can't they put

The Hero

the fire out first and then have the fight coming back?

Mr. Matchett: That's the way them Eyetalians does when two funerals have a race. They always race coming *back* from the graveyard. That there is a better way. It stands to reason.

Mr. Oyster: You would think them boys would stop to think that a house costs money. And them trucks costs money, too.

Mr. Hinsch: And here we got all them Semper Fidelises saying the town had ought to pay Scotty's family a pension, account of him getting beaned like you might say in the line of duty, and all them Water Witches says it's a hell of a note to sock a pension on the taxpayers, account of Scotty being the one that started the fight. And it don't make no difference which way we settle it, we got ourself in Dutch.

Mr. Matchett: A fellow don't hardly know what to do.

Mr. Hinsch: Them companies wasn't so bad before this here Rotary Club butted in with all their lovey-dovey stuff.

Mr. Matchett: Why, no! What I mean, they had a fight now and then, but they didn't have nobody get killed or no house burn down, like of that.

Mr. Oyster: But them Rotarys wasn't satisfied. They had to get up a association and have all the firemen belong to it, so them two companies would love one another. Who the hell ever hear tell of a couple of fire companies that love one another?

Mr. Hinsch: I don't think much of that stuff. You got to have competition.

Mr. Oyster: And come to find out, they love each other so damn much they had a fight and the house burns down. And Scotty gets killed.

Mr. Hinsch: Them Rotarys makes me sick. Why the hell does them fellows belong to a order like that?

Mr. Matchett: I hear a fellow say they don't pay no benefits nor nothing.

Mr. Oyster: That's rrght. Jim Peasely, that was presı dent last year, told me so hisself. They ain't got no insurance or nothing like that.

Mr. Matchett: And they ain't got no regalia.

Mr. Oyster: And then another thing, why don't they have their meetings at night? Daytime ain't no time for a order to meet. I'd like to see them try to pull off a initiation, what I mean, a real initiation, with a big class of candidates, like that, in the daytime. Why, you couldn't do it.

Mr. Matchett: All they got is a password.

Mr. Oyster: Password? Why, hell, they ain't got a pass word no more than a snowbird has. They got a motto, that's all they got. "Serve yourself," or something like that, I forget just what it is. But not no regular password, not even a grip.

Mr. Hinsch: Is that right?

Mr. Matchett: I swear to God, I never knowed that. I thought they had a password and a grip.

Mr. Hinsch: Ain't they got nothing at all?

Mr. Oyster: Not a damn thing! And to hear them fellows talk, and read them pieces in the paper, you would think it was something.

Mr. Hinsch: When I get an order, I want something for my money.

Mr. Matchett: Me, too. I'm in the Junior Order and Heptasophs now, and before long—well, I reckon you boys know what I got my eye on. I hope to get took in the Odd Fellows.

Mr. Oyster: Shall we tell him, Hinsch?

Mr. Hinsch: Go ahead and tell him.

Mr. Oyster: We got a little surprise for you, Matchett. It's all fixed up for you with the Odd Fellows. They act on it next meeting. Fact of the matter the committee has already passed on it.

Mr. Matchett: Is that right! . . . Well, boys, that there was sure some surprise, and I tell you it makes a fellow sure feel good. I kind of had an idea, but a fellow can't never be sure.

Mr. Oyster: Yep, she's all fixed up. You'll be right on the steamboat when this summer's excursion pulls out.

Mr. Matchett: It sure does make a fellow feel good.

Mr. Hinsch: What I say, if them Rotarys hadn't of butted in with this here Buddy Association, everything would of been all right. Them firemen didn't need no association. They ought to of kept them companies separate. But then they got in this here bum argument about what color plumes they're going to have on their hats and then everything is balled up like hell.

Mr. Oyster: That there is a hot thing to have a argument about, ain't it, what color plumes they're going to have? My God! What difference does it make what color plumes they have? They could have green plumes and it wouldn't make no difference to me.

Mr. Hinsch: Me neither. But I say them Water Witches had one thing on their side. White plumes gets dirty awful quick.

Mr. Oyster: Well, Hinsch, I say it's according as according. If a fellow takes care of his hat right, what I mean, not make no football outen it and use it to dust off the back porch, why them plumes stays clean about as long as a man could expect. Me, I kind of like them white plumes. They show off good on parade.

Mr. Hinsch: They don't show off as good as red plumes. A fellow can see a red plume a long ways off.

Mr. Oyster: The trouble with them red plumes was that Myersville had them.

Mr. Hinsch: Myersville ain't got no red plumes no more. They changed them to blue this year.

Mr. Oyster: I know they changed them, but the trouble is nobody out in the state don't know about it. What them Semper Fidelises was thinking about was the state carnival.

Them boys is taken first prize on appearance for three years now, and they didn't want nobody getting them mixed up with Myersville. Well, yes, it's a shame the way things is all shot to hell since them Rotarys butted in the way they done. Them companies ain't got no more show at the carnival now than a snowball in hell.

Mr. Hinsch: I hear them Semper Fidelises ain't going down to the carnival if they don't get what they want for Scotty Akers.

Mr. Oyster: Yeah, I hear that too. First time in fifteen years we ain't had two companies at the carnival. I would think them Rotarys would be ashamed of theirself.

Mr. Matchett: Well, boys, this sure is good news. What I say, a fellow had ought to go in the Junior Order first. The place for a young fellow is in the Junior Order. Then, when he gets so's he can take on another one, he ought to get took in the Heptasophs. Anyway, that's what I done, and if I had the thing to do over again, I would do it the same way. Then, when he gets a little older and he knows where he's at, it's time to get took in the Odd Fellows. Ain't that right?

Mr. Hinsch: A fellow hadn't ought to be in no hurry about the Odd Fellows. Junior Order first, I say.

Mr. Oyster: It don't pay to be in no hurry.

Mr. Hinsch: Fact of the matter, Oyster, I ain't never got it straight in my head whether Scotty died in line of duty or not. That there is a question.

Mr. Oyster: The way I look at it, Scotty was there when the bell rang. Then Scotty drove the truck out and got to the fire. And he was at the fire. We know that much, and there can't be no argument about it. Well, suppose Scotty had of been squirting water on the fire? The string-piece might of beaned him just the same.

Mr. Hinsch: That's so, all right. Fact of the matter, you might say the string-piece would of been more liable to of beaned him if he was squirting water on the fire than like it was. A fellow runs a awful risk, taking a hose in close on a fire when it gets started good.

Mr. Oyster: And then another thing. Take where Scotty was standing. He didn't have to pull that nozzle in close to the fire like that, just to sock it on them Water Witches. It looks to me like Scotty was just getting ready to turn it on the fire anyhow.

Mr. Hinsch: That's right. I was thinking about that myself.

Mr. Oyster: And then, it don't make no difference if Scotty started the fight, he helped to put out a whole lot of fires, and a fellow don't hardly know which fire he's going to get killed at.

Mr. Hinsch: It's just like lynching a nigger. Some of them says you ought not to lynch him, account of maybe he ain't the right nigger, but I always say if a nigger hadn't ought to be lynched for one thing he ought to be lynched for something else he done, so it don't pay to figure it down too close. It's just the same way with Scotty. He might of got beaned some other time.

Mr. Oyster: Or later on, maybe.

Mr. Hinsch: Of course, I ain't saying Scotty didn't make a whole lot of trouble the way he talked. If Scotty could of kept his trap shut he would of been a hell of a sight better fellow.

Mr. Oyster: Scotty had a-plenty to say all right. But in a way you might say he done a lot for the town.

Mr. Hinsch: I say anybody that went to fires regular like Scotty done, why, he done a lot for the town, even if he did have a lot to say.

Mr. Oyster: If it was only me, I would say pay the pension and glad to do it.

Mr. Hinsch: That's right. I would be the first one to vote for it.

Mr. Oyster: The trouble is them goddam Water Witches.

Mr. Hinsch: Them Water Witches sure would raise hell. And what makes it bad, them Water Witches is all from the upper end of town and they pay the taxes.

Mr. Oyster: Them Semper Fidelises ain't got no money.

Mr. Hinsch: Most of them Semper Fidelises pays rent. It's them Water Witches owns the property, or their people does.

Mr. Oyster: They pay rent when they pay it. I swear to God, I don't see how half of them boys get along.

Mr. Hinsch: Now what I say, it ain't nothing against them boys that they're poor people, like of that. But when them people that pays taxes comes in here and puts up a holler, why you got to pay some attention to it.

Mr. Oyster: They put up a holler all right. You could hear them a mile. They plumb wore me out.

Mr. Matchett: There wasn't no trouble about it, was there? What I mean, nobody didn't drop no blackball against me, did they?

Mr. Hinsch: Not a one.

Mr. Oyster: I don't believe I ever saw a application go through as quick as hisn, did you, Hinsch?

Mr. Hinsch: Same as a greased pig.

Mr. Matchett: You know what I would tell them Rotarys if they was to come along and ask me to get in it? I'd tell them to go plumb to hell. The Odd Fellows is good enough for me.

Mr. Hinsch: I wouldn't stay up late nights waiting for them to ask you to get in it. They wouldn't have such a no-account piece of trash as you in it.

Mr. Oyster: Oh, no! Them Rotarys is a sassiety order. A-setting around the lunch table, making speeches and trying to make out like they knowed what all the tools was for.

Mr. Hinsch: They brung Jim Peasely a bowl of water to wash the fish smell offen his fingers and he drunk it.

Mr. Oyster: Thought it was soup.

Mr. Matchett: Don't it beat all, the way them fellows does? I wouldn't trade off one good order, like the Odd Fellows, for a dozen of them Rotarys.

Mr. Oyster: It's a wonder them Rotarys wouldn't help finish what they started. But nobody ain't heard a word out of them since this trouble started.

Mr. Hinsch: Then there's another way to look at it. If we listen to them Water Witches and don't allow no pension, why, then we got all them Semper Fidelises saying Scotty got killed in line of duty, same as a soldier, and the town won't do nothing for him.

Mr. Oyster: Say, Hinsch. That there is what they said, ain't it? "Same as a soldier." That there gives me a idea.

Mr. Hinsch: I hope to hell somebody's got a idea. I ain't.

Mr. Oyster: Hinsch, next Tuesday come a week is Decoration Day. Well, why not us get up a resolution, what I mean a real fancy resolution, saying Scotty died in line of duty same as a soldier, and appropriate some money to put a wreaf on his grave Decoration Day, and then say all the firemen had ought to have a festival to raise some money for Scotty's family. How's that hit you?

Mr. Hinsch: That ain't so bad. How much is wreaves?

Mr. Oyster: They put up as pretty a wreaf as you want to see for twenty-five dollars. The town can afford twenty-five dollars.

Mr. Hinsch: Them Water Witches couldn't hardly put up no squawk on twenty-five dollars. And that there would certainly help to satisfy them Semper Fidelises. They can make a whole lot of money on a festival, this time of year, if everybody gets out and works.

Mr. Oyster: And then we could put in that the commissioners has looked up the law and found it ain't legal for the town to pay out a pension for Scotty. That there would make it look like we wanted to pay out a pension, only we couldn't.

Mr. Hinsch: That's right. And so far as that goes, they ain't none of us don't want to see something done for Scotty's family.

Mr. Oyster: You and me was just saying if it was only us, we would give a pension and glad to do it.

Mr. Hinsch: And fact of the matter is, I ain't no ways sure the commissioners is got power to pay out a pension. I ain't said nothing about it, but if them Water Witches was to take it to court, I don't believe it would stand up.

Mr. Oyster: Why, Hinsch, it stands to reason it ain't legal. Them is the things people never think about.

Mr. Hinsch: That's right. What makes me sick is this here no-account element, always kicking and putting up a holler, and you try to please them, and nothing ever suits them, and come to find out, they don't know what they want.

Mr. Oyster: And then another thing. We'll put in that them Rotarys had ought to help out with the festival. They done raised so much hell, now let them do a little work.

Mr. Hinsch: That's right. Now le's get this here resolution wrote up. This here has got to be a pretty good resolution, what I mean, not no regular resolution, but a fancy one, if it's going to do the work. You write it.

Mr. Oyster: Not me. I ain't much on writing. You write it.

Mr. Hinsch: All right.

(*He sighs, and slowly collects pen and paper. Presently he starts to write. Mr. Oyster lights a cigar and watches him. Mr. Matchett dreamily looks out the window.*)

Mr. Matchett (*after a very long time, in the tempo of the intermezzo out of* Cavalleria Rusticana): Boys . . . I tell you there ain't nothing will do as much for a fellow . . . as a good fraternal order. . . . If I was a young fellow . . . first thing I would join . . . would be the Junior Order . . . then the Heptasophs . . . or maybe the Red Men . . . then . . . the Odd Fellows. . . . You can't beat a good order . . . to help a young fellow along. . . . Take, for instance . . . if you was to land broke . . . in some town . . . them lodge brothers . . . wouldn't never let you jump no freight . . . to get home. . . . I remember one time . . . over in Myersville . . . I lost forty-seven dollars . . . at a shell game . . . in the county fair . . . and when I got done . . . I didn't have a damn nickel . . . to buy myself a hot dog with . . . and the Junior Order seen me through. . . . You can't beat a good order . . . to help a young fellow . . . along. . . .

Mr. Hinsch: I got something wrote out here. But it seems to me it's too damn long.

Mr. Oyster: Why, hell, it ought to be long. That pleases a whole lot of people. Read it.

Mr. Hinsch (*in an impressive voice*): "Whereas, in the wisdom of Almighty God—"

Mr. Oyster: That's the stuff.

Mr. Hinsch: "—there has been taken from our midst one of our most valuable and beloved citizens, Winfield Scott Akers, snatched to his reward from the bosom of a sorrowing wife and five small children—"

Mr. Oyster: Six.

Mr. Hinsch: Did Scotty have another kid? Damn, I never knowed that. "—a sorrowing wife and six small children, but done his duty to the last, in the manner of a soldier on the field of battle—"

Mr. Oyster: Them Semper Fidelises will eat that up.

Mr. Hinsch: "—in order that precious property might be saved from the flames, and might of been, except for things not under human control—"

Mr. Oyster: That kind of makes that goddam fight look better.

Mr. Hinsch: "—and whereas public-spirited citizens has appeared before the Board at a public hearing, whereof due notice was given three days in advance, according to law, and petitioned that the sorrowing family of the said beloved brother, Winfield Scott Akers, be given a pension of thirty-five dollars a month—"

Mr. Oyster: I would put in that we would of give it anyhow, only it was illegal.

Mr. Hinsch: I got that in here "—and whereas the Board is fully of the same sentiment in regards to the matter, and believe the sorrowing family of the said beloved brother, Winfield Scott Akers, is entitled to a pension, but regret to note, after looking up the charter, that the Board has not got power to grant same, unless amended—"

Mr. Oyster: I would cross out that "unless amended." We don't want them Semper Fidelises trying to amend the charter. Things is bad enough like they are.

Mr. Hinsch: That's right "—therefore be it resolved, that the Board appropriates the sum of twenty-five dollars for a wreaf to be placed on the grave of the said beloved brother, Winfield Scott Akers, May thirtieth, Decoration Day, account of him dying in line of duty, same as a soldier, and hereby calls on both fire companies to hold a parade and lay the said wreaf on the grave, and further recommends that a festival be held that night, to be assisted in by both fire companies and all fraternal orders and civic societies, and that the Rotary Club take charge of same and see it is put over right. And be it further resolved, that this resolution be spread on the minutes of the Board and a copy sent to the sorrowing family of the said beloved brother, Winfield Scott Akers, and advertised in the press. Done under our hand and seal." How's that?

Mr. Oyster: Seems to me we could get some more fancy stuff in it. Something like "borne aloft to his reward for his labors on this earth." Only Scotty never labored none, if he could help it.

Mr. Hinsch: I'm going to write the first part over again. I got some Odd Fellow resolutions home that has got some good stuff in them.

Mr. Oyster: That's right. Some of them Memorial Service resolutions would have a whole lot of that stuff in them.

Mr. Hinsch: Well, that fixes it, don't it? Damn, I sure thought they had us in a hole for a while. Now let them goddam Rotary buttinskis take off their coat and go to work.

Mr. Oyster: That there'll fix them.

Mr. Matchett: Boys, did you ever stop to think what a real good fraternal order can do for a man?

Theological Interlude

CHARACTERS: Mr. Nation
             Mrs. Nation
             Mr. Barlow

The scene is the porch of "The Anchorage," a boarding-house run by the Nations in a Christian summer resort in the state of Delaware. It is about nine o'clock of an evening in late spring. Few sounds relieve the loneliness, except the restless swash of waves on the nearby beach. In the gathering darkness Mr. Barlow has been peering around in an interested way, asking questions now and then about the things that meet his eye. He is Mrs. Nation's brother, and apparently has not visited the locality in a long time. He gets only mechanical answers to his queries, both Mr. and Mrs. Nation seeming distracted. When it is quite dark, he knocks the ashes out of his pipe in a businesslike way, and puts it in his pocket.

Mr. Barlow: Well, now, what's this all about? 'Cause you two sure did pick a bad time to bring me all the way up

Theological Interlude

here from Delmar, and I want to get to it. What I mean, I don't want to spend no more time up here than I have to.

Mr. Nation: I reckon Laura can tell you.

Mrs. Nation: Tell him yourself. You sent for him.

Mr. Nation: You're the one has got the squawk. Go on and tell him.

Mr. Barlow: Now, now, that ain't no way to talk. Come on, Laura, let's have it.

Mrs. Nation: It's about Eva.

Mr. Barlow: Where's she at? I been waiting for her, and I ain't saw her.

Mr. Nation: Never mind where she's at. We'll get to that part in a minute. She ain't here, anyway.

Mrs. Nation: Well, it all started with what happened last summer. You remember that?

Mr. Barlow: I heard them talking about it at home, but I kinda forgot how it was. I reckon you better start at the beginning, so I can get it all straight.

Mrs. Nation: She had the typhoid fever. She was took just this time a year ago.

Mr. Barlow: Yeah, I remember that.

Mr. Nation: She was took a little earlier than this. First part of May, and she was getting better around the middle of June.

Mrs. Nation: She was getting better when the first boarders begin to come. Dr. Winship said all danger was past, and we was all set she should get well.

Mr. Nation: Only we was kidding ourself.

Mr. Barlow: How old is Eva now? I ain't saw her in five or six years, I do believe.

Mrs. Nation: Eva's sixteen now. But she was only fifteen then.

Mr. Barlow: Sixteen! Who could believe it! And last time I seen her she was a little bit of a thing.

Mrs. Nation: So she was took sick again.

Mr. Nation: Sudden.

Mrs. Nation: Real sudden. Dr. Winship said maybe it was something she et, on account their stomach is always tender after typhoid fever.

Mr. Barlow: Yep, I tell you, you got to watch them after typhoid fever.

Mrs. Nation: But anyway, she looks at me one night and says "Ma! . . . Ma!" just like that, and I knowed she had a sinking spell. And lands sakes, I was legging it down the boardwalk to Dr. Winship's office before I really knowed I was out the door!

Mr. Nation: And me trying to raise him by telephone! I'll never forget that night.

Mrs. Nation: So when Dr. Winship got here she was white as a sheet and he didn't hardly get his gripsack open before she up and died.

Mr. Barlow: *(vastly surprised)*: Hanh?

Mr. Nation: Almost before you could say Jack Robinson.

Mr. Barlow: Who? You mean Eva?

Mrs. Nation: Yes, Eva.

Mr. Barlow: Eva dead and I ain't heared nothing about it?

Mrs. Nation: Well of course she ain't dead *now*, if that's what you mean.

Mr. Barlow: *(staggered)*: Well . . . this beats *me*!

Mr. Nation: There's a-plenty more to it yet. Go on, Laura.

Mrs. Nation: So when Dr. Winship listened to her heart and it didn't beat no more—

Mr. Nation: He pronounced her dead, don't forget that. Official.

Mrs. Nation: That's right. When he pronounced her dead, then he left. And then Hal called up the undertaker, the one in Greenwood.

Theological Interlude

Mr. Nation: I was blubbering same as a baby. I couldn't hardly talk.

Mrs. Nation: So then a young fellow what was one of the boarders, he come in the room.

Mr. Nation: Mr. Travis. He was a doctor. Anyway, he went to the medical school.

Mrs. Nation: He took a look at her, and then he shook Hal by the arm and sent him down the beach where they keep the pulmotor, what they use when somebody gets drowned.

Mr. Nation: And I run. I hope my die I did.

Mrs. Nation: And then Mr. Travis, he commence to work on her. He run up to his room and got a gripsack and when he come back I don't think I hardly ever seen anybody work like he did.

Mr. Nation: We never took no more offen Travis after that. We give him his board free.

Mrs. Nation: And when Hal come back with the pulmotor he went to work on her with that too. And then he stuck a needle in her. And pretty soon she came to.

Mr. Barlow: Gosh! I'm glad you come to that part at last!

Mrs. Nation: So when the undertaker come she was setting up.

Mr. Nation: That there finished me with undertakers. You know what that boy done? He got sore because she wasn't dead no more. Can you beat that?

Mrs. Nation: So then, after a couple of weeks, she begun to tell me about—

Mr. Nation: You forgot something. You forgot them pieces in the papers.

Mrs. Nation: Oh yes. You see we was so excited we forgot all about Dr. Winship. To call him up, I mean, and tell him about it. And before he went to bed that night he wrote up the death certificate and dropped it in the mailbox and it come out in the papers she was dead. And maybe Eva weren't sore! 'Cause some of them papers from Dover and Salisbury, they had it in about the funeral and how many flowers there was. And Eva, she said, she hear tell all her life you couldn't believe nothing you seen in the papers, but that time they sure did have a crust.

Mr. Barlow: It beats all how many things them fellows puts in the papers. Sometimes I wonder how they find time to make up all the stuff what they put in.

Mrs. Nation: So then, after a couple weeks, she commences talking about the dream she had. And me, I don't take stock in dreams, but one day I asked her what it was. And she said that night when she was took that way, she dreamed she been to Heaven. And still we didn't pay no attention to it, until that night, when I happened to think about what she said, and I told Hal about it. And all of a sudden he seen the meaning of it. Or thought he did anyway.

Mr. Nation: And you thought so, too. Ain't no reason for you to talk so big all of a sudden.

Mrs. Nation: There's a-plenty reason. If it hadn't been for you and your—

Mr. Barlow: Now wait a minute, wait a minute! Just what was this meaning, Hal, what you seen? Or thought you seen anyway?

Mr. Nation: Well . . . well . . . I kind of figured out . . . that she . . . that maybe she . . . really *had* been to Heaven.

Mr. Barlow: Oh! How come you to figure that out?

Mr. Nation: Well, we'll get to that part in a minute. That ain't all of it.

Mrs. Nation: So we kind of told a few people about it, and they let on they wanted to hear about it too. So when company come—

Mr. Nation: Yeah, when company come! Who was it all the time a-egging Eva on to tell the company about it? Who was a-saying "Get out your banjer now, Eva, and let the folks hear it?"

Theological Interlude 73

Mr. Barlow: Her banjer? What the hell did she want with a banjer? Did she bring that back with her from Heaven?

Mr. Nation: She can pick a banjer.

Mrs. Nation: She picks a banjer to them pieces what she speaks in school. She puts the banjer on her knees and while she picks it she talks.

Mr. Barlow: But this wasn't no piece.

Mrs. Nation: Well, I'm a-trying to tell it.

Mr. Nation: It was something like a piece. You see, after a while she kind of learned it by heart. And then she put the banjer in. And then after a while she put in a couple of songs what she knowed. The first one come right after the part where she come to the pearly gates, and that was a piece called "The Portal Left Ajar." And the second one come right after the Angel of the Lord tooken her by the hand and told her she had to come back to earth, 'cause all the people down here couldn't bear to see her go. And that was a piece called "He Calleth Me." Or something like that. And believe me, when she got through with it, it took pretty near a hour, and if there was anybody listening what wasn't busting out crying at the end, why he wasn't human, that was all. He just wasn't human.

Mr. Barlow: I see. She kind of put it up fancy. Damn, I never knowed that girl could pick a banjer.

Mr. Nation: Oh, she's smart. Ain't nothing that girl can't do.

Mr. Barlow: Well, what next?

Mrs. Nation: So then a preacher what was holding a revival over in Greenwood last month, he heared about her.

Mr. Nation: Reverend Day.

Mr. Barlow: Day? Sure. I know him.

Mrs. Nation: And he come around one afternoon and listened at her. And then nothing wouldn't do him but she had to go over and tell it at his meeting. And then nothing wouldn't do Hal but she had to go.

Mr. Nation: Aw Laura, why you tell it like that? You know yourself you was tickled to death she had the chance.

Mrs. Nation: I was tickled to death she had the chance for *one* night. But I didn't know she was going over there for the whole revival. You know I didn't. You and her, you kept that from me.

Mr. Barlow: Well, but what then?

Mrs. Nation: So then she run off with this Day.

Mr. Barlow: How you mean, run off?

Mrs. Nation: Mean run off, that's what I mean

Mr. Nation: And not a thing to show that it's so. Now listen. What happened? He moved to Easton, for to hold a revival there, and she went with him. And he went to Cambridge, and she went with him there, and that's where she's at now. And for what? To tell about it some more, same as she done in Greenwood. That there is a big card, that is. That there brings in the money, and it saves a whole lot of souls. And she's getting paid for it. And how can you tell she run off with him?

Mrs. Nation: I can tell by the cut of her jib.

Mr. Nation: You ain't got a thing to show—

Mr. Barlow: And what next?

Mr. Nation: Nothing next. That's all. 'Cepting my life ain't been worth living for the last month, what with Laura a-whooping and a-hollering and a-carrying on—

Mrs. Nation: Why, Hal Nation!—

Mr. Nation: And it got so bad I sent for you to come up here and see if you could straighten us out.

Mrs. Nation: Why, Hal Nation, I never heared no man talk the way you do. Some time I wonder if you got good sense. Don't nothing mean nothing to you what all the people is a-saying? Ain't you got no respect for your own daughter's vircher?

Mr. Barlow: Have you had the law on him?

Mr. Nation: Can't get no law on him. Can't prove nothing.

Theological Interlude

Mrs. Nation. My land, Hal! My land! And all on account of you in the first place. You and your figuring out the meaning of it—

Mr. Nation: Stop! Stop right there! That's the first thing what we got to have out. And it ain't no use going further till we do. (*He turns earnestly to Mr. Barlow, takes careful thought before he speaks, and then proceeds in a solemn voice.*) Now I ask you, and if you don't see it my way I'm a-perfectly willing to say I was wrong, but if she weren't in Heaven in the time when she was dead, then where the hell was she?

Mr. Barlow: I swear, Hal, now you're coming at me pretty strong. That there is kind of out of my line.... What you say to that, Laura?

Mrs. Nation: I don't say nothing.

Mr. Nation: You said a-plenty till Day come along. You couldn't see it no other way. Funny you ain't got nothing to say.

Mr. Barlow: Have you asked any preachers about it?

Mr. Nation: We asked five or six preachers about it, not counting Day. And they all said the same thing. Said there could be no doubt about it at all. Said it had to be so.

Mr. Barlow: Still, you can't go by none of them preachers. I never seen one of them as what wouldn't jump up and holler amen for anything they heared, didn't make no difference what it was. Them bums if they had sense enough to figure anything out, why they wouldn't be preachers.... Well, now, le's see. Maybe we can figure it out for ourself. How was it now again?

Mr. Nation: She died.

Mr. Barlow: You're sure of that, now. 'Cause look like to me that was pretty important.

Mr. Nation: If her heart didn't beat no more, then she died, didn't she? You never seen nobody what was *half* dead, did you? Winship said it didn't beat no more, and so did Travis. And Winship sent the death certificate in to the county clerk's office, and a hell of a time I had getting it out so she could get on the school rolls again, and be alive legal and all like of that.

Mr. Barlow: Well then, looks like she *was* dead. Nobody couldn't hardly be deader than that.

Mr. Nation: That's right. That's all I'm trying to say. She was dead.

Mr. Barlow: All right then, she was dead. We know that much anyway. Now le's see. The next thing to figure out is where she could of been before she come back to life.

Mr. Nation: That's right. Now keep right on going.

Mr. Barlow: Well, first off, she could of been in Heaven, where she said she was.

Mr. Nation: That's right. Now where else?

Mr. Barlow: Then . . . well, ain't no sense saying that.

Mr. Nation: Go on say it. What I want is to figure this thing out right, oncet and for all. And if a thing has got to be said, then it just as well be said.

Mr. Barlow: What I started to say, she might of been in Hell. But ain't no sense talking like that.

Mr. Nation: Might just as well say it. She might of been in Hell. We ain't going to get nowheres pussyfooting.

Mr. Barlow: Well then, she might of been in Hell. Now where else?

Mr. Nation: All right. Where else?

Mr. Barlow: Dogged if I know. Where the hell else do they go when they die, anyway?

Mr. Nation: Onliest place I can think of is she might of been still on this earth. Now can you think of any other places?

Mr. Barlow: Nope. Damned if I can.

Mr. Nation: All right, she might of been in Heaven, she might of been in Hell, and she might of been down here on the earth. Ain't no other place she could of been. Now then, take Hell. What the hell would a girl fifteen year old what had always gone to church regular be doing in Hell? Tell me that oncet?

Mr. Barlow: Well, I told you already that ain't reasonable. Ain't no use talking about that. Why no. 'Cause look. You mean to tell me anybody could be in Hell and not know it?

Mr. Nation: What I tell you, Laura? Ain't them the very same words I said not more'n two weeks ago?

Mrs. Nation: If them is the same words you said two weeks ago, then I know there ain't no sense to it.

Mr. Barlow: Nope. From what I hear, when somebody goes to Hell, they're going to get scorched, and you can bank on that. Go on, Hal.

Mr. Nation: All right, then, she ain't been in Hell. Now that leaves Heaven and this earth. And if she was on this earth, that means she was a ghost. And me, I don't care what people say, I don't believe in no ghosts.

Mr. Barlow: By gosh! that's right. I never thought of that. She would of been a ghost, wouldn't she? That there wouldn't be so good, would it? What do you think about that, Laura? Do you believe in ghosts?

Mrs. Nation: Never mind what I believe in. I ain't had my say yet.

Mr. Barlow: Well now, there ain't no use being bull-headed about it. We're a-trying to figure this thing out, and we ain't getting nowhere with you setting there rocking like you had a pain in your big toe and not doing nothing to help. The big thing now is, was she a ghost or not?

Mrs. Nation: I ain't never said I believed in ghosts.

Mr. Barlow: Well me, I never believed in them neither. . . . But Hal, I tell you I hear tell of some funny things in my time.

Mrs. Nation: Me too. Me too.

Mr. Barlow: Did I ever tell you about the time I was driving along the road on the other side of the Maryland line?

Mr. Nation: No. What was it?

Mr. Barlow: Well, that beat anything I ever hear tell of in my life. It was about three o'clock in the morning, and I had tooken a girl to a dance. I was a young fellow then. And I was driving back, after I dropped her where she lived, and believe me it was lonely. And I come to a piece of road what run through a woods. And the woods was mostly scrub pine, but right alongside the road was a big oak tree. It was a fine-looking tree, and had a big limb what hung out over the road. And I was letting my horse walk, 'cause it was a sandy piece of road, and I kept looking at the tree, and thinking how fine it looked, and kind of wild, 'cause the limbs was kind of swaying a lot, and the leaves was rustling, and every now and then turning gray in the moonlight, when the undersides would show up in the wind. And then I drove right under a big limb, and went on a little ways, and then all of a sudden I turned right cold. 'Cause, Hal, *there wasn't no wind!* . . . Well, when I got in and turned my plug over to the fellow in the livery stable, I told him about it, and I swear he turned green. And then he told me that was the tree where they had lynched a nigger about ten year before, and it was a windy night, and he swung around like he was drunk before they cut him down to take the souvenirs off him, and sometimes now that tree still shakes in the same wind.

    Mr. Nation: I'd of dropped dead! I'd of dropped dead!

    Mr. Barlow: Some funny things, I tell you.

    Mr. Nation: Gosh! And no wind a-blowing!

    Mr. Barlow: Fellow told me one time you can always tell if there's a ghost in the house by the way the cat acts. Cat won't stay in no house with a ghost. Did you take notice of the cat when all this was going on?

    Mr. Nation: No, we didn't. No, we didn't. Yes, by gosh we did! Yes, we did! Laura, remember what you said when you come back from the kitchen with that hot-water bottle? Remember? Remember? You said it sure was funny how that cat was still asleep alongside the stove after all that fuss what we had upstairs. Remember?

    Mrs. Nation: I don't recollect.

Mr. Barlow: Well now, Laura, try just this oncet to see if you can't be some help. You—

Mrs. Nation: The cat was asleep, if that's all you want to know.

Mr. Nation: Well then, that settles it. She couldn't of been no ghost. And that leaves Heaven.

Mr. Barlow: I swear, Hal, I don't see nothing wrong with that. It kind of went a little funny when you first mentioned it, but now we figured on it awhile, it don't seem like it could have been no other way. Anyhow, not no other way that I can think of.

Mr. Nation: All right. All right. Then how about all this here about running off? Does that sound right? Would a girl what had been to Heaven take and run off with the first preacher who come along? Would she, now?

Mr. Barlow. Well . . .

Mrs. Nation. Well nothing! Now I have to have *my* say. All right, she's been in Heaven. Is she ever going back there after she run off with Day? Tell me that.

Mr. Barlow: Well now, maybe she will at that. You know, I was talking not long ago with a fellow what had just put up a kind of a short Bible for Sunday school classes, or something like that. And he had made a kind of a study of it. And he says to me, he says, "It's a funny thing, but there ain't a word in the Bible agin a little cutting up. Yes," he says, "I know most people think there is, but it's a fact there ain't."

Mrs. Nation: Then there ought to be.

Mr. Barlow: Laura, try to act like you was a little bit bright. If we got to write the whole Bible over again to suit you, that's right where I quit.

Mr. Nation: Me too. . . . I swear, that there bellering around all the time has got my goat.

Mr. Barlow: And suppose she *is* a-cutting up a little with Day? What of it? There's always got to be some cutting up before people gets married. And she could do a whole lot worse than marry Day.

Mrs. Nation: Ain't he married?

Mr. Barlow: He is not. Anyway, not when I seen him last, about six months ago. I think he did have a wife oncet but he ain't got her no more. And I say this for Day. He may be a preacher but he's got enough git-up-and-git to buy hisself a tent and go out and hustle and that's more'n you can say for many young bucks here in Delaware what want to cut up with a girl.

Mr. Nation: Ain't nothing wrong with the fellow. I always said so, right from the beginning.

Mr. Barlow: Look like to me, the thing for you two to do is to invite him over here. Him and Eva together. That would kind of smooth things out a bit, and at the same time git it in his head that you got your eye on him.

Mrs. Nation: Well, we could run over and get them in the car, I reckon. And have them here to dinner. And put them back in time for the night meeting.

Mr. Barlow: That's the stuff, Laura. Now you're talking something what has got some sense to it.

Mr. Nation: That there sounds pretty good to me. That there is the thing to do.

Mrs. Nation: I ain't wanted to believe it of her nohow.... 'Cause I loved it so, about her having been to ... to Heaven ... and all.... And she told it so sweet.... And when she puts them songs in and all.... It was so beautiful.

Mr. Barlow: Why sure, I swear, I been setting here tonight, thinking to myself it's just about the beautifulest thing I ever hear tell of in my life. I wish one of my daughters could of done it, and could pick a banjer and all....

Mr. Nation: Now Laura, ain't no use crying. What you crying about?

Mr. Barlow: Hal, looks like to me the thing for you to do is to take Laura in and put her to bed. And I don't know

Theological Interlude

but I'm ready to turn in myself if you two think you're all straightened out now. 'Cause I got to catch that early train down from Greenwood. . . .

(*They rise, Mr. Barlow stretching and winding his watch, Mrs. Nation sniffling, and Mr. Nation awkwardly guiding her into the house.*)

Mr. Nation: Come on, now, Laura. . . . Why, sure she was up in Heaven! . . . Couldn't of been nowheres else. . . . Why sure. . . . Stands to reason. . . .

SHORT STORIES

Cain's first published short story—"Pastorale"—was written for H. L. Mencken while Cain was still working on the *New York World*, and it grew out of a profile of William Gilbert Patten that Cain did for the *Saturday Evening Post*. Patten, who wrote under the pseudonym Burt L. Standish, created the fictional hero Frank Merriwell, and Cain was probably drawn to him because they both started their careers in the same manner—trying to sell short stories to magazines. During their interview, Patten told Cain a story about a couple of western roughnecks who committed a gruesome crime. Patten's point in telling the story was to illustrate a friend's fiendish sense of humor, but to Patten's horror Cain took the anecdote as truly hilarious and, furthermore, asked Patten if he could use it someday in a piece of fiction. Patten said he did not mind, and Cain thought about it for several months before shifting the story to his favorite locale and telling it in the first person, through the eyes of an Eastern Shore roughneck. He called it "Pastorale," a deceptively benign title for its grisly doings, and submitted it to Mencken, who published it in the March 1928 *Mercury*. It is a very funny tale, told in the Ring Lardner manner, and David Madden, author of the only full-length literary study of Cain, considers it Cain's best short story. It was also an extremely important event in Cain's evolution as a writer of fiction. In the first place, he now found that he could tell a story in some manner other than dialogue or one-act plays by writing in the first person, preferably the voice of some "low-life character," as his mother called the type. "The only way I can keep on the track at all," he said, trying to explain this idiosyncrasy, "is to pretend to be somebody else—to put it in dialect and thus get it told. If I try to do it in my own language I find that I have none. A style that seems to be personal enough for ordinary gassing refuses to get going for an imaginary narrative. So long as I merely report what people might have said under certain circumstances, I am all right; but the moment I have to step in myself, and try to create the impression that what happened to those people really matters, then I am sunk. I flounder about, not knowing whether I should skip to the scene at the church or pile in a little more of the talk at the post office. The reason is . . . I don't care what happened. It doesn't matter to me. Narratively, I do not exist, I have no impulse to hold an audience."

In "Pastorale," Cain not only managed to make his narrator care what happened, enabling the story to move, he also found his favorite theme: Although two people may get away with committing a crime, they cannot live with it.

"Pastorale" was also important to Cain as a demonstration that his style was in no way influenced by or copied from Ernest Hemingway, as some critics charged. "Pastorale" was written in late 1927, and by then Cain's narrative technique and ear for dialogue—which in a few years would constitute one of the most widely discussed and imitated literary styles in the country—were clearly established. His realistic, colloquial dialogue had gradually emerged from the pieces he had been writing for Mencken since 1924, and the technique he used in most of his novels, themselves written in the first person, originated more or less with "Pastorale." He says—and there is no reason not to believe him—that he did not read Hemingway until *Men Without Women* appeared in 1928, and he was tremendously impressed. But what surprised him was "an echo I found in it, of something I couldn't place." Then he remembered the voice: It was Roxy Stimson, the divorced wife of Jess Smith, a lackey of Attorney General Harry Daugherty, one of the key figures in the Teapot Dome scandal. In 1924 Roxy testified at the Senate Hearings on Teapot Dome and her manner of speech, as Cain recalled, "burst on the country like a July Fourth rocket." Her tale, describing Smith's slow deterioration as he was caught up in the scandal and his own foolish speculations in the stock market, electrified the country, especially the literary world, for which Roxy briefly became the object of a cult. "She could come popping out with some bromide," Cain said, "a cornball expression that should have been pure hush puppy, and somehow transform it, the way Dvořak transformed folk music, so it stayed in your ear as a classic."

Roxy's testimony was carried in full in the *New York Times*, and Cain assumed it reached Paris, where he was certain Hemingway had absorbed it. He became convinced that his theory was correct when he finally read "Fifty Grand" and noted the similarity in its plot, especially in an incident described by Roxy Stimson, prior to Jess Smith's suicide. As for Roxy's influence on Cain's style: "She taught me respect for the cliché. I'd say she influenced me plenty," he said.

The good response to "Pastorale" encouraged Cain to write another short story, this one based on an experience in France on the night of September 26, 1918, during the opening of the Meuse-Argonne offensive. Again, Cain elected to tell the story in the first-person narration of an Eastern Shore rube, although the incident actually happened to him and he could just as easily have told it in his own near-perfect diction. "The Taking of Montfaucon" also appeared in the *Mercury* and was reprinted in 1929 and 1942 in the *Infantry Journal*, which said, "[It] has never been excelled as an accurate description of conditions in the war and few stories of any aspect of the war will stand beside it."

After "Montfaucon," Cain worked exclusively on dialogues to round out his book *Our Government*, then moved to California, where, for the first year or so, he tried to establish himself as a screenwriter. When Paramount let him go—after six months of unsuccessful scriptwriting efforts—he decided to resume his fiction. His first story ideas grew out of the automobile trips around Southern California he and his wife, Elina, used to take, sometimes with the two kids. One place they liked to stop was the Goebels Lion Farm on the road to Ventura. Cain had a lifelong fascination with cats—especially big ones. His feelings for them bordered on fanaticism: "I find it impossible," he said, "to believe in a life after death, and if you don't accept that, the Christian theology goes up in smoke. . . . To me, God is life, and if no immortal soul figures in, then all must be included in the concept. So animals to me take on a mystic meaning, more perhaps than they do to most people." Cain wrote editorials and several short stories about tigers; he wrote Hearst columns about panthers; and late in life he wrote an unpublished novel about a little girl who is given a tiger cub, which she raises as a pet.

Out at Goebels, Cain conceived an idea for a story about a couple who run a gas station and lunchroom on the road to Ventura. Their trouble starts when the husband, Duke, decides to add some big cats to interest the children and draw more customers. Cain called his story "The Baby in the Icebox," and although he also wrote it in his first-person, Ring Lardner style, he found that when he moved from the Eastern Shore and put his story in the mouth of a western roughneck, a type he was beginning to observe in California, he was writing in a comfortable, natural style that had distinctive flavor and pace. The famous James M. Cain momentum began to emerge.

"The Baby in the Icebox" is a tribute to Cain's ability to tell an improbable tale believably—and to make it eminently readable. It was also an important link in the chain that eventually led to Cain's phenomenal career as a novelist. When Mencken showed Knopf the galleys of "The Baby in the Icebox," the publisher wrote Cain that the story "is a whopper—one of the best I have read, and it encourages me to believe that one of these days you may try your hand at a novel."

Cain replied that he still did not think he could write long fiction, but added that Knopf's note might be just the encouragement he needed. Then he outlined an idea for a story which would soon become *The Postman Always Rings Twice*.

"The Baby in the Icebox" sold immediately to Paramount, but when the movie—*She Made Her Bed*—based on the story was released in the spring of 1934, it was panned by the critics. This did not affect Cain, who by that time was riding the crest of the wave created by the publication of *Postman*. Usually, the leads to the movie reviews referred to Cain or "the most famous story by James M. Cain" rather than to the movie itself, and most reviewers relieved Cain of all responsibility for the film's failure. Said Bosley Crowther in the *New York Times*: "Though it is fastened upon a story by James M. Cain, the blame for this picture is too large, too richly complicated to be attached to one person."

With the publication of *Postman*, James M. Cain was suddenly famous and in demand. His agent, James Geller, quickly sold two of his stories, written at about the time he wrote "The Baby in the Icebox" but rejected by several editors ("Come Back," about a bit player trying to make a comeback in Hollywood riding a famous horse; and "The Whale, the Cluck and the Diving Venus," about an Eastern Shore hustler who tries to promote a tourist attraction by putting a whale in a swimming pool). Cain was working at a furious pace—"the fastest two-finger typist I ever saw," says his stepson, Leo Tyszecki. He started a series of food articles, which drove Edith Haggard, his new agent, nearly frantic. "You have made me an old woman, lad. With the magazine world at your feet, with their hands raised high over their heads pleading for short stories, you want to write food articles."

He was also writing a three-times-a-week syndicated column for the Hearst papers, working on a play to be based on *Postman*, beginning a magazine serial to be called *Double Indemnity*, and taking studio assignments, during one of which he dictated a short story, "Hip, Hip, Hippo," about a Hollywood bit player who tried to make a comeback riding a hippopotamus in a big movie, not one of Cain's better efforts.

By this time, Cain had also outlined a novel, eventually to be called *Serenade*, for Knopf, and the publisher was urging him to finish it and take advantage of all the publicity surrounding the publication of *Postman*. But Cain was still not satisfied that the basic idea for *Serenade* was sound, and he settled down to respond to his New York agent's plea that he write more short stories. But once again, as with his food articles, he flabbergasted Ms. Haggard, this time by writing a third-person story about a girl and a boy and the boy's fear of diving off high places. He called it "The Birthday Party" and sent it off to New York. An amazed Edith Haggard replied, "It's a new writer who signs himself James M. Cain!" She had been pleading for more stories—but a children's birthday party? Most of New York's magazine editors agreed. "It would be hard to imagine anything more different from *The Postman Always Rings Twice*," wrote the assistant editor of *This Week* in rejecting the story. "Although we are by no means demanding that he spend the rest of his life rewriting *Postman*, we had hoped for something as swift-moving and full of action." Ms.

Haggard finally sold "The Birthday Party" to the *Ladies' Home Journal* for $750.

After that, with Ms. Haggard still pleading for a murder story, he finished *Double Indemnity*, then started to work on another short story that he expected would be more to the agent's liking. He recalled how, when he was living in Burbank, he would drive home from one of the studios and be detained night after night by the freight trains at the crossings. As he sat there watching the boxcars go by, he was appalled by the hoboes—"the hundreds of human derelicts silhouetted against the Verdugo Hills, perched like crows on top of the cars, going nowhere and knowing they were going nowhere." As he thought about these men, his mind—with the usual Cain twist—began to play on an idea: What would happen if one of these hoboes, perhaps unwittingly, became involved in some scrape, such as a murder? Characteristically, Cain was more interested in the hobo's subjective reaction than in his battle with the law. "When a murderer comes to grips with the law," Cain thought, "he has a better than even chance to win. But, because of forces inside of him, his crime eventually catches up with him"—again, Cain's favorite theme.

By now Cain had firmly established his style and milieu. After "The Birthday Party" had satisfied him that he could write salable stories in the third person, he decided to try his hobo tale, which he called "Dead Man," in the third person. Ms. Haggard wrote back one of what Cain called "those Mama-knows-best letters," suggesting the story would have a much better chance of selling if he made the ending more pleasant. Cain must have wanted the money badly because in uncharacteristic fashion he changed the ending to make it commercial. But still it did not sell. Then one day, when he was in New York working on his play based on *Postman*, he received a call from Paul Palmer, the new editor of the *Mercury*. Palmer was calling about "Dead Man," which Edith

Haggard had finally submitted to him. "Jim, I like it fine," Palmer said, "and want to run it in the next issue, except that this damned Pollyanna ending doesn't sound like you. . . . Could you fix me up another?" Cain restored the original ending, and the story appeared in the March 1936 *Mercury*. It is perhaps his best third-person story and has been reprinted at least half a dozen times, including an appearance in the O. Henry collection.

By the mid-1930s, after the publication of *Serenade*, Cain was giving most of his writing energy to novels and to trying to make it as a screenwriter, which he never did. But responding to Edith Haggard's pleadings, he wrote a few more short stories—all in the third person—which she sold to *Liberty*: "Brush Fire," "Coal Black," "Everything but the Truth," and "The Girl in the Storm."

The last short story in this section ("Joy Ride to Glory") was probably written sometime in the late 1930s. It was never published but turned up in a collection of Cain manuscripts purchased in Los Angeles by Stuart and Roger Birnbaum. In that the Birnbaums have, to the best of my knowledge, the only copy of the story in existence, their cooperation was necessary, and I wish to thank them for giving me permission to include it in this collection. The story is written in the first person and concerns a young man who, in escaping from prison, takes a perilous underground journey through a storm sewer. The idea for this story must have grown out of an experience Cain had when he lived on Belden Drive in Hollywood Hills. One day after a storm, he was appalled to look out of his window and see a little girl being swept by the swollen waters in a gutter toward a large open drain that would have carried her underground. Suddenly, one of his neighbors, the composer George Antheil, came rushing from his house in his underwear and scooped the little girl up in his arms just before she would have disappeared into the sewer. Earlier, when Cain was an editorial writer for the *New York World*, he had met Antheil after he had written a critical editorial about Antheil's composition *Ballet Mechanique*. Cain did not like the composer or his music, but after the incident at the storm sewer, he said he felt kindly disposed toward him the rest of his life.

After returning to the East in 1948 and becoming mired in a Civil War novel, Cain returned to short-story writing, hoping to make some quick money. He wrote several stories, some of which were sold to *Esquire* and adventure magazines such as *Manhunt*. They were consciously commercial stories, not up to his earlier work. But this did not bother Cain; he always felt that stories written primarily for magazines did not count.

R.H.

Pastorale

I

WELL, IT LOOKS LIKE BURBIE is going to get hung. And if he does, what he can lay it on is, he always figured he was so damn smart.

You see, Burbie, he left town when he was about sixteen year old. He run away with one of them travelling shows, "East Lynne" I think it was, and he stayed away about ten years. And when he come back he thought he knowed a lot. Burbie, he's got them watery blue eyes what kind of stick out from his face, and how he killed the time was to sit around and listen to the boys talk down at the poolroom or over at the barber shop or a couple other places where he hung out, and then wink at you like they was all making a fool of theirself or something and nobody didn't know it but him.

But when you come right down to what Burbie had in his head, why it wasn't much. 'Course, he generally always had a

Pastorale

job, painting around or maybe helping out on a new house, like of that, but what he used to do was to play baseball with the high school team. And they had a big fight over it, 'cause Burbie was so old nobody wouldn't believe he went to the school, and them other teams was all the time putting up a squawk. So then he couldn't play no more. And another thing he liked to do was sing at the entertainments. I reckon he liked that most of all, 'cause he claimed that a whole lot of the time he was away he was on the stage, and I reckon maybe he was at that, 'cause he was pretty good, 'specially when he dressed hisself up like a old-time Rube and come out and spoke a piece what he knowed.

Well, when he come back to town he seen Lida and it was a natural. 'Cause Lida, she was just about the same kind of a thing for a woman as Burbie was for a man. She used to work in the store, selling dry goods to the men, and kind of making hats on the side. 'Cepting only she didn't stay on the dry goods side no more'n she had to. She was generally over where the boys was drinking Coca-Cola, and all the time carrying on about did they like it with ammonia or lemon, and could she have a swallow outen their glass. And what she had her mind on was the clothes she had on, and was she dated up for Sunday night. Them clothes was pretty snappy, and she made them herself. And I heard some of them say she wasn't hard to date up, and after you done kept your date why maybe you wasn't going to be disappointed. And why Lida married the old man I don't know, lessen she got tired working at the store and tooken a look at the big farm where he lived at, about two mile from town.

By the time Burbie got back she'd been married about a year and she was about due. So her and him commence meeting each other, out in the orchard back of the old man's house. The old man would go to bed right after supper and then she'd sneak out and meet Burbie. And nobody wasn't supposed to know nothing about it. Only everybody did, 'cause

Burbie, after he'd get back to town about eleven o'clock at night, he'd kind of slide into the poolroom and set down easy like. And then somebody'd say, "Yay, Burbie, where you been?" And Burbie, he'd kind of look around, and then he'd pick out somebody and wink at him, and that was how Burbie give it some good advertising.

So the way Burbie tells it, and he tells it plenty since he done got religion down to the jailhouse, it wasn't long before him and Lida thought it would be a good idea to kill the old man. They figured he didn't have long to live nohow, so he might as well go now as wait a couple of years. And another thing, the old man had kind of got hep that something was going on, and they figured if he throwed Lida out it wouldn't be no easy job to get his money even if he died regular. And another thing, by that time the Klux was kind of talking around, so Burbie figured it would be better if him and Lida was to get married, else maybe he'd have to leave town again.

So that was how come he got Hutch in it. You see, he was afeared to kill the old man hisself and he wanted some help. And then he figured it would be pretty good if Lida wasn't nowheres around and it would look like robbery. If it would of been me, I would of left Hutch out of it. 'Cause Hutch, he was mean. He'd been away for a while too, but him going away, that wasn't the same as Burbie going away. Hutch was sent. He was sent for ripping a mail sack while he was driving the mail wagon up from the station, and before he come back he done two years down to Atlanta.

But what I mean, he wasn't only crooked, he was mean. He had a ugly look to him, like when he'd order hisself a couple of fried eggs over to the restaurant, and then set and eat them with his head humped down low and his arm curled around his plate like he thought somebody was going to steal if off him, and handle his knife with his thumb down near the tip, kind of like a nigger does a razor. Nobody didn't have much to say to Hutch, and I reckon that's why he ain't heard nothing about Burbie and Lida, and et it all up what Burbie told him about the old man having a pot of money hid in the fireplace in the back room.

So one night early in March, Burbie and Hutch went out and done the job. Burbie he'd already got Lida out of the way. She'd let on she had to go to the city to buy some things, and she went away on No. 6, so everybody knowed she was gone. Hutch, he seen her go, and come running to Burbie saying now was a good time, which was just what Burbie wanted. 'Cause her and Burbie had already put the money in the pot, so Hutch wouldn't think it was no put-up job. Well, anyway, they put $23 in the pot, all changed into pennies and nickels and dimes so it would look like a big pile, and that was all the money Burbie had. It was kind of like you might say the savings of a lifetime.

And then Burbie and Hutch got in the horse and wagon what Hutch had, 'cause Hutch was in the hauling business again, and they went out to the old man's place. Only they went around the back way, and tied the horse back of the house so nobody couldn't see it from the road, and knocked on the back door and made out like they was just coming through the place on their way back to town and had stopped by to get warmed up, 'cause it was cold as hell. So the old man let them in and give them a drink of some hard cider what he had, and they got canned up a little more. They was already pretty canned, 'cause they both of them had a pint of corn on their hip for to give them some nerve.

And then Hutch he got back of the old man and crowned him with a wrench what he had hid in his coat.

II

Well, next off Hutch gets sore as hell at Burbie 'cause there ain't no more'n $23 in the pot. He didn't do nothing. He just set there, first looking at the money, what he had piled up on a table, and then looking at Burbie.

And then Burbie commences soft-soaping him. He says hope my die he thought there was a thousand dollars anyway in the pot, on account the old man being like he was. And he says hope my die it sure was a big surprise to him how little there was there. And he says hope my die it sure does make him feel bad, on account he's the one had the idea first. And he says hope my die it's all his fault and he's going to let Hutch keep all the money, damn if he ain't. He ain't going to take none of it for hisself at all, on account of how bad he feels. And Hutch, he don't say nothing at all, only look at Burbie and look at the money.

And right in the middle of while Burbie was talking, they heard a whole lot of hollering out in front of the house and somebody blowing a automobile horn. And Hutch jumps up and scoops the money and the wrench off the table in his pockets, and hides the pot back in the fireplace. And then he grabs the old man and him and Burbie carries him out the back door, hists him in the wagon, and drives off. And how they was to drive off without them people seeing them was because they come in the back way and that was the way they went. And them people in the automobile, they was a bunch of old folks from the Methodist church what knowed Lida was away and didn't think so much of Lida nohow and come out to say hello. And when they come in and didn't see nothing, they figured the old man had went in to town and so they went back.

Well, Hutch and Burbie was in a hell of a fix all right. 'Cause there they was, driving along somewheres with the old man in the wagon and they didn't have no more idea than a bald-headed coot where they was going or what they was going to do with him. So Burbie, he commence to whimper. But Hutch kept a-setting there, driving the horse, and he don't say nothing.

So pretty soon they come to a place where they was building a piece of county road, and it was all tore up and a whole lot of toolboxes laying out on the side. So Hutch gets out and twists the lock off one of them with the wrench, and takes out a pick and a shovel and throws them in the wagon. And then he got in again and drove on for a while till he come to the Whooping Nannie woods, what some of them says has got a ghost in it on dark nights, and it's about three miles from the old man's farm. And Hutch turns in there and pretty soon he come to a kind of a clear place and he stopped. And then, first thing he's said to Burbie, he says,

"Dig that grave!"

So Burbie dug the grave. He dug for two hours, until he got so damn tired he couldn't hardly stand up. But he ain't hardly made no hole at all. 'Cause the ground is froze and even with the pick he couldn't hardly make a dent in it scarcely. But anyhow Hutch stopped him and they throwed the old man in and covered him up. But after they got him covered up his head was sticking out. So Hutch beat the head down good as he could and piled the dirt up around it and they got in and drove off.

After they'd went a little ways, Hutch commence to cuss Burbie. Then he said Burbie'd been lying to him. But Burbie, he swears he ain't been lying. And then Hutch says he *was* lying and with that he hit Burbie. And after he knocked Burbie down in the bottom of the wagon he kicked him and then pretty soon Burbie up and told him about Lida. And when Burbie got done telling him about Lida, Hutch turned the horse around. Burbie asked then what they was going back for and Hutch says they're going back for to git a present for Lida. So they come back to the grave and Hutch made Burbie cut off the old man's head with the shovel. It made Burbie sick, but Hutch made him stick at it, and after a while Burbie had it off. So Hutch throwed it in the wagon and they get in and start back to town once more.

Well, they wasn't no more'n out of the woods before Hutch takes hisself a slug of corn and commence to holler. He kind of raved to hisself, all about how he was going to make Burbie put the head in a box and tie it up with a string and take it out to Lida for a present, so she'd get a nice surprise when she opened it. Soon as Lida comes back he says Burbie has got to do it, and then he's going to kill Burbie. "I'll kill you!" he says. "I'll kill you, damn you! I'll kill you!" And he says it kind of singsongy, over and over again.

And then he takes hisself another slug of corn and stands up and whoops. Then he beat on the horse with the whip and the horse commence to run. What I mean, he commence to gallop. And then Hutch hit him some more. And then he commence to screech as loud as he could. "Ride him, cowboy!" he hollers. "Going East! Here come old broadcuff down the road! Whe-e-e-e-e!" And sure enough, here they come down the road, the horse a-running hell to split, and Hutch a-hollering, and Burbie a-shivering, and the head a-rolling around in the bottom of the wagon, and bouncing up in the air when they hit a bump, and Burbie damn near dying every time it hit his feet.

III

After a while the horse got tired so it wouldn't run no more, and they had to let him walk and Hutch set down and commence to grunt. So Burbie, he tries to figure out what the hell he's going to do with the head. And pretty soon he remembers a creek what they got to cross, what they ain't crossed on the way out 'cause they come the back way. So he figures he'll throw the head overboard when Hutch ain't looking. So he done it. They come to the creek, and on the way down to the bridge there's a little hill, and when the wagon tilted going down the hill the head rolled up between Burbie's feet, and he held it there, and when they got in the middle of the bridge he reached down and heaved it overboard.

Next off, Hutch give a yell and drop down in the bottom of the wagon. 'Cause what it sounded like was a pistol shot. You see, Burbie done forgot that it was a cold night and the creek done froze over. Not much, just a thin skim about a inch thick, but enough that when that head hit it it cracked pretty loud in different directions. And that was what scared Hutch. So when he got up and seen the head setting out there on the ice in the moonlight, and got it straight what Burbie done, he let on he was going to kill Burbie right there. And he reached for the pick. And Burbie jumped out and run, and he didn't never stop till he got home at the place where he lived at, and locked the door, and climbed in bed and pulled the covers over his head.

Well, the next morning a fellow come running into town and says there's hell to pay down at the bridge. So we all went down there and first thing we seen was that head laying out there on the ice, kind of rolled over on one ear. And next thing we seen was Hutch's horse and wagon tied to the bridge rail, and the horse damn near froze to death. And the next thing we seen was the hole in the ice where Hutch fell through. And the next thing we seen down on the bottom next to one of the bridge pilings, was Hutch.

So the first thing we went to work and done was to get the head. And believe me a head laying out on thin ice is a pretty damn hard thing to get, and what we had to do was to lasso it. And the next thing we done was to get Hutch. And after we fished him out he had the wrench and the $23 in his pockets and the pint of corn on his hip and he was stiff as a board. And near as I can figure out, what happened to him was that after Burbie run away he climbed down on the bridge piling and tried to reach the head and fell in.

But we didn't know nothing about it then, and after we done got the head and the old man was gone and a couple of boys that afternoon found the body and not the head on it, and the pot was found, and them old people from the Methodist church done told their story and one thing and another, we figured out that Hutch done it, 'specially on account he must of been drunk and he done time in the pen and all like of that, and nobody ain't thought nothing about Burbie at all. They had the funeral and Lida cried like hell and everybody tried to figure out what Hutch wanted with the head and things went along thataway for three weeks.

Then one night down to the poolroom they was having it some more about the head, and one says one thing and one says another, and Benny Heath, what's a kind of a constable around town, he started a long bum argument about how Hutch must of figured if they couldn't find the head to the body they couldn't prove no murder. So right in the middle of it Burbie kind of looked around like he always done and then he winked. And Benny Heath, he kept on a-talking, and after he got done Burbie kind of leaned over and commence to talk to him. And in a couple of minutes you couldn't of heard a man catch his breath in that place, accounten they was all listening at Burbie.

I already told you Burbie was pretty good when it comes to giving a spiel at a entertainment. Well, this here was a kind of a spiel too. Burbie act like he had it all learned by heart. His voice trimmled and ever couple of minutes he'd kind of cry and wipe his eyes and make out like he can't say no more, and then he'd go on.

And the big idea was what a whole lot of hell he done raised in his life. Burbie said it was drink and women what done ruined him. He told about all the women what he knowed, and all the saloons he's been in, and some of it was a lie 'cause if all the saloons was as swell as he said they was they'd of throwed him out. And then he told about how sorry he was about the life he done led, and how hope my die he come home to his old home town just to get out the devilment and settle down. And he told about Lida, and how she wouldn't let him cut it out. And then he told how she done led him on till he got the idea to kill the old man. And then he told about how him and Hutch done it, and all about the money and the head and all the rest of it.

And what it sounded like was a piece what he knowed called "The Face on the Floor," what was about a bum what drawed a picture on the barroom floor of the woman what done ruined him. Only the funny part was that Burbie wasn't ashamed of hisself like he made out he was. You could see he was proud of hisself. He was proud of all them women and all the liquor he'd drunk and he was proud about Lida and he was proud about the old man and the head and being slick enough not to fall in the creek with Hutch. And after he got done he give a yelp and flopped down on the floor and I reckon maybe he thought he was going to die on the spot like the bum what drawed the face on the barroom floor, only he didn't. He kind of lain there a couple of minutes till Benny got him up and put him in the car and tooken him off to jail.

So that's where he's at now, and he's went to work and got religion down there, and all the people what comes to see him, why he sings hymns to them and then he speaks them his piece. And I hear tell he knows it pretty good by now and has got the crying down pat. And Lida, they got her down there too, only she won't say nothing 'cepting she done it same as Hutch and Burbie. So Burbie, he's going to get hung, sure as hell. And if he hadn't felt so smart, he would of been a free man yet.

Only I reckon he done been holding it all so long he just had to spill it.

The Taking of Montfaucon

I

I BEEN ASKED DID I GET A DSC in the late war, and the answer is no, but I might of got one if I had not run into some tough luck. And how that was is pretty mixed up, so I guess I better start at the beginning, so you can get it all straight and I will not have to do no backtracking. On the 26th of September, 1918, when the old 79th Division hopped off with the rest of the AEF on the big drive that started that morning, the big job ahead of us was to take a town named Montfaucon, and it was the same town where the Crown Prince of Germany has his PC [Post of Command] in 1916, when them Dutch was hammering on Verdun and he was watching his boys fight by looking up at them through a periscope. And our doughboys was in two brigades, the 157th and 158th, with two regiments in each, and the 157th Brigade was in front. But they ain't took the town because it was up on a high hill, and on the side of the hill was a whole lot of pillboxes and barbed wire what made it a tough job. Only I ain't seen none of that, because I spent the whole day on the water wagon, along with another guy name of Armbruster, and we was driving it up from the Division PC what we left to the Division PC where we was going. And that there weren't so good, because neither him, me, nor the horse hadn't had no sleep, account of the barrage shooting off all night, and every time we come to one of them sixteen-inch guns going through the woods and a Frog would squat down and pull the cord, why the horse would pretty near die and so would we. But sometime we seen a little of what was going on, like when a Jerry aviator come over and shot down four of our balloons and then flew over the road where we was and everybody tooken a shot at him, only I didn't because I happen to look at my gun after I pulled the bolt and it was all caked up with mud and I kind of changed my mind about taking a shot.

So after a while we come to a place in a trench and they said it was the new Division PC, and Ryan, who was the stable sergeant, come along and took the horse, and we got something to eat and there was still plenty shelling going on, but not bad like it was, and we figured we could get some sleep. So then it was about six o'clock in the evening. But pretty soon Captain Madeira, he come to me and says I was to go on duty. And what I was to do was to go with another guy, name of Shepler, to find the PC of the 157th Brigade, what was supposed to be one thousand yards west of where we was, and then report back. And why we was to do that was so we could find the Brigade PC in the night and carry messages to it. Because us in the Headquarters Troops, what we done in the fighting was act as couriers and all like of that, and what we done in between the fighting was curry horse belly. So me and Shepler started out. And as the Brigade PC was supposed to be one thousand yards west, and where we was was in a trench, and the trench run east and west, it looked like all we had to do was to follow the trench right into where the sun was setting and it wouldn't be no hard job to find what we was looking for.

And it weren't. In about ten minutes we come to the Brigade PC and there was General Nicholson [Brigadier General William J. Nicholson, commanding 157th Infantry Brigade] and his aides, and a bunch of guys what was in Brigade Headquarters, all setting around in the trench. But they was moving. They was all set to go forwards somewheres, and had their packs with them.

"Well," says Shep, "we ain't got nothing to do with that. Let's go back."

"Right," I says. But then I got to thinking. "What the hell good is it," I says, "for us to go back and tell them we found this PC when in a couple of minutes there ain't going to be nobody in it?"

"What the hell good is the war?" says Shep. "We was told to find this PC and we've found it. Now we go back and let them figure out what the hell good it is."

"This PC," I says, "soon as the General clears out, is same as a last year's bird nest."

"That's jake with me," says Shep. "In this man's army you do what you're told to do, and we've done it. We ain't got nothing to do with what kind of a bird's nest it is."

"No," I says, "we ain't done it. We was told to find a PC. And soon as Nick gets out this ain't going to be no PC, but only a dugout. We got to go with him. We got to find where his new PC is at, and then we go back."

"Well, if we ain't done it," says Shep, "that's different."

So in a couple of minutes Nick started off, and we went with him, and a hell of a fine thing we done for ourself that we ain't went back in the first place, like Shep wanted to do. Because where we went, it weren't over no road and it weren't through no trench. It was straight up toward the front line over No Man's Land, and a worse walk after supper nobody ever took this side of Hell. How we went was single file, first Nick, and then them aides, and then them headquarters guys, and then us. About every fifty yards, a runner would pick us up, and point the way, and then fall back and let us pass. And what we was walking over was all shell holes and barbed wire, and you was always slipping down and busting your shin, and then all them dead horses and things was laying around, and you didn't never see one till you had your foot in it, and then it made you sick. And dead men. The first one we seen was in a trench, kind of laying up against the side, what was on a slant. And he was sighting down his gun just like he was getting ready to pull the trigger, and when you come to him you opened your mouth to beg his pardon for bothering him. And then you didn't.

Well, we went along that way for a hell of a while. And pretty soon it seemed like we wasn't nowheres at all, but was slugging along through some kind of black dream what didn't have no end, and them goddam runners look like ghosts what was standing there to point, only we wasn't never going to get where they was pointing nor nowheres else.

But after a while we come to a road and on the side of the road was a piece of corrugated iron. And Nick, soon as he come to that, unslung his musette bag and sat down on it. And then all them other guys sat down too. So me and Shep, we figured on that awhile, because at first we thought they was just taking a rest, but then Shep let on it looked like to him they was expecting to stay awhile. So then we went up to Nick.

"Sir," I says, "is this the new Brigade PC?"

"Who are you?" he says.

"We're from Division Headquarters," I says. "We was ordered to find the Brigade PC and report back."

"This is the new PC," he says.

"This piece of iron?" I says.

"Yes," says he.

"Thank you, sir," I says, and me and Shep saluted and left him.

"A hell of a looking PC," says Shep, soon as we got where he couldn't hear us.

"A hell of a looking PC all right," I says, "but it's pretty looking alongside of that trip we got going back."

"I been thinking about that," he says.

So then we sat down by the road a couple of minutes.

"Listen," he says. "I ain't saying I like that trip none. But what I'm thinking about is suppose we get lost. I don't mind telling you I can't find my way back over them shell holes."

"I got a idea," I says.

"Shoot," he says.

"This here road we're setting on," I says, "must go somewheres."

"They generally do," he says.

"If we can find someplace what's on one end of it," I says, "I can take you back if you don't mind a little walking. Be cause I know all these roads around here like a book." And how that was, was because I had been on observation post before the drive started, and had to study them maps, and even if I hadn't never been on the roads I knowed how they run.

"I'll walk with you to sunup," he says, "if it's on a road and we know where we're going. But I ain't going to try to get back over that No Man's Land, boy, I'll tell you that. Because I just as well try to fly."

So we asked a whole lot of guys did they know where the road run, and not none of them knowed nothing about it. But pretty soon we found a guy in the engineers, what was fixing the road, and he said he thought the road run back to Avocourt.

"Let's go," I says to Shep. "I know where we're at now."

So we started out, and sure enough after a while we come to Avocourt. And I knowed there was a road run east from

Avocourt over the ridge to Esnes, if we could only figure out which the hell way was east. So the moon was coming up about then, and we remembered the moon come up in the east, and we headed for it, and hit the road. And a bunch of rats come outen a trench and began going up the road in front of us, hopping along in a pretty good line, and Shep said they was trench camels, and that give us a laugh, and we felt better. And pretty soon, sure enough we come to Esnes, and turned left, and in a couple minutes we was right back in the Division PC what we had left after supper, and it weren't much to look at, but it sure did feel like home.

II

Well, we weren't no sooner there than a bunch of guys begun to holler out to Captain Madeira that here we was, and he came a-running, and if we had of been a letter from home he couldn't of been more excited about us.

"Thank God, you've come," he says.

"Sure we've come," says Shep; "you wasn't really worried about us, was you?"

But I seen it was more than us the Captain was worrying about, so I says:

"What's the matter?"

"General Nicholson has broken liaison," he says, "and we've got not a way on earth to reach him unless you fellows can do it."

"Well, I guess we can, hey kid?" I says to Shep.

But Shep shook his head. "Maybe you can," he says, "but I ain't got no more idea where we been than a blind man. I'll keep you company, though, if you want."

"Company hell," says the Captain. "Here," he says to me, "you come in and see the General."

So he brung me into the dugout what was the PC to see

General Kuhn [Major General Joseph E. Kuhn, commanding general, 79th Division]. And most of the time, the General was a pretty snappy-looking soldier. He was about medium size, and he had a cut to his jaw and a swing to his back what look like them pictures you see in books. But he weren't no snappy-looking soldier that night. He hadn't had no shave, and his eyes was all sunk in, and no wonder. Because when the Division ain't took Montfaucon that day, like they was supposed to, it balled everything up like hell. It put a pocket in the American advance, a kind of a dent, what was holding up the works all along the line. And the General was getting hell from Corps, and he had lost a lot of men, and that was why he was looking like he was.

"Do you know where General Nicholson is?" he says to me, soon as Captain Madeira had told him who I was.

"Yes, sir," I says, "but I don't think *he* does."

Now what the General said to that I ain't sure, but he mumbled something to hisself what sound like he be damned if he did either.

"I want you to take a message to him," he says.

"Yes, sir," I says.

So he commenced to write the message. And while I was standing there I was so sleepy everything look like it was turning around, like them things you see in a dream. It was a couple of aides in there, and maybe an orderly, and Captain Madeira, and it was in behind a lot of blankets, what they wet and hang over the door of a dugout to keep out gas. And in the middle of it was General Kuhn, writing on a pad in lead pencil, and I remember thinking how old he looked setting there, and then that would blank out and I couldn't see nothing but his whiskers, and then that would blank out and I would be thinking it was pretty tough on him, and I would do my best to help him out. It weren't no more than a minute, mind. Why I was thinking all them things jumbled up together was because I hadn't had no sleep.

The Taking of Montfaucon   111

"All right," he says to me; listen now while I read it to you."

And why they read it to you is so if you lose it you can tell them what was in it and you ain't no worse off. And he hadn't no sooner started to read it then I snapped out of that dream pretty quick. Because it was short and sweet. It said that Nick was to attack right away soon as he got it. And I knowed a little about this Montfaucon stuff from hearing them brigade guys talk while we was going over No Man's Land, so I knowed I weren't carrying no message what just said good morning.

"Is that clear to you?" he says.

"Yes, sir," I says.

"Captain, give this man a horse. As good a horse as you've got."

"Yes, sir," says the Captain.

"You better ride pretty lively. And report back to me here."

"Yes, sir."

"No, wait a minute. I'm moving my PC to Malancourt in the next hour. Do you know where Malancourt is?"

"Yes, sir."

"Hunh," he says, like he meant thank God there was somebody in the outfit what knowed right from left and I was glad I had studied them maps good like I had and could be some use to him.

"Then report to me in Malancourt." And me and the Captain saluted and went out.

So the Captain took me to Ryan, and Ryan saddled me a horse, and while he was doing it Shep came up and begun to talk about the argument we had about whether we was going with Nick or not, and he handed it to me for figuring out the right thing to do, and the Captain said he was goddam proud of us both for carrying out orders with some sense when everybody else act like they had went off their nut and things was all shot to hell, and I felt pretty good. So pretty soon Ryan come with the horse, and I started out, and after I had went about a couple of miles it was commencing to get light, so I dug my heels in, because I knowed I didn't have much time.

III

Well, in another five minutes I come to Avocourt. And soon as I rode around the bend I got a funny feeling in my stomach. Because I seen something I had forgot when me and Shep was there, and that was that there was two roads what run from Avocourt up to the front line, one of them running north and the other running northeast, and they kind of forked off from each other in such a way that when you was coming down one of them like we done you wouldn't notice the other one at all. And I knowed as soon as I looked at them that I didn't have no idea which one we had come over and it weren't no way to find out.

So I pulled in and figured. And I closed my eyes and tried to remember how that road had looked when we was coming back down it into Avocourt with the moon rising on our left before we hit the road to Esnes, and that was damn hard, because I was so blotto from not having no sleep that soon as I closed my eyes all I got was a bellering in my ears. But I squinted them up good, and pretty soon it jumped in front of me, how that road looked, and right near Avocourt was a bunch of holes in the middle of it, what look like a tank had got stuck there and dug them up trying to get out. So I opened my eyes and was all set to hit for them holes. But then I knowed I was in for it good. Because in between while we had been over the road, them engineers had surfaced it, and it weren't no holes, because they was all covered up with stone.

But it weren't doing no good setting on top of the horse figuring, so I picked the right-hand road and started up it. I

The Taking of Montfaucon 113

figured I would go about as far as me and Shep had come, and then maybe I would run into Nick, or somebody that could tell me where he was at, or what the right road was to take, and that the main thing was to get a move on. But that there sounds easier than it was. Because once you start out somewheres, and get to wondering are you headed right or not, you're bad off, and you might just as well be standing still for all you're going to get there.

I kept pushing the horse on, and every step he took I would look around to see if I could see something that me and Shep had seen, and about all I seen was tanks and engineers forking stone, what was what we had saw the night before, but it didn't prove nothing because you could see tanks and engineers on any road. And them engineers wasn't no help, because engineers is dumb as hell and then they ain't got nothing to do with fighting outfits and 157th Brigade sounds just the same to them as any other brigade, and a hell of a wonder me and Shep had found one the night before that could even tell us which way the road run.

Well, after I had went a ways, about as far as I thought me and Shep had come, and ain't seen a thing that I could say for certain we had saw the night before, and no sign of Nick or his piece of corrugated iron, what might be covered up with stone too for all I knowed, I figured I was on the wrong road sure as hell, and I got a awful feeling that I would have to go back to Avocourt and start over again. Because that order in my pocket, it weren't getting no cooler, I'm here to tell you. It was damn near burning a hole in my leg, and a funny hiccuppy noise would come up out of my neck every time I thought of it.

But I went a little bit further, just to make sure, and then I come to something that I thought straightened me all out. It was kind of a crossroads, bearing off to the left. And I couldn't remember that we had passed it the night before, so I figured I must of gone wrong when I tooken the right-hand fork at

Avocourt. But this road, I thought, will put me right, because it leads right acrost to the other one and I won't have to lose all that time going back to Avocourt. So I helloed down it, and for the first time since I left Avocourt I felt I was going right. And sure enough, pretty soon I come to the other road, and it weren't no new stone on it at that place, so I turned right, toward the front, and started up it. And I worked on the horse a little bit, because without no loose stone under his foot he could go better, and kind of patted him on the neck and talked to him, because he hadn't had no sleep neither and he was tired as hell by this time, and then I lifted him along so he went in a good run. And it weren't quite light yet, and I thought thank God I'll be in time.

IV

So pretty soon I come to some soldiers what wasn't engineers. So I pulled up and hollered out:

"What way to the Hundred and fifty-seventh Brigade PC?"

"The what?" they says.

"The Hundred and fifty-seventh Brigade PC," I says. "General Nicholson's PC."

"Never hear tell of it," they says.

"The hell you say," I says. "And you're a hell of a goddam comical outfit, ain't you?"

Because that was one of them gags they had in the army. They would ask a guy what his outfit was, and then when he told them they would say they never hear tell of it.

So I rode a little further and come to another bunch. "Which way is the Hundred and fifty-seventh Brigade PC?" I says. "General Nicholson's PC?"

But they never said nothing at all. Because they was doughboys going up in the lines, and when you hear somebody talk about doughboys singing when they're going to fight, you can tell him he's a damn liar and say I said so. Doughboys when they're going up in the lines they look straight in front of them and they swaller every third step and they don't say nothing.

So pretty soon I come to another bunch what wasn't doughboys and I asked them. "Search me, buddy," they says, and I went on. And I done that a couple of times, and I ain't found out nothing. So then I figured it weren't no use asking for the Brigade PC no more, because a lot of them guys they wouldn't never of hear tell of the Hundred and fifty-seventh Brigade even if they was in it, so I figured I would find out what outfit they was in and then I could figure out from that about where I was at. So that's what I done.

"What outfit, buddy?" I says to the next bunch I come to. But all they done was look dumb, so I didn't waste no more time on them, but went on till I come to another bunch, and I asked them.

"AEF," a guy sings out.

"What the hell," I says. "You think I'm asking for fun?"

"YMCA," says another, and I went on. And then all of a sudden I knowed why them guys was acting like that, and why it was was this: Ever since they come to France, they had been told if somebody up in the front lines asks you what your outfit is, don't you tell him because maybe he's a German spy trying to find out something. Because of course they wasn't really worried none that I was a German spy. What they was worried about was that maybe I was a MP or something what was going around finding out how they was minding the rule, and they wasn't taking no chances. Later on, when a whole hell of a lot of couriers had got lost and the American Army didn't know was it coming or going, they changed that rule. They marked all the PC's good so you could see them, and had arrows pointing to them a couple miles away so you couldn't get lost. But the rule hadn't been changed that morning, and that was why them guys wouldn't say nothing.

Well, was you ever in a lunatic asylum? That was what it was like for me from that time on. I would ask and ask, and all I ever got was "YMCA," or "Company B," or something like that, and it getting later all the time, and me with that order in my pocket. And after a while I thought well I got to pretend to be an officer and scare somebody into telling me where I'm at. So the first ones I come to was a captain and a lieutenant setting by the side of the road, and they was wearing bars. But me not having no bars didn't make no difference, because up at the front some officers wore bars but most of them didn't, and if you take the bars off, one guy without a shave looks pretty much like another. So I went up to them and saluted and spoke sharp, like I had been bawling out orders all my life.

"Which way is General Nicholson's PC?" I says, and the captain jumped up and saluted.

"General Nicholson?" he says. "Not around here, I'm pretty sure, sir," he says.

"Hundred and fifty-seventh Brigade?" I says, pretty short, like he must be asleep or something if he didn't know where that was.

"Oh, no," he says. "That wouldn't be in this Division. This is all Thirty-seventh."

So then I knowed I was sunk. The 37th Division, it was on our left, and that meant I had been on the right road all the time when I left Avocourt, as I seen many a time since by checking it up on the maps, and had went wrong by wondering about that fork. And it weren't nothing to do but cut across again, and hope I might bump into General Nicholson somehow, and if I didn't to keep on beating to Malancourt, so I could report to General Kuhn like I had been told to do. And what I done from then on I ain't never figured out, even from them maps, because I was thinking about that order all the time, and how it ought to been delivered already if it was going to do any good, and I got a little wild. I put the horse over the ditch and went through the woods, and never went back to the crossroads at all. And them woods was all full of shell holes, so you couldn't go straight, and the day was still cloudy, so you couldn't tell by the sun which way you was headed, and it weren't long before I didn't know which the hell way I was going. One time I must of been right up with the fighting, because a guy got up out of a shell hole and yelled at me for Christ sake not go over the top of that hill with the horse, because there was a sniper a little ways away, and I would get knocked off sure as hell. But by that time a sniper, if he only knowed where the hell he was sniping from, would of looked like a brother, so I went over. But it weren't no sniper, because I didn't get knocked off.

And another time I come to the rim of a shell hole what was so big you could of dropped a two-story house in it, and right new, but it weren't no dirt around it and you couldn't see no place the dirt had went. And right then the horse he wheeled and begun to cut back toward where he had come from. Because he was so tired by then he was stumbling every step and didn't want to go on. So I had to fight him. And then I got off and begun to beat him. And then I begun to blubber. And then I begun to blubber some more on account of how I was treating the horse, because he ain't done nothing and it was up to me to make him go.

And while I was standing there blubbering, near as I can figure out, the 313th, what was part of the 157th Brigade, was taking Montfaucon. Because General Kuhn he ain't sat back and waited for me. Soon as I left him he got on a horse and rode up to the front line hisself, there in the dark, and passed the word over they was to advance, and then relieved a general what didn't seem to be showing no signs of life, and put a colonel in command at that end of the line, and pretty soon things were moving. So Nick, he got the order that way and went on, and the boys, if they had Nick in command, they would take the town. So they took it.

V

It must of been after eleven o'clock when I got in to Malancourt. And there by the side of the road was General Kuhn, all smeared up with mud and looking like hell. And I went up to him and saluted.

"Did you deliver that message?" he says.

"No, sir," I says.

"What!" he says. "Then what are you doing coming in here at this hour?"

"I got lost," I says.

He never said nothing. He just looked at me, starting in from my eyes and going clear down to my feet, and that there was the saddest look I ever seen one man turn on another. And it weren't nothing to do but stand there and hold on to the reins of the goddam horse, and wish to hell the sniper had got me.

But just then he looked away quick, because somebody was saluting in front of him and commencing to talk. And it was Nick. And what he was talking about was that Montfaucon had been took. But he didn't no more than get started before General Kuhn started up hisself.

"What do you mean!" he says, "by breaking liaison with me? And where have you been anyway?"

"Where have I been?" says Nick. "I've been taking that position, that's where I've been. And I did not break liaison with you!"

So come to find out, them runners what had showed us the way over No Man's Land was supposed to keep liaison, only it was their first day of fighting, same as it was everybody else's, and what they done was keep liaison with that last year's bird nest what Nick had left, and didn't get it straight they was supposed to space out a little bit till they reached to the Division PC.

"And, anyway," says Nick, "there was a couple of

The Taking of Montfaucon

your own runners that knew where I was. Why didn't you use them?"

So of course that made me feel great.

So they began to cuss at each other, and the generals can outcuss the privates, I'll say that for them. So I kind of saluted and went off, and then Captain Madeira, he come to me.

"What's the matter?" he says.

"Nothing much," I says.

"You didn't make it, hey?"

"No. Didn't make it."

"Don't worry about it. You did the best you could."

"Yeah, I done the best I could."

"You're not the only one. It's been a hell of a night and a hell of a day."

"Yeah, it sure has."

"Well—don't worry about it."

"Thanks."

So that is how I come not to get no DSC in the late war. If I had of done what I was sent to do, maybe they would of give me one, because Shep, he got cited, and they sure needed me bad. But I never done it, and it ain't no use blubbering over how things might be if only they was a little different.

The Baby in the Icebox

OF COURSE THERE WAS PLENTY PIECES in the paper about what happened out at the place last summer, but they got it all mixed up, so I will now put down how it really was, and 'specially the beginning of it, so you will see it is not no lies in it.

Because when a guy and his wife begin to play leapfrog with a tiger, like you might say, and the papers put in about that part and not none of the stuff that started it off, and then one day say X marks the spot and next day say it wasn't really no murder but don't tell you what it was, why, I don't blame people if they figure there was something funny about it or maybe that somebody ought to be locked up in the booby hatch. But there wasn't no booby hatch to this, nothing but plain onriness and a dirty rat getting it in the neck where he had it coming to him, as you will see when I get the first part explained right.

Things first begun to go sour between Duke and Lura

when they put the cats in. They didn't need no cats. They had a combination auto camp, filling station, and lunchroom out in the country a ways, and they got along all right. Duke run the filling station, and got me in to help him, and Lura took care of the lunchroom and shacks. But Duke wasn't satisfied. Before he got this place he had raised rabbits, and one time he had bees, and another time canary birds, and nothing would suit him now but to put in some cats to draw trade. Maybe you think that's funny, but out here in California they got every kind of a farm there is, from kangaroos to alligators, and it was just about the idea that a guy like Duke would think up. So he begun building a cage, and one day he showed up with a truckload of wildcats.

I wasn't there when they unloaded them. It was two or three cars waiting and I had to gas them up. But soon as I got a chance I went back there to look things over. And believe me, they wasn't pretty. The guy that sold Duke the cats had went away about five minutes before, and Duke was standing outside the cage and he had a stick of wood in his hand with blood on it. Inside was a dead cat. The rest of them was on a shelf, that had been built for them to jump on, and every one of them was snarling at Duke.

I don't know if you ever saw a wildcat, but they are about twice as big as a house cat, brindle gray, with tufted ears and a bobbed tail. When they set and look at you they look like a owl, but they wasn't setting and looking now. They was marching around, coughing and spitting, their eyes shooting red and green fire, and it was a ugly sight, 'specially with that bloody dead one down on the ground. Duke was pale, and the breath was whistling through his nose, and it didn't take no doctor to see he was scared to death.

"You better bury that cat," he says to me. "I'll take care of the cars."

I looked through the wire and he grabbed me. "Look out!" he says. "They'd kill you in a minute."

"In that case," I says, "how do I get the cat out?"

"You'll have to get a stick," he says, and shoves off.

I was pretty sore, but I begun looking around for a stick. I found one, but when I got back to the cage Lura was there. "How did that happen?" she says.

"I don't know," I says, "but I can tell you this much: If there's any more of them to be buried around here, you can get somebody else to do it. My job is to fix flats, and I'm not going to be no cat undertaker."

She didn't have nothing to say to that. She just stood there while I was trying the stick, and I could hear her toe snapping up and down in the sand, and from that I knowed she was choking it back, what she really thought, and didn't think no more of this here cat idea than I did.

The stick was too short. "My," she says, pretty disagreeable, "that looks terrible. You can't bring people out here with a thing like that in there."

"All right," I snapped back. "Find me a stick."

She didn't make no move to find no stick. She put her hand on the gate. "Hold on," I says. "Them things are nothing to monkey with."

"Huh," she says. "All they look like to me is a bunch of cats."

There was a kennel back of the cage, with a drop door on it, where they was supposed to go at night. How you got them back there was bait them with food, but I didn't know that then. I yelled at them, to drive them back in there, but nothing happened. All they done was yell back. Lura listened to me awhile, and then she give a kind of gasp like she couldn't stand it no longer, opened the gate, and went in.

Now believe me, that next was a bad five minutes, because she wasn't hard to look at, and I hated to think of her getting mauled up by them babies. But a guy would of had to of been blind if it didn't show him that she had a way with cats. First thing she done, when she got in, she stood still,

The Baby in the Icebox

didn't make no sudden motions or nothing, and begun to talk to them. Not no special talk. Just "Pretty pussy, what's the matter, what they been doing to you?"—like that. Then she went over to them.

They slid off, on their bellies, to another part of the shelf. But she kept after them, and got her hand on one, and stroked him on the back. Then she got ahold of another one, and pretty soon she had give them all a pat. Then she turned around, picked up the dead cat by one leg, and come out with him. I put him on the wheelbarrow and buried him.

Now, why was it that Lura kept it from Duke how easy she had got the cat out and even about being in the cage at all? I think it was just because she didn't have the heart to show him up to hisself how silly he looked. Anyway, at supper that night, she never said a word. Duke, he was nervous and excited and told all about how the cats had jumped at him and how he had to bean one to save his life, and then he give a long spiel about cats and how fear is the only thing they understand, so you would of thought he was Martin Johnson just back from the jungle or something.

But it seemed to me the dishes was making quite a noise that night, clattering around on the table, and that was funny, because one thing you could say for Lura was: she was quiet and easy to be around. So when Duke, just like it was nothing at all, asks me by the way how did I get the cat out, I heared my mouth saying, "With a stick," and not nothing more. A little bird flies around and tells you, at a time like that. Lura let it pass. Never said a word. And if you ask me, Duke never did find out how easy she could handle the cats, and that ain't only guesswork, but on account of something that happened a little while afterward, when we got the mountain lion.

A mountain lion is a cougar, only out here they call them a mountain lion. Well, one afternoon about five o'clock this one of ours squat down on her hunkers and set up the worst squalling you ever listen to. She kept it up all night, so you wanted to go out and shoot her, and next morning at breakfast Duke come running in and says come on out and look what happened. So we went out there, and there in the cage with her was the prettiest he mountain lion you ever seen in your life. He was big, probably weighed a hundred and fifty pounds, and his coat was a pearl gray so glossy it looked like a pair of new gloves, and he had a spot of white on his throat. Sometimes they have white.

"He come down from the hills when he heard her call last night," says Duke, "and he got in there somehow. Ain't it funny? When they hear that note nothing can stop them."

"Yeah," I says. "It's love."

"That's it," says Duke. "Well, we'll be having some little ones soon. Cheaper'n buying them."

After he had went off to town to buy the stuff for the day, Lura sat down to the table with me. "Nice of you," I says, "to let Romeo in last night."

"Romeo?" she says.

"Yes, Romeo. That's going to be papa of twins soon, out in the lion cage."

"Oh," she says, "didn't he get in there himself?"

"He did not. If she couldn't get out, how could he get in?"

All she give me at that time was a dead pan. Didn't know nothing about it at all. Fact of the matter, she made me a little sore. But after she brung me my second cup of coffee she kind of smiled. "Well?" she says. "You wouldn't keep two loving hearts apart, would you?"

So things was, like you might say, a little gritty, but they got a whole lot worse when Duke come home with Rajah, the tiger. Because by that time he had told so many lies that he begun to believe them hisself, and put on all the airs of a big animal trainer. When people come out on Sundays, he would take a black snake whip and go in with the mountain lions and wildcats, and snap it at them, and they would snarl and yowl, and Duke acted like he was doing something. Before he went in, he would let the people see him strapping on a big six-shooter, and Lura got sorer by the week.

For one thing, he looked so silly. She couldn't see nothing to going in with the cats, and 'specially she couldn't see no sense in going in with a whip, a six-shooter, and a ten-gallon hat like them cow people wears. And for another thing, it was bad for business. In the beginning, when Lura would take the customers' kids out and make out the cat had their finger, they loved it, and they loved it still more when the little mountain lions come and they had spots and would push up their ears to be scratched. But when Duke started that stuff with the whip it scared them to death, and even the fathers and mothers was nervous, because there was the gun and they didn't know what would happen next. So business begun to fall off.

And then one afternoon he put down a couple of drinks and figured it was time for him to go in there with Rajah. Now it had took Lura one minute to tame Rajah. She was in there sweeping out his cage one morning when Duke was away, and when he started sliding around on his belly he got a bucket of water in the face, and that was that. From then on he was her cat. But what happened when Duke tried to tame him was awful. The first I knew what he was up to was when he made a speech to the people from the mountain lion cage telling them not to go away yet, there was more to come. And when he come out he headed over to the tiger.

"What's the big idea?" I says. "What you up to now?"

"I'm going in with that tiger," he says. "It's got to be done, and I might as well do it now."

"Why has it got to be done?" I says.

He looked at me like as though he pitied me.

"I guess there's a few things about cats you don't know yet," he says. "You got a tiger on your hands, you got to let him know who's boss, that's all."

"Yeah?" I says. "And who is boss?"

"You see that?" he says, and cocks his finger at his face.

"See what?" I says.

"The human eye," he says. "The human eye, that's all. A cat's afraid of it. And if you know your business, you'll keep him afraid of it. That's all I'll use, the human eye. But, of course, just for protection, I've got these too."

"Listen, sweetheart," I says to him. "If you give me a choice between the human eye and a Bengal tiger, which one I got the most fear of, you're going to see a guy getting a shiner every time. If I was you, I'd lay off that cat."

He didn't say nothing: hitched up his holster, and went in. He didn't even get a chance to unlimber his whip. That tiger, soon as he saw him, begun to move around in a way that made your blood run cold. He didn't make for Duke first, you understand. He slid over, and in a second he was between Duke and the gate. That's one thing about a tiger you better not forget if you ever meet one. He can't work examples in arithmetic, but when it comes to the kinds of brains that mean meat, he's the brightest boy in the class and then some. He's born knowing more about cutting off a retreat than you'll ever know, and his legs do it for him, just automatic, so his jaws will be free for the main business of the meeting.

Duke backed away, and his face was awful to see. He was straining every muscle to keep his mouth from sliding down in his collar. His left hand fingered the whip a little, and his right pawed around, like he had some idea of drawing the gun. But the tiger didn't give him time to make up his mind what his idea was, if any.

He would slide a few feet on his belly, then get up and trot a step or two, then slide on his belly again. He didn't make no noise, you understand. He wasn't telling Duke, "Please go away"; he meant to kill him, and a killer don't generally make no more fuss than he has to. So for a few seconds you could even hear Duke's feet sliding over the floor. But all of a sudden a kid begun to whimper, and I come to my senses. I run around to the back of the cage, because that was where the tiger was crowding him, and I yelled at him.

"Duke!" I says. "In his kennel! Quick!"

He didn't seem to hear me. He was still backing, and the tiger was still coming. A woman screamed. The tiger's head went down, he crouched on the ground, and tightened every muscle. I knew what that meant. Everybody knew what it meant, and 'specially Duke knew what it meant. He made a funny sound in his throat, turned, and ran.

That was when the tiger sprung. Duke had no idea where he was going, but when he turned he fell through the trapdoor and I snapped it down. The tiger hit it so hard I thought it would split. One of Duke's legs was out, and the tiger was on it in a flash, but all he got on that grab was the sole of Duke's shoe. Duke got his leg in somehow and I jammed the door down tight.

It was a sweet time at supper that night. Lura didn't see this here, because she was busy in the lunchroom when it happened, but them people had talked on their way out, and she knowed all about it. What she said was plenty. And Duke, what do you think he done? He passed it off like it wasn't nothing at all. "Just one of them things you got to expect," he says. And then he let on he knowed what he was doing all the time, and the only lucky part of it was that he didn't have to shoot a valuable animal like Rajah was. "Keep cool, that's the main thing," he says. "A thing like that can happen now and then, but never let a animal see you excited."

I heard him, and I couldn't believe my ears, but when I looked at Lura I jumped. I think I told you she wasn't hard to look at. She was a kind of medium size, with a shape that would make a guy leave his happy home, sunburned all over, and high cheekbones that give her eyes a funny slant. But her eyes was narrowed down to slits, looking at Duke, and they shot green where the light hit them, and it come over me all of a sudden that she looked so much like Rajah, when he was closing in on Duke in the afternoon, that she could of been his twin sister.

Next off, Duke got it in his head he was such a big cat man now that he had to go up in the hills and do some trapping. Bring in his own stuff, he called it.

I didn't pay much attention to it at the time. Of course, he never brought in no stuff, except a couple of raccoons that he probably bought down the road for two dollars, but Duke was the kind of a guy that every once in a while has to sit on a rock and fish, so when he loaded up the flivver and blew, it wasn't nothing you would get excited about. Maybe I didn't really care what he was up to, because it was pretty nice, running the place with Lura with him out of the way, and I didn't ask no questions. But it was more to it than cats or 'coons or fish, and Lura knowed it, even if I didn't.

Anyhow, it was while he was away on one of them trips of his that Wild Bill Smith, the Texas Tornado, showed up. Bill was a snake doctor. He had a truck, with his picture painted on it, and two or three boxes of old rattlesnakes with their teeth pulled out, and he sold snake oil that would cure what ailed you, and a Indian herb medicine that would do the same. He was a fake, but he was big and brown and had white teeth, and I guess he really wasn't no bad guy. The first I seen of him was when he drove up in his truck, and told me to gas him up and look at his tires. He had a bum differential that made a funny rattle, but he said never mind and went over to the lunchroom.

He was there a long time, and I thought I better let him know his car was ready. When I went over there, he was setting on a stool with a sheepish look on his face, rubbing his hand. He had a snake ring on one finger, with two red eyes, and on the back of his hand was red streaks. I knew what that meant. He had started something and Lura had fixed him. She had a pretty arm, but a grip like iron, that she said come from milking cows when she was a kid. What she done when a guy got fresh was take hold of his hand and squeeze it so the bones cracked, and he generally changed his mind.

She handed him his check without a word, and I told him what he owed on the car, and he paid up and left.

"So you settled his hash, hey?" I says to her.

"If there's one thing gets on my nerves," she says, "it's a man that starts something the minute he gets in the door."

"Why didn't you yell for me?"

"Oh, I didn't need no help."

But the next day he was back, and after I filled up his car I went over to see how he was behaving. He was setting at one of the tables this time, and Lura was standing beside him. I saw her jerk her hand away quick, and he give me the bright grin a man has when he's got something he wants to cover up. He was all teeth. "Nice day," he says. "Great weather you have in this country."

"So I hear," I says. "Your car's ready."

"What I owe you?" he says.

"Dollar twenty."

He counted it out and left.

"Listen," says Lura, "we weren't doing anything when you come in. He was just reading my hand. He's a snake doctor, and knows about the zodiac."

"Oh, wasn't we?" I says. "Well, wasn't we nice!"

"What's it to you?" she says.

"Nothing," I snapped at her. I was pretty sore.

"He says I was born under the sign of Yin," she says. You would of thought it was a piece of news fit to put in the paper.

"And who is Yin?" I says.

"It's Chinese for tiger," she says.

"Then bite yourself off a piece of raw meat," I says, and slammed out of there. We didn't have no nice time running the joint *that* day.

Next morning he was back. I kept away from the lunchroom, but I took a stroll and seen them back there with the tigers. We had hauled a tree in there by that time for Rajah to sharpen his claws on, and she was setting on that. The tiger had his head in her lap, and Wild Bill was looking through the wire. He couldn't even draw his breath. I didn't go near enough to hear what they was saying. I went back to the car and begin blowing the horn.

He was back quite a few times after that, in between while Duke was away. Then one night I heard a truck drive up. I knowed that truck by its rattle. And it was daylight before I heard it go away.

Couple weeks after that, Duke come running over to me at the filling station. "Shake hands with me," he says, "I'm going to be a father."

"Gee," I says, "that's great!"

But I took good care he wasn't around when I mentioned it to Lura.

"Congratulations," I says. "Letting Romeos into the place seems to be about the best thing you do."

"What do you mean?" she says.

"Nothing," I says. "Only I heard him drive up that night. Look like to me the moon was under the sign of Cupid. Well, it's nice if you can get away with it."

"Oh," she says.

"Yeah," I says. "A fine double cross you thought up. I didn't know they tried that any more."

She set and looked at me, and then her mouth begin to twitch and her eyes filled with tears. She tried to snuffle them up but it didn't work. "It's not any double cross," she says. "That night I never went out there. And I never let anybody in. I was supposed to go away with him that night, but—"

She broke off and begin to cry. I took her in my arms. "But then you found this out?" I says. "Is that it?" She nodded her head. It's awful to have a pretty woman in your arms that's crying over somebody else.

From then on, it was terrible. Lura would go along two or three days pretty well, trying to like Duke again on account of the baby coming, but then would come a day when she looked like some kind of a hex, with her eyes all sunk in so you could hardly see them at all, and not a word out of her.

Them bad days, anyhow when Duke wasn't around, she would spend with the tiger. She would set and watch him sleep, or maybe play with him, and he seemed to like it as much as she did. He was young when we got him, and mangy and thin, so you could see his slats. But now he was about six years old, and had been fed good, so he had got his growth, and his coat was nice, and I think he was the biggest tiger I ever seen. A tiger, when he is really big, is a lot bigger than a lion, and sometimes when Rajah would be rubbing around Lura, he looked more like a mule than a cat.

His shoulders come up above her waist, and his head was so big it would cover both legs when he put it in her lap. When his tail would go sliding past her it looked like some kind of a constrictor snake. His teeth were something to make you lie awake nights. A tiger has the biggest teeth of any cat, and Rajah's must have been four inches long, curved like a cavalry sword, and ivory white. They were the most murderous-looking fangs I ever set eyes on.

When Lura went to the hospital it was a hurry call, and she didn't even have time to get her clothes together. Next day Duke had to pack her bag, and he was strutting around, because it was a boy, and Lura had named him Ron. But when he come out with the bag he didn't have much of a strut. "Look what I found," he says to me, and fishes something out of his pocket. It was the snake ring.

"Well?" I says. "They sell them in any ten-cent store."

"H'm," he says, and kind of weighed the ring in his hand. That afternoon, when he come back, he says: "Ten-cent store, hey? I took it to a jeweler today, and he offered me two hundred dollars for it."

"You ought to sold it," I says. "Maybe save you bad luck."

Duke went away again right after Lura come back, and for a little while things was all right. She was crazy about the little boy, and I thought he was pretty cute myself, and we got along fine. But then Duke come back and at lunch one day he made a crack about the ring. Lura didn't say nothing, but he kept at it, and pretty soon she wheeled on him.

"All right," she says. "There was another man around here, and I loved him. He give me that ring, and it meant that he and I belonged to each other. But I didn't go with him, and you know why I didn't. For Ron's sake, I've tried to love you again, and maybe I can yet, God knows. A woman can do some funny things if she tries. But that's where we're at now. That's right where we're at. And if you don't like it, you better say what you're going to do."

"When was this?" says Duke.

"It was quite a while ago. I told you I give him up, and I give him up for keeps."

"It was just before you knowed about Ron, wasn't it?" he says.

"Hey," I cut in. "That's no way to talk."

"Just what I thought," he says, not paying no attention to me. "Ron. That's a funny name for a kid. I thought it was funny, right off when I heard it. Ron. Ron. That's a laugh, ain't it?"

"That's a lie," she says. "That's a lie, every bit of it. And it's not the only lie you've been getting away with around here. Or think you have. Trapping up in the hills, hey? And what do you trap?"

But she looked at me and choked it back. I begun to see that the cats wasn't the only things had been gumming it up.

"All right," she wound up. "Say what you're going to do. Go on. Say it!"

But he didn't.

"Ron," he cackles, "that's a hot one," and walks out.

Next day was Saturday, and he acted funny all day. He wouldn't speak to me or Lura, and once or twice I heard him mumbling to himself. Right after supper he says to me, "How are we on oil?"

"All right," I says. "The truck was around yesterday."

"You better drive in and get some," he says. "I don't think we got enough."

"Enough?" I says. "We got enough for two weeks."

"Tomorrow is Sunday," he says, "and there'll be a big call for it. Bring out a hundred gallon and tell them to put it on the account."

By that time I would give in to one of his nutty ideas rather than have an argument with him, and besides, I never tumbled that he was up to anything. So I wasn't there for what happened next, but I got it out of Lura later, so here is how it was:

Lura didn't pay much attention to the argument about the oil, but washed up the supper dishes, and then went in the bedroom to make sure everything was all right with the baby. When she come out she left the door open, so she could hear if he cried. The bedroom was off the sitting room, because these here California houses don't have but one floor, and all the rooms connect. Then she lit the fire, because it was cool, and sat there watching it burn. Duke come in, walked around, and then went out back. "Close the door," she says to him. "I'll be right back," he says.

So she sat looking at the fire, she didn't know how long, maybe five minutes, maybe ten minutes. But pretty soon she felt the house shake. She thought maybe it was a earthquake, and looked at the pictures, but they was all hanging straight. Then she felt the house shake again. She listened, but it wasn't no truck outside that would cause it, and it wouldn't be no state-road blasting or nothing like that at that time of night. Then she felt it shake again, and this time it shook in a regular movement, one, two, three, four, like that. And then all of a sudden she knew what it was, why Duke had acted so funny all day, why he had sent me off for the oil, why he had left the door open, and all the rest of it. There was five hundred pound of cat walking through the house, and Duke had turned him loose to kill her.

She turned around, and Rajah was looking at her, not five foot away. She didn't do nothing for a minute, just set there thinking what a boob Duke was to figure on the tiger doing his dirty work for him, when all the time she could handle him easy as a kitten, only Duke didn't know it. Then she spoke. She expected Rajah to come and put his head in her lap, but he didn't. He stood there and growled, and his ears flattened back. That scared her, and she thought of the baby I told you a tiger has that kind of brains. It no sooner went through her head about the baby than Rajah knowed she wanted to get to that door, and he was over there before she could get out of the chair.

He was snarling in a regular roar now, but he hadn't got a whiff of the baby yet, and he was still facing Lura. She could see he meant business. She reached in the fireplace, grabbed a stick that was burning bright, and walked him down with it. A tiger is afraid of fire, and she shoved it right in his eyes. He backed past the door, and she slid in the bedroom. But he was right after her, and she had to hold the stick at him with one hand and grab her baby with the other.

But she couldn't get out. He had her cornered, and he was kicking up such a awful fuss she knowed the stick wouldn't stop him long. So she dropped it, grabbed up the baby's covers, and threw them at his head. They went wild, but they saved her just the same. A tiger, if you throw something at him with a human smell, will generally jump on it and bite at it before he does anything else, and that's what he done now. He jumped so hard the rug went out from under him, and while he was scrambling to his feet she shot past him with the baby and pulled the door shut after her

She run in my room, got a blanket, wrapped the baby in it, and run out to the electric icebox. It was the only thing around the place that was steel. Soon as she opened the door she knowed why she couldn't do nothing with Rajah. His meat was in there; Duke hadn't fed him. She pulled the meat out, shoved the baby in, cut off the current, and closed the door.

The Baby in the Icebox

Then she picked up the meat and went around the outside of the house to the window of the bedroom. She could see Rajah in there, biting at the top of the door, where a crack of light showed through. He reached to the ceiling. She took a grip on the meat and drove at the screen with it. It give way, and the meat went through. He was on it before it hit the floor.

Next thing was to give him time to eat. She figured she could handle him once he got something in his belly. She went back to the sitting room. And in there, kind of peering around, was Duke. He had his gun strapped on, and one look at his face was all she needed to know she hadn't made no mistake about why the tiger was loose.

"Oh," he says, kind of foolish, and then walked back and closed the door. "I meant to come back sooner, but I couldn't help looking at the night. You got no idea how beautiful it is. Stars is bright as anything."

"Yeah," she says. "I noticed."

"Beautiful," he says. "Beautiful."

"Was you expecting burglars or something?" she says, looking at the gun.

"Oh, that," he says. "No. Cat's been kicking up a fuss. I put it on, case I have to go back there. Always like to have it handy."

"The tiger," she says. "I thought I heard him, myself."

"Loud," says Duke. "Awful loud."

He waited. She waited. She wasn't going to give him the satisfaction of opening up first. But just then there come a growl from the bedroom, and the sound of bones cracking. A tiger acts awful sore when he eats. "What's that?" says Duke.

"I wonder," says Lura. She was hell-bent on making him spill it first.

They both looked at each other, and then there was more growls, and more sound of cracking bones. "You better go in there," says Duke, soft and easy, with the sweat standing out on his forehead and his eyes shining bright as marbles. "Something might be happening to Ron."

"Do you know what I think it is?" says Lura.

"What's that?" says Duke. His breath was whistling through his nose like it always done when he got excited.

"I think it's that tiger you sent in here to kill me," says Lura. "So you could bring in that woman you been running around with for over a year. That redhead that raises rabbit fryers on the Ventura road. That cat you been trapping!"

"And 'stead of getting you he got Ron," says Duke. "Little Ron! Oh my, ain't that tough? Go in there, why don't you? Ain't you got no mother love? Why don't you call up his pappy, get him in there? What's the matter? Is he afraid of a cat?"

Lura laughed at him. "All right," she says. "Now you go." With that she took hold of him. He tried to draw the gun, but she crumpled up his hand like a piece of wet paper and the gun fell on the floor. She bent him back on the table and beat his face in for him. Then she picked him up, dragged him to the front door, and threw him out. He run off a little ways. She come back and saw the gun. She picked it up, went to the door again, and threw it after him. "And take that peashooter with you," she says.

That was where she made her big mistake. When she turned to go back to the house, he shot, and that was the last she knew for a while.

Now, for what happened next, it wasn't nobody there, only Duke and the tiger, but after them state cops got done fitting it all together, combing the ruins and all, it wasn't no trouble to tell how it was, anyway most of it, and here's how they figured it out:

Soon as Duke seen Lura fall, right there in front of the house, he knowed he was up against it. So the first thing he done was run to where she was and put the gun in her hand, to make it look like she had shot herself. That was where he made *his* mistake, because if he had kept the gun he might of had a chance. Then he went inside to telephone, and what he

The Baby in the Icebox

said was, soon as he got hold of the state police: "For God's sake come out here quick. My wife has went crazy and throwed the baby to the tiger and shot herself and I'm all alone in the house with him and—*oh, my God, here he comes!*"

Now that last was something he didn't figure on saying. So far as he knowed, the tiger was in the room, having a nice meal off his son, so everything was hotsy-totsy. But what he didn't know was that that piece of burning firewood that Lura had dropped had set the room on fire and on account of that the tiger had got out. How did he get out? We never did quite figure that out. But this is how I figure it, and one man's guess is good as another's:

The fire started near the window, we knew that much. That was where Lura dropped the stick, right next to the cradle, and that was where a guy coming down the road in a car first seen the flames. And what I think is that soon as the tiger got his eye off the meat and seen the fire, he begun to scramble away from it, just wild. And when a wild tiger hits a beaverboard wall, he goes through, that's all. While Duke was telephoning, Rajah come through the wall like a clown through a hoop, and the first thing he seen was Duke, at the telephone, and Duke wasn't no friend, not to Rajah he wasn't.

Anyway, that's how things was when I got there with the oil. The state cops was a little ahead of me, and I met the ambulance with Lura in it, coming down the road seventy mile an hour, but just figured there had been a crash up the road, and didn't know nothing about it having Lura in it. And when I drove up, there was plenty to look at all right. The house was in flames, and the police was trying to get in, but couldn't get nowheres near it on account of the heat, and about a hundred cars parked all around, with people looking, and a gasoline pumper cruising up and down the road, trying to find a water connection somewhere they could screw their hose to.

But inside the house was the terrible part. You could hear

Duke screaming, and in between Duke was the tiger. And both of them was screams of fear, but I think the tiger was worse. It is a awful thing to hear a animal letting out a sound like that. It kept up about five minutes after I got there, and then all of a sudden you couldn't hear nothing but the tiger. And then in a minute that stopped.

There wasn't nothing to do about the fire. In a half hour the whole place was gone, and they was combing the ruins for Duke. Well, they found him. And in his head was four holes, two on each side, deep. We measured them fangs of the tiger. They just fit.

Soon as I could I run in to the hospital. They had got the bullet out by that time, and Lura was laying in bed all bandaged around the head, but there was a guard over her, on account of what Duke said over the telephone. He was a state cop. I sat down with him, and he didn't like it none. Neither did I. I knowed there was something funny about it, but what broke your heart was Lura, coming out of the ether. She would groan and mutter and try to say something so hard it would make your head ache. After a while I got up and went in the hall. But then I see the state cop shoot out of the room and line down the hall as fast as he could go. At last she had said it. The baby was in the electric icebox. They found him there, still asleep and just about ready for his milk. The fire had blacked up the outside, but inside it was as cool and nice as a new bathtub.

Well, that was about all. They cleared Lura, soon as she told her story, and the baby in the icebox proved it. Soon as she got out of the hospital she got a offer from the movies, but 'stead of taking it she come out to the place and her and I run it for a while, anyway the filling-station end, sleeping in the shacks and getting along nice. But one night I heard a rattle from a bum differential, and I never even bothered to show up for breakfast the next morning.

I often wish I had. Maybe she left me a note.

The Birthday Party

He bounced the tennis ball against the garage with persistence, but no enthusiasm. He would have gone swimming, but Red would be there, and he owed Red ten cents. Red drove the ice-cream truck evenings, and so swam in midafternoon; debtors, therefore, used the creek mornings, late afternoons, and, if there was a moon, nights. Between times they passed away the hours bouncing tennis balls against garages.

He bounced the ball with sudden zeal. There had come a call from the house: "Burwell!" It was repeated, twice, and then amended: "Burwell Hope!"

He slowed the tempo. "You call me, ma?"

"I don't see why you can't answer when I call."

"I was practicing strokes," he told her.

"Well, don't stand there yelling so the whole neighborhood can hear you; and, besides, I don't think that's any place for practicing strokes. It makes an awful noise and I don't wonder people are annoyed."

He slouched slowly into the house, practicing a trick that involved mashing the ball into the ground, hitting it with the edge of the racket as it sprang up, and catching it in the pants pocket as it bounced waist-high.

"Have you bathed?"

"It's too hot to bathe now. I'll be all perspired up again. I'll bathe after supper."

"You ought to bathe now."

"It's too hot."

"Did you black your shoes as I told you?"

"Not yet."

"Not yet, what?"

"Not yet, ma."

"Well, there's the pen and ink; sit down and write the card now so I can wrap it up. I've got a minute now and I don't want to have to think about it later."

"Wrap what up?"

"Burwell, how many times have I got to tell you you must stop this habit of asking useless questions? It's annoying, and you have to stop it. Marjorie's birthday present, of course. I can't wrap it up until I have the card, and you're giving it to her, so you have to write the card."

"I'm not giving it to her. I don't even know what it is."

"It's a very nice bottle of perfume. Want to see it?"

"Phooie!"

"Stop—using—that—word!"

"I don't want to see it."

"Very well. Then as soon as you write the card you can black your shoes."

"What for?"

"Will you stop asking those useless questions! For the party, of course. Didn't I tell you? Answer me. Didn't I tell you not two hours ago that Mrs. Lucas stopped by, told me they were giving a little surprise party for Marjorie tonight because it's her birthday, and that she especially wanted you to be there? Didn't I tell you that?"

"I'm not going."

"You're—"

"Sure, you told me, but I never said I would go."

"Why, Burwell Hope, the very idea. And after Mrs. Lucas said she especially wanted you to go. And after I made a trip downtown to buy a nice present. Why, I never heard of such a thing. All her friends are going. Spencer, and Jackie, and Junior LeGrand, and—"

"Bunch of sissies."

"Is every boy a sissy that has some kind of manners and does what his mother tells him to once in a while without always having to argue?"

"I'm not going."

"What will Marjorie think?"

"Marjorie Lucas. The belle of Home Room Twenty-nine."

"Why do you always have to be so mean to Marjorie? What has she ever done to you?"

"The face that only a mother could love."

"I haven't time to stand around and argue with you. You write the card right now—'Happy Birthday to Marjorie from Burwell'—and then you go out and black your shoes. They're on the back porch, and there's a new can of blacking in the things that came up from the market."

He wrote the card, then went out on the back porch and looked at his shoes. Then he looked at the sun. Then he looked at the sun again, making certain calculations based on its position in the heavens and its relation to the general progress of the afternoon. Then he drifted into the backyard, took his swimming suit off the line, and slipped quickly through the hole in the hedge.

The creek was deserted, but damp spots on the boat landing showed that Red, to say nothing of his more solvent customers, wasn't long gone. Burwell peeled off his clothes, had a moment of wild determination to go in naked, but compromised on trunks, without shirt. The water felt queer, and all his tricks seemed shriveled: He kept opening his mouth to yell, "Hey, look at this one," but there was nobody to look. He tried a back dive, but all he got out of it was a pair of smarting shins, where they slapped the water as he came over. He tried a feat of his own, for which he imagined he had acquired quite a local reputation: to go down under and stay down under, with only his feet sticking out; but something seemed to be wrong with it. As a rule, he could stay down under at least five minutes—or, at any rate, so he frequently asserted, in the absence of any watch to time him, and in the absence also of any knowledge that even one minute is a prodigious time for holding the breath; but now, for some unexplainable reason, he was no sooner down than he had to come up again, puffing grievously.

Treading water, about to try again, he felt a tingle in his back: somebody, he knew, was watching him. This time, as he lazily flipped himself under, all was as it should be. He stayed down at least ten minutes, crossing his feet as they stuck out in the air, wiggling his toes, sending up bubbles, and in other ways putting in subtle artistic touches. When he came up he tossed the hair out of his eyes nonchalantly and breathed through his nose—to conceal the puffing, and to show that, staggering though the performance might be, it had been done with ease.

Marjorie was on the boat landing. "Hello."

"Hello."

"My, but you scared me."

"Me scare you?"

"I thought something had happened to you. When I saw your toes wiggle I thought something had you. I thought I would die."

"Oh, that. That wasn't nothing."

He put his face in the water and blew through his mouth, at the same time uttering loud noises. He conceived this to be a peculiarly terrifying experience for the beholder.

However, she didn't seem to be paying much attention. "I wish I could go in."

The Birthday Party

"Well, come on."

"I didn't bring my suit."

He became a steamboat, churning up a great deal of foam, but stopped when she wandered into the canoe house. When she came out she had his swimming shirt.

"Are you going to be wearing this?"

"Only sissies wear shirts."

"I could pin it at the bottom. It's pretty big for me, and I could pin it so it would be all right."

"I don't mind."

She went back into the canoe house again, and he began doing all his tricks, one after the other. Presently she came out, a bit suggestive of diapers and safety pins here and there, but in the main clad neatly in a one-piece bathing suit, made of his shirt. He let go with a jackknife; then climbed out with an air of triumph mixed with boredom.

She climbed down the cleats and felt the water with one toe.

"What's the matter? You scared?"

"I'm not scared. But I always like to know if it's cold or not."

"You're scared."

"Well, I always am. A little."

"If you're scared, you've got to dive in."

"I'm going to."

"Well, why don't you?"

"I'm going to. In a minute."

He had a moment of vast, soul-warming contempt, but it congealed within him to a drop of bitter, cruel gall. She was climbing the piling. He watched her, stunned, saw her poise far above his head, then go off and cut the water so cleanly that only a high spurt of foam marked her entering it.

Nobody had told him that little girls dive better than little boys. Nobody had told him that little girls could possibly do anything better than little boys. All he knew was that he had never had the nerve to climb the piling and dive off, and here she had done it; and not only done it, but done it, apparently, without even knowing that it was hard.

He jumped up, as soon as her head came out of the water, and yelled at her: "So you think you're smart, hey? That's nothing. I can do it too. I've done it plenty of times. I can even do a back dive from up there."

"Can you really?"

She said it with honest admiration, and he climbed up. But when he got there a sick feeling swept down his throat and into his stomach. It was higher than he imagined. It was higher than he had ever imagined anything could be. The water was way, way down, far removed from anything that he could possibly dive into.

He tried to get set for a dive, but couldn't even stand up. All he could do was squat there, holding the tops of the piles with his hands, and gulp.

"If you're scared," she said, "you've got to dive in."

The ancient apothegm, quoted so blandly by himself not two minutes ago, was spoken innocently, yet it floated up from the water with a terrible mockery.

"Who's scared?"

"Well, my goodness, anybody can be scared."

"I'm not scared. I'm just taking it easy."

"It just comes from being dizzy."

"Why don't you kick your feet when you swim? That's no way to swim. Why don't you kick your feet like I do?"

"I can't swim very well, but I like to dive."

"Well, anybody can dive. Swimming's the important thing. If you can swim good you might save somebody from drowning, but what good is diving?"

"Maybe if you sat down on the big pile and then let go, it would be like jumping off."

"Who's asking you?"

She climbed up beside him. "What makes you dizzy is looking down. Why don't you look up at the sky and try it? Like this."

The Birthday Party

She threw back her head, gripped the pile with her toes, stiffened, sprang. But he didn't see her swash into the water. The pilings shuddered so sickeningly from her leap that he had to clutch them tight with his fingers, looking cravenly into the cracks of the wood. When the swaying stopped he looked up at the sky and tried to stand. He couldn't. She climbed up there again. This time she turned her back to the water, leaned out. He knew it was a back dive, but he didn't see that one either. She stretched herself out on the boat landing to rest, and there was nothing he could do but climb down. He was panting when he reached her, not from exertion, but from rage.

"I know what you're doing here. I know why you're not home. It's your birthday, and they're giving you a surprise party, and they ran you out of the house so you wouldn't see them getting ready for it. Yah! Got run out of the house. Yah!"

"I knew it all the time, but I think it was mean of you to tell me."

"Whole lot of cake and stuff coming in and they didn't want you to see it. Bum old cake from the bakery."

"It's not bum old cake. It's a special birthday cake with my name on it in icing."

"How do you know?"

"I peeped and saw it. It's going to have candles on it and they're going to bring it out in front of everybody and then I'm going to cut it."

"Old stale cake they had left over from last week and then they put your name on it in icing."

"It is not."

"Phooie!" He spat in the water and sat there laughing, mumbling, and shaking his head, as though the ignoble tricks of the whole human race were quite beyond him.

She sat up and began to fluff out her hair. "Are you invited, Burwell?"

"Wouldn't you like to know?"

"I kind of said one or two things so they wouldn't forget to invite you."

"Wouldn't you like to know?"

"Are you coming?"

"Is that a laugh! Is that a laugh!"

"I don't see anything funny."

"Am I coming? Say, is that a laugh! Me come to a bum birthday party with a lot of sissies and an old stale cake the bakery couldn't give away but your old man came and bought it cheap and had your name put on it in icing. Well! Is that a laugh!"

"Aren't you really coming, Burwell?"

"Who, me?"

"I was going to give you the first piece of cake."

"That stale stuff."

"Tell me, Burwell. Why aren't you coming?"

"Phooie! I'm busy."

"How do you mean, busy?"

"Don't you wish you knew? Don't you wish you knew?"

She looked at him and he had a sensation of having to think fast. "Are you really busy, Burwell?"

"Sure, I'm busy."

"Doing what?"

"Why—I got to work."

The agreeable degree of her astonishment surprised even him. "Have you got a job, Burwell?"

"Sure I got a job."

"What kind of a job? Tell me."

"Helping Red."

Now this wasn't true. The only relation it had to truth was that he had been considering a plan whereby he would offer to help Red for a night or two, in return for the extinguishment of the ten-cent debt. But actually he had made no such offer, and whether he would ever make it was problematical for Red was a brisk young man, rather hard to talk to, despite his professional affability.

The Birthday Party

"Honest?"

"Busy guy these days. Me go to a party? Say, is that a laugh!"

"I haven't seen you with Red."

"I'm inside the truck."

"What doing?"

"Oh, lot of things."

"Tell me."

"Well, I pass out the stuff to him. Drive the old bus, so he don't all the time have to be jumping in and out, saves him a lot of time. Keep things going. Ring up the cash. Lot of things."

"Do you get paid for it?"

"You think I'm doing all that for nothing?"

"Well, I didn't know. I thought he might just give you ice cream. You know. A free cake if you wanted it."

"A fat chance."

"When did you start?"

"Oh, I don't just remember. I've been at it quite a while. Maybe a week."

"Just think! And I didn't know a thing about it."

He rather fancied his new job now. As a matter of fact, the truck had a wheel that had always taken his eye; it was a big, horizontal wheel, something like the wheel on the rear end of a hook-and-ladder, and there now leaped into his mind a picture of himself behind it.

"Say, you ought to see me in there, swinging her around corners, dodging traffic, shooting her up beside the curb, ringing the bell—I forgot that. I'm the one that rings the bell."

He acted it out, his feet hanging over the water, his hands caressing the wheel. He shifted gears, pedaled the brake, sounded the bell, pulled up short just in time to avoid a collision with a lady pushing a gocart containing an infant, went on with a noble, though worried, look on his face. A captious listener might have reflected that evening was a strange time for infants to be abroad in gocarts; might have taken exception, too, to a certain discrepancy between the critical situations in which this ice-cream truck seemed always to find itself, and the somewhat innocuous tinkle of the bell which accompanied its doings. However, his listener wasn't captious. She gazed at him with wide-open eyes, and a rapture so complete that all she could think of to say was an oft-repeated "My!"

They took turns dressing, and as they started home he glowed pleasantly under her admiration. Yet admiration, even now, was not quite enough. He craved definite superiority.

"Beat you to the edge of the woods."

"No you can't."

She started so suddenly he was taken by surprise, and as she raced ahead of him he had one twinge of fear that she not only could dive better than he could, but run faster. But the distance was in his favor. She tired, and as he clattered past her he had at last what he had craved all afternoon: the hot, passionate feeling that he was better than she was; that from now on she must be his creature, to worship him without question, to look on from a distance while he dazzled her with tricks. It was short-lived. He felt a jolting, terrible pain in his face, having tripped on the wet bathing suit and slammed down in the road, the dust grinding into his mouth, the little stones cutting his cheek. He set his jaws, closed his eyes, screwed up his face in an agony of effort not to cry.

"It's all right, Burwell. You're not hurt bad. You're just scratched up a little bit. Here, I'll wipe it off for you."

He felt the wet bathing suit wiping his face, then the soft dry dabs of her handkerchief. The effort not to cry was becoming more than he could stand. He clenched his fists.

"Open your mouth and close your eyes, I'll give you something to make you wise." A quick, warm little kiss alighted on his mouth, stayed a moment, pressed hard, and then left.

A wave of happiness swept over him. The strain eased, he

The Birthday Party

hadn't cried. He opened his eyes. She was gone.

They were at supper when he got home, and his mother jumped up when she saw him. "Mercy, Burwell, what on earth has happened to you?"

"I fell down."

"Mercy! Mercy!"

"I'm all right."

"Are you sure? My, I'll have to put something on your face before you come to the table."

"I don't want any supper."

She felt his brow.

"I'm going to bed."

"I don't think he has any fever."

"I'm all right, but I'm going to bed."

However, at this point Liza, the cook, appeared with a platterful of sliced watermelon, then hastily backed out: "Ah thought you-all was th'oo."

His eye caught the wet redness, and he couldn't shake it out of his mind. "Well, maybe I could eat a little bit."

"Then sit right down, and I'll put something on your face later."

He sat down, and permitted himself to be coaxed into eating three pieces of fried chicken, two new potatoes, four ears of corn on the cob, a dish of pickled beets, and two big slices of watermelon.

While he was putting this away, his mother kept up a sort of running soliloquy: "I wonder if I ought to let him go to that party tonight. It seems a pity to have him miss it, and yet—we'll see."

It annoyed him that his mother seemed to have forgotten he didn't want to go to the party, and discussed it as though it were something he had been looking forward to for his whole life. However, there was nothing to do but fall in with that view of it, and dodge the main issue, if possible.

"It's all right. I don't mind. I'm going to bed."

"Did you shine your shoes?"

"No'm. I was going to, but—I fell down."

"Well, I'll shine them. You keep quiet after supper, and then we'll see."

"It's all right. I don't want to go."

"Why, Burwell! You know you want to go."

"I do not! I'm going to bed!"

He had overplayed it, and he knew it. At his insistent shout his father, who had been eyeing him narrowly for some time, suddenly spoke: "Burwell."

"Yes, sir."

"What's this about the party?"

"Nothing."

"When you get through supper you're to shine your shoes. You're to bathe and dress. When you're ready, come to me, and we'll get some collodion on that face so it'll have a beauty suitable to the festivities. Then you're going to the party."

"Yes, sir."

Bathed, shined, dressed, and patched, he started out, but he was in no hurry to get there. He was troubled, and he fingered the birthday present in his pocket most uneasily. How to explain his absence from his job wasn't what bothered him. He already had a plan that would take care of it handsomely. He was at an age when it would be sufficient to say, "Yah, were you kidded! Did you bite! Yah!" and this would settle anything. But somehow he didn't like it. He didn't know it, but what ailed him was that he had already tasted triumph, or anyhow some sort of triumph, and what he craved now was humility, the sweet sacrifice of love: the sensation of being unselfish, and noble, and wan about the eyes.

He loitered outside the billiard hall watching the mysterious business of white balls clicking against red; scuffled past the picture show, examining all the posters; dillied and dallied, but after a while he had it. He would put the first plan into effect almost as soon as he got there, but he would combine it with another plan, to be uncorked later. After Marjorie had had an hour of moping brokenheartedly trying to be gay with her guests, he would call her aside and tell her the truth, or what at the moment seemed to be the truth. He had worked for Red. He had helped him on the truck; had helped him for two weeks, as a matter of fact; and all because he knew that tonight would be her birthday, and he wanted to give her something out of his own money, and—well, here it is. Then she would know she had cruelly misjudged him, and they would sit there in the shadows, happy, but in a soft dreamy way, since she would be aware at last of his lofty nature.

So it was quite dark when he got there and the party was in full swing out in the backyard. The yard had been strung with lanterns, and as he slipped back of the house he could see them all out there dancing on the clipped grass, to the radio. He paused in the shadows and looked for Marjorie. She wasn't there. He kept looking and looking, and then a sound caught his ear, so close he jumped. He turned, and found himself looking in the dining-room window. In front of it on a small table, not three feet from him, was the big cake, with Marjorie's name on it, the unlit candles spaced around its edge, with one in the middle.

And approaching that cake, in the dark room, was Marjorie. She got to it, picked up the knife, hesitated. Then he felt creepy at the enormity of the thing she was about to do. She was cutting the cake that was to be carried out before the guests as the grand surprise of the evening.

He was numb with shocked astonishment as he saw the knife go in twice, saw Marjorie pick up the wedge of cake in her hands and hurry out of the room. He was still staring at the mutilated cake when he heard a step, saw her run out of the front of the house, flit down the lawn to the pillar of the driveway, and wait. Then shame, panic, fear, and love shot through him in one terrible stab. He crept to the edge of the porch. He slipped the present under the rail. He ran blindly to the street, into the night.

From the distance, up the street, came the bell of the ice-cream truck.

Dead Man

I

He felt the train check, knew what it meant. In a moment, from up toward the engine, came the chant of the railroad detective: "Rise and shine, boys, rise and shine." The hoboes began dropping off. He could hear them out there in the dark, cursing as the train went by. That was what they always did on these freights: let the hoboes climb on in the yards, making no effort to dislodge them there; for that would have meant a foolish game of hide-and-seek between two or three detectives and two or three hundred hoboes, with the hoboes swarming on as fast as the detectives put them off. What they did was let the hoboes alone until the train was several miles under way; then they pulled down to a speed slow enough for men to drop off, but too fast for them to climb back on. Then the detective went down the line, brushing them off, like caterpillars from a twig. In two minutes they would all be ditched, a crowd of bitter men in a lonely spot, but they always cursed, always seemed surprised.

He crouched in the coal gondola and waited. He hadn't boarded a flat or a refrigerator with the others, back in the Los Angeles yards, tempting though this comfort was. He wasn't long on the road, and he still didn't like to mix with the other hoboes, admit he was one of them. Also, he couldn't shake off a notion that he was sharper than they were, that playing a lone hand he might think of some magnificent trick that would defeat the detective, and thus, even at this ignoble trade, give him a sense of accomplishment, of being good at it. He had slipped into the gond not in spite of its harshness, but because of it; it was black, and would give him a chance to hide, and the detective, not expecting him there, might pass him by. He was nineteen years old, and was proud of the nickname they had given him in the poolroom back home. They called him Lucky.

"Rise and shine, boys, rise and shine."

Three dropped off the tank car ahead, and the detective climbed into the gond. The flashlight shot around, and Lucky held his breath. He had curled into one of the three chutes for unloading coal. The trick worked. These chutes were dangerous, for if you stepped into one and the bottom dropped, it would dump you under the train. The detective took no chances. He first shot the flash, then held on to the side while he climbed over the chutes. When he came to the last one, where Lucky lay, he shot the flash, but carelessly, and not squarely into the hole, so that he saw nothing. Stepping over, he went on, climbed to the boxcar behind, and resumed his chant: there were more curses, more feet sliding on ballast on the roadbed outside. Soon the train picked up speed. That meant the detective had reached the caboose, that all the hoboes were cleared.

Lucky stood up, looked around. There was nothing to see, except hot-dog stands along the highway, but it was pleasant to poke your head up, let the wind whip your hair, and reflect how you had outwitted the detective. When the click of the rails slowed and station lights showed ahead, he squatted down again, dropped his feet into the chute. As soon as lights flashed alongside, he braced against the opposite side of the chute: that was one thing he had learned, the crazy way they shot the brakes on these freights. When the train jerked to a shrieking stop, he was ready, and didn't get slammed. The bell tolled, the engine pulled away, there was an interval of silence. That meant they had cut the train, and would be picking up more cars. Soon they would be going on.

"Ah-ha! Hiding out on me, hey?"

The flashlight shot down from the boxcar. Lucky jumped, seized the side of the gond, scrambled up, vaulted. When he hit the roadbed, his ankles stung from the impact, and he staggered for footing. The detective was on him, grappling. He broke away, ran down the track, past the caboose, into the dark. The detective followed, but he was a big man and began to lose ground. Lucky was clear, when all of a sudden his foot drove against a switch bar and he went flat on his face, panting from the hysteria of shock.

The detective didn't grapple this time. He let go with a barrage of kicks.

"Hide out on me, will you? Treat you right, give you a break, and you hide out on me. I'll learn you to hide out on me."

Lucky tried to get up, couldn't. He was jerked to his feet, rushed up the track on the run. He pulled back, but couldn't get set. He sat down, dug in with his sliding heels. The detective kicked and jerked, in fury. Lucky clawed for something to hold on to, his hand caught the rail. The detective stamped on it. He pulled it back in pain, clawed again. This time his fingers closed on a spike, sticking an inch or two out of the tie. The detective jerked, the spike pulled out of the hole, and Lucky resumed his unwilling run.

Lemme go! Why don't you lemme go?"

"Come on! Hide out on me, will you? I'll learn you to hide out on Larry Nott!"

"Lemme go! Lemme—"

Lucky pulled back, braced with his heels, got himself stopped. Then his whole body coiled like a spring and let go in one convulsive, passionate lunge. The spike, still in his hand, came down on the detective's head, and he felt it crush. He stood there, looking down at something dark and formless, lying across the rails.

II

Hurrying down the track, he became aware of the spike, gave it a toss, heard it splash in the ditch. Soon he realized that his steps on the ties were being telegraphed by the listening rail, and he plunged across the ditch to the highway. There he resumed his rapid walk, trying not to run. But every time a car overtook him his heels lifted queerly, and his breath first stopped, then came in gasps as he listened for the car to stop. He came to a crossroads, turned quickly to his right. He let himself run here, for the road wasn't lighted as the main highway was, and there weren't many cars. The running tired him, but it eased the sick feeling in his stomach. He came to a sign that told him Los Angeles was seventeen miles, and to his left. He turned, walked, ran, stooped down sometimes, panting, to rest. After a while it came to him why he had to get to Los Angeles, and so soon. The soup kitchen opened at seven o'clock. He had to be there, in that same soup kitchen where he had had supper, so it would look as though he had never been away.

When the lights went off, and it came broad daylight with the suddenness of Southern California, he was in the city, and a clock told him it was ten minutes after five. He thought

Dead Man

he had time. He pressed on, exhausted, but never relaxing his rapid, half-shuffling walk.

It was ten minutes to seven when he got to the soup kitchen, and he quickly walked past it. He wanted to be clear at the end of the line, so he could have a word with Shorty, the man who dished out the soup, without impatient shoves from behind, and growls to keep moving.

Shorty remembered him. "Still here, hey?"

"Still here."

"Three in a row for you. Holy smoke, they ought to be collecting for you by the month."

"Thought you'd be off."

"Who, me?"

"Sunday, ain't it?"

"Sunday? Wake up. This is Saturday."

"Saturday? You're kidding."

"Kidding my eye, this is Saturday, and a big day in this town, too."

"One day looks like another to me."

"Not this one. Parade."

"Yeah?"

"Shriners. You get that free."

"Well, that's my name, Lucky."

"My name's Shorty, but I'm over six feet."

"Nothing like that with me. I really got luck."

"You sure?"

"Like, for instance, getting a hunk of meat."

"I didn't give you no meat."

"Ain't you going to?"

"Shove your plate over quick. Don't let nobody see you."

"Thanks."

"Okay, Lucky. Don't miss the parade."

"I won't."

He sat at the rough table with the others, dipped his bread in the soup, tried to eat, but his throat kept contracting from excitement and he made slow work of it. He had what he wanted from Shorty. He had fixed the day, and not only the day but the date, for it would be the same date as the big Shriners' parade. He had fixed his name, with a little gag. Shorty wouldn't forget him. His throat relaxed, and he wolfed the piece of meat.

Near the soup kitchen he saw signs: LINCOLN PARK PHARMACY, LINCOLN PARK CAFETERIA.

"Which way is the park, buddy?" If it was a big park, he might find a thicket where he could lie down, rest his aching legs.

"Straight down, you'll see it."

There was a fence around it, but he found a gate, opened it, slipped in. Ahead of him was a thicket, but the ground was wet from a stream that ran through it. He crossed a small bridge, followed a path. He came to a stable, peeped in. It was empty, but the floor was thickly covered with new hay. He went in, made for a dark corner, burrowed under the hay, closed his eyes. For a few moments everything slipped away, except warmth, relaxation, ease. But then something began to drill into the back of his mind: Where did he spend last night? Where would he tell them he spent last night? He tried to think, but nothing would come to him. He would have said that he spent it where he spent the night before, but he hadn't spent it in Los Angeles. He had spent it in Santa Barbara, and come down in the morning on a truck. He had never spent a night in Los Angeles. He didn't know the places. He had no answers to the questions that were now pounding at him like sledge hammers:

"What's that? Where you say you was?"

"In a flophouse."

"Which flophouse?"

"I didn't pay no attention which flophouse. It was just a flophouse."

"Where was this flophouse at?"

"I don't know where it was at. I never been to Los Angeles before. I don't know the names of no streets."

"What this flophouse look like?"

"Looked like a flophouse."

"Come on, don't give us no gags. What this flophouse look like? Ain't you got eyes, can't you say what this here place looked like? What's the matter, can't you talk?"

Something gripped his arm, and he felt himself being lifted. Something of terrible strength had hold of him, and he was going straight up in the air. He squirmed to get loose, then was plopped on his feet and released. He turned, terrified.

An elephant was standing there, exploring his clothes with its trunk. He knew then that he had been asleep. But when he backed away, he bumped into another elephant. He slipped between the two elephants, slithered past a third to the door, which was open about a foot. Out in the sunlight, he made his way back across the little bridge, saw what he hadn't noticed before: pens with deer in them, and ostriches, and mountain sheep, that told him he had stumbled into a zoo. It was after four o'clock, so he must have slept a long time in the hay. Back on the street, he felt a sobbing laugh rise in his throat. *That* was where he had spent the night. "In the elephant house at Lincoln Park."

"*What?*"

"That's right. In the elephant house."

"What you giving us? A stall?"

"It ain't no stall. I was in the elephant house."

"With them elephants?"

"That's right."

"How you get in there?"

"Just went in. The door was open."

"Just went in there, seen the elephants, and bedded down with them?"

"I thought they was horses."

"You thought them elephants was horses?"

"It was dark. I dug in under the hay. I never knowed they was elephants till morning."

"How come you went in this place?"

"I left the soup kitchen, and in a couple of minutes I came to the park. I went in there, looking for some grass to lie down on. Then I come to this here place, looked to me like a stable. I peeped in, seen the hay, and hit it."

"And you wasn't scared of them elephants?"

"It was dark, I tell you, and I could hear them eating the hay, but I thought they was horses. I was tired, and I wanted someplace to sleep."

"Then what?"

"Then when it got light, and I seen they was elephants, I run out of there, and beat it."

"Couldn't you tell them elephants by the smell?"

"I never noticed no smell."

"How many elephants was there?"

"Three."

III

He brushed wisps of hay off his denims. They had been fairly new, but now they were black with the grime of the coal gond. Suddenly his heart stopped, a suffocating feeling swept over him. The questions started again, hammered at him, beat into his brain.

"Where that coal dust come from?"

"I don't know. The freights, I guess."

"Don't you know it ain't no coal ever shipped into this part of the state? Don't you know that here all they burn is gas? Don't you know it ain't only been but one coal car shipped in here in six months, and that come in by a misread train order? Don't you know that car was part of that train this here detective was riding that got killed? *Don't you know that?* Come on, out with it. WHERE THAT COAL DUST COME FROM?"

Getting rid of the denims instantly became an obsession. He felt that people were looking at him on the street, spying the coal dust, waiting till he got by, then running into drugstores to phone the police that he had just passed by. It was like those dreams he sometimes had, where he was walking through crowds naked, except that this was no dream, and he wasn't naked, he was wearing these denims, these telltale denims with coal dust all over them. He clenched his hands, had a moment of terrible concentration, headed into a filling station.

"Hello."

"Hello."

"What's the chances on a job?"

"No chances."

"Why not?"

"Don't need anybody."

"That's not the only reason."

"There's about forty-two other reasons, one of them is I can't even make a living myself, but it's all the reason that concerns you. Here's a dime, kid. Better luck somewhere else."

"I don't want your dime. I want a job. If the clothes were better, that might help, mightn't it?"

"If the clothes were good enough for Clark Gable in the swell gambling-house scene, that wouldn't help a bit. Not a bit. I just don't need anybody, that's all."

"Suppose I got better clothes. Would you talk to me?"

"Talk to you any time, but I don't need anybody."

"I'll be back when I get the clothes."

"Just taking a walk for nothing."

"What's your name?"

"Hook s my name Oscar Hook."

"Thanks, Mr. Hook. But I'm coming back. I just got a idea I can talk myself into a job. I'm some talker."

"You're all that, kid. But don't waste your time. I don't need anybody."

"Okay. Just the same, I'll be back."

He headed for the center of town, asked the way to the cheap clothing stores. At Los Angeles and Temple, after an hour's trudge, he came to a succession of small stores in a Mexican quarter that were what he wanted. He went into one. The storekeeper was a Mexican, and two or three other Mexicans were standing around smoking.

"Mister, will you trust me for a pair of white pants and a shirt?"

"No trust. Hey, scram."

"Look. I can have a job Monday morning if I can show up in that outfit. White pants and a white shirt. That's all."

"No trust. What you think this is, anyway?"

"Well, I got to get that outfit somewhere. If I get that, they'll let me go to work Monday. I'll pay you soon as I get paid off Saturday night."

"No trust. Sell for cash."

He stood there. The Mexicans stood there, smoked, looked out at the street. Presently one of them looked at him. "What kind of job, hey? What you mean, got to have white pants a white shirt a hold a job?"

"Filling station. They got a rule you got to have white clothes before you can work there."

"Oh. Sure. Filling station."

After a while the storekeeper spoke. "Ha! Is a joke. Job in filling station, must have a white pants, white shirt. Ha! Is a joke."

"What else would I want them for? Holy smoke, these are better for the road, ain't they? Say, a guy don't want white pants to ride freights, does he?"

"What filling station? Tell me that."

"Guy name of Hook, Oscar Hook, got a Acme station. Main near Twentieth. You don't believe me, call him up."

"You go to work there, hey?"

"I'm *supposed* to go to work. I *told* him I'd get the white pants and white shirt, somehow. Well—if I don't get them, I don't go to work."

"Why you come to me, hey?"

"Where else would I go? If it's not you, it's another guy down the street. No place else I can dig up the stuff over Sunday, is there?"

"Oh."

He stood around. They all stood around. Then once again the storekeeper looked up. "What size you wear, hey?"

He had a wash at a tap in the backyard, then changed there, between piled-up boxes and crates. The storekeeper gave him a white shirt, white pants, necktie, a suit of thick underwear, and a pair of shoes to replace his badly worn brogans. "Is pretty cold, nighttime, now. A thick underwear feel better."

"Okay. Much obliged."

"Can roll this other stuff up."

"I don't want it. Can you throw it away for me?"

"Is pretty dirty."

"Plenty dirty."

"You no want?"

"No."

His heart leaped as the storekeeper dropped the whole pile into a rubbish brazier and touched a match to some papers at the bottom of it. In a few minutes, the denims and everything else he had worn were ashes.

He followed the storekeeper inside. "Okay, here is a bill, I put all a stuff on a bill, no charge you more than anybody else. Is six dollar ninety-eight cents, then is a service charge one dollar."

All of them laughed. He took the "service charge" to be a gyp overcharge to cover the trust. He nodded. "Okay on the service charge."

The storekeeper hesitated. "Well, six ninety-eight. We no make a service charge."

"Thanks."

"See you keep a white pants clean till Monday morning."

"I'll do that. See you Saturday night."

"*Adios.*"

Out in the street, he stuck his hand in his pocket, felt something, pulled it out. It was a $1 bill. Then he understood about the "service charge," and why the Mexicans had laughed. He went back, kissed the $1 bill, waved a cheery salute into the store. They all waved back.

He rode a streetcar down to Mr. Hook's, got turned down for the job, rode a streetcar back. In his mind, he tried to check over everything. He had an alibi, fantastic and plausible. So far as he could recall, nobody on the train had seen him, not even the other hoboes, for he had stood apart from them in the yards, and had done nothing to attract the attention of any of them. The denims were burned, and he had a story to account for the whites. It even looked pretty good, this thing with Mr. Hook, for anybody who had committed a murder would be most unlikely to make a serious effort to land a job.

But the questions lurked there, ready to spring at him, check and recheck as he would. He saw a sign, 5-COURSE DINNER, 35 CENTS. He still had ninety cents, and went in, ordered steak and fried potatoes, the hungry man's dream of heaven. He ate, put a ten-cent tip under the plate. He ordered cigarettes, lit one, inhaled. He got up to go. A newspaper was lying on the table.

He froze as he saw the headline:

L. R. NOTT, R. R. MAN, KILLED.

IV

On the street, he bought a paper, tried to open it under a street light, couldn't, tucked it under his arm. He found Highway 101, caught a hay truck bound for San Francisco. Going out Sunset Boulevard, it unexpectedly pulled over to the curb and stopped. He looked warily around. Down a side street, about a block away, were the two red lights of a police station. He was tightening to jump and run, but the driver wasn't looking at the lights. "I told them bums that air hose was leaking. They set you nuts. Supposed to keep the stuff in shape and all they ever do is sit around and play blackjack."

The driver fished a roll of black tape from his pocket and got out. Lucky sat where he was a few minutes, then climbed down, walked to the glare of the headlights, opened his paper. There it was:

L. R. NOTT, R. R. MAN. KILLED

The decapitated body of L. R. Nott, 1327 De Soto Street, a detective assigned to a northbound freight, was found early this morning on the track near San Fernando station. It is believed he lost his balance while the train was shunting cars at the San Fernando siding and fell beneath the wheels. Funeral services will be held tomorrow from the De Soto Street Methodist Church.

Mr. Nott is survived by a widow, formerly Miss Elsie Snowden of Mannerheim, and a son, L. R. Nott, Jr., 5.

He stared at it, refolded the paper, tucked it under his arm, walked back to where the driver was taping the air hose. He was clear, and he knew it. "Boy, do they call you Lucky? Is your name Lucky? I'll say it is."

He leaned against the trailer, let his eye wander down

the street. He saw the two red lights of the police station—glowing. He looked away quickly. A queer feeling began to stir inside him. He wished the driver would hurry up

Presently he went back to the headlights again, found the notice, re-read it. He recognized that feeling now; it was the old Sunday-night feeling that he used to have back home, when the bells would ring and he would have to stop playing hide in the twilight, go to church, and hear about the necessity for being saved. It shot through his mind, the time he had played hookey from church, and hid in the livery stable; and how lonely he had felt, because there was nobody to play hide with; and how he had sneaked into church, and stood in the rear to listen to the necessity for being saved.

His eyes twitched back to the red lights, and slowly, shakily, but unswervingly he found himself walking toward them.

"I want to give myself up."

"Yeah, I know, you're wanted for grand larceny in Hackensack, New Jersey."

"No, I—"

"We quit giving them rides when the New Deal come in. Beat it."

"I killed a man."

"You—? . . . When was it you done this?"

"Last night."

"Where?"

"Near here. San Fernando. It was like this—"

"Hey, wait till I get a card. . . . Okay, what's your name?

"Ben Fuller."

"No middle name?"

"They call me Lucky."

"Lucky like in good luck?"

"Yes, sir. . . . Lucky like in good luck."

Brush Fire

He banged sparks with his shovel, coughed smoke, cursed the impulse that had led him to heed that rumor down in the railroad yards that CCC money was to be had by all who wanted to fight this fire the papers were full of, up in the hills. Back home he had always heard them called forest fires, but they seemed to be brush fires here in California. So far, all he had got out of it was a suit of denims, a pair of shoes, and a ration of stew, served in an army mess kit. For that he had ridden twenty miles in a jolting truck out from Los Angeles to these parched hills, stood in line an hour to get his stuff, stood in line another hour for the stew, and then labored all night, the flames singeing his hair, the ground burning his feet through the thick brogans, the smoke searing his lungs, until he thought he would go frantic if he didn't get a whiff of air.

Still the thing went on. Hundreds of them smashed out flames, set backfires, hacked at bramble, while the bitter complaint went around: "Why don't they give us brush hooks if we got to cut down them bushes? What the hell good are these damn shovels?" The shovel became the symbol of their torture. Here and there, through the night, a grotesque figure would throw one down, jump on it, curse at it, then pick it up again as the hysteria subsided.

"Third shift, this way! Third shift, this way. Bring your shovels and turn over to shift number four. Everybody in the third shift, right over here."

It was the voice of the CCC foreman, who, all agreed, knew as much about fighting fires as a monkey did. Had it not been for the state fire wardens, assisting at critical spots, they would have made no progress whatever.

"All right. Answer to your names when I call them. You got to be checked off to get your money. They pay today two o'clock, so yell loud when I call your name."

"Today's Sunday."

"I said they pay today, so speak up when I call your name."

The foreman had a pencil with a little bulb in the end of it which he flashed on and began going down the list.

"Bub Anderson, Lonnie Beal, K. Bernstein, Harry Deever. . . ." As each name was called there was a loud "Yo," so when his name was called, Paul Larkin, he yelled "Yo" too. Then the foreman was calling a name and becoming annoyed because there was no answer. "Ike Pendleton! Ike Pendleton!"

"He's around somewhere."

"Why ain't he here? Don't he know he's got to be checked off?"

"Hey, Ike! Ike Pendleton!"

He came out of his trance with a jolt. He had a sudden recollection of a man who had helped him to clear out a brier patch a little while ago, and whom he hadn't seen since. He raced up the slope and over toward the fire.

Near the brier patch, in a V between the main fire and a

backfire that was advancing to meet it, he saw something. He rushed, but a cloud of smoke doubled him back. He retreated a few feet, sucked in a lungful of air, charged through the backfire. There, on his face, was a man. He seized the collar of the denim jacket, started to drag. Then he saw it would be fatal to take this man through the backfire that way. He tried to lift, but his lungful of air was spent: he had to breathe or die. He expelled it, inhaled, screamed at the pain of the smoke in his throat.

He fell on his face beside the man, got a little air there, near the ground. He shoved his arm under the denim jacket, heaved, felt the man roll solidly on his back. He lurched to his feet, ran through the backfire. Two or three came to his aid, helped him with his load to the hollow, where the foreman was, where the air was fresh and cool.

"Where's his shovel? He ought to have turned it over to—"
"His shovel! Give him water!"
"I'm gitting him water; but one thing at a time—"
"Water! Water! Where's that water cart?"

The foreman, realizing belatedly that a life might be more important than the shovel tally, gave orders to "work his arms and legs up and down." Somebody brought a bucket of water, and little by little Ike Pendleton came back to life. He coughed, breathed with long shuddering gasps, gagged, vomited. They wiped his face, fanned him, splashed water on him.

Soon, in spite of efforts to keep him where he was, he fought to his feet, reeled around with the hard, terrible vitality of some kind of animal. "Where's my hat? Who took my hat?" They clapped a hat on his head, he sat down suddenly, then got up and stood swaying. The foreman remembered his responsibility. "All right, men, give him a hand, walk him down to his bunk."

"Check him off!"
"Check the rest of us! You ain't passed the *P*'s yet!"

O.K. Sing out when I call. Gus Ritter!"

"Yo!"

When the names had been checked, Paul took one of Ike's arms and pulled it over his shoulder; somebody else took the other, and they started for the place, a half mile or so away on the main road, where the camp was located. The rest fell in behind. Dawn was just breaking as the little file, two and two, fell into a shambling step.

"Hep! . . . Hep!"

"Hey, cut that out! This ain't no lockstep."

"Who says it ain't?"

When he woke up, in the army tent he shared with five others, he became aware of a tingle of expectancy in the air. Two of his tent mates were shaving; another came in, a towel over his arm, his hair wet and combed.

"Where did you get that wash?"

"They got a shower tent over there."

He got out his safety razor, slipped his feet in the shoes, shaved over one of the other men's shoulders, then started out in his underwear. "Hey!" At the warning, he looked out. Several cars were out there, some of them with women standing around them, talking to figures in blue denim.

"Sunday, bo. Visiting day. This is when the women all comes to say hello to their loved ones. You better put something on."

He slipped on the denims, went over to the shower tent, drew towel and soap, stripped, waited his turn. It was a real shower, the first he had had in a long time. It was cold, but it felt good. There was a comb there. He washed it, combed his hair, put on his clothes, went back to his tent, put the towel away, made his bunk. Then he fell in line for breakfast—or dinner, as it happened, as it was away past noon. It consisted of corned beef, cabbage, a boiled potato, apricot pie, and coffee.

He wolfed down the food, washed up his kit, began to

feel pretty good. He fell into line again, and presently was paid, $4.50 for nine hours' work, at fifty cents an hour. He fingered the bills curiously. They were the first he had had in his hand since that day, two years before, when he had run away from home and begun this dreadful career of riding freights, bumming meals, and sleeping in flophouses.

He realized with a start they were the first bills he had ever earned in his twenty-two years; for the chance to earn bills had long since departed when he graduated from high school and began looking for jobs, never finding any. He shoved them in his pocket, wondered whether he would get the chance that night to earn more of them.

The foreman was standing there, in the space around which the tents were set up, with a little group around him. "It's under control, but we got to watch it, and there'll be another call tonight. Any you guys that want to work, report to me eight o'clock tonight, right here in this spot."

By now the place was alive with people, dust, and excitement. Cars were jammed into every possible place, mostly second-, third-, and ninth-hand, but surrounded by neatly dressed women, children, and old people, come to visit the fire fighters in denim. In a row out front, ice-cream, popcorn, and cold-drink trucks were parked, and the road was gay for half a mile in both directions with pennants stuck on poles, announcing their wares. Newspaper reporters were around too, with photographers, and as soon as the foreman had finished his harangue, they began to ask him questions about the fire, the number of men engaged in fighting it, and the casualties.

"Nobody hurt. Nobody hurt at all. Oh, early this morning, fellow kind of got knocked out by smoke, guy went in and pulled him out, nothing at all."

"What was his name?"

"I forget his name. Here—here's the guy that pulled him out. Maybe he knows his name."

In a second he was surrounded, questions being shouted

at him from all sides. He gave them Ike's name and his own, and they began a frantic search for Ike, but couldn't find him. Then they decided he was the main story, not Ike, and directed him to pose for his picture. "Hey, not there; not by the ice-cream truck. We don't give ice cream a free ad in this paper. Over there by the tent."

He stood as directed, and two or three in the third shift told the story all over again in vivid detail. The reporters took notes, the photographers snapped several pictures of him, and a crowd collected. "And will you put it in that I'm from Spokane, Washington? I'd kind of like to have that in, on account of my people back there. Spokane, Washington."

"Sure, we'll put that in."

The reporters left as quickly as they had come, and the crowd began to melt. He turned away, a little sorry that his big moment had passed so quickly. Behind him he half heard a voice: "Well, ain't *that* something to be getting his picture in the paper?" He turned, saw several grins, but nobody was looking at him. Standing with her back to him, dressed in a blue silk Sunday dress, and kicking a pebble, was a girl. It was a girl who had spoken, and by quick elimination he decided it must be she.

The sense of carefree goofiness that had been growing on him since he got his money, since the crowd began to jostle him, since he had become a hero, focused somewhere in his head with dizzy suddenness. "Any objections?"

This got a laugh. She kept her eyes on the pebble but turned red and said: "No."

"You sure?"

"Just so you don't get stuck up."

"Then that's O.K. How about an ice-cream cone?"

"I don't mind."

"Hey, mister, two ice-cream cones."

"Chocolate."

"Both of them chocolate and both of them double."

When they got their cones he led her away from the guffawing gallery which was beginning to be a bit irksome. She looked at him then, and he saw she was pretty. She was small, with blue eyes, dusty blonde hair that blended with the dusty scene around her, and a spray of freckles over her forehead. He judged her to be about his own age. After looking at him, and laughing rather self-consciously and turning red, she concentrated on the cone, which she licked with a precise technique. He suddenly found he had nothing to say, but said it anyhow: "Well, say—what are you doing here?"

"Oh—had to see the fire, you know."

"Have you seen it?"

"Haven't even found out where it is, yet."

"Well, my, my! I see I got to show it to you."

"You know where it is?"

"Sure. Come on."

He didn't lead the way to the fire, though. He took her up the arroyo, through the burned-over area, where the fire had been yesterday. After a mile or so of walking, they came to a little grove of trees beside a spring. The trees were live oak and quite green and cast a deep shade on the ground. Nobody was in sight, or even in earshot. It was a place the Sunday trippers didn't know about.

"Oh, my! Look at these trees! They didn't get burnt."

"Sometimes it jumps—the fire, I mean. Jumps from one hill straight over to the other hill, leaves places it never touched at all."

"My, but it's pretty."

"Let's sit down."

"If I don't get my dress dirty."

"I'll put this jacket down for you to sit on."

"Yes, that's all right."

They sat down. He put his arm around her, put his mouth against her lips.

It was late afternoon before she decided that her family

might be looking for her and that she had better go back. She had an uncle in the camp, it seemed, and they had come as much to see him as to see the fire. She snickered when she remembered she hadn't seen either. They both snickered. They walked slowly back, their little fingers hooked together. He asked if she would like to go with him to one of the places along the road to get something to eat, but she said they had brought lunch with them, and would probably stop along the beach to eat it, going back.

They parted, she to slip into the crowd unobtrusively; he to get his mess kit, for the supper line was already formed. As he watched the blue dress flit between the tents and disappear, a gulp came into his throat; it seemed to him that this girl he had held in his arms, whose name he hadn't even thought to inquire, was almost the sweetest human being he had ever met in his life.

When he had eaten, and washed his mess kit and put it away, he wanted a cigarette. He walked down the road to a Bar-B-Q shack, bought a package, lit up, started back. Across a field, a hundred yards away, was the ocean. He inhaled the cigarette, inhaled the ocean air, enjoyed the languor that was stealing over him, wished he didn't have to go to work. And then, as he approached the camp, he felt something ominous.

Ike Pendleton was there, and in front of him this girl, this same girl he had spent the afternoon with. Ike said something to her, and she backed off. Ike followed, his fists doubled up. The crowd was silent, seemed almost to be holding its breath. Ike cursed at her. She began to cry. One of the state police came running up to them, pushed them apart, began to lecture them. The crowd broke into a buzz of talk. A woman, who seemed to be a relative, began to explain to all and sundry: "What if she *did* go with some guy to look at the fire? He don't live with her no more! *He* don't support her—never *did* support her! She didn't come up here to see *him*; never even knew he was *up* here! My land, can't the poor child have a good time once in a while?"

It dawned on him that this girl was Ike's wife.

He sat down on a truck bumper, sucked nervously at his cigarette. Some of the people who had guffawed at the ice-cream-cone episode in the afternoon looked at him, whispered. The policeman called over the woman who had been explaining things, and she and the girl, together with two children, went hurriedly over to a car and climbed into it. The policeman said a few words to Ike, and then went back to his duties on the road.

Ike walked over, picked up a mess kit, squatted on the ground between tents, and resumed a meal apparently interrupted. He ate sullenly, with his head hulked down between his shoulders. It was almost dark. The lights came on. The camp was not only connected to county water but to county light as well. Two boys went over to Ike, hesitated, then pointed to Paul. "Hey, mister, that's him. Over there, sitting on the truck."

Ike didn't look up. When the boys came closer and repeated their news, he jumped up suddenly and chased them. One of them he hit with a baked potato. When they had run away he went back to his food. He paid no attention to Paul.

In the car, the woman was working feverishly at the starter. It would whine, the engine would start and bark furiously for a moment or two, then die with a series of explosions. Each time it did this, the woman would let in the clutch, the car would rock on its wheels, and then come to rest. This went on for at least five minutes, until Paul thought he would go insane if it didn't stop, and people began to yell: "Get a horse!" "Get that damn oil can out of here and stop that noise!" "Have a heart! This ain't the Fourth of July!"

For the twentieth time it was repeated. Then Ike jumped up and ran over there. People closed in after him. Paul, propelled by some force that seemed completely apart from himself, ran after him. When he had fought his way through the crowd, Ike was on the running board of the car, the chilren screaming, men trying to pull him back. He had the knife from the mess kit in his hand. "I'm going to kill her! I'm going to kill her! If it's the last thing I do on earth, I'm going to kill her!"

"Oh, yeah!"

He seized Ike by the back of the neck, jerked, and slammed him against the fender. Then something smashed against his face. It was the woman, beating him with her handbag. "Go away! Git away from here!"

Ike faced him, lips writhing, eyes glaring a slaty gray against the deep red of the burns he had received that morning. But his voice was low, even if it broke with the intensity of his emotion. "Get out of my way, you! You got nothing to do with this."

He lunged at Ike with his fist—missed. Ike struck with the knife. He fended with his left arm, felt the steel cut in. With his other hand he struck, and Ike staggered back. There was a pile of shovels beside him, almost tripping him up. He grabbed one, swung, smashed it down on Ike's head. Ike went down. He stood there, waiting for Ike to get up, with that terrible vitality he had shown this morning. Ike didn't move. In the car the girl was sobbing.

The police, the ambulance, the dust, the lights, the doctor working on his arm, all swam before his eyes in a blur. Somewhere far off, an excited voice was yelling: "But I *got* to use your telephone, I *got* to, I tell you! Guy saves a man's life this morning, kills him tonight! It's a *hell* of a story!" He tried to comprehend the point of this; couldn't.

The foreman appeared, summoned the third shift to him in loud tones, began to read names. He heard his own name called, but didn't answer. He was being pushed into the ambulance, handcuffed to one of the policemen.

Coal Black

FROM UP THE ENTRY CAME A WHIR, the blackness was shot with blue sparks, a cluster of lights appeared and approached. Lonnie opened the trap and the motor passed through. He closed the trap, sat down, and wished he was a motorman. Then he debated whether to eat one of his remaining sandwiches, but decided to wait awhile. Then he whistled "In the Shade of the Old Apple Tree." It was one of the three tunes he knew, so he whistled it again. Then he just sat there, and found this pleasant. Of course, *you* might not have found it pleasant to be alone in a tunnel so dark its coal walls sparkled by comparison, with only a carbide lamp to see by and nothing whatever to keep you company. But *he* minded neither the dark nor the solitude: he was so used to both that he hardly noticed them.

As for the tunnel, it had its points. It was always the same even temperature, winter or summer; the air was fresh, the intricate system of blowers and traps taking care of that. He had helped dig it, shore it, and wire it, so that it seemed a part of him—as the whole mine did for that matter. For this was the only world he had known in all his nineteen years; and he was just as at home in it as you are in your world, and found it just as familiar, just as real, just as satisfying to the soul.

After a while he heard something on the other side of the trap. Instinctively he looked at the rails. If a rat scuttled by, that meant run for his life; for a rat knows, before anybody else knows, when something is about to crack, and it is time to move, and move fast. But no rat appeared, and in a moment he got up, opened the door in the center of the trap, and peered through. At first he saw nothing. He unhooked the lamp from his hat and shot the light around. Huddled against a toolbox, her face smeared with coal dust, her dress torn so that in places her skin showed through, was a girl he judged about sixteen. She stared at him, then began to whimper:

"I'll go away, honest I will, if you just show me the way out. I don't mean nothing. I just come in to peep."

"Who let you in here?"

"Nobody. I hid in a car."

"Where? You mean you hid in it outside?"

"I don't know. Yes, of course it was outside. I hid in it, and then the train ran a whole lot further than I thought it was going to. And then I slid out. And then my matches give out, and it was dark and I got lost. And then I kept falling down, and—oh my, look at my dress! Please show me how to get out. I want to go home."

"Where you live?"

"In the north end of town."

"I never seen you before."

"We just moved in. My father, he enlarges pictures. We move from one town to the other. I wanted to see a mine. Please show me how to get out."

"Set down."

She sat down dejectedly beside the trap, and he pondered. You see, it's bad luck for a woman to enter a mine, and whenever this happens, the mine has to be "blown out," as it is blown out when somebody gets killed; that is, all hands have to quit work for the day, lest some dreadful catastrophe ensue. The trouble was that this was the first day's work the mine had had in two weeks, and the last it would have for an indefinite period; indeed, all they were doing now was loading empties for the tipple, so the men could have a little work and stray orders could be filled. If he reported this, and they blew the mine out, it might go hard with this girl; for desperate housewives, counting on a full day's pay to replenish empty shelves, might not be amused if they found they had been cheated by a ninny who merely wanted to peep.

On the next creek a woman who had dashed into a drift to say something to her husband had been so badly beaten she had to be taken to a hospital.

"You know what it means? A woman in a mine?"

"Yes; but I didn't mean nobody to see me."

"Ain't no way you can get out. I can't leave this here trap, and that place you come in, it's at least two mile away, and you can't find it, and anyway you got no light. Ain't no way you can get out, except we wait till quitting time, and then I take you out by the old drift mouth."

"All right."

"You got to stay hid. You heard what I said? They find you in here, something's going to happen to you. And they find out I let you stay, something's going to happen to *me*, too. After they turn me loose, I can't work in this mine no more, and maybe I can't work in *no* mine."

"Somebody's coming."

"In the toolbox—quick!"

She climbed in the toolbox, and he closed the cover, wedging a stone under it so she could have a little air. He sat down and with elaborate nonchalance resumed his rendition of "In the Shade of the Old Apple Tree." Han Biloxi was approaching. Of course, all that was visible was a bobbing point of light; but to Lonnie a bobbing point of light had special and personal motions, so that he knew it was Han Biloxi without knowing how he knew it or even wondering how he knew it. When Han was within hailing distance he stopped whistling and yelled, "Yah, Han!" There was no answer. Han came on, and when his face could be seen, it was grave. "All right, kid. We're blowing out. Jake's train is on the main tunnel, third entry down. He'll hold for ten minutes."

"Blowing out? What for?"

"Eckhart got it."

"*What?*"

"Rolled ag'in' the rib."

". . . When?"

"Just now. I seen it myself. Car jumped the switch and got him. He didn't have a chance."

"Gee, I rode in with him."

"You got ten minutes."

Han stepped through the trap, went on to notify miners farther up the entry.

Lonnie lifted the toolbox cover. "You heard him?"

"Yes."

"All right. Now you see what you done!"

"Please don't say that."

"He's dead, ain't he?"

"You don't have to put it on me."

"I'm putting it where it belongs."

She stood up, climbed out of the box, and faced him. "It's not true. Just because I'm in here, it don't mean that's why he got killed. I won't believe it!"

"Whose fault is it?"

"All right: What are you going to do now?"

"I got to go out on Jake's train."

"And leave me in here all alone?"

"I got to go on Jake's train. If I don't show up, they start looking for me. If they don't find me, they think something happened to me."

"And no light. And pitch dark."

"Nobody asked you in here."

"My, but you're hateful."

She turned her back to him, and the nape of her neck looked disturbingly childish. He felt a twinge of guilt. She walked around, shaking her head angrily, and then dashed for the toolbox. She didn't have time to climb into it. She crouched behind it as six or eight miners, following Han Biloxi, stepped through the trap in gloomy silence.

Lonnie called to Han: "Tell Jake not to wait for me. I'm going out by the old drift mouth."

"What's the matter—you crazy?"

"There's a roll of wire up there I want. I'm making myself some rabbit traps. Maybe catch something while we're laid off."

"Come on, boy—stop acting like you got no sense. Whoever hear'n tell of that, going through all them old dead entries just to get a roll of wire? Can't you go up there tomorrow, from the outside?"

"I want the wire tonight."

"Cut the jawing and let's go."

"That's right; if the kid's crazy, let him do what he wants—and come on, let's get out of here."

They went on, their footsteps growing fainter, the splotches of light contracting until they were a small cluster of luminous blurs, when abruptly they disappeared.

She stood up. "My, but it's lonely in here!"

"Come on."

He picked up his lunch bucket and they started down the entry. He led the way on the footpath beside the track, she stumbling along behind. When they had gone a short distance he glanced back, and was just in time to see her reel and wave crazily with her arms to keep her balance. Like a cat striking at prey, he batted her arm down, and she fell, snarling. "What you hit me for? I'm doing as good as I can. That lamp, it don't give me no light. You can see, but I can't."

"Watch that wire."

"What wire?"

"The feed wire—can't you see it? Up there on the side, at the top of the rib. That's why I knocked your arm down. You touch that thing, it'll kill you so quick you won't even know what hit you."

"Oh."

"We better walk on the track, if that's how careless you are. If you can't see behind, walk up beside me. And anyway, why didn't you say so?"

Side by side they walked between the rails, stepping from one slippery metal tie to the next. He put his arm around her to steady her, and unexpectedly found himself touching her bare flesh. Hastily he shifted his grip, taking her arm. He began trying not to think how soft her skin was, and how warm.

Soon he turned into another entry, and abruptly the top dipped. The height of a mine tunnel depends on the thickness of the coal from which it is dug. The seven-foot seam they had been in now thinned to less than five feet, so that it was impossible for them to stand. He went along at a sidewise shamble, his back bent to clear the top; for low entries were an everyday affair to him and he slipped through them without effort. But she kept bumping her head, and presently broke into hysterics. "I can't stand it no more! I got to stand up! It's pressing down on me! And my back hurts!"

"Ain't much more of the low top. Set down a few minutes, then you won't feel that way."

They sat down, she panting and convulsively straightening her aching back. He didn't look at her. But he was thoroughly aware of her now—of every detail of her slim shape, of those places where her dress was torn, of the heady, sweetly sensuous scent that hung about her. Presently they went on. The top lifted, and he turned again. She gasped at what she saw.

A dead entry is indeed a terrifying spectacle, and could serve as a chamber in some horrible inferno. Untended by man, the top erodes from the air and forms great blisters, like the blisters on paint, except that each blister is five or six feet across and five or six inches thick. The blisters then crack and fall, piece by piece, to the floor, which is thus covered with jagged shards of stone that look like gigantic shark teeth. Add that one touch can bring a blister crashing down; that the fragments underfoot can cut through the thickest shoe; that wiring, timber, rails, and all other signs of human activity have long since been removed; and that in fact nothing human ever comes here—and you can form some idea of what the abandoned parts of a coal mine are like. They proceeded slowly, hugging the wall, he ahead, she at his heels, holding tight to his denim jacket. Then they turned into another, worse than this, and then into still another. They had gone only a short distance in this when there was a report like a cannon shot and the lamp went out. She screamed.

"It's all right. Some top fell down, that's all. Stick close to the rib, like I do. It generally falls in the middle."

"Is the lamp busted? Why did it go out?"

"Air. Concussion blew it out."

"Please light it. The dark scares me so."

"Sure."

He had, in fact, already unhooked the lamp from his hat and was banging the flint with the palm of his hand. Sparks appeared, but no light. She moaned: "I knew it was busted."

"It ain't busted. Carbide needs water, that's all."

He opened his lunch bucket, to pour in water. Then he remembered he had drunk all his water. He waited, hoping a few drops might still be left. Nothing happened.

He closed the bucket, set it down, puckered his lips, preparatory to priming the lamp with spit. Then his mouth went dry with fright and he couldn't spit. For what he had touched, when he set down the bucket, was a hand, cold and unmoving. She felt his breath stop. "What's the matter?"

"We took the wrong turn."

"Are we lost?"

"No, we ain't lost. But we're in the haunted entry."

"The—"

He placed her hand over the cold thing he had touched. She screamed, and screamed again. "That's the stone—the stone they put up for him because they couldn't get him out. With the hand chiseled on it, holding a palm. And he's in there, and he keeps tamping his powder."

"I don't hear nothing," she whispered.

"You will. . . . He tamped in his powder, and lit his fuse, and started out here to wait for the shot. Then the whole room caved in. And he keeps going back there to see why it don't go off, and then he tamps in his powder again, and—"

"I still don't hear—"

But her words froze in her throat, for off in the rock somewhere began a faint *clink, clink, clink*. Then it stopped. "That's it—that's the needle. Now comes the tamping iron." The sound resumed, reached a brisk crescendo, and stopped again. "Now he's coming out! Now he's coming this way! *And we can't move; we got no light!*"

They were crouched on the floor now, locked in each other's arms, in an ecstasy of terror. Several times the sound was repeated, and they strained closer as they listened and waited. But fear is a peculiar emotion: it cannot be sustained indefinitely at the same high pitch. In spite of his horror of the ghost, he gradually became aware that there was something distinctly pleasurable about this: lying in the dark with this girl in his arms, shuddering in unison with her, mingling his breath with hers; indeed, with an almost exquisite agony he began to look forward to each repetition of the sound. He thought of her flesh again, and in a moment his hand was touching her side, patting the torn place in her dress, as though this were what the circumstances called for. She didn't seem to mind. On the contrary, his thick paw apparently soothed her; so that she relaxed slightly, and put her head on his shoulder, and sighed. He patted and patted again, and each time the sound would resume they would draw together.

Suddenly, though, she sat up, listened, and turned to him. "That ain't no miner."

"Oh, yes, it is. He—"

"That ain't no miner. That's water. I can tell by how it sounds."

"Gee, if we could only get some! But I can't even start the lamp. I'm scared so bad I can't spit."

"Give me that lamp. I can spit."

She took the lamp, and he heard it hiss from plenty of good wet spit. He struck the flint, and flame punctured the darkness. "We got to hurry. That won't last long."

"Keep still, so I can hear."

He held the light, and she crawled on her hands and knees, cocking her head now and then to listen. The flame grew smaller and smaller. Suddenly she thrust her hand under a slab of rock. "There it is."

"You sure?"

"Give me the bucket."

She took the bucket and thrust it under, and at once came the loud *clank* of water on tin. They looked at each other, and he spoke breathlessly: "That's it! That's how it sounded, only now it's in the bucket." The lamp went out, and they waited in the dark while there came a few drops, then a pause, then a few more drops, then the rapid staccato of a full trickle, then a long pause, then the separate drops again. After a long time she shook the bucket, and they heard the water slosh. "That's enough. That'll get us out."

They poured water in the lamp, struck the flint, and a fine big flame spurted out. They were off at once. They went through more dead entries, then came to where the going was better. He laughed—a high nervous giggle. "Ain't that a joke? Won't them miners feel silly when I tell them that haunt ain't nothing but water?"

"It come to me, just like that, that them was drops."

"And think of that—that was why they stopped working that coal. That's why the company had to close down them entries. Not no miner would work in there."

"Gee, that's funny."

When, still laughing at this, they popped suddenly on to the old drift mouth, it was nearly dark outside, and snowing. They said stiff good-byes; she thanked him for helping her out, and promised to protect him in his guilty secret. She started down the mountain toward the part of the camp where she lived. He watched her a moment, and then something rose in his throat, an overwhelming recollection—of a naked patch of flesh, lovely smell, and brave, hissing spit.

He called in a queer strained voice: "Yay!"

"What?"

"Come back here a minute."

She ran back and stood in front of him. He wanted to say something; didn't know what it was; then heard himself talking, in the same queer voice, about his hope there was no hard feelings about what he had said, back there in the mine, before they started out. She didn't answer. She kept looking at him. And then, to his astonishment, she came up and put her arms around him. Then he said it. He pulled her to him, pushed his lips against hers for the first time, and the words came jerkily: "Listen. . . . The hell with going home. . . . Let's not go home. . . . Let's get married. . . . Let's . . . be together."

She stayed near him, touched his face with her fingers, then looked away. "We can't get married."

"Why not?"

"We got no money. You got no money. I got no money, nobody in a coal camp has got any money. . . Gee, I'd love to be with you."

"My old man would take us in."

"And your old lady would throw us out."

"All right, never mind the married part. Let's not go home tonight. Let's stay up here, in one of these shacks."

"They'll be looking for us."

"Let them look."

"We'd be awful cold and hungry."

"We can build a fire, and I got two sandwiches left."

". . . All right."

They tried to say something else, but found themselves unexpectedly embarrassed. But then he began shaking her, his eyes shining. "Who says we can't get married? Who says we got no money? Why, I'll have a job! I'll have a real job! I'll have a company job!"

"How will you get a company job?"

"The haunt! Don't you get it? *I'll* prove to them miners that haunt is nothing but water! Then they can get that coal! Boy, will they give me a company job for doing that! Will they!"

"Gee. I bet they will."

"Listen. Do you really mean it? About camping out tonight?"

"I don't want we should be separated, ever."

"Kiss me again. Maybe we can catch a rabbit. Can you cook a rabbit?"

"Yes."

Inside, an astral miner picked up an astral bucket and sadly prepared to join the great army of unemployed.

The Girl in the Storm

He woke up suddenly, feeling that ice had touched him, but it was an interval before his mind caught up with what he saw. Through the open door of the boxcar it was pouring rain: that much was as he remembered it from the night before. But on the floor was a spreading puddle. It was the puddle, indeed, which had touched his ribs and awakened him; he was edging away from it, even while he was blinking his eyes. When he scrambled to his feet and looked out, the breath left his body in a wailing moan. For as far as he could see no land was visible, nothing but brown, swirling water full of trees, bushes, and what might have been houses, moving in the direction of the bridge, off to his right. It was already lapping at the door of the boxcar; it was what was causing the rapidly deepening puddle.

He stood staring out at it, and became fascinated by a pile of ties across from the car. One by one the flood lifted them, as though some invisible elephant were riding it, and

The Girl in the Storm

carried them spinning into the current, to bang against the boxcar at his feet, then go swiftly on to the bridge. He watched several go by, then turned his back to them and caught the roof of the car with his hands. He chinned himself, in an effort to climb to the roof, but there was no support for his feet, and he dropped back.

When the next tie came by, he stooped down and caught it. Hugging it to his stomach, he dragged it into the car. Then he jammed it across the door slantwise, one end at the bottom, the other halfway up. He caught the roof of the car again and, clambering up the slanting tie, pushed up high enough to get his chin over the edge. Then he managed to reach the catwalk on the roof of the car, and pulled himself toward it. Wriggling on his belly, he was safely on the walk in a few moments, and stood up.

All around him was the flood, and behind him he could hear it thunder under the bridge. About a quarter of a mile ahead of him was a loading platform, and beyond that the station. No locomotive was in sight; he had been shunted with a string of empties onto a siding and left there. Beyond the station, on higher ground, was what appeared to be a village, and he could see trucks backed up there, evidently evacuating whole families. He wondered if he could get a place on a truck. But it took him ten minutes, clambering down from boxcars to flatcars, and then over boxcars again, to reach the loading platform, and when he ran around it to yell at them, they were gone.

He stood looking at the station, read the name of the place: Hildalgo, California. For the moment he was sheltered from the rain; but his respite was short. The loading platform was only a few inches higher than the floor of the cars, and even while he was standing there another puddle appeared and he was retreating from it. He found himself facing the county road. It was higher than the platform, and although water was running over it in a sheet, and back toward the bridge it dipped into the flood, between this point and the village it was not inundated. To reach it he would have to go through water at least waist-deep, and he eyed it dismally. Then he squatted down, held his breath, and plunged in.

When he scrambled up on the concrete he was so wet he could feel the weight of his denim pants hanging off his hips. He started up the road at a half trot, the storm driving him from behind. He didn't know where he was going, except that he had to find shelter. And who would shelter him he had no idea, for he knew from bitter experience that nineteen-year-old hoboes are seldom welcome guests, whether rain-soaked or not.

He passed a stalled car, with nobody in it. He passed several houses, in front of which he had seen the trucks. They were obviously empty, but they were below road level and surrounded by yellow ponds pocked with rain. He came to a sidewalk, but between him and the curbs was a torrent, and he stayed in the center of the road. He came to a filling station, but it was deserted and six inches deep in water. Next to the filling station was a store, a chain grocery store. He headed for it, going in up to his knees in the torrent. The force of it almost upset him and forced him several paces below his goal. When he gained the sidewalk he ran at the door, wrenching at the knob and driving against it with one motion.

It was locked. As his face smashed against the glass, he remembered it was Sunday.

He stood there, furiously rattling the door. Facing him, inside, he could see the clock: ten minutes to three. But nothing answered his rattling except the rain. He kicked the door, dashed away, and in a second was under cover. Next to the store was a half-finished house, and his dive for the porch was automatic. He turned in anger at the rain, stood stamping the water off his legs, then went inside. The floor was laid, but the walls were only half finished and there was a damp smell of plaster. Off to one side were piled lumber, tar paper, and sawbucks. But the doors and windows were not in place yet, and the air felt even colder than the air outside.

He stood shivering in his soaking denims; started to take off the coat. As the air met his wet chest, he pulled it around him again. At the touch of the clammy cloth he gritted his teeth and took it off. He took off his shoes and his pants. He wore no socks or undershirt. He was left in a pair of tattered shorts, and while he was draping the denims over a sawbuck he collapsed on the tar paper, shaking with chill. But soon he was quiet, and he could think of but one thing: that he had to get warm. He thought of fire, and looked around.

On one side of the room was a fireplace, the mortar in it still damp. The tar paper would do to start it, all right, and there were bricks outside he could use to build it on. The lumber would burn, if there were any pieces short enough to go in the fireplace. He spied a kit of carpenter's tools in one corner, went over to examine it, wincing as the crumbs of plaster hurt his feet.

The main tool in the kit was a saw. Quickly he set up two sawbucks, laid a joist between them and cut it up with the saw. The exercise made him feel better. When he had a pile of wood, he got two bricks and began to build the fire. He tore up tar paper and laid it on the bricks, found the carpenter's trimming knife and whittled kindling, laid the big pieces he had sawed on top. But when he went to his coat and fished the matches out of the pocket, the tips were nothing but smelly wet smears.

He cursed, screamed, and pounded his fist against the wall. He went all through the house, searching every place he could think of, trying to find a match. He began to shake from chill again, and ran to the front door to shake his fist at the rain.

Down the road, creeping slowly, came a car, its lights on. It was a small sedan, and it went cautiously past him. Bitterly he wondered where the driver thought he was going, for the lake of floodwaters down by the station would make further progress impossible. About this time the driver seemed to see the flood too, for a little beyond the grocery store the car came to a stop. Then, as though it were part of a slow movie, it began to slide. It slid into the torrent, lurched against the curb, stopped. Almost at once the taillight went out. That, he decided, was because the water had shorted the ignition. This car, like the other one, was there to stay awhile.

He watched, wondered if the guy would have a match. Then the door opened, the left-hand door, next to the road, and a foot appeared, then a leg. It wasn't a man's leg; it was a woman's. A girl got out, and staggered as the storm hit her. She was a smallish girl, in a raincoat. She slammed the door shut and started toward him, around the back of the car, heading for the curb. He opened his mouth to yell at her, but he was too late. The water staggered her and she went down. She tried to get up; the current tumbled her under the wheels of the car.

He leaped from the porch, went scampering to her in his shorts. Taking her by the hand, he jerked her to her feet, put his arms around her, ran her to the house. As he pulled her into the cold interior, her teeth chattered. He grabbed her dripping handbag, clawed it open. "You got a match? We'll freeze if we don't get a match!"

"There's some in the car."

He dashed out again, ran down to the car, jerked the door open, jumped inside. In the dashboard compartment he found a package of paper matches, wiped his hand dry on the seat before he touched them. He looked around for something to wrap them in, to keep the rain off them. On the back seat he saw robes. He grabbed them, wrapped them around the matches.

When he got back to the house he waited only to open the robes and dry his hands again, pawing with them on the wool. Then he struck a match, and it lit. He touched the tar paper with it. A blue flame appeared, hesitated, spread out, and licked the wood. The fire crackled. It turned yellow and light filled the room. He felt warmth. He crowded so close he was almost in the fireplace.

"Come on, kid, you better get warm."

"I'm already here."

She picked up one of the robes, held it in front of the fire to warm it, put it around him. Then she warmed the other one, pulled it around herself, squatted down beside him. He sat down on the robe, tucked it around his feet. The fire burned up, scorched his face. He didn't move. The heat reached him through the robe. His shivering stopped, he relaxed with a long, quavering sigh. She looked at him.

"My, you must have been cold."

"You don't know the half of it."

"I almost died, myself. If you hadn't come, I don't know what I would have done. I went clear down in that water."

"I yelled at you, but you was already in it."

"I don't know what's going to happen to the car."

"It'll be all right soon as it dries out."

"You think so?"

"Just got water in it, that's all."

"I hope that's all."

"Some rain!"

"It's awful, and it's going to get worse. I had the radio on in the car. They're warning people. Over in Hildalgo they took everybody out. Half the town's washed away."

"Yeah, I seen them."

"You were in Hildalgo?"

"Yeah. . . . What you talking about? This *is* Hildalgo."

"This is Hildalgo?"

"That's what it says on the sign at the station."

"Oh, my! I thought Hildalgo was on the other road."

"Well? So it's Hildalgo."

"But there's nobody here. They took them all away."

"O.K. Then it's us.

"Suppose this washes away?"

"Till it does, we got a fire."

She got up, holding the robe tightly around her, and pulled a sawbuck over to the fire. On it, he noticed for the first time, were her sweater, stockings, and skirt. She must have taken them off while he was down in the car. She looked around.

"Are those your things over there? Don't you want me to move them closer to the fire, so they'll dry?"

"I'll do it."

The sight of her absurdly small things had made him suddenly aware of her as a person, and he was afraid to let her move his denims to the fire for fear that in the heat they would stink. He got up, pulled the pile of tar paper to the fire for her to sit on. Then he took the denims off the sawbuck and went back with them to the kitchen. The fixtures were in, though caked with grit, and on his previous tour of the place he had seen a bucket and some soap. He dumped the denims on the floor, filled the bucket with water, carried it to where she was. By poking with a piece of flooring he made a place for it on the fire, and while it was heating, studied her.

She wasn't a pretty girl exactly. She was small, with sandy hair, and freckles on her nose. But she had a friendly smile, and she wasn't bawling at her plight. Indeed, she seemed to take it more philosophically than he did. He took her to be about his own age.

"What's your name?"

"Flora. Flora Hilton. . . . It's really Dora, but they all began calling me Dumb Dora, so I changed it."

"Yes, I guess that was bad."

"What's yours?"

"Jack. Jack Schwab."

"You come from California?"

"Pennsylvania. I—kind of travel around."

"Hitchhike?"

"Sometimes. Other times I ride the freights."

"I didn't think you talked like California."

"What you doing out in this storm?"

"I went over to my uncle's. I went over there last night, to stay till Monday. But when it started to rain I thought I better get back. It wasn't so bad over where he lives, and I didn't know it was going to be like this. They've got no radio or anything. But then, when I turned the car radio on, I found out. I still thought I could make it, though. I thought I was on the main road. I didn't know I was coming through Hildalgo."

"Well, they'll be coming for you. The cops, or somebody. We'll see them when they find the car."

"I don't know if they'll be coming for me."

"Oh, they will."

"My father, he don't even know I started out, and my uncle, he probably thinks I'm home by now."

"Then we got it to ourselves."

"Sure looks like it."

The water was steaming by now. He wrapped the hot bucket handle in tar paper, lifted it off the fire, and went back to the kitchen with it. First washing out the sink, then using a piece of tar paper as a stopper, he soaped the denims and washed them. The water turned so black he felt a sense of shame. He put them through two or three waters, wrung them dry. The last of the hot water he saved for the shorts he had on. With a quick glance toward the front of the house, he stepped out of them, washed them, wrung them out. Then he spread them, to step back into them. They were no wetter than when he took them off, but he hated the idea of having them touch him. However, they were hot from the water, and felt unexpectedly pleasant when he buttoned them up.

Back at the fire, he draped the denims on the sawbuck, beside her things, to dry.

"Well, Flora, nice climate you got."

"Sunny California! It can rain harder here than any place on earth. Well, you know what they say. We only have two kinds of weather in California, magnificent and unusual."

"I'll say it's unusual."

"Just listen to that rain come down."

"What do you do with yourself, Flora?"

"Me? Oh, I work. I got a job in a drive-in."

"Slinging hot dogs, hey?"

"I wish you'd talk about something else."

"A hot dog sure would go good now, wouldn't it?"

"I was the one that played dumb this morning. They wanted me to wait for breakfast, but I was in such a hurry to get away I wouldn't listen to them. I haven't had anything to eat all day."

"Breakfast? Say, that's a laugh."

"Haven't you had anything to eat either?"

"I haven't et a breakfast in so long I've forgot what it tastes like. By the time they get around to me it's always dinnertime, and even then, when they get to me, sometimes they close the window in my face."

"I guess it's hard, hitchhiking and—"

"Flora! Are we the couple of dopes!"

"What's the matter, Jack?"

"Talking about hot dogs and breakfast. That store! There's enough grub in there to feed an army!"

"You mean—just take it?"

"You think it's going to walk over here and ask us to eat it? Come on! Here's where we eat!"

When he seized the largest of the carpenter's chisels and the hammer, she still sat there, watching him, and didn't follow when he went outside. He splashed around to the rear of the store, drove the chisel into the crack of the door, pulled. Something snapped, and he pushed the door open. He waited a moment, the rain pouring on him from the roof, for the sound of the burglar alarm, but he heard nothing. He

The Girl in the Storm

groped for the light switch, found it, snapped it, but nothing happened. If all wires were down in the storm, that might explain the silent burglar alarm. He began to grope his way toward the shelves. Suddenly he felt her beside him, there in the murk.

"If you've got the nerve, I have."

She was looking square into his eyes, and he felt a throb of excitement.

"The worst they can do is put us in jail. Well—I been there before, haven't I? Plenty of times—but I'm still here."

He turned to the shelves again, didn't see her look at him queerly, hesitate, and start to leave before deciding to follow him. His hand touched something and he gave an exclamation.

"What is it, Jack?"

"Matches! Now we're coming."

Lighting matches, poking and peering, they located the canned goods section.

"Here's soup. My, Jack, that'll be good!"

"O.K. on soup."

"What kind do you like?

"Any kind. So it's got meat in it."

"Mulligatawny?"

"Take two. Small size, so they'll heat quick."

"Peas?"

"O.K."

She set the cans on the counter, but he continued searching, and presently yelled:

"Got it, Flora, got it! I knew it had to be there!"

"What is it, Jack?"

"Chicken! Canned chicken! Just look at it!"

He found currant jelly, found instant coffee, condensed milk, a package of lump sugar, found cigarettes.

"O.K., Flora. Anything else you want?"

"I can't think of anything else, Jack."

"Let's go."

When they got back to the house again, it was dark. He put more wood on the fire, went back to the kitchen, filled the bucket again. When he returned, to put it on the fire, he noticed she had put on her stockings, sweater, and skirt. He felt his own denims. They were dry. He put them on. But when he went to put on his shoes his feet recoiled from their cold dampness. He let them lie, sat down, and pulled the robe over his feet. She started to laugh.

"Wonder what we're going to eat off of?"

"We'll soon fix that."

He found the saw, found a piece of smooth board, sawed off two squares. "How's that?"

"Fine. Just like plates."

"Here's a couple of chisels for forks."

"We sure do help ourselves."

"If you don't help yourself, nobody'll do it for you."

When the water began to steam, they dropped the cans in—the big can of chicken shaped like a flatiron first, the others on top of it. They sat side by side and watched. After a while they fished out the soup, and he took a chisel and hammer and neatly excised the tops. "Take it easy, Flora. Watch you don't cut your lip."

They put the cans to their mouths, drank. "Oh, is that good! Is that good!" Her voice throbbed as she spoke.

Panting, they gulped the soup, tilting the cans to let the meat and vegetables slip down their throats.

They fished out the other cans then, and he opened them, the chicken last. She took it by a leg and quickly lifted it to one of their plates.

"Don't spill the juice. We'll drink that out of the can."

"I haven't spilled a drop, Flora. Wait a minute. There's a knife here, I'll cut it in half."

He jumped up, looked for the carpenter's trimming knife he had used to whittle the kindling. He couldn't find it.

"Damn it, there was a knife here. What did I do with it?"

She said nothing.

The Girl in the Storm

He cut the chicken in half with the hammer and chisel. They ate like a pair of animals, sometimes stopping to gasp for breath. Presently nothing was left but wet spots on the board plates. He got fresh water and set it on the fire. It heated quickly. He went to the kitchen, washed out the soup cans, came back, made the coffee in them. He opened the milk and sugar, gave each can a judicious dose.

"There you are, Flora. You can stir it with a chisel."

"That's just what I was wishing for all the time—that I could have a good cup of coffee, and then it would be perfect."

"Is it O.K.?"

"Grand."

He offered her a cigarette, but she said she didn't smoke. He lit up, inhaled, lay back on the couch of tar paper. He was warm, full, and content. He watched her when she got up and cleared away the cans and bucket. She found a rag in the tool kit, dipped it in the last of the hot water.

"Don't you want me to wipe the grease off your hands?"

He held out his hands, and she wiped them. She wiped her own hands, put the rag with the other stuff, sat down beside him. He held out his hand, open. She hesitated, looked at him a moment as she had looked at him in the store, put her hand in his.

"We ain't got it so bad, Flora."

"I'll say we haven't. Not to what we might have. We could have been drowned."

He put his arm around her, drew her to him. She let her head fall on his shoulder. He could smell her hair, and his throat contracted, as though he were going to cry. For the first time in his short battered life he was happy. His grip on her tightened, he pushed his cheek against hers. She buried her face in his neck. He kept nuzzling her, felt his lips nearing her mouth. Then he pulled her to him hard, felt her yield, turn her head for his kiss.

Convulsively he winced. There was a sharp pain in the

pit of his stomach. He looked down, saw something rough and putty-stained about the neck of her sweater. Instantly he knew what it was, what it was there for. He jumped up.

"So—that's where the knife was. I pull you out of the gutter, feed you, take you in my arms, and all the time you're getting ready to stick me in the back with that thing."

She started to cry. "I never saw you before. You said you'd been in jail, and I didn't know what you were fixing to do to me!"

He lit a cigarette, walked around the room. Once more he felt cold, forlorn, and bitter, the way he felt on the road. He looked out. The rain was slackening. He threw away the cigarette, sat down on the floor, drove his feet into the cold clammy shoes. Savagely he knotted the stiff laces. Then, without a word to her, he went slogging out into the night.

Joy Ride to Glory

I WAS ASSIGNED TO THE KITCHEN, dipping grub for the guards, not the cons like the radio said I was. I had been in the laundry, but my fingers and toes all swelled up and I got a ringing in the ears from the liquid soap, so they switched me to the kitchen. My name is Red Conley. If you don't quite recollect who Red Conley is, go down to the public library and look him up in the Los Angeles newspapers. You'll find out a funny thing about him. According to them write-ups, Red Conley is dead.

It had been raining all morning, and around eleven the meat truck drives up. They let it right in the yard, and Cookie yells for me and Bugs Calenso to unload it. Bugs, he's got three concurrents and two consecutives running against him, and some of it's violation of parole, so they don't bother to figure it up any more. Along about 2042, with good behavior and friends on the outside, he's eligible. Me, I'm in for rolling six tires down the hill from Mullins's Garage, which seemed to be a good idea at the time, but I was doing a one-to-five before we even got the papers off them. Still, I had served a year, and was up for parole, and it looked O.K., and if I'd let it ride I'd have been out in a month.

So me and Bugs, we split it up with me handling the meat, account I'm younger, and him handling the hooks, account he knows how. I'd pull out a quarter of beef, then brace under it, then come up. Then I'd tote it to the cold storage room, and Bugs would catch it with the hook that swiveled to the overhead trolley. Then he'd throw the switch and I'd shove the stuff in place, the forequarters on one rail, the hindquarters on another. There was four steers on the truck, two of them for someplace down the line, two of them for the prison. That meant eight quarters of meat, and I guess I took ten minutes, because beef is not feathers, and I needed a rest in between. But then it was all moved, and Bugs give a yelp for the driver, who was not outside, where he generally waited, but inside, account of the rain. So he yelped back, from inside the corridors someplace, and then we hollered some more and said what was he doing, stalling around so he could get a free meal off the taxpayers of the state of California, and why don't he take away his truck? So Cookie joins in, and quite a few joins in, and some very good gags was made, and it was against the rules but it felt good to holler.

So Bugs was grinning at me, standing there in the door, but then all of a sudden he wasn't grinning any more and he was looking at me hard. Then overhead I hear the planes. You understand how this was? The kitchen door is out back, and there's a guard on that part of the wall. But he's a spotter, see? He's a spotter for the army, and just to make sure, he spots everything, and there he is now, with his rifle over one arm and his head thrown back, to see what's coming. Three fast ones break out of a cloud, the split-tail jobs with two motors, but Bugs, he don't wait. He motions to me and we take two steps. Then he checks front and I check rear. Then he vaults

Joy Ride to Glory

in the truck and I follow him. Then we lay down, in between quarters of beef.

We were hardly flat when the driver came out, still yelling gags at the guys in the kitchen. He climbs in, starts, rolls a little way, and stops, and we hear him say something to the guards at the gate. Then he gets going again, and starts down the hill on the motor, so it begins to backfire. He goes so fast I have to lock my throat to keep the wind from being shook out of me, ha-ha-ha-ha like that. Bugs, he seems to be having the same kind of trouble, but we both hang on and choke it back, whatever the driver might hear. He's a little fat guy, and he sings the "Prisoner's Song" pretty lousy, but he slows down for the boulevard stop at the bottom of the hill. That was when Bugs grabs my neck for a handhold and stands up. He stands right over me, so I can see his face, where it's all twisted with this maniac look, and his hands, where they were hooked to come in on the driver's neck.

Then I woke up for the first time to the spot I was in. Here, with one month to go only, I had got myself in the same truck with this killer, and made myself just as guilty of whatever was done as he was. I yelled at the driver then, as loud as I could scream. He hit the brake and turned around, but he was too late. That jerk threw Bugs right on top of him, and them hooks came together so his tongue popped out of his mouth. I grabbed at Bugs and begged him to quit, but then I woke up to what was going on outside. The truck was still rolling, and if something wasn't done in about two seconds it was going over in the ditch. I reached over and grabbed the wheel, then I slid over the seat on my belly till I was on the right-hand side beside the driver, so with my left foot I could shove down the brake.

All during that time the driver was being pulled over backwards, so he arched up till his knees touched the wheel. Then something cracked, and I felt sick to my stomach. Then it wasn't the driver back of the wheel, it was Bugs. He was panting like some kind of an animal, but he threw it in gear and we started off. Pretty soon he says: "Get back there, go through his pockets, and find his cigarettes."

"Get back there yourself."

"Oh, just a passenger, hey?"

"Just a fall guy, maybe."

"O.K., fall guy, suppose you keep an eye out behind, see if they're following us. Because if they're not, maybe we still got a little time, before it's a general alarm."

"Haven't you got a mirror?"

"Oh, just a passenger after all, hey?"

"What you kill that guy for?"

"What you think I killed him for? So he cooperates, and he's doing it. Like he is now, he don't give no trouble."

"We could have tied him up, or dropped him off, or knocked him out. We could have handled him somehow, so they wouldn't have this on us."

"You done all you could."

"You bet I did."

"I hope he appreciates it."

"Shut up and drive."

"Says who?"

I hauled off and let him have it, right in the mouth. His foot came off the gas, and we slowed, and I stamped on the brake, and we stopped. I let him have it again, so the blood spurted out of his lip. Then I grabbed him, jerked him out from behind the wheel, and drove my fist in till my arm was numb and his face looked like something the butcher would pitch in the bucket. Then I kicked him into my seat, took the wheel myself, and went on. It didn't do any good. We were in the same old truck, with the rain pouring down in front, a dead man in behind, and headed nowhere. But it made me feel better.

On the dashboard was a button at the top of what looked like a grill, and I give it a twist. Plenty of drivers have shortwave, so they can pick up the police calls, and I figured I could find out what was being done about us. But 'stead of a grill it was a panel, and it opened up on a compartment full of cigarettes, chewing gum, maps, apples, and what looked to me like a flashlight. I took the cigarettes and lit up, and had me a deep inhale, and all the time he was looking at me, and I was wondering whether to give him one, just because he couldn't help being like he was, and anyway I'd done all I wanted to do to him, and maybe more than I really wanted to do. I began sliding one out of the pack, when he moved. When I looked up I knew that flashlight wasn't a flashlight at all, it was a automatic. Because I was looking straight into it.

"Rat, you listening what I say?"

"I hear every word, Bugs."

"Drive."

"I'm driving."

"Drive like I tell you to drive."

"Just say it, Bugs."

He told me, and we began a zigzag course, part on the main highways, part on the crossroads, but as near as I could tell we were zigzagging for Los Angeles, and getting there. Then we had to stop for a freight that was crossing. Ahead of us was a green sedan, and for a while Bugs sat there looking at it and bearing down on some chocolate bars he found in with the apple. Then he sits up and says: "Bump him! *Bump him!*"

"What do you mean, bump him?"

"Bump him so he has to get out!"

I came up slow, then stepped on it so I smacked right into the rear bumper of the sedan. I no sooner untangled than Bugs jumped out and ran around front, shoving the gun in his pants as he went. Sure enough, the guy gets out, and Bugs began yelling and pointing at the truck. But the guy can't make any sense out of it because he's looking at Bugs's face, where it's still running blood, and he can't connect all that grief with the little bump he felt. Bugs just keeps on talking.

All that time the freight is going by, and he can't take a chance the train crew might hop off to help some guy out. But soon as the bell stops he whips out the gun and tells the guy to peel off his clothes and hand over his dough. I hop out then, and run around the right-hand side and jump in the sedan and slide over behind the wheel. But Bugs thought of that. By the time I was set he had the guy out front, blocking me off. The guy's taking orders now, and each piece of his clothes he peels, Bugs lays it on the hood and covers it with the guy's raincoat. When the guy's stripped naked, so his teeth are chattering and he's begging Bugs not to keep him out there in the rain any more, Bugs plugs him. It was like something in a movie. First I could see them in front, on the other side of this pile of clothes on the hood, then comes the shot, and I can see Bugs and I can't see him. Then Bugs has scooped up the clothes under his arm and is jumping in the back door of the sedan, telling me to drive. I start up, and I cut the wheel hard left. But the right side of the car goes up, then bumps down, as we go over something soft.

When Bugs climbed up in the front seat, maybe a half hour later, he was all dressed up in the guy's clothes and his face was wiped off a little. He didn't really look good, but he wasn't in prison denims, like I was, and he could take out some money and count it. There was quite a little money, and he took quite a while. Then he says: "I guess you wonder why you killed *him* too?"

"You're running it, Bugs."

"Nekkid like he is, they may be quite a while identifying him, see? Without any driver's license, or Elks' pin, or tailor's label, or that stuff they generally go on, they might be some little time. Well, all that time we're moving, you get it, stupid? We're on our way, and they don't know what car we got, or the number of it, or anything at all, except we're not no longer hauling meat. Pretty, isn't it?"

"Oh, it's clever. I can see that."

"I killed him so he can't talk to the cops and tell them what they might want to know. Of course, we all know *you* killed him."

"Yeah, that's right."

"What do you mean, 'that's right'?"

"I mean if you say I killed him."

"Quit cracking smart."

"O.K."

"And quit chattering them teeth."

Changing cars I had got wet, and he hadn't give me any chocolate bars, and I was cold and hungry and weak, and my teeth were chattering all right. I bit down on them, and they stopped. It was four or five in the afternoon by then, and we were in Los Angeles already, and I began wondering why he didn't kill me. He had everything he wanted, a car, a suit, a raincoat, and dough. He didn't need me any more. Then I got this awful sensation in the pit of my stomach, when I saw he *was* going to kill me, and it was just a question of when. He sat there staring at me, the gun in his lap, and I figured it would be at the next stop. So when we come to it I went right through. He snarled like a mad dog. "What's the big idea, going through that light?"

"I didn't see it."

"I told you quit cracking smart."

"I swear I didn't see it."

"You want some cops stopping us?"

"If you don't see it, why would you stop?"

"You stop at the next one, though."

"Oh, sure."

The next one, I went through at seventy, and he began to scream. He'd have plugged me right there, but at that speed he was afraid. But I had the mirror and he didn't, and back of us I see a light, just a single. Then behind that there's another one, and then still another. I hold on seventy, but they begin closing in. The next light, I come off the gas, like I'm going to do like I'm told, and stop. I feel him tighten, and aim the gun. When we dropped to forty I hit the brake and cut the wheel. We spun around like something crazy. Inside, it's like we've exploded, because he's thrown on the floor but he shoots just the same. Whether I'm hit I don't know, but I throw open the door and jump. Inside there's more shots, and outside the motorcycles deploy, all three guns barking. I start to run, then I go down. But I don't lay there. Because it was the torrent in the gutter that threw me, and it rushed me along like I was a hunk of rubble. I try to get up and can't. Then all of a sudden it's pitch dark and I'm falling. Then I crash down, so I think my back is broken. Then the water is rushing me along again, and I tumble where I am.

I'm in a storm drain.

They have them all over the city, some little, made out of terra-cotta pipe, some big, made out of concrete sections. They run under streets, and every so often there's a manhole, so they can clean them out, and off under the sidewalks are intakes, to tap the flow in the gutter. In the intakes, they got handholds and bars, just in case somebody did fall in, and if I'd been quick I might have saved myself, but I was too crossed up. How big the pipe was that I was in I don't know, but at a guess I would say three feet, maybe. In that was running about a foot of water, and I was bumping along with it, feet first. I kept trying to stop, but I couldn't. Over my face all the time the water kept pouring, and I kept gasping for air, and every time I'd gasp I'd swallow a gallon and then start over again.

How long that went on I don't know. It seemed like an hour, but figuring it up now, I'd say about a minute. Then I see some gray light, and almost before I knew it, I was shooting past another intake pipe. I caught it, and four or five feet away, I could see bars. I reached and tried to grab one, but the water was pulling me back. I slipped off and went helloing down the black pipe again, still trying to breathe, still strangling from the water that was pouring over me. But my mind began to work, anyway a little bit. I knew there'd be another intake further on, and I set myself to watch for it and grab for a handhold. But I was watching on the right-hand side, where the other one had come in, and I shot right by one on the left. Then a couple more went by and I began to scream. It came to me, somehow, what a no-account life I'd led, and here I was, winding it up like a rat in a sewer, and even with the water in my mouth I began to scream like a maniac.

I saw light again, and got ready, but it wasn't an intake this time. It was a grating over a big square drain that my pipe spilled me into, and then I really began to move, and for just that long I could breathe better and my back didn't bump any more, because it was deeper. I put my head up, and there must have been two feet of clearance above me. But then I noticed there wasn't that much, and pretty soon I knew why. Every so often pipes came roaring in, and each one filled the big drain fuller, and pretty soon it would be running full with no air, like a water pipe. I wasn't screaming any more. I had just give up. I was going along, but I didn't care any more.

Pretty soon something clipped my nose, and I put up my hands. I almost died then, because the top was only six inches from my face. There was a roar, and I figured another pipe was coming in. I knew I was up tight, and drew the biggest breath I could. When the top bumped my face I pushed down under to keep it away. Then I rolled over. I could feel the top bumping my back, and I kept telling myself I mustn't breathe. I had that many seconds to live till I breathed, and I clamped down on my throat like I had in the truck, when we were bumping down the hill. Then something bumped my belly, and I breathed. But what I breathed was air. I opened my eyes and it was almost dark, and street lights were on, and I was washed up on a slab of concrete in the middle of water that was boiling all around me. About twenty feet away I could see the square mouth of a drain, and I figured it was what I come out of. It was at least five minutes, I guess, before I doped it out I was in the middle of the Los Angeles River.

I won't tell you much about how I got out of there, about the guy that seen me, and stopped his car, and found a length of rubber hose, and threw me one end of it, and then ran me home, and wrapped me in blankets, and opened up a can of hot soup, and then give me hot coffee and hot milk mixed, and then put me to bed. If I told you too much, maybe you could figure out who he is, and he'd be in more trouble than I'm worth. And anyway, what I want to tell about, what I been leading up to all this time, was next morning, when he come in the little room he had put me in, and sat down beside the bed, and it was just him and me. He kind of mentioned that his wife and little boy were visiting her folks over the weekend, and I got the idea that was what he was trying to tell me, that it was just him and me, that nobody else knew anything. After a while he says: "What's your name?"

". . . Bud O'Brien's my name."

"Funny. I thought it was Conley."

"What made you think that?"

"There was a convict named Conley that made his escape yesterday. From the stencil marks on those denims you were wearing, I figured you came from a prison yourself."

"In that case, you might be right."

"Want to read about it, Conley?"

"Yeah, I'd kind of like to."

He went out and came back with the papers, and it was all plastered over the front pages how me and Bugs had slipped out in the meat truck, killed the driver, then killed another guy and taken his car, then been shot by the cops, with Bugs wounding a cop before they got him, and my body washing down the storm drain. Identification was certain, though, it said, because a cop recognized me before I went down. So I read all that stuff, and then I started to talk, and I told the guy what I've just told you, and 'specially I tried to make him believe I never killed anybody, which I didn't. He listened, and sat there a long time, and then he said: "I figured it might be something like that. 'Specially when I read that item that covered Calenso's record and your record.... All right, let's say it's true, the way you tell it. Well—O.K. I guess I really believe it. You didn't kill anybody, and you're dead. So far as the cops are concerned, they know they got you, and that means that today, this Sunday morning, you can, if I say the word, begin a new life. Suppose I do say the word, what then? What are you going to do with this life?"

Well, what was I going to say? The last I did any thinking about my life, I was ten feet under the street, in a drain pipe that was drowning me so fast I couldn't see myself sink, and I wasn't ready to talk. I began mumbling about I hope I would die if I ever pulled any crooked stuff again, and how I sure was going to get a job and go to work, and he listened, and then cut me off short. "That's not good enough, Conley."

"It's all I know to do."

"How old are you?"

"Twenty-three."

"There's just one place for a guy your age, these days, with your country in a war. Just one place, and you haven't once mentioned it."

"Well, I'm all registered up."

"You sure of that?"

"You bet I'm registered up. O.K., so it's the army, but don't you think I'd have been in it long ago if it hadn't been for that rap I was doing?"

"Which is your draft board?"

We talked for a minute about that, and then we both seen that wouldn't do, because even if I give a new name to the draft board, the fingerprints would trip me, and then all of a sudden I said: "O.K., mister, I got it. This man's army, the one we got, it can't take me, because before it does, it's got to turn me over to the state of California to die for what Bugs Calenso done. But that's not the only army. There's other armies—"

He looked up and come over and shook hands. So that's

where I am now, on my way to another army, that's fighting for the same thing and that needs guys just as much as our army does. And I'm writing this on the deck of a freighter headed west, and the agreement is I mail it to him, to prove I did like I promised. If it all goes O.K., he keeps this locked up, and that's that. If something goes wrong, and the ship gets it, or maybe my number goes up and I check in over there, why then maybe he hands it to some guy, to be printed if somebody wants to read it. So—

Say, that's a funny one. Them reporters, they generally get it right, don't they? Because now, if you happen to read this, why then Red Conley, he is dead!

SERIAL

JAMES M. CAIN wrote six magazine serials, all while he was in California, and he considered them "commercial stories"—written primarily for quick money from either a magazine, studio, or both. But Cain also considered "Old Man Posterity" the only judge of literary merit, and by the Old Man's measure some of these stories have had a surprising life of their own. *Double Indemnity*, for example: It was Cain's first serial, written strictly for a quick sale in the hope of capitalizing on his fame as the author of the controversial, best-selling *Postman*. The editor of *Redbook*, especially, had been pressing Ms. Haggard for a Cain mystery. But when Cain sent *Double Indemnity* to New York, *Redbook* declined it. This annoyed Cain, who told Alfred A. Knopf that he considered the story "a piece of tripe [that] will never go between hardcovers while I live. The penalty, I suppose, for doing something like this is that you don't even sell it to magazines."

Cain gave serious thought to rewriting *Double Indemnity*

in the manner of Thornton Wilder's *The Bridge of San Luis Rey*, exploring "what forces of destiny brought these particular people to this dreadful spot, at this particular time, on this particular day." But before he could rework it, Edith Haggard sold *Double Indemnity* to *Liberty*, and when it came out over eight weeks in early 1936, it created a sensation. *Liberty* immediately wanted another, and Cain by then needed money to finance a trip to Mexico to research his still-evolving *Serenade*. So he wrote a serial about a female opera star whose businessman husband suddenly discovers his voice is better than his wife's. Cain called this one *Two Can Sing*, but when he sent it to New York, *Liberty* turned it down. The editor wanted more murder. Then 20th Century-Fox bought *Two Can Sing* for $8,000. (It was made twice into movies, in 1939 as *Wife, Husband and Friend* starring Loretta Young, Warner Baxter, Binnie Barnes, and Cesar Romero, and in 1949 as *Everybody Does It* starring Linda Darnell, Paul Douglas, and Celeste Holm.) Later, after it sold to the *American*, it proved the most popular short novel the magazine ever published. The editor, Albert Benjamin, pleaded with Cain for another. By now, *Serenade* had been published, creating almost as much excitement as *Postman*, and Cain was hotter than ever.

His next serial grew out of a conversation he once had with a *Collier's* editor ("How about a Cinderella story with a modern twist? What about a waitress marrying a Harvard man?"). He wrote it specifically with *Collier's* in mind, but when his agent sent the magazine the story—called *Modern Cinderella*—*Collier's* turned it down, primarily, Cain thought, because it was also concerned with organized labor. But Universal bought it for $17,500 late in 1937 and made it into a soppy little film called *When Tomorrow Comes*, starring Irene Dunne and Charles Boyer.

The following year, Cain wrote *Money and the Woman*, which *Liberty* bought immediately. It was also sold to Warner Brothers, and the studio assigned the script to Robert Presnell.

When the film, starring Jeffrey Lynn and Brenda Marshall, was released in 1940, *Variety* said the script was all right and the story okay, "but somewhere along the line, the plot went askew. Result is a mild 'B' film."

Cain did not attempt another serial until late 1941, when, recuperating from an operation and needing money, he wrote *Love's Lovely Counterfeit*. It was, he said, the only story he ever wrote with the movies in mind. But it was also a story about the seamier side of city politics, and after Japan attacked Pearl Harbor and America entered World War II, neither the magazines nor the studios were interested in fiction criticizing American institutions, and the story never sold.

The following year, still needing money and having a difficult time adjusting to the mood of wartime America, Cain wrote another serial, a story about the involvement between a Reno sheriff and a movie star whose husband is murdered. It was essentially a rewrite of his unproduced play, *7-11*, about a Broadway actress, a New York writer, and a murder in a nightclub similar to "21." He called the story *Galloping Domino*, but it also failed to sell to either the magazines or a studio.

His next and final attempt at a serial came four years later. By then, *Double Indemnity* had been published in hardcover and made into a movie, and one of its stars, Edward G. Robinson, had been asking Cain if he would write another story featuring Keyes, the insurance agent Robinson plays in the film. Cain wrote a story about an insurance agent named Ed Horner and a beautiful woman involved in a complicated divorce action in Reno. It also included the character Keyes and several references, in the first draft, at least, to *Double Indemnity*. But Robinson did not like the story, which Cain called *Nevada Moon* and, like *Galloping Domino*, it never sold to either a magazine or a studio.

Cain's curious career as a magazine serial writer is even stranger when you consider the book-publishing history of these six serials. In 1943, Knopf gathered three of them—*Dou-*

ble Indemnity, Two Can Sing (now called Career in C Major), and Money and the Woman (changed to The Embezzler)—into a single hardcover volume titled Three of a Kind. Considering that Cain thought Double Indemnity a "piece of tripe," and that all his magazine serials were written as commercial quickies, the collection was given a remarkable reception. It was highly praised by the critics, with John K. Hutchens calling Cain "a writer who holds you by the sheer, dazzling pace he sets." Of the three serials in the Knopf hardcover collection, only Double Indemnity had not already been made into a movie. But the literary response to Three of a Kind enabled Cain's Hollywood agent, H. N. Swanson, to revive studio interest in the story, which resulted in the now-classic Billy Wilder–Raymond Chandler film.

In 1949 the Saturday Review and the American Library Association compiled a list of books by American authors published in the previous quarter century that librarians felt were the most popular with their readers, and Three of a Kind was the only Cain title on the list. Then, in 1969, Knopf republished Double Indemnity in a hardcover collection called Cain X 3. It was a Book-of-the-Month Club selection and, more than any other of his books, helped create Cain's "Re-Incarnation," as he called it, in the 1970s. Today Double Indemnity and Postman continue to live as American classics of suspense writing and will probably give Cain the literary renown which he felt was the only thing that mattered to a writer—other than making a good living at his trade.

Cain's four other serials also had a curious publishing history. In 1942, after the success of Three of a Kind, Knopf decided to publish Love's Lovely Counterfeit, despite its anti-American flavor. Although reviewers were hard on the book, it sold very well, and Mencken thought it was one of the best Cain ever wrote. Then, in the late 1940s, with Cain at the height of his fame, Avon published as paperback originals the other serials which Cain had not been able to sell. All three were given new titles—Modern Cinderella became The Root of

His Evil, *Galloping Domino* became *Sinful Woman*, and *Nevada Moon* became *Jealous Woman*. Cain did not like the new titles, but by then he did not really care. He felt that being published as a paperback original was the same as being published in magazines; it did not really count in the literary sweepstakes. Recently, G. K. Hall brought out the three serials in a hardcover volume called *Hard Cain*, and the three serials, as well as most of his other books, continue to be published in reprint editions around the world, including a series of Cain titles now selling very well in Vintage paperbacks. In fact, paperbacks have been primarily responsible for giving Cain the worldwide literary reputation he valued.

The serial included in this collection—*Money and the Woman*—was written in early 1938 after Cain had experienced one of the few writer's blocks of his long career. He had just come back from a trip to Europe and had driven through West Virginia to gather material for *The Butterfly*, which he was finding impossible to write. He had also been hired briefly by Universal Pictures to work on a script, *The Victoria Docks at 8*, but then was abruptly fired for reasons unknown. He went back to his typewriter, but could not seem to get going, until finally he had an idea for a story ("The Girl in the Storm") and then a serial. The serial was triggered by a friend who worked for the same insurance company in Baltimore where Cain's father had worked. The friend had sent him a study—"1001 Embezzlers"—asking Cain to comment on it. Cain responded with an excellent critique and then began to think about a story involving a man who mortgages his house to help a woman *return* $9,000 to a bank. *Liberty* bought it for $4,000, and by the time it finally appeared in *Three of a Kind*, Cain had decided it was one of his favorite stories. "In *The Embezzler*," he wrote in a preface to the Knopf collection, "I find writing that is much simpler, much freer from calculated effect, than I find in the other two [*Double Indemnity* and *Career in C Major*]."

Cain was pleased with the collection when it was pub

lished in 1941, and he wrote Knopf: "Later, if some of my writing kicks me into prominence, it may be a title that will have occasional spurts of activity."

Three of a Kind has long been out of print, but the three stories—as most of Cain's fiction—continue to live.

R.H.

Money and the Woman
(The Embezzler)

I

I FIRST MET HER WHEN SHE came over to the house one night, after calling me on the telephone and asking if she could see me on a matter of business. I had no idea what she wanted, but supposed it was something about the bank. At the time, I was acting cashier of our little Anita Avenue branch, the smallest of the three we've got in Glendale, and the smallest branch we've got, for that matter. In the home office, in Los Angeles, I rate as vice president, but I'd been sent out there to check up on the branch, not on what was wrong with it, but what was right with it. Their ratio of savings deposits to commercial deposits was over twice what we had in any other branch, and the Old Man figured it was time somebody went out there and found out what the trick was, in case they'd invented something the rest of the banking world hadn't heard of.

I found out what the trick was soon enough. It was her husband, a guy named Brent that rated head teller and had charge of the savings department. He'd elected himself little White Father to all those workmen that banked in the branch, and kept after them and made them save until half of them were buying their homes and there wasn't one of them that didn't have a good pile of dough in the bank. It was good for us, and still better for those workmen, but in spite of that I didn't like Brent and I didn't like his way of doing business. I asked him to lunch one day, but he was too busy, and couldn't come. I had to wait till we closed, and then we went to a drugstore while he had a glass of milk, and I tried to get out of him something about how he got those deposits every week, and whether he thought any of his methods could be used by the whole organization. But we got off on the wrong foot, because he thought I really meant to criticize, and it took me half an hour to smooth him down. He was a funny guy, so touchy you could hardly talk to him at all, and with a hymn-book-salesman look to him that made you understand why he regarded his work as a kind of a missionary job among these people that carried their accounts with him. I would say he was around thirty, but he looked older. He was tall and thin, and beginning to get bald, but he walked with a stoop and his face had a gray color that you don't see on a well man. After he drank his milk and ate the two crackers that came with it, he took a little tablet out of an envelope he carried in his pocket, dissolved it in his water, and drank it.

But even when he got it through his head I wasn't sharpening an axe for him, he wasn't much help. He kept saying that savings deposits have to be worked up on a personal basis, that the man at the window has to make the depositor feel that he takes an interest in seeing the figures mount up, and more of the same. Once he got a holy look in his eyes, when he said that you can't make the depositor feel that way unless you really feel that way yourself, and for a few seconds he was a little excited, but that died off. It looks all right, as I write it, but it didn't sound good. Of course, a big corporation doesn't like to put things on a personal basis, if it can help it. Institutionalize the bank, but not the man, for the good reason that the man may get an offer somewhere else, and then when he quits he takes all his trade with him. But that wasn't the only reason it didn't sound good. There was something about the guy himself that I just didn't like, and what it was I didn't know, and didn't even have enough interest to find out.

So when his wife called up a couple of weeks later, and asked if she could see me that night, at my home, not at the bank, I guess I wasn't any sweeter about it than I had to be. In the first place, it looked funny she would want to come to my house, instead of the bank, and in the second place, it didn't sound like good news, and in the third place, if she stayed late, it was going to cut me out of the fights down at the Legion Stadium, and I kind of look forward to them. Still, there wasn't much I could say except I would see her, so I did. Sam, my Filipino houseboy, was going out, so I fixed a highball tray for myself, and figured if she was as pious as he was, that would shock her enough that she would leave early.

It didn't shock her a bit. She was quite a lot younger than he was, I would say around twenty-five, with blue eyes, brown hair, and a shape you couldn't take your eyes off of. She was about medium size, but put together so pretty she looked small. Whether she was really good-looking in the face I don't know, but if she wasn't good-looking, there was something about the way she looked at you that had that thing. Her teeth were big and white, and her lips were just the least little bit thick. They gave her a kind of a heavy, sullen look, but one eyebrow had a kind of twitch to it, so she'd say something and no part of her face would move but that, and yet it meant more than most women could put across with everything they had.

All that kind of hit me in the face at once, because it was

the last thing I was expecting. I took her coat, and followed her into the living room. She sat down in front of the fire, picked up a cigarette and tapped it on her nail, and began looking around. When her eye lit on the highball tray she was already lighting her cigarette, but she nodded with the smoke curling up in one eye. "Yes, I think I will."

I laughed, and poured her a drink. It was all that had been said, and yet it got us better acquainted than an hour of talk could have done. She asked me a few questions about myself, mainly if I wasn't the same Dave Bennett that used to play halfback for U.S.C., and when I told her I was, she figured out my age. She said she was twelve years old at the time she saw me go down for a touchdown on an intercepted pass, which put her around twenty-five, what I took her for. She sipped her drink. I put a log of wood on the fire. I wasn't quite so hot about the Legion fights.

When she'd finished her drink she put the glass down, motioned me away when I started to fix her another, and said: "Well."

"Yeah, that awful word."

"I'm afraid I have bad news."

"Which is?"

"Charles is sick."

"He certainly doesn't look well."

"He needs an operation."

"What's the matter with him—if it's mentionable?"

"It's mentionable, even if it's pretty annoying. He has a duodenal ulcer, and he's abused himself so much, or at least his stomach, with this intense way he goes about his work, and refusing to go out to lunch, and everything else that he shouldn't do, that it's got to that point. I mean, it's serious. If he had taken better care of himself, it's something that needn't have amounted to much at all. But he's let it go, and now I'm afraid if something isn't done—well, it's going to be very serious. I might as well say it. I got the report today, on the examination he had. It says if he's not operated on at once, he's going to be dead within a month. He's—verging on a perforation."

"And?"

"This part isn't so easy."

". . . How much?"

"Oh, it isn't a question of money. That's all taken care of. He has a policy, one of these clinical hook-ups that entitles him to everything. It's Charles."

"I don't quite follow you."

"I can't seem to get it through his head that this has to be done. I suppose I could, if I showed him what I've just got from the doctors, but I don't want to frighten him any more than I can help. But he's so wrapped up in his work, he's such a fanatic about it, that he positively refuses to leave it. He has some idea that these people, these workers, are all going to ruin if he isn't there to boss them around, and make them save their money, and pay up their installments on their houses, and I don't know what all. I guess it sounds silly to you. It does to me. But—he won't quit."

"You want me to talk to him?"

"Yes, but that's not quite all. I think, if Charles knew that his work was being done the way he wants it done, and that his job would be there waiting for him when he came out of the hospital, that he'd submit without a great deal of fuss. This is what I've been trying to get around to. Will you let me come in and do Charles's work while he's gone?"

". . . Well—it's pretty complicated work."

"Oh no, it's not. At least not to me. You see, I know every detail of it, as well as he does. I not only know the people, from going around with him while he badgered them into being thrifty, but I used to work in the bank. That's where I met him. And—I'll do it beautifully, really. That is, if you don't object to making it a kind of family affair."

I thought it over a few minutes, or tried to. I went over

in my mind the reasons against it, and didn't see any that amounted to anything. In fact, it suited me just as well to have her come in, if Brent really had to go to the hospital, because it would peg the job while he was gone, and I wouldn't have to have a general shake-up, with the other three in the branch moving up a notch, and getting all excited about promotions that probably wouldn't last very long anyway. But I may as well tell the truth. All that went through my mind, but another thing that went through my mind was her. It wasn't going to be a bit unpleasant to have her around for the next few weeks. I liked this dame from the start, and for me anyway, she was plenty easy to look at.

"Why—I think that's all right."

"You mean I get the job?"

"Yeah—sure."

"What a relief. I hate to ask for jobs."

"How about another drink?"

"No, thanks. Well—just a little one."

I fixed her another drink, and we talked about her husband a little more, and I told her how his work had attracted the attention of the home office, and it seemed to please her. But then all of a sudden I popped out: "Who are you, anyway?"

"Why—I thought I told you."

"Yeah, but I want to know more."

"Oh, I'm nobody at all, I'm sorry to say. Let's see, who am I? Born, Princeton, New Jersey, and not named for a while on account of an argument among relatives. Then when they thought my hair was going to be red they named me Sheila, because it had an Irish sound to it. Then—at the age of ten, taken to California. My father got appointed to the history department of U.C.L.A."

"And who is your father?"

"Henry W. Rollinson—"

"Oh, yes, I've heard of him."

"Ph.D. to you, just Hank to me. And—let's see. High school, valedictorian of the class, tagged for college, wouldn't go. Went out and got myself a job instead. In our little bank. Answered an ad in the paper. Said I was eighteen when I was only sixteen, worked there three years, got a one-dollar raise every year. Then—Charles got interested, and I married him."

"And, would you kindly explain *that*?"

"It happens, doesn't it?"

"Well, it's none of my business. Skip it."

"You mean we're oddly assorted?"

"Slightly."

"It seems so long ago. Did I mention I was nineteen? At that age you're very susceptible to—what would you call it? Idealism?"

". . . Are you still?"

I didn't know I was going to say that, and my voice sounded shady. She drained her glass and got up.

"Then, let's see. What else is there in my little biography? I have two children, one five, the other three, both girls, and both beautiful. And—I sing alto in the Eurydice Women's Chorus. . . . That's all, and now I have to be going."

"Where'd you put your car?"

"I don't drive. I came by bus."

"Then—may I drive you home?"

"I'd certainly be grateful if you would. . . . By the way, Charles would kill me if he knew I'd come to you. About him, I mean. I'm supposed to be at a picture show. So tomorrow, don't get absent-minded and give me away."

"It's between you and me."

"It sounds underhanded, but he's very peculiar."

I live on Franklin Avenue in Hollywood, and she lived on Mountain Drive, in Glendale. It's about twenty minutes, but when we got in front of her house, instead of stopping, I drove on. "I just happened to think; it's awful early for a picture show to let out."

"So it is, isn't it?"

We drove up in the hills. Up to then we had been plenty gabby, but for the rest of the drive we both felt self-conscious and didn't have much to say. When I swung down through Glendale again the Alexander Theatre was just letting out. I set her down on the corner, a little way from her house. She shook hands. "Thanks ever so much."

"Just sell him the idea, and the job's all set."

". . . I feel terribly guilty, but—"

"Yes?"

"I've had a grand time."

II

She sold me the idea, but she couldn't sell Brent, not that easy, that is. He squawked, and refused to go to the hospital, or do anything about his ailment at all, except take pills for it. She called me up three or four times about it, and those calls seemed to get longer every night. But one day, when he toppled over at the window, and I had to send him home in a private ambulance, there didn't seem to be much more he could say. They hauled him off to the hospital, and she came in next day to take his place, and things went along just about the way she said they would, with her doing the work fine and the depositors plunking down their money just like they had before.

The first night he was in the hospital I went down there with a basket of fruit, more as an official gift from the bank than on my own account, and she was there, and of course after we left him I offered to take her home. So I took her. It turned out she had arranged that the maid should spend her nights at the house, on account of the children, while he was in the hospital, so we took a ride. Next night I took her down, and waited for her outside, and we took another ride. After they got through taking X-rays they operated, and it went off all right, and by that time she and I had got the habit. I found a newsreel right near the hospital, and while she was with him, I'd go in and look at the sports, and then we'd go for a little ride.

I didn't make any passes, she didn't tell me I was different from other guys she'd known, there was nothing like that. We talked about her kids, and the books we'd read, and sometimes she'd remember about my old football days, and some of the things she'd seen me do out there. But mostly we'd just ride along and say nothing, and I couldn't help feeling glad when she'd say the doctors wanted Brent to stay there until he was all healed up. He could have stayed there till Christmas, and I wouldn't have been sore.

The Anita Avenue branch, I think I told you, is the smallest one we've got, just a little bank building on a corner, with an alley running alongside and a drugstore across the street. It employs six people, the cashier, the head teller, two other tellers, a girl bookkeeper, and a guard. George Mason had been cashier, but they transferred him and sent me out there, so I was acting cashier. Sheila was taking Brent's place as head teller. Snelling and Helm were the other two tellers, Miss Church was the bookkeeper, and Adler the guard. Miss Church went in for a lot of apple-polishing with me, or anyway what I took to be apple-polishing. They had to stagger their lunch hours, and she was always insisting that I go out for a full hour at lunch, that she could relieve at any of the windows, that there was no need to hurry back, and more of the same. But I wanted to pull my oar with the rest, so I took a half hour like the rest of them took, and relieved at whatever window needed me, and for a couple of hours I wasn't at my desk at all.

One day Sheila was out, and the others got back a little early, so I went out. They all ate in a little cafe down the street, so I ate there too, and when I got there she was alone at a table. I would have sat down with her, but she didn't look up, and I took a seat a couple of tables away. She was looking out the window, smoking, and pretty soon she doused her cigarette and came over where I was. "You're a little stand-offish today, Mrs. Brent."

"I've been doing a little quiet listening."

"Oh—the two guys in the corner?"

"Do you know who the fat one is?"

"No, I don't."

"That's Bunny Kaiser, the leading furniture man of Glendale. 'She Buys 'Er Stuff from Kaiser.'"

"Isn't he putting up a building or something? Seems to me we had a deal on, to handle his bonds."

"He wouldn't sell bonds. It's his building, with his own name chiseled over the door, and he wanted to swing the whole thing himself. But he can't quite make it. The building is up to the first floor now, and he has to make a payment to the contractor. He needs a hundred thousand bucks. Suppose a bright girl got that business for you, would she get a raise?"

"And how would *she* get that business?"

"Sex appeal! Do you think I haven't got it?"

"I didn't say you haven't got it."

"You'd better not."

"Then that's settled."

"And—?"

"When's this payment on the first floor due?"

"Tomorrow."

"Ouch! That doesn't give us much time to work."

"You let *me* work it, and *I'll* put it over."

"All right, you land that loan, it's a two-dollar raise."

"Two-fifty."

"O.K.—two-fifty."

"I'll be late. At the bank, I mean."

"I'll take your window."

So I went back and took her window. About two o'clock a truck driver came in, cashed a pay check with Helm, then came over to me to make a $10 deposit on savings. I took his book, entered the amount, set the $10 so she could put it with her cash when she came in. You understand: They all have cash boxes, and lock them when they go out, and that cash is checked once a month. But when I took out the card in our own file, the total it showed was $150 less than the amount showing in the passbook.

In a bank, you never let the depositor notice anything. You've got that smile on your face, and everything's jake, and that's fair enough, from his end of it, because the bank is responsible, and what his book shows is what he's got, so he can't lose no matter how you play it. Just the same, under that pasted grin, my lips felt a little cold. I picked up his book again, like there was something else I had to do to it, and blobbed a big smear of ink over it. "Well, that's nice, isn't it."

"You sure decorated it."

"I tell you what, I'm a little busy just now—will you leave that with me? Next time you come in, I'll have a new one ready for you."

"Anything you say, Cap."

"This one's kind of shopworn, anyway."

"Yeah, getting greasy."

By that time I had a receipt ready for the book, and copied the amount down in his presence, and passed it out to him. He went and I set the book aside. It had taken a little time, and three more depositors were in line behind him. The first two books corresponded with the cards, but the last one showed a $200 difference, more on his book than we had on our card. I hated to do what he had seen me do with the other guy, but I had to have that book. I started to enter the deposit, and once more a big blob of ink went on that page.

"Say, what you need is a new pen."

"What they need is a new teller. To tell you the truth, I'm a little green on this job, just filling in till Mrs. Brent gets back, and I'm hurrying it. If you'll just leave me this book, now—"

"Sure, that's all right."

I wrote the receipt, and signed it, and he went, and I put that book aside. By that time I had a little breathing spell, with nobody at the window, and I checked those books against the cards. Both accounts, on our records, showed withdrawals, running from $25 to $50, that didn't show on the passbooks. Well, brother, it had to show on the passbooks. If a depositor wants to withdraw, he can't do it without his book, because that book's his contract, and we're bound by it, and he can't draw any dough unless we write it right down there, what he took out. I began to feel a little sick at my stomach. I began to think of the shifty way Brent had talked when he explained about working the departments up on a personal basis. I began to think about how he refused to go to the hospital, when any sane man would have been begging for the chance. I began to think of that night call Sheila made on me, and all that talk about Brent's taking things so seriously, and that application she made, to take things over while he was gone.

All that went through my head, but I was still thumbing the cards. My head must have been swimming a little when I first checked them over, but the second time I ran my eye over those two cards I noticed little light pencil checks beside each one of those withdrawals. It flashed through my mind that maybe that was his code. He had to have a code, if he was trying to get away with anything. If a depositor didn't have his book, and asked for his balance, he had to be able to tell him. I flipped all the cards over. There were light pencil checks on at least half of them, every one against a withdrawal, none of them against a deposit. I wanted to run those checked amounts off on the adding machine, but I didn't. I was afraid Miss Church would start her apple-polishing again, and offer to do it for me. I flipped the cards over one at a time, slow, and added the amounts in my head. If I was accurate I didn't know. I've got an adding machine mind, and I can do some of those vaudeville stunts without much trouble, but I was too excited to be sure. That didn't matter, that day. I wouldn't be far off. And those little pencil checks, by the time I had turned every card, added up to a little more than $8,500.

Just before closing time, around three o'clock, Sheila came in with the fat guy, Bunny Kaiser. I found out why sex appeal had worked, where all our contact men, trying to make a deal for bonds a few months before, had flopped. It was the first time he had ever borrowed a dollar in his life, and he not only hated it, he was so ashamed of it he couldn't even look at me. Her way of making him feel better was not to argue about it at all, but to pat him on the hand, and it was pathetic the way he ate it up. After a while she gave me the sign to beat it, so I went back and got the vault closed, and chased the rest of them out of there as fast as I could. Then we fixed the thing up, I called the main office for O.K.'s, and around four-thirty he left. She stuck out her hand, pretty excited, and I took it. She began trucking around the floor, snapping her fingers and singing some tune while she danced. All of a sudden she stopped, and made motions like she was brushing herself off.

"Well—is there something *on* me?"

". . . No. Why?"

"You've been *looking* at me—for an *hour*!"

"I was—looking at the dress."

"Is there anything the *matter* with it?"

"It's different from what girls generally wear around a bank. It—doesn't look like an office dress."

"I made it myself."

"Then that accounts for it."

III

Brother, if you want to find out how much you think of a woman, just get the idea she's been playing you for a sucker. I was trembling when I got home, and still trembling when I went up to my room and lay down. I had a mess on my hands, and I knew I had to do something about it. But all I could think of was the way she had taken me for a ride, or I thought she had anyway, and how I had fallen for it, and what a sap I was. My face would feel hot when I thought of those automobile rides, and how I had been too gentlemanly to start anything. Then I would think how she must be laughing at me, and dig my face into the pillow. After a while I got to thinking about tonight. I had a date to take her to the hospital, like I had for the past week, and wondered what I was going to do about that. What I wanted to do was give her a stand-up and never set eyes on her again, but I couldn't. After what she had said at the bank, about me looking at her, she might tumble I was wise if I didn't show up. I wasn't ready for that yet. Whatever I had to do, I wanted my hands free till I had time to think.

So I was waiting, down the street from her house, where we'd been meeting on account of what the neighbors might think if I kept coming to the door, and in a few minutes here she came, and I gave the little tap on the horn and she got in. She didn't say anything about me looking at her, or what had been said. She kept talking about Kaiser, and how we had put over a fine deal, and how there was plenty more business of the same kind that could be had if I'd only let her go out after it. I went along with it, and for the first time since I'd known her, she got just the least little bit flirty. Nothing that meant much, just some stuff about what a team we could make if we really put our minds to it. But it brought me back to what my face had been red about in the afternoon, and when she went in the hospital I was trembling again.

I didn't go to the newsreel that night. I sat in the car for the whole hour she was in there, paying her visit to him, and the longer I sat the sorer I got. I hated that woman when she came out of the hospital, and then, while she was climbing in beside me, an idea hit me between the eyes. If that was her game, how far would she go with me? I watched her light a cigarette, and then felt my mouth go dry and hot. I'd soon find out. Instead of heading for the hills, or the ocean, or any of the places we'd been driving, I headed home.

We went in, and I lit the fire without turning on the living-room light. I mumbled something about a drink, and went out in the kitchen. What I really wanted was to see if Sam was in. He wasn't, and that meant he wouldn't be in till one or two o'clock, so that was all right. I fixed the highball tray, and went in the living room with it. She had taken off her hat, and was sitting in front of the fire, or to one side of it. There are two sofas in my living room, both of them half facing the fire, and she was on one of them swinging her foot at the flames. I made two highballs, put them on the low table between the sofas, and sat down beside her. She looked up, took her drink, and began to sip it. I made a crack about how black her eyes looked in the firelight, she said they were blue, but it sounded like she wouldn't mind hearing more. I put my arm around her.

Well, a whole book could be written about how a woman blocks passes when she doesn't mean to play. If she slaps your face, she's just a fool, and you might as well go home. If she hands you a lot of stuff that makes *you* feel like a fool, she doesn't know her stuff yet, and you better leave her alone. But if she plays it so you're stopped, and yet nothing much has happened, and you don't feel like a fool, she knows her stuff, and she's all right, and you can stick around and take it as it comes, and you won't wake up next morning wishing that you hadn't. That was what she did. She didn't pull away, she didn't act surprised, she didn't get off any bum gags. But she didn't come to me either, and in a minute or two she leaned forward to pick up her glass, and when she leaned back she wasn't inside of my arm.

I was too sick in my mind though, and too sure I had her sized up right for a trollop, to pay any attention to that, or even figure out what it meant. It went through my mind, just once, that whatever I had to do, down at the bank, I was putting myself in an awful spot, and playing right into her hands, to start something I couldn't stop. But that only made my mouth feel drier and hotter.

I put my arm around her again, and pulled her to me. She didn't do anything about it at all, one way or the other. I put my cheek against hers, and began to nose around to her mouth. She didn't do anything about that either, but her mouth seemed kind of hard to reach. I put my hand on her cheek, and then deliberately let it slide down to her neck, and unbuttoned the top button of her dress. She took my hand away, buttoned her dress, and reached for her drink again, so when she sat back I didn't have her.

That sip took a long time, and I just sat there, looking at her. When she put the glass down I had my arm around her before she could even lean back. With my other hand I made a swipe, and brushed her dress up clear to where her garters met her girdle. What she did then I don't know, because something happened that I didn't expect. Those legs were so beautiful, and so soft, and warm, that something caught me in the throat, and for about one second I had no idea what was going on. Next thing I knew she was standing in front of the fireplace, looking down at me with a drawn face. "Will you kindly tell me what's got into you tonight?"

"Why—nothing particular."

"Please, I want to know."

"Why, I find you exciting, that's all."

"Is it something I've done?"

"I didn't notice you doing anything."

"Something's come over you, and I don't know what. Ever since I came in the bank today, with Bunny Kaiser, you've been looking at me in a way that's cold, and hard, and ugly. What is it? Is it what I said at lunch, about my having sex appeal?"

"Well, you've got it. We agreed on that."

"Do you know what I think?"

"No, but I'd like to."

"I think that remark of mine, or something, has suddenly wakened you up to the fact that I'm a married woman, that I've been seeing quite a little of you, and that you think it's now up to you to be loyal to the ancient masculine tradition, and try to make me."

"Anyway, I'm trying."

She reached for her drink, changed her mind, lit a cigarette instead. She stood there for a minute, looking into the fire, inhaling the smoke. Then:

". . . I don't say it couldn't be done. After all, my home life hasn't been such a waltz dream for the last year or so. It's not so pleasant to sit by your husband while he's coming out of ether, and then have him begin mumbling another woman's name, instead of your own. I guess that's why I've taken rides with you every night. They've been a little breath of something pleasant. Something more than that. Something romantic, and if I pretended they haven't meant a lot to me, I wouldn't be telling the truth. They've been—little moments under the moon. And then today, when I landed Kaiser, and was bringing him in, I was all excited about it, not so much for the business it meant to the bank, which I don't give a damn about, or the two-dollar-and-a-half raise, which I don't give a damn about either, but because it was something you and I had done together, something we'd talk about tonight, and it would be—another moment under the moon, a very bright moon. And then, before I'd been in the bank more than a minute or two, I saw that look in your eye. And tonight, you've been—perfectly horrible. It could have been done, I think. I'm afraid I'm only too human. But not this way. And not any more. Could I borrow your telephone?"

I thought maybe she really wanted the bath, so I took her to the extension in my bedroom. I sat down by the fire quite a while, and waited. It was all swimming around in my head, and it hadn't come out at all like I expected. Down somewhere inside of me, it began to gnaw at me that I had to tell her, I had to come out with the whole thing, when all of a sudden the bell rang. When I opened the door a taxi driver was standing there.

"You called for a cab?"

"No, nobody called."

He fished out a piece of paper and peered at it, when she came downstairs. "I guess that's my cab."

"Oh, you ordered it?"

"Yes. Thanks ever so much. It's been so pleasant."

She was as cold as a dead man's foot, and she was down the walk and gone before I could think of anything to say. I watched her get in the cab, watched it drive off, then closed the door and went back in the living room. When I sat down on the sofa I could still smell her perfume, and her glass was only half drunk. That catch came in my throat again, and I began to curse at myself out loud, even while I was pouring myself a drink.

I had started to find out what she was up to, but all I had found out was that I was nuts about her. I went over and over it till I was dizzy, and nothing she had done, and nothing she had said, proved anything. She might be on the up-and-up, and she might be playing me for a still worse sucker than I had thought she was, a sucker that was going to play her game for her, and not even get anything for it. In the bank, she treated me just like she treated the others, pleasant, polite, and pretty. I didn't take her to the hospital any more, and that was how we went along for three or four days.

Then came the day for the monthly check on cash, and I tried to kid myself that was what I had been waiting for, before I did anything about the shortage. So I went around with Helm, and checked them all. They opened their boxes, and Helm counted them up, and I counted his count. She stood there while I was counting hers, with a dead pan that could mean anything, and of course it checked to the cent. Down in my heart I knew it would. Those false entries had all been made to balance the cash, and as they went back for a couple of years, there wasn't a chance that it would show anything in just one month.

That afternoon when I went home I had it out with myself, and woke up that I wasn't going to do anything about that shortage, that I couldn't do anything about it, until at least I had spoken to her, anyway acted like a white man.

So that night I drove over to Glendale, and parked right on Mountain Drive where I had always parked. I went early, in case she started sooner when she went by bus, and I waited a long time. I waited so long I almost gave up, but then along about half past seven, here she came out of the house, and walking fast. I waited till she was about a hundred feet away, and then I gave that same little tap on the horn I had given before. She started to run, and I had this sick feeling that she was going by without even speaking, so I didn't look. I wouldn't give her that much satisfaction. But before I knew it the door opened and slammed, and there she was on the seat beside me, and she was squeezing my hand, and half whispering:

"I'm so glad you came. So glad."

We didn't say much going in. I went to the newsreel, but what came out on the screen I couldn't tell you. I was going over and over in my mind what I was going to say to her, or at least trying to. But every time when I'd get talking about it, I'd find myself starting off about her home life, and trying to find out if Brent really had taken up with another woman, and more of the same that only meant one thing. It meant I wanted her for myself. And it meant I was trying to make myself believe that she didn't know anything about the shortage, that she had been on the up-and-up all the time, that she really liked me. I went back to the car, and got in, and pretty soon she came out of the hospital, and ran down the steps. Then she stopped, and stood there like she was thinking. Then she started for the car again, but she wasn't running now. She was walking slow. When she got in she leaned back and closed her eyes.

"Dave?"

It was the first time she had ever called me by my first name. I felt my heart jump. "Yes, Sheila?"

"Could we have a fire tonight?"

"I'd love it."

"I've—I've got to talk to you."

So I drove to my house. Sam let us in, but I chased him out. We went in the living room, and once more I didn't turn on the light. She helped me light the fire, and I started into the kitchen to fix something to drink, but she stopped me.

"I don't want anything to drink. Unless you do."

"No. I don't drink much."

"Let's sit down."

She sat on the sofa, where she had been before, and I sat beside her. I didn't try any passes. She looked in the fire a long time, and then she took my arm and pulled it around her. "Am I terrible?"

"No."

"I want it there."

I started to kiss her, but she raised her hand, covered my lips with her fingers, then pushed my face away. She dropped her head on my shoulder, closed her eyes, and didn't speak for a long time. Then: "Dave, there's something I've got to tell you."

"What is it?"

"It's pretty tragic, and it involves the bank, and if you don't want to hear it from me, this way, just say so and I'll go home."

". . . All right. Shoot."

"Charles is short in his accounts."

get me where you wanted me. Well—that clears *that* up."

She was sitting up now, looking at me hard.

"Dave, I *didn't* know it."

"I know you didn't—*now*, I know it."

"I knew about *her*—this woman he's been—going around with. I wondered sometimes where he got the money. But this, I had no idea. Until two or three days ago. Until I began to notice discrepancies in the passbooks."

"Yeah, that's what I noticed."

"And that's why you turned seducer?"

"Yeah. It's not very natural to me, I guess. I didn't fool you any. What I'm trying to say is I don't feel that way about you. I want you every way there is to want somebody, but—I mean it. Do you know what I'm getting at, if anything?"

She nodded, and all of a sudden we were in each other's arms, and I was kissing her, and she was kissing back, and her lips were warm and soft, and once more I had that feeling in my throat, that catch like I wanted to cry or something. We sat there a long time, not saying anything, just holding each other close. We were halfway to her house before we remembered about the shortage and what we were going to do about it. She begged me once more to give her a chance to save her children from the disgrace. I told her I'd have to think it over, but I knew in my heart I was going to do anything she asked me to.

IV

"Where are you going to get this money?"
"There's only one place I can possibly get it."
"Which is?"
"My father."
"Has he got that much dough?"
"I don't know. . . . He owns his house. Out in Westwood.

He could get something on that. He has a little money. I don't know how much. But for the last few years his only daughter hasn't been any expense. I guess he can get it."

"How's he going to feel about it?"

"He's going to hate it. And if he lets me have it, it won't be on account of Charles. He bears no goodwill to Charles, I can tell you that. And it won't be on account of me. He was pretty bitter when I even considered marrying Charles, and when I actually went and did it—well, we won't go into that. But for his grandchildren's sake, he might. Oh, what a mess. What an awful thing."

It was the next night, and we were sitting in the car, where I had parked on one of the terraces overlooking the ocean. I suppose it was around eight-thirty, as she hadn't stayed at the hospital very long. She sat looking out at the surf, and then suddenly I said I might as well drive her over to her father's. I did, and she didn't have much to say. I parked near the house, and she went in, and she stayed a long time. It must have been eleven o'clock when she came out. She got in the car, and then she broke down and cried, and there wasn't much I could do. When she got a little bit under control, I asked, "Well, what luck?"

"Oh, he'll do it, but it was awful."

"If he got sore, you can't blame him much."

"He didn't get sore. He just sat there, and shook his head, and there was no question about whether he'd let me have the money or not. But—Dave, an old man, he's been paying on that house for fifteen years, and last year he got it clear. If he wants to, he can spend his summers in Canada, he and Mamma both. And now—it's all gone, he'll have to start paying all over again, all because of this. And he never said a word."

"What did your mother say?"

"I didn't tell her. I suppose he will, but I couldn't. I waited till she went to bed. That's what kept me so long.

"How much?"

"A little over nine thousand dollars. Nine one one three point two six, if you want the exact amount. I've been suspecting it. I noticed one or two things. He kept saying I must have made mistakes in my bookkeeping, but tonight I made him admit it."

"Well. That's not so good."

"How bad is it?"

"It's pretty bad."

"Dave, tell me the truth about it. I've got to know. What will they do to him? Will they put him in prison?"

"I'm afraid they will."

"What, actually, does happen?"

"A good bit of what happens is up to the bonding company. If they get tough, he needn't expect much mercy. It's dead open-and-shut. They put him under arrest, have him indicted, and the rest of it's a question of how hard they bear down, and how it hits the court. Sometimes, of course, there are extenuating circumstances—"

"There aren't any. He didn't spend that money on me, or on the children, or on his home. I've kept all expenses within his salary, and I've even managed to save a little for him, every week."

"Yeah, I noticed your account."

"He spent it on another woman."

"I see."

"Does it make any difference if restitution is made?"

"All the difference in the world."

"If so, would he get off completely free?"

"There again, it all depends on the bonding company, and the deal that could be made with them. They might figure they'd make any kind of a deal, to get the money back, but as a rule they're not lenient. They can't be. The way they look at it, every guy that gets away with it means ten guys next year that'll try to get away with it."

"Suppose they never knew it?"

"I don't get you."

"Suppose I could find a way to put the money back, I mean suppose I could get the money, and then found a way to make the records conform, so nobody ever knew there was anything wrong."

"It couldn't be done."

"Oh yes, it could."

"The passbooks would give it away. Sooner or later."

"Not the way I'd do it."

"That—I would have to think about."

"You know what this means to me, don't you?"

"I think so."

"It's not on account of me. Or Charles. I try not to wish ill to anybody, but if he had to pay, it might be what he deserves. It's on account of my two children. Dave, I can't have them spend the rest of their lives knowing their father was a convict, that he'd been in prison. Do you, can you, understand what that means, Dave?"

For the first time since she had begun to talk, I looked at her then. She was still in my arms, but she was turned to me in a strained, tense kind of way, and her eyes looked haunted. I patted her head, and tried to think. But I knew there was one thing I had to do. I had to clear up my end of it. She had come clean with me, and for a while, anyway, I believed in her. I had to come clean with her.

"Sheila?"

"Yes?"

"I've got to tell *you* something."

"... What is it, Dave?"

"I've known this all along. For at least a week."

"Is that why you were looking at me that day?"

"Yes. It's why I acted that way, that night. I thought you knew it. I thought you had known it, even when you came to me that night, to ask for the job. I thought you were playing me for a sucker, and I wanted to find out how far you'd go, to

Fifteen years, paying regularly every month, and now it's to go, all because Charles fell for a simpleton that isn't worth the powder and shot to blow her to hell."

I didn't sleep very well that night. I kept thinking of the old history professor, and his house, and Sheila, and Brent lying down there in the hospital with a tube in his belly. Up to then I hadn't thought much about him. I didn't like him, and he was washed up with Sheila, and I had just conveniently not thought of him at all. I thought of him now, though, and wondered who the simpleton was that he had fallen for, and whether he was as nuts about her as I was about Sheila. Then I got to wondering whether I thought enough of her to embezzle for her, and that brought me sitting up in bed, staring out the window at the night. I could say I wouldn't, that I had never stolen from anybody, and never would, but here I was already mixed up in it some kind of way. It was a week since I uncovered that shortage, and I hadn't said a word about it to the home office, and I was getting ready to help her cover up.

Something popped in me then, about Brent, I mean, and I quit kidding myself. I did some hard figuring in bed there, and I didn't like it a bit, but I knew what I had to do. Next night, instead of heading for the ocean, I headed for my house again, and pretty soon we were back in front of the fire. I had mixed a drink this time, because at least I felt at peace with myself, and I held her in my arms quite a while before I got to it. Then: "Sheila?"

"Yes?"

"I've had it out with myself."

"Dave, you're not going to turn him in?"

"No, but I've decided that there's only one person that can take that rap."

"Who do you mean?"

"Me."

"I don't understand you."

"All right, I drove you over to see your father last night, and he took it pretty hard. Fifteen years, paying on that house, and now it's all got to go, and he don't get anything out of it at all. Why should he pay? I got a house, too, and I do get something out of it."

"What do *you* get out of it?"

"You."

"What are you talking about?"

"I mean I got to cough up that nine thousand bucks."

"You *will* not!"

"Look, let's quit kidding ourselves. All right, Brent stole the dough, he spent it on a cutie, he treated you lousy. He's father of two children that happen also to be your father's grandchildren, and that means your father's got to pay. Well, ain't that great. Here's the only thing that matters about this: Brent's down and out. He's in the shadow of the penitentiary, he's in the hospital recovering from one of the worst operations there is, he's in one hell of a spot. But me—I'm in love with his wife. While he's down, I'm getting ready to take her away from him, the one thing he's got left. O.K., that's not so pretty, but that's how I feel about it. But the least I can do is kick in with that dough. So, I'm doing it. So, quit bothering your old man. So, that's all."

"I can't let you do it."

"Why not?"

"If you paid that money, then I'd be bought."

She got up and began to walk around the room. "You've practically said so yourself. You're getting ready to take a man's wife away from him, and you're going to salve your conscience by replacing the money he stole. That's all very well for him, since he doesn't seem to want his wife anyway. But can't you see where it puts me? What can I say to you now? Or what could I say, if I let you put up that money? I can't pay you back. Not in ten years could I make enough to pay you nine thousand dollars. I'm just your—creature."

I watched her as she moved around, touching the furniture with her hands, not looking at me, and then all of a sudden a hot, wild feeling went through me, and the blood began to pound in my head. I went over and jerked her around, so she was facing me. "Listen, there's not many guys that feel for a woman nine thousand dollars' worth. What's the matter with that? Don't you want to be bought?"

I took her in my arms, and shoved my lips against hers. "Is that so tough?"

She opened her mouth, so our teeth were clicking, and just breathed it: "It's grand, just grand."

She kissed me then, hard. "So it was just a lot of hooey you were handing me?"

"Just hooey, nothing but hooey. Oh, it's so good to be bought. I feel like something in a veil, and a harem skirt—and I just love it."

"Now—we'll put that money back."

"Yes, together."

"We'll start tomorrow."

"Isn't that funny. I'm completely in your power. I'm your slave, and I feel so safe, and know that nothing's going to happen to me, ever."

"That's right. It's a life sentence for you."

"Dave, I've fallen in love."

"Me, too."

V

If you think it's hard to steal money from a bank, you're right. But it's nothing like as hard as it is to put the money back. Maybe I haven't made it quite clear yet what that bird was doing. In the first place, when there's a shortage in a bank, it's always in the savings, because no statements are rendered on them. The commercial depositor, the guy with a checking account, I mean, gets a statement every month. But no statements are rendered to savings depositors. They show up with their passbooks, and plunk their money down, and the deposit is entered in their books, and their books are their statements. They never see the bank's cards, so naturally the thing can go on a long time before it's found out, and when it's found out, it's most likely to be by accident, like this was, because Brent didn't figure on his trip to the hospital.

Well, what Brent had done was fix up a cover for himself with all this stuff about putting it on a personal basis, so no savings depositor that came in the bank would ever deal with anybody but him. That ought to have made George Mason suspicious, but Brent was getting the business in, and you don't quarrel with a guy that's doing good. When he got that part the way he wanted it, with him the only one that ever touched the savings file, and the depositors dealing only with him, he went about it exactly the way they all go about it. He picked accounts where he knew he wouldn't be likely to run into trouble, and he'd make out a false withdrawal slip, generally for somewhere around fifty bucks. He'd sign the depositor's name to it, just forge it, but he didn't have to be very good at that part, because nobody passed on those signatures but himself. Then he'd put fifty bucks in his pocket, and of course the false withdrawal slip would balance his cash. Our card had to balance too, of course, so he'd enter the withdrawal on that, but beside each false entry he'd make that little light pencil check that I had caught, and that would tell him what the right balance ought to be, in case the depositor made some inquiry.

Well, how were you going to get that money put back, so the daily cash would balance, so the cards would balance, and so the passbooks would balance, and at the same time leave it so nothing would show later, when the auditors came around? It had me stumped, and I don't mind telling you for a while I began to get cold feet. What I wanted to do was report it, as

Money and the Woman (The Embezzler)

was, let Sheila fork up the dough, without saying where she got it, and let Brent get fired and go look himself up a job. It didn't look like they would do much to him, if the money was put back. But she wouldn't hear of that. She was afraid they might send him up anyway, and then I would be putting up the money all for nothing, her children would have to grow up under the disgrace, and where we would be was nowhere. There wasn't much I could say to that. I figured they would probably let him off, but I couldn't be sure.

It was Sheila that figured out the way. We were riding along one night, just one or two nights after I told her I was going to put up the dough myself, when she began to talk. "The cards, the cash, and the passbooks, is that it?"

"That's all."

"The cards and the cash are easy."

"Oh yeah?"

"That money goes back the same way it came out. Only instead of false withdrawals, I make out false deposits. The cash balances, the posting balances, and the card balances."

"And the passbooks don't balance. Listen. If there's only one passbook—just one—that can tell on us after you're out of there, and I'm out, we're sunk. The only chance we've got is that the thing is never suspected at all—that no question is ever raised. And, what's more, we don't dare make a move till we see every one of the passbooks on those phoney accounts. We think we've got his code, how he ticked his false withdrawals, but we can't be sure, and maybe he didn't tick them all. Unless we can make a clean job of this, I don't touch it. Him going to jail is one thing. All three of us going, and me losing my job and nine thousand bucks—oh no."

"All right then, the passbooks."

"That's it—the passbooks."

"Now when a passbook gets filled up, or there's some mistake on it, what do we do?"

"Give him a new one, don't we?"

"Containing how many entries?"

"One, I suppose. His total as of that date."

"That's right. And that one entry tells no tales. It checks with the card, and there's not one figure to check against all those back entries—withdrawals and deposits and so on, running back for years. All right, then; so far, perfect. Now what do we do with his old book? Regularly, I mean."

"Well—what *do* we do with it?"

"We put it under a punch, the punch that goes through every page and marks it void, and give it back to him."

"And then he's got it—any time an auditor calls for it. Gee, that's a big help."

"But if he doesn't want it?"

"What are you getting at?"

"If he doesn't want it, we destroy it. It's no good to us, is it? And it's not ours, it's his. But he doesn't want it."

"Are you *sure* we destroy it?"

"I've torn up a thousand of them. . . . And that's just what we're going to do now. Between now and the next check on my cash, we're going to get all those books in. First we check totals, to know exactly where we're at. Then the depositor gets a new book that tells no tales."

"Why does he get a new book?"

"He didn't notice it when he brought the old one in, but the stitching is awfully strained, and it's almost falling apart. Or I've accidentally smeared lipstick on it. Or I just think it's time he got one of our nice new books, for luck. So he gets a new book with one entry in it—just his total, that's all. Then I say: 'You don't want this, do you?' And the way I'll say it, that old book seems positively *contaminated*. And then right in front of his eyes, as though it's the way we do it every day, I'll tear it up, and drop it in the wastebasket."

"Suppose he *does* want it?"

"Then I'll put it under the punch, and give it to him. But somehow that punch is going to make its neat little holes in the exact place where the footings are, and it's going to be impossible for him, or an auditor, or anybody else, to read those figures. I'll punch five or six times, you know, and his book will be like Swiss cheese, more holes than anything else."

"And all the time you're getting those holes in exactly the right place, he's going to be on the other side of the window looking at you, wondering what all the hocus-pocus is about."

"Oh no—it won't take more than a second or two. You see, I've been practicing. I can do it in a jiffy. . . . But he won't want that book back. Trust me. I know how to do it."

There was just a little note of pleading on that, as she said it. I had to think it over. I did think it over, for quite a while, and I began to have the feeling that on her end of it, if that was all, she could put it over all right. But then something else began to bother me. "How many of these doctored accounts are there?"

"Forty-seven."

"And how are you going to get those passbooks in?"

"Well, interest is due on them. I thought I could send out little printed slips—signed 'per Sheila Brent,' in ink, so they'd be sure to come to me about it—asking them to bring in their books for interest credits. I never saw anybody that wouldn't bring in his book if it meant a dollar and twenty-two cents. And a printed slip looks perfectly open and aboveboard, doesn't it?"

"Yeah, a printed slip is about the most harmless, open, and aboveboard thing there is. But this is what I'm thinking: You send out your printed slips, and within a couple of days all those books come in, and you can't hold them forever. You've got to hand them back—or the new ones they're going to get —or somebody's going to get suspicious. That means the money's got to be put back all at once. That's going to make one awful bulge in your cash. Everybody in the bank is going to wonder at the reason for it, because it's going to show in the posting."

"I've thought of that. I don't have to send out all those slips at once. I can send out four or five a day. And then, even if they do come in bunches—the passbooks I mean—I can issue the new books, right away as the old ones are presented, but make the adjustments on the cards and in my cash little by little—three or four hundred dollars a day. That's not much."

"No, but while that's going on, we're completely defenseless. We've got our chins hanging out and no way in the world of putting up a guard. I mean, while you're holding out those adjustment entries, so you can edge them in gradually, your cash doesn't balance the books. If then something happened—so I had to call for a cash audit on the spot, or if I got called away to the home office for a couple of days, or something happened to you, so you couldn't come to work—then watch that ship go out of water. You may get away with it. But it'll have to be done, everything squared up, before the next check on your cash. That's twenty-one days from now. And at that, a three- or four-hundred-dollar bulge in your cash every day is going to look mighty funny. In the bank, I mean."

"I could gag it off. I could say I'm keeping after them, to keep their deposits up, the way Charles always did. I don't think there's any danger. The cash will be there."

So that was how we did it. She had the slips printed, and began mailing them out, three or four at a time. For the first few days' replacement, the cash replacement I mean, I had enough in my own checking account. For the rest, I had to go out and plaster my house. For that I went to the Federal people. It took about a week, and I had to start an outside account, so nobody in the bank would know what I was up to. I took eight thousand bucks, and if you don't think that hurt, you never plastered your house. Of course, it would be our luck that when the first of those books came in, she was out to lunch, and I was on the window myself. I took in the book, and receipted for it, but Church was only three or four feet away, running a column on one of the adding machines. She heard what I said to the depositor, and was at my elbow before I even knew how she got there.

"I can do that for you, Mr. Bennett. I'll only be a minute, and there'll be no need for him to leave his book."

"Well—I'd rather Mrs. Brent handled it."

"Oh, *very* well, then."

She switched away then, in a huff, and I could feel the sweat in the palms of my hands. That night I warned Sheila. "That Church can bust it up."

"How?"

"Her damned apple-polishing. She horned in today, wanted to balance that book for me. I had to chase her."

"Leave her to me."

"For God's sake, don't let her suspect anything."

"I won't, don't worry."

From then on, we made a kind of routine out of it. She'd get in three or four books, ask the depositors to leave them with her till next day. She'd make out new cards, and tell me the exact amount she needed, that night. I'd hand her that much in cash. Next day, she'd slip it into her cash box, make out new cards for the depositors, slip them in the file, then make out new passbooks and have them ready when the depositors called. Every day we'd be that much nearer home, both praying that nothing would tip it before we got the whole replacement made. Most days I'd say we plugged about $400 into the cash, one or two days a little more.

One night, maybe a week after we started putting the money back, they had the big dinner dance for the whole organization. I guess about a thousand people were there, in the main ballroom of one of the Los Angeles hotels, and it was a pretty nice get-together. They don't make a pep meeting out of it. The Old Man doesn't like that kind of thing. He just has a kind of a family gathering, makes them a little speech, and then the dancing starts, and he stands around watching them enjoy themselves. I guess you've heard of A. R. Ferguson. He's founder of the bank, and the minute you look at him you know he's a big shot. He's not tall, but he's straight and stocky, with a little white moustache that makes him look like some kind of a military man.

Well, we all had to go, of course. I sat at the table with the others from the branch, Miss Church, and Helm, and Snelling, and Snelling's wife, and Sheila. I made it a point not to sit with Sheila. I was afraid to. So after the banquet, when the dancing started, I went over to shake hands with the Old Man. He always treated me fine, just like he treats everybody. He's got that natural courtesy that no little guy ever quite seems capable of. He asked how I was, and then: "How much longer do you think you'll be out there in Glendale? Are you nearly done?"

An icy feeling began to go over me. If he yanked me now, and returned me to the home office, there went all chance of covering that shortage, and God only knew what they would find out, if it was half covered and half not.

"Why, I tell you, Mr. Ferguson, if you can possibly arrange it, I'd like to stay out there till after the first of the month."

". . . So long?"

"Well, I've found some things out there that are well worth making a thorough study of, it seems to me. Fact of the matter, I had thought of writing an article about them in addition to my report. I thought I'd send it to the *American Banker*, and if I could have a little more time—"

"In that case, take all the time you want."

"I thought it wouldn't hurt us any."

"I only wish more of our officials would write."

"Gives us a little prestige."

"—and makes them *think*!"

My mouth did it all. I was standing behind it, not knowing what was coming out from one minute to the next. I hadn't thought of any article, up to that very second, and I give you one guess how I felt. I felt like a heel, and all the worse on account of the fine way he treated me. We stood there a few minutes, he telling me how he was leaving for Honolulu the next day, but he'd be back within the month, and looked forward to reading what I had to say as soon as he came back. Then he motioned in the direction of the dance floor. "Who's the girl in blue?"

"Mrs. Brent."

"Oh yes, I want to speak to her."

We did some broken-floor dodging, and got over to where Sheila was dancing with Helm. They stopped, and I introduced the Old Man, and he asked how Brent was coming along after the operation, and then cut in on Helm, and danced Sheila off. I wasn't in much of a humor when I met her outside later and took her home. "What's the matter, Dave?"

"Couldn't quite look the Old Man in the eye, that's all."

"Have you got cold feet?"

"Just feeling the strain."

"If you have got cold feet, and want to quit, there's nothing I can say. Nothing at all."

"All I got to say is I'll be glad when we're clear of that heel, and can kick him out of the bank and out of our lives."

"In two weeks it'll be done."

"How is he?"

"He's leaving the hospital Saturday."

"That's nice."

"He's not coming home yet. The doctor insists that he go up to Arrowhead to get his strength back. He'll be there three or four weeks. He has friends there."

"What have you told him, by the way?"

"Nothing."

"Just nothing?"

"Not one word."

"He had an ulcer, is that what you said?"

"Yes."

"I was reading in a medical magazine the other day what causes it. Do you know what it is?"

"No."

"Worry."

"So?"

"It might help the recuperating process if he knew it was O.K. about the shortage. Lying in a hospital, with a thing like that staring you in the face, that may not be so good. For his health anyway."

"What am I to tell him?"

"Why, I don't know. That you've fixed it up."

"If I tell him I've fixed it up, so nobody is going to know it, he knows I've got some kind of assistance in the bank. That'll terrify him, and I don't know what he's likely to do about it. He may speak to somebody, and the whole thing will come out. And who am I going to say has let me have the money, so I can put it back? You?"

"Do you have to say?"

"No. I don't have to say anything at all, and I'm not going to. The less you're involved in this the better. If he worries, he ought to be used to it by now. It won't hurt that young man to do quite a little suffering over what he's done to me—and to you."

"It's up to you."

"He knows something's cooking, all right, but he doesn't know what. I look forward to seeing his face when I tell him I'm off to—where did you say?"

". . . I said Reno."

"Do you still say Reno?"

"I don't generally change my mind, once it's made up."

"You can, if you want to."

"Shut up."

"I don't want you to."

"Neither do I."

VI

We kept putting the money back, and I kept getting jitterier every day. I kept worrying that something would happen, that maybe the Old Man hadn't left a memo about me before he went away, and that I'd get a call to report to the home office; that maybe Sheila would get sick and somebody else would have to do her work; that some depositor might think it was funny, the slip he had got to bring his book in, and begin asking about it somewhere.

One day she asked me to drive her home from the bank. By that time I was so nervous I never went anywhere with her in the daytime, and even at night I never met her anywhere that somebody might see us. But she said one of the children was sick, and she wanted a ride in case she had to get stuff from the drugstore that the doctor had ordered, and that anyway nobody was there but the maid and she didn't matter. By that time Brent had gone to the lake, to get his strength back, and she had the house to herself.

So I went. It was the first time I'd ever been in her home, and it was fixed up nice, and smelled like her, and the kids were the sweetest little pair you ever saw. The oldest was named Anna, and the younger was named Charlotte. She was the one that was sick. She was in bed with a cold, and took it like a little soldier. Another time, it would have tickled me to death to sit and watch her boss Sheila around, and watch Sheila wait on her, and take the bossing just like that was how it ought to be. But now I couldn't even keep still that long. When I found out I wasn't needed I ducked, and went home and filled up some more paper with the phoney article I had to have ready for the Old Man when he got back. It was called, "Building a Strong Savings Department."

We got to the last day before the monthly check on cash. Six hundred dollars had to go into her box that day, over and above the regular day's receipts. It was a lot, but it was a

Wednesday, the day the factories all around us paid off, and deposits were sure to be heavy, so it looked like we could get away with it. We had all the passbooks in. It had taken some strong-arm work to get the last three we needed, and what she had done was go to those people the night before, like Brent had always done, and ask where they'd been, and why they hadn't put anything on savings. By sitting around a few minutes she managed to get their books, and then I drove her over to my place and we checked it all up. Then I gave her the cash she needed, and it looked like she was set.

But I kept wanting to know how she stood, whether it had all gone through like we hoped. I couldn't catch her eye and I couldn't get a word with her. They were lined up at her window four and five deep all day long, and she didn't go out to lunch. She had sandwiches and milk sent in. On Wednesday they send out two extra tellers from the home office, to help handle the extra business, and every time one of them would go to her for help on something, and she'd have to leave her window for a minute, I'd feel the sweat on the palms of my hands, and lose track of what I was doing. I'm telling you it was a long day.

Along about two-thirty, though, it slacked off, and by five minutes to three there was nobody in there, and at three sharp Adler, the guard, locked the door. We went on finishing up. The home office tellers got through first, because all they had to do was balance one day's deposits, and around three-thirty they turned in their sheets, asked me to give them a count, and left. I sat at my desk, staring at papers, doing anything to keep from marching around and tip it that I had something on my mind.

Around quarter to four there came a tap on the glass, and I didn't look up. There's always that late depositor trying to get in, and if he catches your eye you're sunk. I went right on staring at my papers, but I heard Adler open and then who should be there but Brent, with a grin on his face, a satchel in

Money and the Woman (The Embezzler)

one hand, and a heavy coat of sunburn all over him. There was a chorus of "Hey's," and they all went out to shake hands, all except Sheila, and ask him how he was, and when he was coming back to work. He said he'd got home last night, and would be back any time now. There didn't seem to be much I could do but shake hands too, so I gritted my teeth and did it, but I didn't ask him when he was coming back to work.

Then he said he'd come in for some of his stuff, and on his way back to the lockers he spoke to Sheila, and she spoke, without looking up. Then the rest of them went back to work.

"Gee, he sure looks good, don't he?"

"Different from when he left."

"He must have put on twenty pounds."

"They fixed him up all right."

Pretty soon he came out again, closing his grip, and there was some more talk, and he went. They all counted their cash, turned in their sheets, and put their cash boxes into the vault. Helm wheeled the trucks in, with the records on them, and then he went. Snelling went back to set the time lock.

That was when Church started some more of her apple-polishing. She was about as unappetizing a girl as I ever saw. She was thick, and dumpy, with a delivery like she was making a speech all the time. She sounded like a dietician demonstrating a range in a department store basement, and she started in on a wonderful new adding machine that had just come on the market, and didn't I think we ought to have one. I said it sounded good, but I wanted to think it over. So then she said it all over again, and just about when she got going good she gave a little squeal and began pointing at the floor.

Down there was about the evilest-looking thing you ever saw in your life. It was one of these ground spiders you see out here in California, about the size of a tarantula and just about as dangerous. It was about three inches long, I would say, and was walking toward me with a clumsy gait but getting there all the time. I raised my foot to step on it, and she gave another squeal and said if I squashed it she'd die. By that time they were all standing around—Snelling, Sheila, and Adler. Snelling said get a piece of paper and throw it out the door, and Sheila said yes, for heaven's sake do something about it quick. Adler took a piece of paper off my desk, and rolled it into a funnel, and then took a pen and pushed the thing into the paper. Then he folded the funnel shut and we all went out and watched him dump the spider into the gutter. Then a cop came along and borrowed the funnel and caught it again and said he was going to take it home to his wife, so they could take pictures of it with their home movie camera.

We went back in the bank, and Snelling and I closed the vault, and he went. Church went. Adler went back for his last tour around before closing. That left me alone with Sheila. I stepped back to where she was by the lockers, looking in the mirror while she put on her hat. "Well?"

"It's all done."

"You put back the cash."

"To the last cent."

"The cards are all in?"

"It all checks to the last decimal point."

That was what I'd been praying for, for the last month, and yet as soon as I had it, it took me about one-fifth of a second to get sore, about Brent.

"Is he driving you home?"

"If so, he didn't mention it."

"Suppose you wait in my car. There's a couple of things I want to talk to you about. It's just across the street."

She went, and Adler changed into his street clothes, and he and I locked up, and I bounced over to the car. I didn't head for her house, I headed for mine, but I didn't wait till we got there before I opened up.

"Why didn't you tell me he was back?"

"Were you interested?"

"Yeah, plenty."

"Well, since you ask me, I didn't know he was back—when I left you last night. He was there waiting for me when I got in. Today, I haven't had one minute to talk to you, or anybody."

"I thought he was due to spend a month up there."

"So did I."

"Then what's he doing back?"

"I haven't the faintest idea. Trying to find out what's going to happen to him, perhaps. Tomorrow, you may recall, you'll check the cash, and he knows it. That may account for why he cut his recuperation short."

"Are you sure he didn't have a date with you, now he's feeling better? To be waiting for you after you said goodnight to me?"

"I stayed with the children, if that's what you mean."

I don't know if I believed any of that or not. I think I told you I was nuts about her, and all the money she'd cost me, and all the trouble she'd brought, only seemed to make it worse. The idea that she'd spent a night in the same house with him, and hadn't said anything to me about it, left me with a prickly feeling all over. Since I'd been going around with her, it was the first time that part of it had come up. He'd been in the hospital, and from there he'd gone right up to the lake, so in a way up to then he hadn't seemed real. But he seemed real now, all right, and I was still as sore as a bear when we got to my house, and went in. Sam lit the fire, and she sat down, but I didn't. I kept marching around the room, and she smoked, and watched me.

"All right, this guy's got to be told."

"He will be."

"He's got to be told *everything*."

"Dave, he'll be told, he'll be told everything, and a little more even than you know he's going to be told—when I'm ready to tell him."

"What's the matter with now?"

"I'm not equal to it."

"What's that—a stall?"

"Will you sit down for a moment?"

"All right, I'm sitting."

"Here—beside me."

I moved over beside her, and she took my hand and looked me in the eyes. "Dave, have you forgotten something?"

"Not that I know of."

"I think you have. . . . I think you've forgotten that today we finished what we started to do. That, thanks to you, I don't have to lie awake every night staring at the ceiling, wondering whether my father is going to be ruined, my children are going to be ruined—to say nothing of myself. That you've done something for me that was so dangerous to you I hate to think what would have happened if something had gone wrong. It would have wrecked your career, and it's such a nice, promising career. But it wasn't wrong, Dave. It was wonderfully right. It was decenter than any man I know of would have done, would even have thought of doing. And now it's done. There's not one card, one comma, one missing penny to show—and I can sleep, Dave. That's all that matters to me today."

"O.K.—then you're leaving him."

"Of course I am, but—"

"You're leaving him tonight. You're coming in here, with your two kids, and if that bothers you, then I'll move out. We're going over there now, and—"

"We're doing nothing of the kind."

"I'm telling you—"

"And I'm telling *you*! Do you think I'm going over there now, and starting a quarrel that's going to last until three o'clock in the morning and maybe until dawn? That's going to wander all over the earth, from how horribly he says I've treated him to who's going to have the children—the way I feel now? I certainly shall not. When I'm ready, when I know exactly what I'm going to say, when I've got the children safely over to my father's, when it's all planned and I can do it in one terrible half hour—then I'll do it. In the meantime, if he's biting his fingernails, if he's frightened to death over what's going to happen to him—that's perfectly all right with me. A little of that won't hurt him. When it's all done, then I go at once to Reno, if you still want me to, and then my life can go on. . . . Don't you know what I'm trying to tell you, Dave? What you're worried about just couldn't happen. Why—he hasn't even looked at me that way in over a year. Dave, tonight I want to be happy. With you. That's all."

I felt ashamed of myself at that, and took her in my arms, and that catch came in my throat again when she sighed, like some child, and relaxed, and closed her eyes.

"Sheila?"
"Yes?"
"We'll celebrate."
"All right."

So we celebrated. She phoned her maid, and said she'd be late, and we went to dinner at a downtown restaurant, and then we drove to a night club on Sunset Boulevard. We didn't talk about Brent, or the shortage, or anything but ourselves, and what we were going to do with our lives together. We stayed till about one o'clock. I didn't think of Brent again till we pulled up near her house, and then this same prickly feeling began to come over me. If she noticed anything she didn't say so. She kissed me good-night, and I started home.

VII

I turned in the drive, put the car away, closed the garage, and walked around to go in the front way. When I started for the door I heard my name called. Somebody got up from a bench under the trees and walked over. It was Helm. "Sorry to be bothering you this hour of night, Mr. Bennett, but I've got to talk to you."

"Well, come in."

He seemed nervous as I took him inside. I offered him a drink, but he said he didn't want anything. He sat down and lit a cigarette, and acted like he didn't know how to begin. Then: "Have you seen Sheila?"

". . . Why?"

"I saw you drive off with her."

"Yes—I had some business with her. We had dinner together. I—just left her a little while ago."

"Did you see Brent?"

"No. It was late. I didn't go in."

"She say anything about him?"

"I guess so. Now and then. . . . What's this about?"

"Did you see him leave the bank? Today?"

"He left before you did."

"Did you see him leave the second time?"

". . . He only came in once."

He kept looking at me, smoking and looking at me. He was a young fellow, twenty-four or -five, I would say, and had only been with us a couple of years. Little by little he was losing his nervousness at talking with me.

". . . He went in there twice."

"He came in once. He rapped on the door, Adler let him in, he stood there talking a few minutes, then he went back to get some stuff out of his locker. Then he left. You were there. Except for the extra tellers, nobody had finished up yet. He must have left fifteen minutes before you did."

"That's right. Then I left. I finished up, put my cash box away, and left. I went over to the drugstore to get myself a malted milk, and was sitting there drinking it when he went in."

"He couldn't have. We were locked, and—"

"He used a key."

"... When was this?"

"A little after four. Couple of minutes before you all come out with that spider and dumped it in the gutter."

"So?"

"I didn't see him come out."

"Why didn't you tell me?"

"I haven't seen you. I've been looking for you."

"You saw me drive off with Sheila."

"Yeah, but it hadn't occurred to me, at the time. That cop, after he caught the spider, came in the drugstore to buy some film for his camera. I helped him put the spider in an ice-cream container, and punch holes in the top, and I wasn't watching the bank all that time. Later, it just happened to run through my head that I'd seen all the rest of you leave the bank, but I hadn't seen Brent. I kept telling myself to forget it, that I'd got a case of nerves from being around money too much, but then—"

"Yeah? What else?"

"I went to a picture tonight with the Snellings."

"Didn't Snelling see him leave?"

"I didn't say anything to Snelling. I don't know what he saw. But the picture had some Mexican stuff in it, and later, when we went to the Snellings' apartment, I started a bum argument, and got Snelling to call Charlie to settle it. Brent spent some time in Mexico once. That was about twelve o'clock."

"And?"

"The maid answered. Charlie wasn't there."

We looked at each other, and both knew that twelve o'clock was too late for a guy to be out that had just had a bad operation.

"Come on."

"You calling Sheila?"

"We're going to the bank."

The protection service watchman was due on the hour,

and we caught him on his two o'clock round. He took it as a personal insult that we would think anybody could be in the bank without him knowing it, but I made him take us in there just the same, and we went through every part of it. We went upstairs, where the old records were stored, and I looked behind every pile. We went down in the basement and I looked behind every gas furnace. We went all around back of the windows and I looked under every counter. I even looked behind my desk, and under it. That seemed to be all. The watchman went up and punched his clock and we went out on the street again. Helm kind of fingered his chin.

"Well, I guess it was a false alarm."

"Looks like it."

"Sorry."

"It's all right. Report everything."

"Guess there's no use calling Sheila."

"Pretty late, I'm afraid."

What he meant was, we ought to call Sheila, but he wanted me to do it. He was just as suspicious as he ever was, I could tell that from the way he was acting. Only the watchman was sure we were a couple of nuts. We got in the car, and I took him home, and once more he mumbled something about Sheila, but I decided not to hear him. When I let him out I started for home, but as soon as I was out of sight I cut around the block and headed for Mountain Drive.

A light was on, and the screen door opened as soon as I set my foot on the porch. She was still dressed, and it was almost as though she had been expecting me. I followed her in the living room, and spoke low so nobody in the house could hear us, but I didn't waste any time on love and kisses.

"Where's Brent?"

"... He's in the vault."

She spoke in a whisper, and sank into a chair without looking at me, but every doubt I'd had about her in the beginning, I mean, every hunch that she'd been playing me for a sucker, swept back over me so even looking at her made me tremble. I had to lick my lips a couple of times before I could even talk. "Funny you didn't tell me."

"I didn't know it."

"What do you mean you didn't know it? If you know it now, why didn't you know it then? You trying to tell me he stepped out of there for a couple of minutes, borrowed my telephone, and called you up? He might as well be in a tomb as be in that place, till it opens at eight-thirty this morning."

"Are you done?"

"I'm still asking you why you didn't tell me."

"When I got in, and found he wasn't home, I went out looking for him. Or at any rate, for the car. I went to where he generally parks it—when he's out. It wasn't there. Coming home I had to go by the bank. As I went by, the red light winked, just once."

I don't know if you know how a vault works. There's two switches inside. One lights the overhead stuff that you turn on when somebody wants to get into his safe deposit box; the other works the red light that's always on over the door in the daytime. That's the danger signal, and any employee of the bank always looks to see that it's on whenever he goes inside. When the vault is closed the light's turned off, and I had turned it off myself that afternoon, when I locked the vault with Snelling. At night, all curtains are raised in the bank, so cops, watchman, and passersby can see inside. If the red light went on, it would show, but I didn't believe she'd seen it. I didn't believe she'd even been by the bank. "So the red light winked, hey? Funny it wasn't winking when I left there not ten minutes ago."

"I said it winked once. I don't think it was a signal. I think he bumped his shoulder against it, by accident. If he were signaling, he'd keep on winking it, wouldn't he?"

"How'd he get in there?"

"I don't know."

"I think you do know."

"I don't know, but the only way I can think of is that he slipped in there while we were all gathered around, looking at that spider."

"That you conveniently on purpose brought in there."

"Or that he did."

"What's he doing in there?"

"I don't know."

"Come on, come on, quit stalling me!"

She got up and began walking around. "Dave, it's easy to see you think I know all about this. That I know more than I'm telling. That Charles and I are in some kind of plot. I don't know anything I can say. I know a lot I could say if I wasn't—"

She stopped, came to life like some kind of a tiger, and began hammering her fists against the wall.

"—bought! That was what was wrong! I ought to have cut my heart out, suffered anything rather than let you give me that money! Why did I ever take it? Why didn't I tell you to—"

"Why didn't you do what I begged you to do? Come over here today and let him have it between the eyes—tell him the truth, that you were through, and this was the end of it?"

"Because, God help me, I wanted to be happy!"

"No! . . . Because, God help you, you knew he wasn't over here! Because you knew he was in that vault, and you were afraid I'd find it out!"

"It isn't true! How can you say that?"

"Do you know what I think? I think you took that money off me, day by day, and that not one penny of it ever found its way into your cash box. And then I think you and he decided on a little phoney hold-up, to cover that shortage, and that that's what he's doing in the vault. And if Helm hadn't got into it, and noticed that Brent didn't come out of the bank the second time he went in, I don't see anything that was to stop you from getting away with it. You knew I didn't dare open my trap about the dough *I* had put up. And if he came out of there masked, and made a quick getaway, I don't know who was going to swear it was him, if it hadn't been for Helm. Now it's in the soup. All right, Mrs. Brent, that vault that don't take any messages till eight-thirty, that works both ways. If he can't get any word to you, you can't get any word to him. Just let him start that little game that looked so good yesterday afternoon, and he's going to get the surprise of his life, and so are you. There'll be a reception committee waiting for him when he comes out of there, and maybe they'll include you in it too."

She looked straight at me the whole time I was talking, and the lamplight caught her eyes, so they shot fire. There was something catlike about her shape anyway, and with her eyes blazing like that, she looked like something out of the jungle. But all of a sudden that woman was gone, and she was crumpled up in front of me, on the sofa, crying in a queer, jerky way. Then I hated myself for what I had said, and had to dig in with my fingernails to keep from crying too.

After a while the phone rang. From what she said, I could tell it was her father, and that he'd been trying to reach her all afternoon and all night. She listened a long time, and when she hung up she lay back and closed her eyes. "He's in there to put the money back."

". . . Where'd he get it?"

"He got it this morning. Yesterday morning. From my father."

"Your father had that much—*ready*?"

"He got it after I talked to him that night. Then when I told him I wouldn't need it, he kept it, in his safe deposit box— just in case. Charles went over there yesterday and said he had to have it—against the check-up on my cash. Papa went down to the Westwood bank with him, and got it out, and gave it to him. He was afraid to call me at the bank. He kept trying to reach me here. The maid left me a note, but it was so late when I got in I didn't call. . . . So, now I pay a price for not telling him. Charles, I mean. For letting him worry."

"I was for telling him, you may remember."

"Yes, I remember."

It was quite a while after that before either of us said anything. All that time my mind was going around like a squirrel cage, trying to reconstruct for myself what was going on in that vault. She must have been doing the same thing, because pretty soon she said, "Dave?"

"Yes?"

"Suppose he *does* put the money back?"

"Then—we're sunk."

"What, actually, will happen?"

"If I find him in there, the least I can do is hold him till I've checked every cent in that vault. I find nine thousand more cash than the books show. All right. What then?"

"You mean the whole thing comes out?"

"On what we've been doing, you can get away with it as long as nobody's got the least suspicion of it. Let a thing like this happen, let them really begin to check, and it'll come out so fast it'll make your head swim."

"And there goes your job?"

"Suppose you were the home office, how would you like it?"

". . . I've brought you nothing but misery, Dave."

"I—asked for it."

"I can understand why you feel bitter."

"I said some things I didn't mean."

"Dave."

"Yes?"

"There's one chance, if you'll take it."

"What's that?"

"Charles."

"I don't get it."

"It may be a blessing, after all, that I told him nothing. He can't be sure what I've done while he's been away—whether I carried his false entries right along, whether I corrected them, and left the cash short—and it does look as though he'd check, before he did anything. He's a wizard at books, you know. And every record he needs is in there. Do you know what I'm getting at, Dave?"

"Not quite."

"You'll have to play dummy's hand, and let him lead."

"I don't want anything to do with him."

"I'd like to wring his neck. But if you just don't force things, if you just act natural, and let me have a few seconds with him, so we'll know just what he *has* done, then—maybe it'll all come out all right. He certainly would be a boob to put the money back when he finds out it's already been put back."

"*Has* it been?"

"Don't you know?"

I took her in my arms then, and for that long was able to forget what was staring us in the face, and I still felt close to her when I left.

VIII

For the second time that night I went home, and this time I turned out all the lights, and went upstairs, and took off my clothes, and went to bed. I tried to sleep, and couldn't. It was all running through my mind, and especially what I was going to do when I opened that vault at eight-thirty. How could I act natural about it? If I could guess he was in the vault, Helm must have guessed it. He'd be watching me, waiting for every move, and he'd be doing that even if he didn't have any suspicion of me, which by now he must have, on account of being out that late with Sheila. All that ran through my mind, and after a while I'd figured a way to cover it, by openly saying something to him, and telling him I was going to go along with it, just wait and see what Brent had to say for himself, in case he was really in there. Then I tried once more to go to sleep. But this time it wasn't the play at the vault that was bothering me, it was Sheila. I kept going over and over it, what was said between us, the dirty cracks I had made, how she had taken them, and all the rest of it. Just as day began to break I found myself sitting up in bed. How I knew it I don't know, what I had to go on I haven't any idea, but I knew perfectly well that she was holding out on me, that there was something back of it all that she wasn't telling.

I unhooked the phone and dialed. You don't stay around a bank very long before you know the number of your chief guard. I was calling Dyer, and in a minute or two he answered, pretty sour. "Hello?"

"Dyer?"

"Yeah, who is it?"

"Sorry to wake you up. This is Dave Bennett."

"What do you want?"

"I want some help."

"Well, what the hell is it?"

"I got reason to think there's a man in our vault. Out in the Anita Avenue branch in Glendale. What he's up to I don't know, but I want you out there when I open up. And I'd like you to bring a couple of men with you."

Up to then he'd been just a sleepy guy that used to be a city detective. Now he snapped out of it like something had hit him. "What do you mean you got reason to think? Who is this guy?"

"I'll give you that part when I see you. Can you meet me by seven o'clock? Is that too early?"

"Whenever you say, Mr. Bennett."

"Then be at my house at seven, and bring your men with you. I'll give you the dope, and I'll tell you how I want you to do it."

He took the address, and I went back to bed.

I went to bed, and lay there trying to figure out what it was I wanted him to do anyway. After a while I had it straightened out. I wanted him close enough to protect the bank, and myself as well, in case Sheila was lying to me, and I wanted him far enough away for her to have those few seconds with Brent, in case she wasn't. I mean, if Brent was really up to something, I wanted him covered every way there was, and by guys that would shoot. But if he came out with a foolish look on his face, and pretended he'd been locked in by mistake, and she found out we could still cover up that book-doctoring, I wanted to leave that open too. I figured on it, and after a while I thought I had it doped out so it would work.

Around six o'clock I got up, bathed, shaved, and dressed. I routed out Sam and had him make me some coffee, and fix up some bacon and eggs. I told him to stand by in case the men that were coming hadn't had any breakfast. Then I went in the living room and began to march around it. It was cold. I lit the fire. My head kept spinning around.

Right on the tick of seven the doorbell rang and there they were, Dyer and his two mugs. Dyer's a tall, thin man with a bony face and eyes like gimlets. I'd say he was around fifty. The other two were around my own age, somewhere over thirty, with big shoulders, thick necks, and red faces. They looked exactly like what they were: ex-cops that had got jobs as guards in a bank. One was named Halligan, the other Lewis. They all said yes on breakfast, so we went in the dining room and Sam made it pretty quick with the service.

I gave it to Dyer, as quick as I could, about Brent being off for a couple of months, with his operation, and how he'd come in yesterday to get his stuff, and Helm had seen him go in the bank a second time, and not come out, and how Sheila had gone out looking for him late at night, and thought she saw the red light flash. I had to tell him that much, to protect myself afterward, because God only knew what was going to come out, and I didn't even feel I was safe on Sheila's end of it. I didn't say anything about the shortage, or Sheila's father, or any of that part. I told what I had to tell, and made it short.

"Now what I figure is, Brent got in there somehow just before we closed it up, maybe just looking around, and that he got locked in there by accident. However, I can't be sure. Maybe—it doesn't seem very likely—he's up to something. So what I'd like you guys to do is to be outside, just be where you can see what's going on. If it's all quiet, I'll give you the word, and you can go on home. If anything happens, you're there. Of course, a man spends a night in a vault, he may not feel so good by morning. We may need an ambulance. If so, I'll let you know."

I breathed a little easier. It had sounded all right, and Dyer kept on wolfing down his toast and eggs. When they were gone he put sugar and cream in his coffee, stirred it around, and lit a cigarette. "Well—that's how you got it figured out."

"I imagine I'm not far off."

"All I got to say, you got a trusting disposition."

"What do you make of it?"

"This guy's a regular employee, you say?"

"He's been head teller."

"Then he *couldn't* get locked in by mistake. He couldn't no more do that than a doctor could sew himself up in a man's belly by mistake. Furthermore, you couldn't lock him in by mistake. You take all the usual care, don't you, when you lock a vault?"

"I think so."

"And you done it regular, yesterday?"

"As well as I can recall."

"You looked around in there?"

"Yes, of course."

"And you didn't see nothing?"

"No, certainly not."

Money and the Woman (The Embezzler)

"Then he's in there on purpose."

The other two nodded, and looked at me like I must not be very bright.

Dyer went on: "It's possible for a man to hide hisself in a vault. I've thought of it, many a time, how it could be done. You think of a lot of things in my business. Once them trucks are wheeled in, with the records on them, if he once got in without being seen, he could stoop down behind them, and keep quiet, and when you come to close up you wouldn't see him. But not by accident. Never."

I was feeling funny in the stomach. I had to take a tack I didn't like.

"Of course, there's a human element in it. There's nothing in this man's record that gives any ground whatever for thinking he'd pull anything. Fact of the matter, that's what I'm doing in the branch. I was sent out there to study his methods in the savings department. I've been so much impressed by his work that I'm going to write an article about it."

"When did he get in there, do you think?"

"Well, we found a spider. A big one."

"One of them bad dreams with fur all over them?"

"That's it. And we were all gathered around looking at it. And arguing about how to get it out of there. I imagine he was standing there looking at it too. We all went out to throw it in the street, and he must have gone in the vault. Perhaps just looking around. Perhaps to open his box, I don't know. And— was in there when I closed it up."

"That don't hit you funny?"

"Not particularly."

"If you wanted to get everybody in one place in that bank, and everybody looking in one direction, so you could slip in the vault, you couldn't think of nothing better than one of them spiders, could you? Unless it was a rattlesnake."

"That strikes me as a little farfetched."

"Not if he's just back from the mountains. From Lake Arrowhead, I think you said. That's where they have them spiders. I never seen one around Glendale. If he happened to turn that spider loose the first time he come in, all he had to do was wait till you found it, and he could easy slip in."

"He'd be running an awful risk."

"No risk. Suppose you seen him? He was looking at the spider too, wasn't he? He come in with his key to see what all the fuss was about. Thought maybe there was trouble . . . Mr. Bennett, I'm telling you, he's not locked in by accident. It couldn't happen."

". . . What would you suggest?"

"I'd suggest that me, and Halligan, and Lewis, are covering that vault with guns when you open the door, and that we take him right in custody and get it out of him what he was doing in there. If he's got dough on him, then we'll know. I'd treat him just like anybody else that hid hisself in a vault. I wouldn't take no chances whatever."

"I can't stand for that."

"Why not?"

For just a split second, I didn't know why not. All I knew was that if he was searched, even if he hadn't put his father-in-law's money back in the cash box, they'd find it on him, and a man with nine thousand dollars on him, unaccounted for, stepping out of a bank vault, was going to mean an investigation that was going to ruin me. But if you've got to think fast, you can do it. I acted like he ought to know why not. "Why—morale."

"What do you mean, morale?"

"I can't have those people out there, those other employees, I mean, see that at the first crack out of the box, for no reason whatever, I treat the senior member of the staff like some kind of a bandit. It just wouldn't do."

"I don't agree on that at all."

"Well, put yourself in their place."

"They work for a bank, don't they?"

"They're not criminals."

"Every person that works for a bank is automatically under suspicion from the minute he goes in until he comes out. Ain't nothing personal about it. They're just people that are entrusted with other people's money, and not nothing at all is taken for granted. That's why they're under bond. That's why they're checked all the time—they know it, they want it that way. And if he's got any sense, even when he sees our guns, supposing he is on the up-and-up, and he's in there by mistake, *he* knows it. But he's not on the up-and-up, and you owe it to them other people in there to give them the protection they're entitled to."

"I don't see it that way."

"It's up to you. But I want to be on record, in the presence of Halligan and Lewis, that I warned you. You hear what I say, Mr. Bennett?"

". . . I hear what you say."

My stomach was feeling still worse, but I gave them their orders. They were to take positions outside. They weren't to come in unless they were needed. They were to wait him out.

I led, driving over to the bank, and they followed, in Dyer's car. When I went past the bank I touched the horn and Dyer waved at me, so I could catch him in the mirror. They had wanted me to show them the bank, because they were all from the home office and had never been there. A couple of blocks up Anita Avenue I turned the corner and stopped. They pulled in ahead of me and parked. Dyer looked out. "All right. I got it."

I drove on, turned another corner, kept on around the block and parked where I could see the bank. In a minute or two along came Helm, unlocked the door and went in. He's first in, every morning. In about five minutes Snelling drove up, and parked in front of the drugstore. Then Sheila came walking down the street, stopped at Snelling's car, and stood there talking to him.

The curtains on the bank door came down. This was all

part of opening the bank, you understand, and didn't have anything to do with the vault. The first man in goes all through the bank. That's in case somebody got in there during the night. They've been known to chop holes in the roof even, to be there waiting with a gun when the vault is opened.

He goes all through the bank, then if everything's O.K. he goes to the front door and lowers the curtains. That's a signal to the man across the street, who's always there by that time. But even that's not all. The man across the street doesn't go in till the first man comes out of the bank, crosses over, and gives the word. That's also in case there's somebody in there with a gun. Maybe he knows all about those curtains. Maybe he tells the first man to go lower the curtains, and be quick about it. But if the first man doesn't come out as soon as he lowers the curtains, the man across the street knows there's something wrong, and puts in a call, quick.

The curtains were lowered, and Helm came out, and Snelling got out of his car. I climbed out and crossed over. Snelling and Helm went in, and Sheila dropped back with me.

"What are you going to do, Dave?"

"Give him his chance."

"If only he hasn't done something dumb."

"Get to him. Get to him and find out what's what. I'm going to take it as easy as I can. I'm going to stall, listen to what he has to say, tell him I'll have to ask him to stick around till we check—and then you get at it. Find out. And let me know."

"Do the others know?"

"No, but Helm's guessed it."

"Do you ever pray?"

"I prayed all I know."

Adler came up then and we went in. I looked at the clock. It was twenty after eight. Helm and Snelling had their dust cloths, polishing up their counters. Sheila went back and started to polish hers. Adler went back to the lockers to put on his uniform. I sat down at my desk, opened it, and took out some papers. They were the same papers I'd been stalling with the afternoon before. It seemed a long time ago, but I began stalling with them again. Don't ask me what they were. I don't know yet.

My phone rang. It was Church. She said she wasn't feeling well, and would it be all right if she didn't come in today? I said yeah, perfectly all right. She said she hated to miss a day, but she was afraid if she didn't take care of herself she'd really get sick. I said certainly, she ought to take care of herself. She said she certainly hoped I hadn't forgotten about the adding machine, that it was a wonderful value for the money, and would probably pay for itself in a year by what it would save. I said I hadn't forgotten it. She said it all over again about how bad she felt, and I said get well, that was the main thing. She hung up. I looked at the clock. It was twenty-five after eight.

Helm stepped over, and gave my desk a wipe with his cloth. As he leaned down he said: "There's a guy in front of the drugstore I don't like the looks of, and two more down the street."

I looked over. Dyer was there, reading a paper.

"Yeah, I know. I sent for them."

"O.K."

"Have you said anything, Helm? To the others?"

"No, sir, I haven't."

"I'd rather you didn't."

"No use starting anything, just on a hunch."

"That's it. I'll help you open the vault."

"Yes, sir."

"See the front door is open."

"I'll open it now."

At last the clock said eight-thirty, and the time lock clicked off. Adler came in from the lockers, strapping his belt on over his uniform. Snelling spoke to Helm, and went over to the vault. It takes two men to open a vault, even after the time lock goes off, one to each combination. I opened the second drawer of my desk, took out the automatic that was in there, threw off the catch, slipped it in my coat pocket, and went back there.

"I'll do that, Snelling."

"Oh, that's all right, Mr. Bennett. Helm and I have it down to a fine art. We've got so we can even do it to music."

"I'll try it, just once."

"O.K.—you spin and I'll whistle."

He grinned at Sheila, and began to whistle. He was hoping I'd forgotten the combination, and would have to ask help, and then he'd have a laugh on the boss. Helm looked at me, and I nodded. He spun his dial, I spun mine. I swung the door open.

At first, for one wild second, I thought there was nobody in there at all. I snapped on the switch, and couldn't see anything. But then my eye caught bright marks on the steel panels of the compartments that hold the safe deposit boxes. Then I saw the trucks had all been switched. They're steel frames, about four feet high, that hold the records. They run on rubber wheels, and when they're loaded they're plenty heavy. When they were put in there, they were all crosswise of the door. Now they were end to it, one jammed up against the other, and not three feet away from me. I dropped my hand in my gun pocket, and opened my mouth to call, and right that second the near truck hit me.

It hit me in the pit of the stomach. He must have been crouched behind it, like a runner, braced against the rear shelves and watching the time lock for the exact second we'd be in there. I went over backwards, still trying to get out the gun. The truck was right over me, like it had been shot out of a cannon. A roller went over my leg, and then I could see it crashing down on top of me.

I must have gone out for a split second when it hit my head, because the next thing I knew screams were ringing in my ears, and then I could see Adler and Snelling, against the wall, their hands over their heads.

But that wasn't the main thing I saw. It was this madman, this maniac, in front of the vault, waving an automatic, yelling that it was a stick-up, to put them up and keep them up, that whoever moved was going to get killed. If he had hoped to get away with it without being recognized, I can't say he didn't have a chance. He was dressed different from the way he was the day before. He must have brought the stuff in the grip. He had on a sweat shirt that made him look three times as big as he really was, a pair of rough pants and rough shoes, a black silk handkerchief over the lower part of his face, a felt hat pulled down over his eyes—and this horrible voice.

He was yelling, and the screaming was coming from Sheila. She seemed to be behind me, and was telling him to cut it out. I couldn't see Helm. The truck was on top of me, and I couldn't see anything clear, on account of the wallop on my head. Brent was standing right over me.

Then, right back of his head, a chip fell out of the wall. I didn't hear any shot at all, but he must have, because Dyer fired, from the street, right through the glass window. Brent turned, toward the street, and I saw Adler grab at his holster. I doubled up my legs and drove against the truck, straight at Brent. It missed him, and crashed against the wall, right beside Adler. Brent wheeled and fired. Adler fired. I fired. Brent fired again. Then he made one leap, and heaved the grip, which he had in his other hand, straight through the glass at the rear of the bank. You understand: The bank is on a corner, and on two sides there's glass. There's glass on half the third side too, at the rear, facing the parking lot. It was through that window that he heaved the grip. The glass broke with a crash, and left a hole the size of a door. He went right through it.

I jumped up, and dived after him, through the hole. I could hear Dyer and his two men coming up the street behind me, shooting as they came. They hadn't come in the bank at all. At the first yelp that Sheila let out they began shooting through the glass.

He was just grabbing up the grip as I got there and leveled his gun right at me. I dropped to the ground and shot. He shot. There was a volley of shots from Dyer and Halligan and Lewis. He ran about five steps, and jumped into the car. It was a blue sedan; the door was open and it was already moving when he landed on it. It shot ahead, straight across the parking lot and over to Grove Street. I raised my gun to shoot at the tires. Two kids came around the corner carrying schoolbooks. They stopped and blinked. I didn't fire. The car was gone.

I turned around and stepped back through the hole in the glass. The place was full of smoke, from the shooting. Sheila, Helm, and Snelling were stooped down, around Adler. He was lying a little to one side of the vault, and a drop of blood was trickling down back of his ear. It was the look on their faces that told me. Adler was dead.

IX

I started for the telephone. It was on my desk, at the front of the bank, and my legs felt queer as I walked along toward it, back of the windows. Dyer was there ahead of me. He came through the brass gate, from the other side, and reached for it.

"I'm using that for a second, Dyer."

He didn't answer, and didn't look at me, just picked up the phone and started to dial. So far as he was concerned, I was the heel that was responsible for it all, by not doing what he said, and he was letting me know it. I felt that way about it too, but I wasn't taking anything off him. I grabbed him by the neck of his coat and jerked him back on his heels.

"Didn't you hear what I said?"

His face got white, and he stood there beside me, his nostrils fanning and his little gray eyes drawn down to points. I broke his connection and dialed the home office. When they came in I asked for Lou Frazier. His title is vice president, same as mine, but he's special assistant to the Old Man, and with the Old Man in Honolulu, he was in charge. His secretary said he wasn't there, but then she said wait a minute, he's just come in. She put him on.

"Lou?"

"Yeah?"

"Dave Bennett, in Glendale."

"What is it, Dave?"

"We've had some trouble. You better get out. And bring some money. There'll be a run."

"What kind of trouble?"

"Stick-up. Guard killed. I think we're cleaned."

"O.K.—how much do you need?"

"Twenty thousand, to start. If we need more, you can send for it later. And step on it."

"On my way."

While I was talking, the sirens were screeching, and now the place was full of cops. Outside, an ambulance was pulling in, and about five hundred people standing around, with more coming by the second. When I hung up, a drop of blood ran off the end of my nose on the blotter, and then it began to patter down in a stream. I put my hand to my head. My hair was all sticky and wet, and when I looked, my fingers were full of blood. I tried to think what caused it, then remembered the truck falling on me.

"Dyer?"

". . . Yes, sir."

"Mr. Frazier is on his way out. He's bringing money to

meet all demands. You're to stay here with Halligan and Lewis, and keep order, and hold yourself ready for anything he tells you. Let the police take care of Adler."

"They're taking him out now."

I looked, and two of them, with the ambulance crew, were carrying him out. They were going the front way. Halligan had opened the door. Lewis and five or six cops were already outside, keeping the people back. They put him in the ambulance. Helm started out there, but I called him.

"Get in the vault, check it up."

"We've been in. Snelling and I."

"What did he get?"

'He got it all. Forty-four thousand, cash. And that's not all. He got in the boxes. He left the little boxes alone. He went in the others with a chisel, the ones that had big valuables and securities in them, and he took it all from them, too. He knew which ones."

"Mr. Frazier is on his way out with cash for the depositors. As soon as that's under way, make a list of all the rifled boxes, get the box holders on the phone if you can, send them wires otherwise, and get them in here."

"I'll start on it now."

The ambulance crew came in, and started over toward me. I waved them away, and they went off with Adler. Sheila came over to me.

"Mr. Kaiser wants to speak to you."

He was right behind her, Bunny Kaiser, the guy she had brought in for the $100,000 loan the afternoon I had found the shortage. I was just opening my mouth to tell him that all demands would be met, that he could take his turn with the other depositors as soon as we opened, when he motioned to the windows. Every window on one side was full of breaks and bullet holes, and the back window had the big hole in it where Brent had thrown his grip through it.

"Mr. Bennett, I just wanted to say, I've got my glaziers at

work now, they're just starting on the plate glass windows for my building, they've got plenty of stock, and if you want, I'll send them over and they can get you fixed up here. Them breaks don't look so good."

"That would help, Mr. Kaiser."

"Right away."

"And—thanks."

I stuck out my left hand, the one that wasn't covered with blood, and he took it. I must have been pretty wrung up. For just that long it seemed to me I loved him more than anybody on earth. At a time like that, what it means to you, one kind word.

The glaziers were already ripping out the broken glass when Lou Frazier got there. He had a box of cash, four extra tellers, and one uniformed guard, all he could get into his car. He came over, and I gave it to him quick, what he needed to know. He stepped out on the sidewalk with his cash box, held it up, and made a speech:

"All demands will be met. In five minutes the windows will open, all depositors kindly fall in line, the tellers will identify you, and positively nobody but depositors will be admitted!"

He had Snelling with him, and Snelling began to pick depositors out of the crowd, and the cops and the new guard formed them in line, out on the sidewalk. He came in the bank again, and his tellers set the upset truck on its wheels again, and rolled the others out, and they and Helm started to get things ready to pay. Dyer was inside by now. Lou went over to him, and jerked his thumb toward me.

"Get him out of here."

It was the first time it had dawned on me that I must be an awful-looking thing, sitting there at my desk in the front of the bank, with blood all over me. Dyer came over and called another ambulance. Sheila took her handkerchief and started to wipe off my face. It was full of blood in a second. She took my own handkerchief out of my pocket, and did the best she could with it. From the way Lou looked away every time his eye fell on me, I figured she only made it worse.

Lou opened the doors, and forty or fifty depositors filed in. "Savings depositors on this side, please have your passbooks ready."

He split them up to four windows. There was a little wait, and then those at the head of the line began to get their money. Four or five went out, counting bills. Two or three that had been in line saw we were paying, and dropped out. A guy counting bills stopped, then fell in at the end of the line, to put his money back in.

The run was over.

My head began to go around, and I felt sick to my stomach. Next thing I knew, there was an ambulance siren, and then a doctor in a white coat was standing in front of me, with two orderlies beside him. "Think you can go, or you going to need a little help?"

"Oh, I can go."

"Better lean on me."

I leaned on him, and I must have looked pretty terrible, because Sheila turned away from me, and started to cry. It was the first she had broken down since it happened, and she couldn't fight it back. Her shoulders kept jerking and the doctor motioned to one of the orderlies.

"Guess we better take her along too."

"Guess we better."

They rode us in together, she on one stretcher, me on the other, the doctor riding backwards, between us. As we went he worked on my cut. He kept swabbing at it, and I could feel the sting of the antiseptic. But I wasn't thinking about that. Once out of the bank, Sheila broke down completely, and it was terrible to hear the sound in her voice, as the sobs came out of her. The doctors talked to her a little, but kept on working on me. It was a swell ride.

X

It was the same old hospital again, and they lifted her out, and wheeled her away somewhere, and then they took me out. They wheeled me in an elevator, and we went up, and they wheeled me out of the elevator to a room, and then two more doctors came and looked at me. One of them was an older man, and he didn't seem to be an intern. "Well, Mr. Bennett, you've got a bad head."

"Sew it up, it'll be all right."

"I'm putting you under an anesthetic, for that."

"No anesthetic, I've got things to do."

"Do you want to bear that scar the rest of your life?"

"What are you talking about, scar?"

"I'm telling you, you've got a bad head. Now if—"

"O.K.—but get at it."

He went, and an orderly came in and started to undress me, but I stopped him and made him call my house. When he had Sam on the line I talked, and told him to drop everything and get in there with another suit of clothes, a clean shirt, fresh necktie, and everything else clean. Then I slipped out of the rest of my clothes, and they put a hospital shirt on me, and a nurse came in and jabbed me with a hypodermic, and they took me up to the operating room. A doctor put a mask over my face and told me to breathe in a natural manner, and that was the last I knew for a while.

When I came out of it I was back in the room again, and the nurse was sitting there, and my head was all wrapped in bandages. They hadn't used ether, they had used some other stuff, so in about five minutes I was myself again, though I felt pretty sick. I asked for a paper. She had one on her lap, reading it, and handed it over. It was an early edition, and the robbery was smeared all over the front page, with Brent's picture, and Adler's picture, and my picture, one of my old football pictures. There was no trace of Brent yet, it said, but the preliminary estimate of what he got was put at $90,000. That included $44,000 from the bank, and around $46,000 taken from the private safe deposit boxes. The story made me the hero. I knew he was in the vault, it said, and although I brought guards with me, I insisted on being the first man in the vault, and suffered a serious head injury as a result. Adler got killed on the first exchange of shots, after I opened fire. He left a wife and one child, and the funeral would probably be held tomorrow.

There was a description of Brent's sedan, and the license number. Dyer had got that, as the car drove off, and it checked with the plates issued in Brent's name. There was quite a lot about the fact that the car was moving when he jumped aboard, and how that proved he had accomplices. There was nothing about Sheila, except that she had been taken to the hospital for nervous collapse, and nothing about the shortage at all. The nurse got up and came over to feed me some ice. "Well, how does it feel to be a hero?"

"Feels great."

"You had quite a time out there."

"Yeah, quite a time."

Pretty soon Sam got there with my clothes, and I told him to stand by. Then two detectives came in and began asking questions. I told them as little as I could, but I had to tell them about Helm, and Sheila seeing the red light, and how I'd gone against Dyer's advice, and what happened at the bank. They dug in pretty hard, but I stalled as well as I could, and after a while they went.

Sam went out and got a later edition of the afternoon paper. They had a bigger layout now on the pictures. Brent's picture was still three columns, but my picture and Adler's picture were smaller, and in an inset there was a picture of Sheila. It said police had a talk with her, at the hospital, and that she was unable to give any clue as to why Brent had committed the crime, or as to his whereabouts. Then, at the end, it said: "It was intimated, however, that Mrs. Brent will be questioned further."

At that I hopped out of bed. The nurse jumped up and tried to stop me, but I knew I had to get away from where cops could get at me, anyway, until the thing broke enough that I knew what I was going to do.

"What are you doing, Mr. Bennett?"

"I'm going home."

"But you can't! You're to stay until—"

"I said I'm going home. Now if you want to stick around and watch me dress, that's O.K. by me, but if you're a nice girl, now is the time to beat it out in the hall."

While I was dressing they all tried to stop me, the nurse and the intern, and the head nurse, but I had Sam pitch the bloody clothes into the suitcase he had brought, and in about five minutes we were off. At the desk downstairs I wrote a check for my bill, and asked the woman how was Mrs. Brent.

"Oh, she'll be all right, but of course it was a terrible shock to her."

"She still here?"

"Well, they're questioning her, you know."

"Who?"

"The police. . . . If you ask me, she'll be held."

"You mean—arrested?"

"Apparently she knows something."

"Oh, I see."

"Don't say I told you."

"I won't, of course."

Sam had a taxi by then, and we got in. I had the driver go out to Glendale, and pull up beside my car, where I had left it on Anita Avenue. I had Sam take the wheel, and told him to drive around and keep on driving. He took Foothill, and went on up past San Fernando somewhere, I didn't pay any attention where.

Going past the bank, I saw the glass was all in place, and

a gold-leafer was inside, putting on the lettering. I couldn't see who was in there. Late in the afternoon we came back through Los Angeles, and I bought a paper. My picture was gone now, and so was Adler's, and Brent's was smaller. Sheila's was four columns wide, and in an inset was a picture of her father, Dr. Henry W. Rollinson, of U.C.L.A. The headline stretched clear across the page, and called it a "cover-up robbery." I didn't bother to read any more. If Dr. Rollinson had told his story, the whole thing was in the soup.

Sam drove me home then, and fixed me something to eat. I went in the living room and lay down, expecting cops, and wondered what I was going to tell them.

Around eight o'clock the doorbell rang, and I answered myself. But it wasn't cops, it was Lou Frazier. He came in and I had Sam fix him a drink. He seemed to need it. I lay down on the sofa again, and held on to my head. It didn't ache, and I felt all right, but I was getting ready. I wanted an excuse not to talk any more than I had to. After he got part of his drink down he started in.

"You seen the afternoon papers?"

"Just the headlines."

"The guy was short in his accounts."

"Looks like it."

"She was in on it."

"Who?"

"The wife. That sexy-looking thing known as Sheila. She doctored the books for him. We just locked up a half hour ago. I've just come from there. Well boy, it's a crime what that dame got away with. That system in the savings department, all that stuff you went out there to make a report on—that was nothing but a cover. The laugh's on you, Bennett. Now you got a real article for the *American Banker*."

"I doubt if she was in on it."

"I know she was in on it."

"If she was, why did she let him go to her father for the

dough to cover up the shortage? Looks to me like that was putting it on a little too thick."

"O.K.—it's taken me all afternoon to figure that one out, and I had to question the father pretty sharp. He's plenty bitter against Brent. All right, take it from their point of view, hers and Brent's. They were short on the accounts, and they figured on a phoney hold-up that would cover their deficit, so nobody would even know there *had* been a shortage. The first thing to do was get the books in shape, and I'm telling you she made a slick job of that. She didn't leave a trace, and if it wasn't for her father, we'd never have known how much they were short. All right, she's got to get those books in shape, and do it before you next check on her cash. That was the tough part, they were up against time, but she was equal to it, I'll say that for her. All right, now she brings a spider in, and he slips in the vault and hides there. But they couldn't be sure what was going to happen next morning, could they? He might get away with it clean, with that handkerchief over his face nobody could identify him, and then later she could call the old man up and say please don't say anything, she'll explain to him later, that Charles is horribly upset, and when the cops go to his house, sure enough he is. He's in bed, still recovering from his operation, and all this and that—but no money anywhere around, and nothing to connect him with it.

"But look: They figure maybe he don't get away with it. Maybe he gets caught, and then what? All the money's there, isn't it? He's got five doctors to swear he's off his nut anyway, on account of illness—and he gets off light. With luck, he even gets a suspended sentence, and the only one that's out is her old man. She shuts him up, and they're not much worse off than they were before. Well, thanks to a guy named Helm it all went sour. None of it broke like they expected—he got away, but everybody knew who he was, and Adler got killed. So now he's wanted for murder—*and* robbery, and she's held for the same."

"Is she held?"

"You bet your sweet life she's held. She doesn't know it yet—she's down at that hospital, with a little dope in her arm to quiet her after the awful experience she had, but there's a cop outside the door right now, and tomorrow when she wakes up maybe she won't look quite so sexy."

I lay there with my eyes shut, wondering what I was going to do, but by that time my head was numb, so I didn't feel anything any more. After a while I heard myself speak to him, "Lou?"

"Yeah?"

"I knew about that shortage."

". . . You mean you suspected it?"

"I knew—"

"You mean you suspected it!"

He fairly screamed it at me. When I opened my eyes he was standing in front of me, his eyes almost popping out of their sockets, his face all twisted and white. Lou is a pretty good-looking guy, big and thickset, with brown eyes and a golf tan all over him, but now he looked like some kind of a wild man.

"If you knew about it, and didn't report it, *there goes our bond! Don't you get it, Bennett? There goes our bond!*"

It was the first I had even thought of the bond. I could see it, though, the second he began to scream, that little line in fine type on the bond. We don't make our people give individual bond. We carry a group bond on them, ourselves, and that line reads: ". . . The assured shall report to the Corporation any shortage, embezzlement, defalcation, or theft on the part of any of their employees, within twenty-four hours of the time such shortage, embezzlement, defalcation, or theft shall be known to them, or to their officers, and failure to report such shortage, embezzlement, defalcation, or theft shall be deemed ground for the cancellation of this bond, and the release of the Corporation from liability for such shortage, embezzlement, defalcation, or shortage." I felt my lips go cold, and the sweat stand out on the palms of my hands, but I went on:

"You're accusing a woman of crimes I know damned well she didn't commit, and bond or no bond, I'm telling you—"

"You're not telling me anything, get that right now!"

He grabbed his hat and ran for the door. "And listen: If you know what's good for you, you're not telling anybody else either! If that comes out, there goes our fidelity bond and our burglary bond—we won't get a cent from the bonding company, we're hooked for the whole ninety thousand bucks, and—God, ninety thousand bucks! Ninety thousand bucks!"

He went, and I looked at my watch. It was nine o'clock. I called up a florist, and had them send flowers to Adler's funeral. Then I went upstairs and went to bed, and stared at the ceiling trying to get through my head what I had to face in the morning.

XI

Don't ask me about the next three days. They were the worst I ever spent in my life. First I went in to the Hall of Justice and talked to Mr. Gaudenzi, the assistant district attorney that was on the case. He listened to me, and took notes, and then things began to hit me.

First I was summoned to appear before the Grand Jury, to tell what I had to say there. I had to waive immunity for that, and boy, if you think it's fun to have those babies tearing at your throat, you try it once. There's no judge to help you, no lawyer to object to questions that make you look like a fool, nothing but you, the district attorney, the stenographer, and them. They kept me in there two hours. I squirmed and sweated and tried to get out of admitting why I put up the money for Sheila, but after a while they had it. I admitted I had asked her to divorce Brent and marry me, and that was all they wanted to know. I was hardly home before a long wire from Lou Frazier was delivered, telling me the bonding company had filed notice they denied liability for the money that was gone, and relieving me of duty until further notice. He would have fired me, if he could, but that had to wait till the Old Man got back from Honolulu, as I was an officer of the company, and couldn't be fired until the Old Man laid it before the directors.

But the worst was the newspapers. The story had been doing pretty well until I got in it. I mean it was on the front page, with pictures and all kinds of stuff about clues to Brent's whereabouts, one hot tip putting him in Mexico, another in Phoenix, and still another in Del Monte, where an auto-court man said he'd registered the night of the robbery. But when they had my stuff, they went hog wild with it. That gave it a love interest, and what they did to me was just plain murder. They called it the Loot Triangle, and went over to old Dr. Rollinson's, where Sheila's children were staying, and got pictures of them, and of him, and stole at least a dozen of her, and they ran every picture of me they could dig out of their files, and I cursed the day I ever posed in a bathing suit while I was in college, with a co-ed skinning the cat on each arm, in an "Adonis" picture for some football publicity.

And what I got for all that hell was that the day before I appeared before them, the Grand Jury indicted Sheila for alteration of a corporation's records, for embezzlement, and for accessory to robbery with a deadly weapon. The only thing they didn't indict her for was murder, and why they hadn't done that I couldn't understand. So it all went for nothing. I'd nailed myself to the cross, brought all my Federal mortgage notes to prove I'd put up the money, and that she couldn't have had anything to do with it, and she got indicted just the same. I got so I didn't have the heart to put my face outside the house, except when a newspaperman showed up, and then

I'd go out to take a poke at him, if I could. I sat home and listened to the shortwave radio, tuned to the police broadcasts, wondering if I could pick up something that would mean they were closing in on Brent. That, and the news broadcasts. One of them said Sheila's bail had been set at $7,500 and that her father had put it up, and that she'd been released. It wouldn't have done any good for me to have gone down to put up bail. I'd given her all I had, already.

That day I got in the car and took a ride, just to keep from going nuts. Coming back I drove by the bank and peeped in. Snelling was at my desk. Church was at Sheila's window. Helm was at Snelling's place, and there were two tellers I'd never seen before.

When I tuned in on the news, after supper that night, for the first time there was some sign the story was slackening off. The guy said Brent hadn't been caught yet, but there was no more stuff about me, or about Sheila. I relaxed a little, but then after a while something began to bore into me. Where was Brent? If she was out on bail, was she meeting him? I'd done all I could to clear her, but that didn't mean I was sure she was innocent, or felt any different about her than I had before. The idea that she might be meeting him somewhere, that she had played me for a sucker that way, right from the start, set me to tramping around that living room once more, and I tried to tell myself to forget it, to forget her, to wipe the whole thing off the slate and be done with it, and I couldn't. Around eight-thirty I did something I guess I'm not proud of. I got in the car, drove over there, and parked down the street about half a block, to see what I could see.

There was a light on, and I sat there a long time. You'd be surprised what went on, the newspaper reporters that rang the bell, and got kicked out, the cars that drove by, and slowed down so fat women could rubber in there, the peeping that was going on from upstairs windows of houses. After a while the light went off. The door opened, and Sheila came out. She started down the street, toward me. I felt if she saw me there I'd die of shame. I dropped down behind the wheel, and bent over on one side so I couldn't be seen from the pavement, and held my breath. I could hear her footsteps coming on, quick, like she was in a hurry to get somewhere. They went right on by the car, without stopping, but through the window, almost in a whisper, I heard her say: "You're being watched."

I knew in a flash then, why she hadn't been indicted for murder. If they'd done that, she wouldn't have been entitled to bail. They indicted her, but they left it so she could get out, and then they began doing the same thing I'd been doing: watching her, to see if she'd make some break that would lead them to Brent.

Next day I made up my mind I had to see her. But how to see her was tough. If they were watching her that close, they'd probably tapped in on her phone, and any wire I sent her would be read before she got it, that was a cinch. I figured on it awhile, and then I went down in the kitchen to see Sam. "You got a basket here?"

"Yes sir, a big market basket."

"O.K., I tell you what you do. Put a couple of loaves of bread in it, put on your white coat, and get on over to this address on Mountain Drive. Go in the back way, knock, ask for Mrs. Brent. Make sure you're talking to her, and that nobody else is around. Tell her I want to see her, and will she meet me tonight at seven o'clock, at the same place she used to meet me downtown, after she came from the hospital. Tell her I'll be waiting in the car."

"Yes sir, seven o'clock."

"You got that all straight?"

"I have, sir."

"There's cops all around the house. If you're stopped, tell them nothing, and if possible, don't let them know who you are."

Money and the Woman (The Embezzler)

"Just leave it to me."

I took an hour that night shaking anybody that might be following me. I drove up to Saugus, and coming in to San Fernando I shoved up to ninety, and I knew nobody was back of me, because I could see everything behind. At San Fernando I cut over to Van Nuys, and drove in to the hospital from there. It was one minute after seven when I pulled in to the curb, but I hadn't even stopped rolling before the door opened and she jumped in. I kept right on.

"You're being followed."

"I think not. I shook them."

"I couldn't. I think my taxi driver had his instructions before he came to the house. They're about two hundred yards behind."

"I don't see anything."

"They're there."

We drove on, me trying to think what I wanted to say. But it was she that started it.

"Dave?"

"Yes?"

"We may never see each other again, after tonight. I think I'd better begin. You've—been on my mind, quite a lot. Among other things."

"All right, begin."

"I've done you a great wrong."

"I didn't say so."

"You didn't have to. I felt everything you were thinking in that terrible ride that morning in the ambulance. I've done you a great wrong, and I've done myself a great wrong. I forgot one thing a woman can never forget. I didn't forget it. But I—closed my eyes to it."

"Yeah, and what was that?"

"That a woman must come to a man, as they say in court, with clean hands. In some countries, she has to bring more than that. Something in her hand, something on her back, something on the ox cart—a dowry. In this country we waive that, but we don't waive the clean hands. I couldn't give you them. If I was going to come to you, I had to come with encumbrances, terrible encumbrances. I had to be bought."

"I suggested that."

"Dave, it can't be done. I've asked you to pay a price for me that no man can pay. I've cost you a shocking amount of money, I've cost you your career, I've cost you your good name. On account of me you've been pilloried in the newspapers, you've endured torture. You've stood by me beautifully, you did everything you could for me, before that awful morning and since—but I'm not worth it. No woman can be, and no woman has a right to think she is. Very well, then, you don't have to stand by me any longer. You can consider yourself released, and if it lies in my power, I'll make up to you what I've cost you. The career, the notoriety, I can't do anything about. The money, God willing, someday I shall repay you. I guess that's what I wanted to say. I guess that's all I wanted to say. That—and good-bye."

I thought that over for five or ten miles. It was no time for lolly-gagging. She had said what she meant and I had to say what I meant. And I wasn't kidding myself that a lot of it wasn't true. The whole mess, from the time we had started doctoring those books, and putting the money back, I had just hated, and they weren't love scenes, those nights when we were getting ready for the next day's skulduggery. They were nervous sessions, and she never looked quite so pretty going home as she had coming over. But it still wasn't what was on my mind. If I could be sure she was on the up-and-up with me, I'd still feel she was worth it, and I'd still stand by her, if she needed me and wanted me. I made up my mind I was going to hit it on the nose. "Sheila?"

"Yes, Dave."

"I did feel that way in the ambulance."

"There's no need to tell me."

Money and the Woman (The Embezzler) 299

"Partly on account of what you've been talking about, maybe. There's no use kidding ourselves. It was one awful morning, and we've both had awful mornings since. But that wasn't the main thing."

". . . What was the main thing?"

"I wasn't sure, I haven't been sure from the beginning, and I'm not sure now, that you haven't been two-timing me."

"What are you talking about? Two-timing you with whom?"

"Brent."

"With *Charles*? Are you crazy?"

"No, I'm not crazy. All right, now you get it. I've known from the beginning, and I'm perfectly sure of it now, that you know more about this than you've been telling, that you've held out on me, that you've held out on the cops. All right, now you can put it on the line. Were you in on this thing with Brent or not?"

"Dave, how can you ask such a thing?"

"Do you know where he is?"

". . . Yes."

"That's all I want to know."

I said it mechanically, because to tell you the truth I'd about decided she was on the up-and-up all the way down the line, and when she said that it hit me between the eyes like a fist. I could feel my breath trembling as we drove along, and I could feel her looking at me too. Then she began to speak in a hard, strained voice, like she was forcing herself to talk, and measuring everything she said.

"I know where he is, and I've known a lot more about him than I ever told you. Before that morning, I didn't tell you because I didn't want to wash a lot of dirty linen, even before you. Since that morning I haven't told anybody because—*I want him to escape!*"

"Oh, you do!"

"I pulled you into it, when I discovered that shortage, for

the reason I told you. So my children wouldn't grow up knowing their father was in prison. I'm shielding Charles now, I'm holding out on you, as you put it, because if I don't, they're going to grow up knowing their father was executed for murder. I won't have it! I don't care if the bank loses ninety thousand dollars, or a million dollars, I don't care if your career is ruined—I might as well tell you the truth, Dave—*if there's any way I can prevent it, my children are not going to have their lives blighted by that horrible disgrace.*"

That cleared it up at last. And then something came over me. I knew we were going through the same old thing again, that I'd be helping her cover up something, that I wasn't going to have any more of that. If she and I were to go on, it had to be a clean slate between us, and I felt myself tighten. "So far as I'm concerned I won't have that."

"I'm not asking you to."

"And not because of what you said about me. I'm not asking you to put me ahead of your children, or anything ahead of your children."

"I couldn't, even if you did ask me."

"It's because the game is up, and you may as well learn that your children aren't any better than anybody else."

"I'm sorry. To me they are."

"They'll learn, before they die, that they've got to play the cards God dealt them, and you'll learn it too, if I know anything about it. What you're doing, you're ruining other lives, to say nothing of your own life, and doing wrong, too—to save them. O.K., play it your own way. But that lets me out."

"Then it's good-bye?"

"I guess it is."

"It's what I've been trying to tell you."

She was crying now, and she took my hand and gave it little jerky shake. I loved her more than I'd ever loved her and I wanted to stop, and put my arms around her, and start all over again, but I didn't. I knew it wouldn't get us anywhere at all, and I kept right on driving. We'd got to the beach by then, by way of Pico Boulevard, and I ran up through Santa Monica to Wilshire, then turned back to take her home. We were done, and I could feel it that she had called the turn. We'd never see each other again.

How far we'd got I don't know, but we were somewhere coming in toward Westwood. She had quieted down, and was leaning against the window with her eyes closed, when all of a sudden she sat up and turned up the radio. I had got so I kept it in shortwave all the time now, and it was turned low, so you could hardly hear it, but it was on. A cop's voice was just finishing an order, and then it was repeated: "Car number forty-two, Car number forty-two. . . . Proceed to number six eight two five Sanborn Avenue, Westwood, at once. . . . Two children missing from home of Dr. Henry W. Rollinson . . ."

I stepped on it hard, but she grabbed me.

"Stop!"

"I'm taking you there!"

"Stop! I said stop—will you please stop!"

I couldn't make any sense out of her, but I pulled over and we skidded to a stop. She jumped out. I jumped out. "Will you kindly tell me what we're stopping here for? They're your kids, don't you get it—?"

But she was on the curb, waving back the way we had come. Just then a pair of headlights snapped on. I hadn't seen any car, but it dawned on me this must be that car that had been following us. She kept on waving, then started to run toward it. At that, the car came up. A couple of detectives were inside. She didn't even wait till she stopped before she screamed: "Did you get that call?"

"What call?"

"The Westwood call, about the children?"

"Baby, that was for Car forty-two."

"Will you wipe that grin off your face and listen to me? Those are my children. They've been taken by my husband, and it means he's getting ready to skip, to wherever he's going—"

She never even finished. Those cops hopped out and she gave it to them as fast as she could. She said he'd be sure to stop at his hideout before he blew, that they were to follow us there, that we'd lead the way if they'd only stop talking and hurry. But the cops had a different idea. They knew by now it was a question of time, so they split the cars up. One of them went ahead in the police car, after she gave him the address, the other took the wheel of my car, and we jumped in on the back seat. Boy, if you think you can drive, you ought to try it once with a pair of cops. We went through Westwood with everything wide open, it wasn't five minutes before we were in Hollywood, and we just kept on going. We didn't stop for any kind of a light, and I don't think we were under eighty the whole trip.

All the time she kept holding on to my hand and praying: "Oh God, if we're only in time! If we're only in time!"

XII

We pulled up in front of a little white apartment house in Glendale. Sheila jumped out, and the cops and myself were right beside her. She whispered for us to keep quiet. Then she stepped on the grass, went around to the side of the house, and looked up. A light was on in one window. Then she went back to the garage. It was open, and she peeped in. Then she came back to the front and went inside, still motioning to us to keep quiet. We followed her, and she went up to the second floor. She tiptoed to the third door on the right, stood there a minute, and listened. She tiptoed back to where we were. The cops had their guns out by now. Then she marched right up to the door, her heels clicking on the floor, and rapped. It opened right away, and a woman was standing there. She had a cigarette in one hand and her hat and coat on, like she was getting ready to go out. I had to look twice to make sure I wasn't seeing things. It was Church.

"Where are my children?"

"Well, Sheila, how should I know—?"

Sheila grabbed her and jerked her out into the hall. "Where are my children, I said."

"They're all right. He just wanted to see them a minute before he—"

She stopped when one of the cops walked up behind her, stepped through the open door with his gun ready, and went inside. The other cop stayed in the hall, right beside Sheila and Church, his gun in his hand, listening. After a minute or two the cop that went in came to the door and motioned us inside. Sheila and Church went in, then I went in, then the other cop stepped inside, but stood where he could cover the hall. It was a one-room furnished apartment, with a dining alcove to one side, and a bathroom. All doors were open, even the closet door, where the cop had opened them, ready to shoot if he had to. In the middle of the floor were a couple of suitcases strapped up tight. The cop that went in first walked over to Church.

"All right, Fats, spit it out."

"I don't even know what you're talking about."

"Where are those kids?"

"How should I know—?"

"You want that puss mashed in?"

". . . He's bringing them here."

"When?"

"Now. He ought to be here by now."

"What for?"

"To take with us. We were going to blow."

"He using a car?"

"He's using his car."

"O.K.—open them suitcases."

"I have no key. He—"

"I said open them."

She stooped down and began to unstrap the suitcases. The cop poked her behind with the gun.

"Come on, step on it, step on it!"

When she had them unstrapped, she took keys from her handbag and unlocked them. The cop kicked them open. Then he whistled. From the larger of the two suitcases money began tumbling on the floor, some of it in bundles, with rubber bands around it, some of it with paper wrappers still on, showing the amounts. That was the new money we had had in the vault, stuff that had never even been touched. Church began to curse at Sheila.

"It's all there, and now you've got what you want, haven't you? You think I didn't know what you were doing? You think I didn't see you fixing those cards up so you could send him up when they found that shortage? All right, he beat you to it, and he took your old man for a ride too—that sanctimonious old fool! But you haven't got him yet, and you haven't got those brats! I'll—"

She made a dive for the door, but the cop was standing there and threw her back. Then he spoke to the other one, the one that was stooped down, fingering the money. "Jake!"

"Yeah?"

"He'll be here for that dough. You better put in a call. No use taking chances. We need more men."

"God, I never seen that much dough."

He stepped over to the phone and lifted the receiver to dial. Just then, from outside, I heard a car horn give a kind of a rattle, like they give when they're tapped three or four times quick. Church heard it too, and opened her mouth to scream. That scream never came out. Sheila leaped at her, caught her throat with one hand, and covered her mouth with the other. She turned her head around to the cops.

"Go on, hurry up, he's out there."

The cops dived out and piled down the stairs, and I was right after them. They no sooner reached the door than there was a shot, from a car parked out front, right behind my car. One cop ducked behind a big urn beside the door, the other ran behind a tree. The car was moving now, and I meant to get that guy if it was the last thing I did on earth. I ran off to the right, across the apartment house lawn and the lawn next to it and the lawn next to that, as hard as I could. There was no way he could turn. If he was going to get away, he had to pass me. I got to a car that was parked about fifty feet up the street, and crouched down in front of it, right on the front bumper, so that the car was between him and me. He was in second now, and giving her the gun, but I jumped and caught the door handle.

What happened in the next ten seconds I'm not sure I know myself. The speed of the car threw me back, so I lost my grip on the door handle, and I hit my head on the fender. I was still wearing a bandage, from the other cut, so that wasn't so good. But I caught the rear door handle, and hung on. All that happened quicker than I can tell it, but being thrown back that way, I guess that's what saved me. He must have thought I was still up front, because inside the car he began to shoot, and I saw holes appear in the front door, one by one. I had some crazy idea I had to count them, so I'd know when he'd shot his shells out. I saw three holes, one right after the other. But then I woke up that there were more shots than holes, that some of those shots were coming from behind. That meant the cops had got in it again. I was right in the line of fire, and I wanted to drop off and lay in the street, but I held on. Then these screams began coming from the back seat, and I remembered the kids. I yelled at the cops that the children were back there, but just then the car slacked and gave a yaw to the left, and we went crashing into the curb and stopped.

I got up, opened the front door, and jumped aside, quick.

There was no need to jump. He was lying curled up on the front seat, with his head hanging down, and all over the upholstery was blood. But what I saw, when one of the cops ran up and opened the rear door, was just pitiful. The oldest of the kids, Anna, was down on the floor moaning, and her sister, the little three-year-old, Charlotte, was up on the seat, screaming at her father to look at Anna, that Anna was hurt.

Her father wasn't saying anything.

It seemed funny that the cop, the one that had treated Church so rough, could be so swell when it came to a couple of children. He kept calling them Sissy, and got the little one calmed down in just about a minute, and the other one too, the one that was shot. The other cop ran back to the apartment house, to phone for help, and to collar Church before she could run off with that dough, and he caught her just as she was beating it out the door. This one stayed right with the car, and he no sooner got the children quiet than he had Sheila on his hands, and about five hundred people that began collecting from every place there was.

Sheila was like a wild woman, but she didn't have a chance with that cop. He wouldn't let her touch Anna, and he wouldn't let Anna be moved till the doctors moved her. There on the floor of the car was where she was going to stay, he said, and nothing that Sheila said could change him. I figured he was right, and put my arms around her, and tried to get her quiet, and in a minute or two I felt her stiffen and knew she was going to do everything she could to keep herself under control.

The ambulances got there at last, and they put Brent in one, and the little girl in the other, and Sheila rode in with her. I took little Charlotte in my car. As she left me, Sheila touched my arm.

"More hospitals."

"You've had a dose."

"But this—Dave!"

Money and the Woman (The Embezzler)

It was one in the morning before they got through in the operating room, and long before that the nurses put little Charlotte to bed. From what she said to me on the way in, and what the cops and I were able to piece together, it wasn't one of the cop's shots that had hit Anna at all.

What happened was that the kids were asleep on the back seat, both of them, when Brent pulled up in front of the apartment house, and didn't know a thing till he started to shoot through the door at me. Then the oldest one jumped up and spoke to her father. When he didn't answer she stood up and tried to talk to him on his left side, back of where he was trying to shoot and drive at the same time. That must have been when he turned and let the cops have it over his shoulder. Except that instead of getting the cops, he got his own child.

When it was all over I took Sheila home. I didn't take her to Glendale. I took her to her father's house in Westwood. She had phoned him what had happened, and they were waiting for her. She looked like a ghost of herself, and leaned against the window with her eyes closed. "Did they tell you about Brent?"

She opened her eyes.

". . . No. How is he?"

"He won't be executed for murder."

"You mean—?"

"He died. On the table."

She closed her eyes again, and didn't speak for a while, and when she did it was in a dull, lifeless way.

"Charles was all right, a fine man—until he met Church. I don't know what effect she had on him. He went completely insane about her, and then he began to go bad. What he did, I mean at the bank that morning, wasn't his think-up, it was hers."

"But *why*, will you tell me that?"

"To get back at me. At my father. At the world. At everything. You noticed what she said to me? With her that meant an obsession that I was set to ruin Charles, and if I was, then they would strike first, that's all. Charles was completely under her, and she's bad. Really, I'm not sure she's quite sane."

"What a thing to call a sweetie."

"I think that was part of the hold she had on him. He wasn't a very masculine man. With me, I think he felt on the defensive, though certainly I never gave him any reason to. But with her, with that colorless, dietician nature that she had—I think he felt like a man. I mean, she excited him. Because she is such a frump, she gave him something I could never give him."

"I begin to get it now."

"Isn't that funny? He was my husband, and I don't care whether he's alive or dead—I simply don't care. All I can think of is that little thing down there—"

"What do the doctors say?"

"They don't know. It's entirely her constitution and how it develops. It was through her abdomen, and there were eleven perforations, and there'll be peritonitis, and maybe other complications—and they can't even know what's going to happen for two or three days yet. And the loss of blood was frightful."

"They'll give her transfusions."

"She had one, while they were operating. That was what they were waiting for. They didn't dare start till the donor arrived."

"If blood's what it takes, I've got plenty."

She started to cry, and caught my arm. "Even blood, Dave? Is there anything you haven't given me?"

"Forget it."

"Dave?"

"Yes?"

"If I'd played the cards that God dealt me, it wouldn't have happened. That's the awful part. If I'm to be punished—

all right, it's what I deserve. But if only the punishment—*doesn't fall on her!*"

XIII

The newspapers gave Sheila a break, I'll say that for them, once the cops exonerated her. They played the story up big, but they made her the heroine of it, and I can't complain of what they said about me, except I'd rather they hadn't said anything. Church took a plea and got sent over to Tehachapi for a while. She even admitted she was the one that brought in the spider. All the money was there, so Dr. Rollinson got his stake back, and the bonding company had nothing to pay, which kind of eased off what had been keeping me awake nights.

But that wasn't what Sheila and I had to worry about. It was that poor kid down there in the hospital, and that was just awful. The doctors knew what was coming, all right. For two or three days she went along and you'd have thought she was doing fine, except that her temperature kept rising a little bit at a time, and her eyes kept getting brighter and her cheeks redder. Then the peritonitis broke, and broke plenty. For two weeks her temperature stayed up around 104, and then when it seemed she had that licked, pneumonia set in. She was in oxygen for three days, and when she came out of it she was so weak you couldn't believe she could live at all. Then, at last, she began to get better.

All that time I took Sheila in there twice a day, and we'd sit and watch the chart, and in between we'd talk about what we were going to do with our lives. I had no idea. The mess over the bond was all cleared up, but I hadn't been told to come back to work, and I didn't expect to be. And after the way my name had been plastered on the front pages all over the country, I didn't know where I could get a job, or whether

I could get a job. I knew a little about banking, but in banking the first thing you've got to have is a good name.

Then one night we were sitting there, Sheila and myself, with the two kids on the bed, looking at a picture book, when the door opened, and the Old Man walked in. It was the first time we had seen him since the night he danced with Sheila, just before he sailed for Honolulu. He had a box of flowers, and handed them to Sheila with a bow. "Just dropped in to see how the little girl is getting along."

Sheila took the flowers and turned away quickly to hide how she felt, then rang for the nurse and sent them out to be put in water. Then she introduced him to the children, and he sat on the bed and kidded along with them, and they let him look at the pictures in the picture book. The flowers came back, and Sheila caught her breath, and they were jumbo chrysanthemums all right. She thanked him for them, and he said they came from his own garden in Beverly. The nurse went and the kids kind of quieted down again, and Sheila went over to him, and sat down beside him on the bed, and took his hand. "You think this is a surprise, don't you?"

"Well, I can do better."

He dug in his pocket and fished up a couple of little dolls. The kids went nuts over them, and that was the end of talk for about five minutes. But Sheila was still hanging on to the Old Man's hand, and went on: "It's no surprise at all. I've been expecting you."

"Oh, you have."

"I saw you were back."

"I got back yesterday."

"I knew you'd come."

The Old Man looked at me and grinned. "I must have done pretty well in that dance. I must have uncorked a pretty good rhumba."

"I'd say you did all right."

Sheila laughed, and kissed his hand, and got up and

moved into a chair. He moved into a chair too, and looked at his chrysanthemums and said, "Well, when you like somebody you have to bring her flowers."

"And when you like somebody, you know they'll do it."

He sat there a minute, and then he said, "I think you two are about the silliest pair of fools I ever knew. Just about the silliest."

"We think so too."

"But not a pair of crooks. . . . I read a little about it, in Honolulu, and when I got back I went into it from beginning to end, thoroughly. If I'd been here, I'd have let you have it right in the neck, just exactly where Lou Frazier let you have it, and I haven't one word of criticism to offer for what he did. But I wasn't here. I was away, I'm glad to say. Now that I'm back I can't find it in me to hold it against you. It was against all rules, all prudence, but it wasn't morally wrong. And—it was silly. But all of us, I suppose, are silly now and then. Even I feel the impulse—especially when dancing the rhumba."

He stopped and let his fingertips touch in front of his eyes, and stared through them for a minute or so. Then he went on:

"But—the official family is the official family, and while Frazier isn't quite as sore as he was, he's not exactly friendly, even yet. I don't think there's anything for you in the home office for some little time yet, Bennett—at any rate, until this blows over a little. However, I've about decided to open a branch in Honolulu. How would you like to take charge of *that*?"

Brother, does a cat like liver?

So Honolulu's where we are now, all five of us: Sheila, and myself, and Anna, and Charlotte, and Arthur, a little number you haven't heard about yet, that arrived about a year after we got here, and that was named after the Old Man. They're out there on the beach now, and I can see them from where I'm writing on the veranda, and my wife looks kind of pretty in a bathing suit, if anybody happens to ask you. The Old Man was in a few weeks ago, and told us that Frazier's been moved East, and any time I want to go back, it's all clear, and he'll find a spot for me. But I don't know. I like it here, and Sheila likes it here, and the kids like it here, and the branch is doing fine. And another thing: I'm not so sure I want to make it too handy for Sheila and the Old Man to dance the rhumba.